THE COCAINE PRINCESS 2

King Rio

Lock Down Publications and Ca$h
Presents
The Cocaine Princess 2
A Novel by *King Rio*

King Rio

Lock Down Publications
P.O. Box 944
Stockbridge, Ga 30281
www.lockdownpublications.com

Lock Down Publications
Like our page on Facebook: Lock Down Publications @
www.facebook.com/lockdownpublications.ldp
Book interior design by: **Shawn Walker**

The Cocaine Princess 2

Stay Connected with Us!

Text **LOCKDOWN** to 22828 to stay up-to-date with new releases, sneak peaks, contests and more…

Thank you!

King Rio

Submission Guideline.

Submit the first three chapters of your completed manuscript to ldpsubmissions@gmail.com, subject line: Your book's title. The manuscript must be in a .doc file and sent as an attachment. Document should be in Times New Roman, double spaced and in size 12 font. Also, provide your synopsis and full contact information. If sending multiple submissions, they must each be in a separate email.

Have a story but no way to send it electronically? You can still submit to LDP/Ca$h Presents. Send in the first three chapters, written or typed, of your completed manuscript to:

LDP: Submissions Dept
P.O. Box 944
Stockbridge, Ga 30281

DO NOT send original manuscript. Must be a duplicate.

Provide your synopsis and a cover letter containing your full contact information.

Thanks for considering LDP and Ca$h Presents.

The Cocaine Princess 2

Dedication

This book is dedicated to Annette Bardlett, my wonderful mother. I love you more than words can express.

King Rio

The Cocaine Princess 2

Prologue
Five Months Prior

"How much money is that? Damn, that's gotta be every bit of $50 million. Cash." Blake King could not keep his eyes off the large, green-blue cellophane wrapped bales of cash.

"More like $900 million," Alexus Costilla said matter-of-factly, as she trailed her fiancé out of the elevator and into the 2000 square foot, stainless steel vault. "My granny told me about this vault about a week ago, the day before she passed. She kept it full of money just in case the American government ever turned on her, the way they did Noriega and Freeway Rick Ross."

"$900 million dollars," Blake said, emphasizing each word. He ogled the blocks of cash for a long moment. "Baby, I damn... I could feed my whole city with this much money."

The big cubes of cash, nine in all, were pushed up against the shiny steel wall to their left. Eighty inch flat screen Sony monitors each spaced about a foot over from the next lined the walls. In the far-right corner, a behemoth Honduran mahogany desk sat in front of a big, expensive looking black leather chair; far across from it was a stainless steel refrigerator, a brown marble countered kitchenette, and a fairly small bedroom with an adjoining full bathroom, each room separated by thick glass walls.

"You could feed more than that tiny little city," Alexus said, planting her palms on her hips. She donned a snow-white Herve Léger dress and a black pair of Miu Miu pumps. A 15-carat cushion-cut diamond and platinum ring embellished her ring finger, and several diamond and platinum tennis bracelets bedazzled her wrists. She was a tantalizing blend of Black and Mexican, with an alluring reddish-brown complexion, verdant green eyes, and a derriere that rivaled most Smooth and Straight Stuntin' magazine models.

In addition, her net worth was over $48 million dollars. Not to mention the fact that she was now the official leader of Mexico's most lucrative drug empire: The Costilla Cartel.

"I'm not turnin' myself in," Blake said. He went to the first bale of cash, scrutinized it for a moment, then dug his fingernails into its corner and ripped it open.

"No one's asked you to turn yourself in, Blake. However, we can't be together all the time, either. I just inherited a $48 billion dollar corporation. I own nineteen restaurants, a resort in Cancun, a television network—"

"Baby, you ain't gotta keep tellin' me about that shit," he interrupted,

turning to her with a bundle of bank-new hundred dollar bills in each hand. "I'm not dumb. I understand our situation for what it is: I'm wanted for murder—"

"Twenty-one murders," she corrected.

"—and you got a business to run," Blake finished.

"Screw the business. I'm not going to be running it. That'll be my momma's job. She has the MBA from Harvard. But you know that, the second we get back to the states, you are going to be arrested."

"I'll stay here in Mata or whatever. Feds ain't gon' fuck with me down here."

Blake had smooth tenebrous skin. His dark-brown eyes held an abundance of wisdom, though he was only 18-years old. He had a bulletproof vest draped over his white tank top. His belt, cargo shorts, and loafers were all Louis Vuitton, and he wore enough diamonds to make Gucci Mane jealous.

He tossed the hundred dollar bills bearing Benjamin Franklin's face atop the huge block of cash he'd opened, and his eyes descended to his fiancée's gravid stomach. She was four months pregnant. Momma's baby, daddy's maybe.

"If that's T-Walks baby, you should let him have sole custody. I don't want—"

"What?" Alexus scoffed incredulously. "I am not giving my child away! Are you crazy?"

"That nigga got me shot ten times. He ain't finna be comin' around me like shit good and gravy."

Agitatedly, she turned and stormed into the elevator. Blake flitted in behind her just before the steel doors closed.

"You got me fucked up, Blake. I'm not giving my baby up. I

don't care who my baby's father is. It's either yours or his, and either way, I'm keeping the baby." She pressed and held the up button for thirty seconds, which, she'd explained, was the only way to get to and from the vault.

The elevator was about three times as capacious as the average elevator. Blake leaned back against the rear steel wall and, since Alexus had her back to him, he gazed at her massive, Hottentot-like ass for a moment.

She was thicker than Serena Williams. Alexus was far too classy to pose for any urban magazine or be a video vixen but she could compete with the best in the industry.

He could not keep himself. He reached out and squeezed her ass. She turned around and slapped down his hand, glowering at him.

"Don't fucking touch me, Blake," she said acidly. "You knew before you proposed to me that T-Walk might be my child's father. I'm not about to go through this with you."

Blake grinned, studying his curvaceous fiancé's cantankerous expression. Even when she was angry, she was beautiful.

"Gimme a kiss," he whispered, knowing that her response would be anything but a kiss.

"Kiss my ass, you black bastard."

"Where you want me to kiss it?"

Alexus sighed. "I don't have time to be arguing with you. You're supposed to be helping me get things in order so, you'll be okay when and if they ever get you. And who told the police you killed all those people anyway?"

With a softly reverberating *ding*, the elevator doors parted, and they strode purposefully out into the foyer of Alexus' 32,000 square foot ranch style estate, which sat on 56 acres and included horse stables, an Equestrian course, a lap pool with a spa, a waterfall and outside cabanas, and a 10-car garage. There were 12 bedrooms, 19 fireplaces, and 22 bathrooms. White Carrera marble lined the floors. Recreational facilities included an indoor tennis court, theater, gym, and a full-size playhouse that had been custom-built for Alexus when she was a child.

"I think Tim-Tim told the law about that shit that popped off in

Indianapolis," Blake surmised. He was tailing Alexus into the gym, his eyes on the latest iPhone in his hand.

"But there were only 15 murders in—oh, they must have charged you with the shootings in Michigan City, Indiana, too."

"That's prob'ly it. Shit, it had to be Tim-Tim who snitched. Nobody else knew about everything."

"You should call Attorney Bostic," Alexus suggested.

Blake put the smart phone back inside its Louis Vuitton holder on his hip and stepped over to the weight-lifting section of the gymnasium. "I just sent her a message on Facebook," he said laconically, and got to work curling a set of fifty-pound dumbbells.

Alexus sat down on a weight bench, leaned forward with her elbows on her knees, and dropped her face into her palms. Blake knew that she had to be feeling ripped apart on the inside. She had watched her paternal grandmother, Vida Costilla, a Mexican drug cartel leader, multimillionaire stock market titan, and Costilla family matriarch, get buried yesterday. She had endured the harsh, envious stares of Granny Costilla's many business associates, most of whom were Mexican, all of whom were pissed. Vida's will had left every cent of her fortune to Alexus, a fact that had infuriated several members of the family, so much so that they made numerous attempts to end her life in the months leading up to Vida's death.

Consequently, one attempt at poisoning Alexus at a downtown Chicago restaurant had actually been the cause of Vida Costilla's unfortunate demise.

Dejectedly, Alexus raised her head. She parted her lips to speak, but said nothing. She didn't need to. The bereavement in her eyes was worth a thousand words.

The past few months had been tumultuous for Blake, as well— he'd been robbed, shot at 10 times, daughter was kidnapped and held for a $50 million dollar ransom, and his daughter's mother had not been murdered not even a week prior. His brother and one of their closest friends were currently in Indiana's Marion County Jail, both charged with fifteen counts of murder—but Blake was practically incapable of expressing emotion.

Like most black men, he was tough as nails—at least to any

observant eyes. "I wired fifty grand to your mother to pay for Ashley's funeral expenses," Alexus said, crossing her legs. "She said the police won't stop harassing her with questions concerning your whereabouts, and that Savaria's been crying a lot, but aside from that everything's been fine. I'm flying them to Los Angeles after the funeral. My granny had a mansion out there. I'm just going to give it to your parents so Savaria can have a nice, stable environment to grow up in. And it's in the Brentwood area, not far from Heidi Klum and Seal's hilltop mansion."

"Who?" Blake asked, grimacing as he continued to alternate and lift the heavy dumbbells.

"Never mind who they are. The point is your family will be close."

"I don't want my daughter growing up in a town full of hood haters.

We're from the ghetto, the—"

"Land of no opportunity? Is that what you want for her? Hmm? You want your daughter to grow up in a poor, low-income neighborhood full of criminals and prostitutes?"

Blake was thoughtful for a moment. Of course, he wanted the absolute best for his daughter; that was not what he was thinking about; his was focus was on determining who snitched on him and his crew out to the police, and who murdered his daughter's mother.

He dropped the weights and grabbed his smart phone.

"Is it really taking you that long to come up with an answer?" Alexus asked. She sounded vaguely disappointed.

"Fine, baby," he murmured dismissively. "Fly 'em to L.A."

"Are you blowing me off?"

"I'm on one right now, Lexi. Gimme a minute."

He dialed the number to the last person on Earth he felt like calling and tapped send.

Trintino "T-Walk" Walkson answered on the second ring.

"I need a favor," Blake said, turning away from Alexus and walking onto the full sized basketball court. "I need you to spread the word through Chicago that I got $10 million for the name and location of whoever killed Ashley."

"Cash?" T-Walk asked with disbelief.

"Cash. And when I find out who's snitchin' about those bodies, I got ten on their heads, too."

The Cocaine Princess 2

Chapter 1

On the warm evening of August 12, 2011, death rendezvoused with Phillip "Jazzy" Dolton at precisely 5:50 p.m., in Gary, Indiana. He pulled up to the curb in front of Miller Projects on East 4th Avenue in a rented, caramel-brown Escalade. Although he was 6'3, 250 pounds, and strapped with a .40 caliber Glock, he was replete with fear and nervousness. However, who could blame him? He was a Blood in a neighborhood full of Gangster Disciples, in a city he never visited before.

With his sunroof open, a Kush-stuffed cigarillo trapped between the fat index and middle fingers of his right hand, and an iPhone in his other hand, he reclined in his seat and blew a thick cloud of smoke into the vespertine sky.

"Hurry up and get out here, Kita. You got me around all these fuck niggas," Jazzy accused, eerily fluctuating his eyes around the street.

There were gang members and drug dealers everywhere. "I'm on my way out now. Let me find my shoes," Kita said. "You got four minutes before I pull off."

"Four minutes! Nigga, you just drove three hours from Naptown for some of this pussy; you ain't leaving that fast."

Jazzy let loose an effeminate laugh. Lakita Thomas was right: he was not about to leave G.I. without her. Ever since he'd first laid eyes on her at a Christmas Eve party the previous year, he hadn't been able to get the titillating image of her curvaceous brown body out of his head.

"Just hurry up yo' lil thick ass up," he told her as he puffed on the blunt.

Those were his last words.

Edward "Squirm-G" Hart, Antonio "lil Ant" Harrington, and Reggie Freeman all had a few things in common. For one, they were all Gangster Disciples from Gary, Indiana. For two, all three of them were dressed alike—black ski masks, black shirts, pants and shoes—and each of them had a Ruger P-90 handgun with thirty-round magazines.

King Rio

Squirm-G stopped the stolen, rust laden gray Buick Regal right next to Jazzy's Escalade, rolled down the mirror-tinted windows, and immediately opened fire on the imposing Cadillac SUV. Lil Ant and Reggie followed suit.Together, they sent ninety bullets pinging through the passenger's side of the Escalade, hitting Jazzy sixty-three times.

He was dead long before their magazines depleted.

Chapter 2

"Did you know that, out of the 40 million Blacks in America, over 9 million of us live in poverty? That's almost twenty-five percent!" Rita Mae Bishop exclaimed histrionically.

Richly comported in a white, one-shouldered Filhas de Gaia jumpsuit over red Louboutin heels, she was standing in front of the 86-story MTN International Tower on Wabash Avenue in downtown Chicago. Her 19-year old daughter, Alexus Costilla, and their family attorney were with her, along with three week-old King Neal Costilla, Alexus' newborn son, who was resting comfortably in a stroller.

"That's why I'm not moving to Hollywood. I'd rather spend my money in poor communities." Alexus, decked out in a black plunging- neckline jumpsuit and yellow peep-toe Miu Miu pumps, with a yellow Balenciaga clutch in her hand, looked even more voguish and stuntin' than her 43-year old, dark hued mother. "Black people are supposed to be the wealthiest ethnic group in the United States. This economy was methodically built by the adroit hands of our ancestors. There is no way African-Americans should be as poor as we are today."

"A lot of it has to do with the recession," said Attorney Britney Bostic, a strikingly attractive, lithesome Black woman in a light gray pantsuit. "But you're right, Alexus. This country should compensate us for all the years our families were enslaved. I don't think the government understands how deeply they vitiated the minds of our people during those 400 years, how not allowing us to read book back then has turned into millions of us not even wanting to open a book now, how separating our black men from their pregnant spouses has led to them disclaiming their kids today. Truth is African Americans need that $700 billion dollar stimulus package way more than those investment banks."

"When Lehmen Brothers and Merrill Lynch failed in September of 2008 and sent the global stock market into a nosedive, it was no accident," Rita informed them. She had been a Professor of Economics at Harvard Business School in the early nineties. "The recession was the direct result of avarice in its purest form. These Wall Street CEOs and executives knew exactly what they were doing. They bought seven and eight private jets at a time; they bought helicopters and $30 million dollar Park Avenue penthouses, and multiple yachts and mansions in The Hamptons. And all of their lavish spending sprees were financed by the predatory subprime loans they were making homeowners sign, and the tricky Collateralized Debt Obligations they were selling to their investors."

Alexus squatted on her haunches in front of the stroller and pushed an index finger into the palm of King's tiny little hand. He was asleep with a pacifier in his mouth. His black cotton bib had "King Neal" stitched across it in gold.

"Vida Costilla was a genius when it came to the stock market," said Rita. "She made $23 billion betting against mortgage securities, because she knew that Goldman Sachs, Bear Stearns, Lehman Brothers and several other banks were participating in the biggest monetary heist in history, and she wanted a part of it."

To leave to me, Alexus added mentally, still finding it hard to believe that she was now listed among the top fifty wealthiest Americans in Forbes magazine.

Then she looked to her left, at the black Armani-suited phalanx of ex- CPD officers who her mother had hired as security, and it became evident that she was indeed a multibillionaire. Who else traveled the Windy City with twelve armed bodyguards in tow?

She stood and stepped around to the rear of the stroller. "Break over, Momma. Time to get back to work."

"Let me give my nugget some sugar," Rita requested affably. She poked her head into the stroller and kissed King on his lips. "Cutest little man on the planet. Yes you are."

"Will you please stop calling my son Nugget?" Alexus smiled. "He's my grandson; I'll call him whatever I please."

"Not if you're gonna call him a damn nugget! He'll grow up thinking he's Chuy's long-lost brother."

"Chuy? Who's Chuy?"

"The midget on *Chelsea Lately*." "*Chelsea Lately*?"

Alexus sighed and started toward her car, a powder-white

Rolls- Royce Phantom convertible gaudily situated atop white twenty-four inch Lexani rims. Lined up single file behind it were three triple-white Chevy Tahoes, each one hovering over white painted rims, only theirs measured six inches more than the Phantom's.

White had always been Alexus Costilla's color of choice.

She put King in his car seat then climbed in the back seat next to him while her chauffeur, a gargantuan, bald-headed Black man she called Big Mark, loaded the stroller into the trunk of the Phantom.

Attorney Bostic was walking to her silver Mercedes-Benz E550 Cabriolet when Alexus shouted for her.

"Nuh uh, girl, you won't get away from me that easily. We have business to discuss. I'll have Big Mark bring you back to your car later tonight."

"I wasn't trying to evade you," Britney claimed as she turned around, pocketing her keys. "There is just so much to be done. I have to get together the paperwork and contracts for your television shows, and then I have to fly to London and convince Aesha Jenner to abandon her job as lead designer at Prada and join Niemann Elements."

Britney got in the passenger's seat of the Rolls-Royce, and Big Mark cruised away from the curb, followed by the three SUV's.

"How much is Aesha making with Prada?" Alexus inquired.

"I'm not 100 percent certain, but I'm surmising about $8 million-a-year."

"Offer her $16 million, with a $20 million dollar signing bonus if she accepts."

"That seems a tad bit gratuitous, if you ask me."

"Listen, if we want Niemann Elements to achieve the same level of success as Louis Vuitton, there will have to be heavy investments. We're launching fragrances, clothes and shoes for men and women, swimsuits, lingerie, and even hair and skin care products. An endeavor of such vast proportions requires not only loads of cash, but also the brightest, most experienced minds available."

"I concur," Britney muttered, drumming her fingernails on the outside of her door. With the windows down, and the top back, the warm evening air flowed briskly through the car. "What about the Chicago Housewives contracts? They're asking for ten grand an episode. Your mom thinks sixty-five hundred per sode is fair pay."

"Well, as president of the Minority Television Network, my mother's word is gold. Tell them they'll get a raise next season if the ratings are high enough this season."

They talked about a few other MTN shows—Mariah's Salon, 'Hood Affairs, and Sweet Licks, the latter of which was a critically acclaimed miniseries based on Mario Bardelett's sensational bestselling novel—and Alexus could not repress a grateful smile. Business was good. Her television network was doing well, and her mother had plans to expand the Costilla restaurants by turning it into a franchise. Her construction company, Urban Housing Development, now had offices in Chicago, Los Angeles, New York City, and Las Vegas.

"Contact the CEO of Barclays bank in London," Alexus said. She was fishing in her Clutch for her iPhone4. "Tell him I'm ready to invest another $2 billion."

Britney Bostic knew exactly what that meant.

The Costilla Cartel had *another* $2 billion dollars in drug money that they needed laundered, and Barclay, the world's second largest banking company, could accomplish this feat with ease.

Chapter 3

"If you ever hurt my daughter, I swear on my mother's grave, I will cut off your fucking head and play baseball with it, *comprende?*"

"I love Alexus. I'm not into hurtin' people I love." "Well, make sure you keep it that way."

Blake's expression drew into a petulant scowl. "You got a whole lotta nuts for a 60-year old man. Anybody ever tell you that?"

Juan "Papi" Costilla looked at Blake from the corner of his eye. "Don't let the age fool you. It was not luck that got me this far. Gray hair is a sign of experience."

Yea, and Alzheimer's, thought Blake, as he steered his lime-green Bugatti Veyron Super Sport around to the rear of the Costilla's restaurant. He stopped the $2 million dollar sports car at the tall wrought iron gate, which was centered in the middle of a 15-foot brownstone wall, and waited on the gate to open.

Behind his Bugatti, the burnt orange Bentley Continental GT that belonged to Papi's brother, Flako Costilla, came to a halt on the sandy redbrick ground, followed by two Mercedes-Benz eighteen wheelers.

Each semitrailer contained $10,000 kilograms of cocaine.

As Blake gazed out his window, his eyebrows came together quizzically. He wondered where the 15 Jeeps full of AK-47 wielding Mexican thugs had gone.

Papi seemed to read his mind. "My young soldiers are securing the perimeter, making sure no Zetas are around. I received word that Gamuza himself was here in Matamoros earlier this week. That's the first time he's been seen outside of Ciudad Juarez in years. I don't know why he's shown his old face in my city, but the reason can't be a good one."

"Gamuza?" Blake said in a questioning intonation. "Is he some kinda threat?"

Papi Scoffed at the inquiry. "Gamuza is el jefe of the Zeta Cartel. He is my arch nemesis. He beheaded my father with a chainsaw when I was a little boy, did it right in front of me and my mother. Since then he's had hundreds of my young soldiers killed. I guess you could classify him a threat."

"Damn, I ain't know it was that deep."

"It gets deeper. You see, the U.S. government has been tightening up on border security ever since they killed Bin Laden, and the Zetas are finding it increasingly harder to get their drugs into the States. Meanwhile, we're raking in $200 million dollars every week, and my daughter's beautiful smile is plastered on the cover of nearly every magazine in the world. Gamuza can't be happy about that."

"$200 million every week!" Blake turned to look at the eighteen- wheelers. Then he moved his shocked eyes back to look at the sexagenarian, who was dressed in a dark blue Niemann Elements business suit. "How many bricks is that per week?"

"$20,000, at ten-grand apiece. I move about $30,000 pounds of high-grade marijuana every Monday to take care of all my workers in Mexico, and I pay the American gangs nothing; they make their money by putting taxes on the drugs. I have forty Mexican Mafia lieutenants spread throughout California, Arizona, New Mexico, Texas, Louisiana, Mississippi, Alabama, Georgia and Florida, and each man receives 500 kilos per week."

"That's a helluva connection," Blake said, leaning back in his seat. He donned a bulletproof vest over a black tank top, black denim Niemann Elements shorts with gold NE symbols decorating the back pockets, and black and brown Jordan sneakers. The two gold-plated Sig-Sauer 9 millimeter pistols Papi had given him were tucked away in his shoulder holsters.

The wrought iron gate in front of them swung open, and he stepped gently on the gas pedal. As he and Papi's brother were pulling over to their left, to park next to a large, dark green dumpster, his iPhone4 rang.

Stepping out of the Veyron, Blake answered the call.

A huge, amorous smile burgeoned on Alexus' face the moment she locked eyes with him. With her long, curly mane of hair blowing in a summer breeze, and her makeup professionally applied, she could have passed as Nicki Minaj's twin sister.

"Boy, you know you need to stay out of that sunlight," she japed with a cotton giggle. "You done got blacker than Tyrese."

For a short while, her unprecedented beauty took Blake. He found it hard to believe that the sexy faced young woman he was staring at was his fiancée.

He shut his driver's door and leaned his shoulder against it. "I can't get no blacker than I already am," he said. "When are you coming back to Mexico?"

"Why? You miss me already?" she asked.

"Hell yeah, I miss *all* of you. I miss that throat, that tongue, that gush..." Reflexively, he grabbed his crotch. "It's been nineteen days since the last time you sucked on Monster. You know he gets sick when you don't come around."

"I'll bet he's ready to vomit," she said dubiously. "You're a class-A pervert, you know that?"

"Shots fired." Chuckling aloud, Blake glanced over the roof of the Bugatti and saw that Papi and Flako were talking to each other in Spanish, both of them looking like Wall Street executives in their $10,000 dollar Niemann Elements suits.

Savio and Santiago Costilla, Papi's sister Jennifer's sons, were backing the eighteen-wheelers up to the loading docks behind the opulent restaurant.

"They're putting you on America's Most Wanted tomorrow," Alexus said. "Charles Byrd, the Director of the FBI, called and told me about an hour ago. They believe you and Young-D are hiding out somewhere in Chicago."

"I don't give a fuck what they think." He broached a different subject. "Rita at work?"

Alexus nodded. "Just left her at the MTN tower. Britney's here with me now. She and Nikkia Staples were moving some boxes into their offices at the tower when I showed up."

"They got offices at the tower?"

Alexus nodded again. "They have their own law firm on the 37th floor. Their entire firm has been poring over the paperwork to all those murders you're being charged with. There's absolutely no physical evidence. Every indictment is based solely on the testimonies of Phillip Dolton and Timothy Trice."

"I changed the subject, and you brought it right back up." Blake walked around the back of his car and stood next to the 54-year old Flako Costilla. "Where's my son?"

"He's sleep." She moved the phone to the baby's sleeping face for a brief moment. "We'll be on the plane to Mexico City at nine o'clock tonight, and we'll take a private plane to Matamoros from there."

"Is that my princess?" Papi asked.

"Yup," Blake said. "Baby, I'ma let you talk to your daddy. I'll see you when you get here."

"Okay. Love you."

"Love you, too." He handed the smart phone to Papi, then took a pack of Newport cigarettes—the top brand among African American urbanites—from the front left pocket of his loose-fitting shorts, lit one, and blew the smoke onto the white diamond-flooded face of his watch as he checked the time.

It was 6:30 p.m.

Flako nudged Blake with an elbow. "Mind if I ask you a personal question?"

"Shoot," Blake said, watching as Savio drove a forklift to the open rear door of the semitrailer and pulled back with six staked cardboard boxes.

"Why didn't you have that baby named after you?" Flako asked. He looked a little like George Lopez, only slightly taller, and perilous.

"Her momma said he shouldn't be named after me," replied Blake. "If you Google my name, all kinds of fucked up shit pops up. Shootings, batteries, murders. My name ain't the best name to give a baby."

"So Alexus took your last name and made it the baby's first name." Blake nodded and puffed his cigarette.

"That's a fitting name, I suppose," Flako said. "You know, up to the very moment of her death, my mother was considered Queen of these great Mexican states. King is a rightful name for that first grandson born after her death. Neal must be your middle—"

"Nuh uh. That's the name of Rita's ex. He was a cop, died when those terrorists crashed that plane into Alexus' beach house last year."

"Hmm." A truculent, twisted expression appeared on Flako's toast-brown face. "I would have fucking killed him," he whispered, replete with anger. "I'd have cut off his head, and sent his body through a wood chipper, sliced his fucking tongue out of his mouth, and left his head on Rita's doorstep. That whore knows how we feel about cops."

What the hell is up with these Mexicans wanting to cut everybody's heads off? Black thought.

His second smart phone—the Infuse—rang suddenly, a welcoming interruption, because he didn't want to hear Flako disrespecting his mother- in-law. In Blake's honest opinion, Rita Bishop was the closest thing to an angel he'd ever seen.

He smiled at the number on his phone screen as he answered it. "What is it?" He said, flicking his cigarette to the ground.

"T-Walk says you had a hundred g's on Jazzy's head." The girl's voice was soft but stern. "Well, I just had it done. Three of my guys did it on the east side of Gary. How long before we get the money?"

"A hun'ed g's? You sure he said that?"

"Please don't tell me he lied," she said frantically." These niggas'll kill me, Blake. I can't—"

"Calm down, Lakita. I got you. Let me make sure he's gone, and I'll send you the money."

"He's dead, okay? He's as dead as Amy Winehouse. I took a couple of pictures with my phone." He hung up, and then received five pictures and each one was more ghastly than the last. When he got back on the line with her, in a vacant whisper, he said, "Damn."

"I know," Lakita replied in the same tone. "But hey, you know....

Snitches get what they deserve."

King Rio

Chapter 4

"Alright then, daddy," Alexus said, gazing at her vulpine-eyed father on the iPhone4, "I'll see you in the morning. Give the family my amor. By the way, keep Blake in the house. We can't risk him being spotted."

She tucked the phone away in her Balenciaga clutch, just as her chauffeur decelerated the white Phantom to a stop in front of her west-side Trumbull Street home.

Months prior, it had been a dilapidated, foreclosed yellow-brick apartment building, centered in the middle of Trumbull between Douglas, a bustling yet poverty stricken boulevard flanked by other low-income tenements and duplexes, and 15th street, which was a one-way street that was never void of young Black men, women, and children.

Alexus had purchased the tenement for $140,000. She had invested $750,00 into renovating and turning the building into a massive unit, complete with a newly-built four-car garage in back,19 exterior security cameras, and eye-pleasing artificial lawn, and a12-foot wrought-iron fence that was layered inside with bullet-resistant slabs of eight-inch-thick glass.

"You're the wealthiest woman in the entire continent, Alexus. What the hell are you doing in the middle of the ghetto, in a city where murder is as common as sunshine?" Britney asked as they all exited the car.

"Chicago's a great place to live," Alexus refuted, cradling King in her arms. "And right down there"—she pointed an index finger further down Trumbull—"almost every day. I like to be able to walk to the place where my network's number one show is brought to life. It has five Prime- Time Emmy Award nominations, for Christ's sake!"

Attorney Bostic cast a fleeting glance at her watch. "I need to be getting back to my office. What to do you want me to do about Monique?"

"Who's Monique?"

"The BET talk show host. She still wants to interview you."

"Did you ask mom?"

Britney nodded in the affirmative. "Rita doesn't mind going herself.

She said she'll go if you come with her."

"Well, get it scheduled, and find a way to fit it in my itinerary. I've been wanting to speak with her for a while now—"

The remainder of Alexus' statement became lodged in her throat, and she gasped reflexively, as a Fox News van appeared out of nowhere.

Seconds later, she found herself confronted by a plethora of shoulder- mounted cameras and microphones.

"Miss Costilla, we've just received word that Phillip Dolton, a state witness against your fiancé, was found brutally murdered in Gary, Indiana, a little over an hour ago. Is there any truth to the accusation that Blake has put a $100,000 dollar hit on the heads of every witness in the cases against him?"

"Alexus, is it true that Blake's daughter was kidnapped when her mother was killed earlier this year, and that you paid a ransom to get her back?"

"How did the federal drug charges against your father, his brother, and your friend Tasia Olsen get dismissed? The public wants to know."

"Are you in any way affiliated with the Costilla Cartel in Mexico?"

Alexus declined to comment, and Big Mark and Attorney Bostic hastily ushered her into the house.

"How did they find out about the ransom?" Alexus asked no one in particular.

She sat down at the head of the mahogany table in her exquisitely decorated dining room. Fluctuating her eyes from left to right, from her mulatta friend Tasia Olsen, to her dark-skinned cousin Kenya she leered at the two women... They were on the second floor of the five-story home, in a spacious room that boasted gray marble floors and walls, and overhead crystal chandeliers.

"This is the first time I've heard of the ransom," Tasia said, flipping through newspaper articles on her iPad2. She was high yellow, with a cute face, and *almost* as Steatopygic as Alexus.

"You never mentioned it to me. It's out now, though. The Chicago Tribune, the Chicago Sun-Times, the New York and Los Angeles Times, The Washington Post, The Houston Chronicle—all of them have you on their front page."

"Who'd you tell?" Kenya asked.

"I didn't tell anybody, and the only person Blake told was Young-D. There's no way Young-D said anything; he's way out in Rocky Mount, North Carolina, on the run like Blake," Alexus said.

"Well, one of you talkative bastards said *something*, yo," Tasia, said in her quotidian New York Accent.

"Te odio," Alexus replied dryly. "I hate you."

"Don't start speaking Mexican to me, Lex. You know I can't understand that shit."

"Stop bothering me the. I can never tell if it's your white side or your black side," Alexus snapped.

Kenya dropped her head back and laughed. She and Alexus had not been on the best of terms since mid-February, when Kenya had showed up at a local nightclub with T-Walk. Although their relationship was still ongoing, Alexus was no longer bothered by it. A few months ago, Kenya was drafted to the WNBA's Phoenix Mercury, and her moving to Arizona had allowed the emotional wounds of betrayal in Alexus' heart time to heal a little; however, an inimical scab remained, a scab that was itching to he scratched.

"How much did you pay the kidnappers?" Kenya asked, with her intense brown eyes trained on Alexus' stressful expression.

"Does it really matter?" Alexus had the baby laid over her shoulder, burping him. Like Kenya, she donned t-shirt, gray sweatpants, and Nike sneakers— workout apparel. "Fact is, I wired them the money, and they released Blake's daughter."

"And killed his baby's momma," Tasia added.

"Wait a minute," Kenya said. "You *wired* the ransom money to the kidnappers? Why didn't you have it traced? Police could have had every single one of them in custody by now."

"You know I hate dealing with cops."

"Then why do you have two shifts full of ex-Chicago policemen following you around everywhere?"

Alexus sighed, and continued patting King's back. She could

not reveal the truth about her bodyguards—that all twenty-nine of them had undergone six weeks of murderous training under the tutelage of the Costilla Cartel's number one assassin, Enrique Alémán in Ciudad Juarez, Mexico, during which time, they collectively assassinated 54 Zeta Cartel members.

"They're not cops, anymore, Kenya; they're my bodyguards," Alexus said. "And besides... I did have the money traced from the Panama bank I wired it to. IT was rerouted from there to the accounts of 10 different people in this very neighborhood."

"No shit, yo?" exclaimed Tasia.

Alexus picked a carrot from the bowl of fresh vegetables in front of her and popped it in her mouth. "Yup. Ten percent of the ransom went to each person. Some of it went to an older lady on Drake Street, and the same goes for woman on Homan, Kedzie, Central Park, Albany, Millard, St.

Louis, and even here on Trumbull. Of course, only a few of them still live here in Chicago."

"How many?" Kenya asked, taking a bite of her frittata. "Three as of two weeks ago." Alexus stood and walked to the

window behind her chair. She pushed aside the gray vertical blinds and looked out.

Sawbuck's, a recently built convenience store on the corner of 15th and Trumbull, was overflowing with a crowd of young Blacks. A long white Mercedes was parked in front of the store, and a slim man in his late twenties, presumably its owner, was standing on top of the Benz's truck, making a "T" sign with his hands by incessantly slapping an open palm onto the knuckles of his closed fist. About two or three, dozen others were mimicking his actions, jumping around wildly.

"I wonder why they killed the little girl's mother," Kenya said, as she and Tasia joined Alexus at the window. "That doesn't make any sense to me. I mean they had the money, right?"

"Maybe Ashley knew the kidnappers," Tasia conjectured. "I think that might be why they killed her."

Alexus nodded thoughtfully, noting the plausibility of Tasia's theory. "I know one thing for sure," she murmured, turning away from the window. "Those 10 women didn't kidnap anybody, but I bet they know who did."

King Rio

Chapter 5

When Blake King awoke the next morning, mildly hung-over from all the Glenmorangie Pride scotch he had ingested before retiring to the underground vault last night, he inhaled the alluring scent of his fiancée's $215,000 Clive Christian perfume and smiled.

For ten minutes or so, he remained supine, watching Alexus as she worked his thick, eleven-inch-long ebony phallus in and out of her mouth with the well-honed skills of a veteran porn star.

"Damn, baby...," he moaned ecstatically. "You do know my birthday ain't till next month, right?"

"Mmm hmm." Her oral grip on his dick was unrelenting. She pulled up and teased its crown with a flickering tongue, then drove her head back down until nearly his whole length was wedged in her throat.

"You've been watchin' too many Pinky movies. It's like you get better and better every time."

Blake interlaced his fingers behind his head and tried to relax. He was a nervous wreck.

Last night, Flako Costilla had arrived at the $90 million dollar estate with four Hummer limousines full of Brazilian models and commenced and impromptu pool party. The girls had consumed a lot of alcohol and cocaine while dancing the night away to songs that Blake had found unintelligible. But after drinking a $3,600-bottle of Glenmorangie with Flako, and smoking a blunt of Kush to himself, he'd been far to inebriated to care about anything other than the topless, buxom Brazilian woman who'd been staring at him for half the night. Just as Papí and a cornucopia of other top-echelon Costilla Cartel, members were pulling up in front of the mansion in their black-on-black Rolls-Royce Phantoms and Mercedes Maybachs, Blake had signaled for the Brazilian to follow him to the 10-car garage.

Once there, he had bent her over the hood of his Bugatti and fucked her senseless, then gave her a $1,000 dollars in Benjamin Franklins—roughly the equivalent of eleven grand in Mexican currency, and headed inside for bed.

Now, he deeply lamented his infidelity, and he wondered if Flako, Papí, or someone else would tell Alexus about what happened last night.

Had any of them even noticed?

"What the hell are you thinking about?" Alexus asked. She was holding his dick in her hand, slapping it against her cheek.

"Nothin'", Blake lied.

"Oh, you're thinking about *something*; your dick is going soft, and it's never done that before. What's wrong?"

"Ain't nothin' wrong. I need some pussy. Bad."

"The doctor said we should wait six weeks, Blake. I just gave birth to a seven pound baby three weeks ago."

"Let me taste it then," he said, suddenly feeling the need to please her. It was the least he could do.

Alexus did not bother taking off her skimpy little two-piece bikini.

She moved into a sixty-nine position on top of him, and he took a self-gratifying moment to kiss and lick the already wet fabric over her pussy, to inhale the overwhelming palatable sent of it.

Then he pushed her bikini bottom to the side and feasted.

When Blake and Alexus exited the elevator an hour later, they were shocked to find an overweight, tattoo-covered Mexican man standing naked in the foyer, his arms secured to his sides by a length of barbed wire that was wrapped around his upper body. Papí and Flako flanked him, along with a 10-man team of Costilla Cartel militiamen, all of whom were toting Kalashnikov AK-47s, who were standing near the front door.

"Who the fuck is he, and what is he doing in my house?" Alexus snapped, placing her hands on her hips.

"This here is Señor Ramón Fuentes," Papí said. "Our Mexican Mafia amigo from Columbus."

"Columbus, Georgia, or Columbus, Mississippi?" Slowly, Alexus sauntered closer to the bound and bloodied man. He had golf ball-sized knots all over his bald head, one of his eyes was purple and swollen shut, and his nose, twisted disproportionately and crusted with dried blood, was obviously broken.

"Mississippi," Flako said. "He's been dumping our dope on the gangs in Memphis, Tennessee, for the most part, charging them $14,000 a key'. His gang was also supplying a lot of the top dealers in Biloxi and a few other Mississippi cities."

"So what's the problem?" Alexus said

"The problem is that our amigo thinks he can get away with not paying us $5 million dollars." Papí said, drawing a gold-plated Desert Eagle .50 caliber pistol from somewhere inside his navy-blue suit jacket. "He claims the DEA busted one of his drivers with yesterday's shipment. We would have heard about a 500-kilo drug bust by now, don't you think?"

"He's lying, Lexi." Flako glowered at Ramón." He sold the dope to cover his gambling debts. You see, over the past couple of months, Ramón has lost close to $70 million dollars in Las Vegas. I guess he figured we would sponsor his next gambling spree."

"Well, looks like you figured wrong, señor Ramón." Alexus slapped the man with a gentle flick of her wrist, then stepped around him and headed for the front door. "I haven't had breakfast yet, and I'm not about to stay here and lose my appetite." She left out, leaving Blake behind.

Blake did not feel anything like dealing with this shit, either. For one, he had on an all-white outfit, a white Kevlar vest over a tank top, baggy denim shorts, and Air Force Ones. A spot of blood from Ramón's dripping body would surely vitiate his clean white look. Secondly, he was carrying four Louis Vuitton duffle bags, two in his left hand, two in his right, each containing $3 million in hundred-dollar bills, most of which he planned to give to Lakita and her comrades whenever their plane landed in Brownsville, Texas.

"Who do you think you are, Rick Ross or somebody?" Flako japed laughingly. "What's with all the fuckin' diamonds?"

Instinctively, Blake glanced at the bevy of yellow diamonds that decorated his quarter million-dollar Audemars watch. He had a $300,000 dollar bracelet on his other wrist, which also held a bunch of yellow diamonds, three long, platinum and yellow diamond necklaces, and two 10-karat yellow diamond and platinum Neil Lane pinky rings.

"Don't worry about my jewelry," Blake said, dropping the duffle bags. He flicked his eyes around the room, studying every facial expression for signs of hostility. There was none.

"What do you think we should do with Ramón?" Papí asked Blake.

Blake approached the bleeding man half-knowing that Juan Costilla's question had been a test. "So what it is, pimp? You gon' pay that five mil? It's up to you."

Ramón Fuentes opened his mouth to respond. Blake saw that his tongue was missing.

Blake's mouth went agape a half second before the strident sound of Papí's .50 caliber firing rocked the foyer. A macabre concoction of brain and skull fragments splashed onto Blake. A lot of it entered his mouth. He grabbed his knees and regurgitated all of last night's supper.

Chapter 6

The entire mansion was furnished with a taste and style one would expect from a billionaire. The décor was expensive and replete with African and Mexican art pieces. Yet, it was very cozy, and comfortable. All the rooms were spacious with high-beamed ceilings and wide windows.

Breakfast was waiting for them in the courtyard. It was served at a square redwood picnic table with a Mexican flag umbrella shading it. After Tasia and Alexus had embraced him, Blake sat down. His four year-old daughter, Savaria Chanel King, hopped up onto his gray denim shorted lap.

"I missed you, Daddy." Savaria wrapped her arms around his neck and buried her face in his shoulder. He rubbed her back as she began to cry.

"Daddy missed you, too, baby," Blake whispered through clenched teeth, still indignant and a little sickened over Papí's stunt in the foyer.

"I ended up flying here in my Gulfstream Six," Alexus said. "So, I stopped in L.A. and picked her up."

Blake did not say a word. He felt like breaking Papí's jaw. Mandible *and* maxilla! He was certain the old man had blasted Ramón's brains all over him on purpose. Nevertheless, why had Papí done it? Had it been motivated by last night's infidelity? He had ruminated over these questions while showering and changing into a smoke-gray Louis Vuitton ensemble.

"Can I..." Savaria snuffled. "...go see my horsie?"

"Eat your breakfast first," Blake said. When she didn't budge, he started feeding her from his own plate of steak, cheese-eggs and has browns.

Tasia moved forward in her seat. She was sporting a two-piece swimsuit that was a violet replica of Alexus' white one. Her voice was Charmin soft, yet subtly gangster.

"I'm not over you shooting my boyfriend," she said. "Just thought I should let you know that."

"I'm engaged to his cousin," Blake replied dryly. "That cancels out that beef. In addition, they shot me ten times. You forgot that, huh?"

"How could I? Bookie's facin' 20 to 50 years for that shit."

"Enough about my cousin," Alexus cut in. She had her hand in King's stroller, tickling his stomach, he was smiling his infantile little grin. "I learned some things in Chicago, Blake. Some things you might want to know about."

"Like what?"

"The ransom money, I found out where it went."

Succinctly, she told him about the 10 women in Chicago and how she believed somebody else was responsible for the kidnapping.

"Remember the vacant lot that used to be on the corner of 15th and Trumbull, catty-cornered from that park? There's a corner store on that lot now. A white Mercedes remains parked in front, and that other vacant lot, at the corner of 16th and Trumball, is now a $1 million dollar strip club. Its owner has one of those new Audi R8 convertibles."

Blake nodded; his eyelids squinted. "So everybody got money all of a sudden? On the same street?"

"It's not only on Trumbull; they've been opening businesses all throughout the Lawndale neighborhood."

"Yeah?" After a brief pause, he asked, "Have you called Lil Cholly or Reesie Cup? You know they run that block?"

"I haven't had a chance to contact anybody. I've been too occupied with the business." Alexus looked down at her plate as if it were a source of salmonella. She had been dieting ever since King was born, shedding the extra pounds she'd put on during the pregnancy. Now the mere sight of fatty foods made her so voracious, she had told Blake that she had to convince herself mentally it was poison to keep her from eating it.

Savaria slipped off Blake's lap and zipped around to the other side of the table to play with the baby. Blake silently watched her for a minute, wondering what would become of her if he ended up in prison for the rest of his life. She had already lost her mother. What would her life be like without both parents?

It irked Blake to know that whoever had kidnapped his daughter, and murdered his daughter's mother, was probably laid up in a mansion somewhere, living happily, like an NFL star on some shit.

What he said next made Alexus gasp.

"I'm goin' back to Chicago." He stood and picked up his four duffle bags. "C'mon, Vari. Let's go and see the horses before I…"

"You can't go back!" Alexus was on her feet in an instant. "They're putting you on America's Most Wanted tonight! Have you lost your fucking mind?"

"I ain't lost shit, except my daughter's momma. And you lost $50 million dollars," Blake reminded her. "Some nigga was dumb enough to fuck with my family. A muhfucka gotta pay for that."

He started toward the east wall of the courtyard, passing eight other shaded tables and two hotel-white cabanas on his left, and an Olympic-sized swimming pool on his right, Savaria loped nimbly behind him.

The three French doors on the east wall all led into the 10-car garage.

Blake was opening one of them when Alexus jumped in front of him. "Blake, you are not going back to the States. You're gonna stay right

here in Matamoros, at least until something is done about Tim-Tim."

"I'm goin' wherever the fuck I feel like goin'." He reached over her head and pushed open the door. He froze.

The passenger's door of his Bugatti was ajar, and a viscid red liquid was dripping out of it, creating a crimson pool on a floor of white Carrera marble.

Alexus discerned the sudden change in Blake's eyes. She turned to see what had captured his attention. "Oh, my God, is that blood?"

"Vari, go back over there with Tasia." Blake sat the duffle bags down on the cobblestone walkway, keeping his eyes inside the garage, searching for an intruder.

He waited until Savaria was at Tasia's side, and then grabbed both of the gold-plated 9mm out of his shoulder holsters as he cautiously entered the garage.

Of the ten vehicles inside, half of them – the Bugatti, a Rolls

King Rio

Royce Phantom Drophead Coupe, a Ferrari 458 Italia, a Lamborghini Aventador, and a Lamborghini Spyder Performante – were Blake's. Every one of them had lime-green paint with matching rims. The other five cars were black Phantoms that belonged to Alexus.

Blake visually swept the garage as he walked toward his Bugatti, and when he made it to the passenger's door, a grisly sight confronted him.

The severed breasts and head of the Brazilian woman he had fucked last night were resting on the passenger's seat.

Chapter 7

Blake put the duffle bags in the trunk of his Phantom convertible, while Alexus helped Savaria into the backseat, buckled the little girl's seatbelt then secured King in his seat. She was steaming on the inside, and she was having an arduous time repressing that anger.

She plopped down in the driver's seat and glanced out her window at two middle-aged Mexican men who were busy cleaning up the blood that had dripped from the Bugatti. The few Costilla Cartel members who knew them knew the two of them as "The Cleaners". Their job requirements were simple: clean the murder scene, get rid of the body, and say nothing. It earned them each $1 million dollars every year, so they had no problem abiding by the rules.

When Blake settled into the seat next to Alexus, she offered him an indignant scowl. Her fingers coiled tightly around the steering wheel. Her nostrils flared.

"What?" Blake asked.

Alexus rolled her eyes as she started the engine. Without a word, she accelerated out of the garage. There were 10 triple-white Tahoe's full of heavily armed cartel members waiting near the private landing strip where Alexus' Gulfstream 6 jet was parked. All ten fell in line behind the Phantom as she cruised the curving drive from the rear of the sprawling estate to the road in front of it.

"I can't believe T-Walk," Blake said, scrolling through a string of text messages on his Infuse. "This nigga just sent me a text sayin' he killed that hoe-ass nigga in Gary. He don't even know where the nigga got offed at."

"Shut up talking to me, Blake."

"For what? Fuck, I do this time? 'Cause I sho-the-fuck didn't chop that girl to pieces like that."

Alexus glowered at him again. "Dirty-dick bitch, you know exactly what I'm pissed off a—"

"Will y'all please stop cussin' up there?" 4-year old Savaria King requested pleadingly. She had her tiny palms pressed down over the baby's ears, apparently trying to block the invective from his hearing. "He don't need to be hearin' all that bad words."

There was a fleeting silence.

"We'll discuss whatever it is you're mad about when we make it to the restaurant," Blake said.

"We most definitely will," Alexus snidely replied. Another bout of silence ensued.

Finally, Blake said, "I think I know somebody who can take Ramón's spot. My nigga Pat, a Mafia Insane Vice Lord out of Gary, can probably handle 500 keys every week. He fuck with real niggas all through the Midwest."

"I don't give a... I don't care about any of that, Blake. You know, I used to have a boyfriend named Raul. He cheated on me like it was the cool thing to do. He fucked every slut he ever came across, from the bottom of Texas to the top, and he didn't stop until he found a bunch of chopped off heads and titties in the trunk of his car. He ditched them, but kept the car.

Brownsville P.D. found the eight mutilated bodies a month later. Traces of Raul's semen was in all of them, and there was still blood from the girls in his trunk when he was arrested. They convicted him in '08, executed him last year."

"Damn," Blake said, flabbergasted. "So who whacked the hoes?"

"Doesn't matter. He should have never had sex with them."

Blake's Infuse rang, and he glanced down at it, but not before Alexus saw a lugubrious expression wash over his face. She knew that Papí had more than likely decapitated the woman at the mansion in the same way he had beheaded the eight girls in Brownsville, Texas. Seeing the regret in Blake's eyes compelled her to show a very brief, barely noticeable smile. It served him right. She hoped he would not be able to sleep for months.

He ignored the call and raised his guilt-stricken eyes to study Alexus.

The lugubriousness had subsided. His voice turned affectionate. "Baby, you know I love you, right?"

"Nuh-uh, nigga, forget all that. Who just called you?" She was pulling into the Costilla's' restaurant rear loading area, which was only five miles east of the mansion.

"That was T-Walk," he said, showing her the phone. "The same nigga you cheated on me with when I was in the county jail."

"Don't try to use that against me now, Blake."

Alexus parked the car, turned to him, and released a drab chuckle of disbelief.

"You're gonna throw old dirt in my face? Because you messed up? I'll tell you what." She snatched her engagement ring off and dropped it in his lap. "Propose to me again when you're ready to be faithful."

"Put the ring back on baby." He stared into her sexy green eyes. "And don't ever let me see it off your finger again. We're s'posed to be like Bonnie and Clyde. What happened to all that ride-or-die shit you was talkin' when we first met? One fuck-up ended all that? A *zillion* fuck ups ain't s'posed to end our relationship. If you take off that ring like it's nothin', you *make* it nothin'."

Alexus was already replacing the ring on her finger, feeling like crying, feeling as if she was the one who had done something wrong. She hated it when he made her feel this way, when he turned the tables.

He leaned toward her, and her lips connected. Her disdain for him went away as quickly as it had come. Her skin tingled all over with that warm, inexplicable sensation that only love could create.

As their lips separated, he whispered, "I love you, Alexus. I wouldn't have asked you to marry me if I didn't love you with all my heart."

He reached around to the back seat, unbuckled Savaria's seatbelt, and lifted her out of the car. Alexus watched him as he squatted down in front of his daughter and murmured a sweet goodbye.

Then he retrieved his duffle bags from the trunk and headed into the back door of the two-story restaurant, where he would get on the "Executive Employees Only" elevator that would descend 28 feet below ground, then a half mile north into Alexus' hometown of Brownsville, Texas.

King Rio

Chapter 8

Blake King paced a tight circle in the large elevator, and stared down at his gray leather Louis Vuitton loafers, pondering his situation. He was an undereducated young Black man from a small city in northwest Indiana who had been a low-level dope boy for the majority of his teenage years all the way up to mid-October of the previous year when he had met Alexus Costilla.

Nothing had been the same since.

Now he was engaged to a multibillionaire. Now he was the most talked about American gangster since Al Capone. Now he was an international fugitive, and his face was shown on every news channel across the globe at least once a day. Now he had twenty grand in hundred-dollar bills stuffed into each of the two front pockets on his baggy denim shorts,

$12 million dollars in his four duffle bags, and two 24-karat gold-plated 9mms, not to mention his new body builder-like physique. He was more than ready to return to the United States of America.

The solid steel doors parted, and Blake stepped out into a brightly lit, concrete-floored room that was nearly packed from wall to wall with stacks of cardboard boxes. It was a basement beneath a basement, an esoteric storage room where the Costilla Cartel kept their cache of drugs. A staircase in the corner to Blake's left led up to a trapdoor, which opened in perfect alignment with the tiles on the floor above making it undetectable when closed.

He carried his duffles up the stairs, pushed up the trapdoor, and quietly entered the upper basement. It was dark and cool. A washing machine and dryer rumbled away on one wall; the air was heavily redolent of fabric softener. He kicked the trapdoor shut, checked to make certain it was closed completely, then ascended a second staircase.

Opening the door, which led into the kitchen of a lavishly furnished, 4,200 square-foot ranch-style home, Blake lifted his nose and took in the detectable scent of scrambled eggs and beef sausages.

Flako Costilla's 23- year old daughter, Isabella, was slaving over the stove in an apron, a navy blue Gucci dress, and 6-inch heels. Short and rotund, she was the demure CEO of Feed The Nation, a non profit organization dedicated to supplying canned goods and other victuals to the

$44 million Americans who live in poverty. Although the organization's distribution center was located about a hundred miles, west in McAllen, Texas, hundreds of people regularly mailed their food donations to Bella's Brownsville home.

Nevertheless, there was a Catch-22 to Feed The Nation's philanthropy.

Twice every week, when Bella's brothers, Antoney and Pedro, showed up in Feed The Nation's trucks and began loading boxes into the semitrailers, food donations accounted for only 10 to 15 percent of the load; all the other heavy boxes would contain kilos of cocaine or pounds of high- grade marijuana.

Bella twisted her neck and glanced over her shoulder at Blake. "Buenos días, señor," she said with a beaming smile. "¿Cómo está usted?"

"Muy bien, gracias, ¿y usted?"

"Así, así. Siéntese un momento."

Blake sat down at a yew wood table, eyeing his watch. It read 9:15 a.m. Lakita's plane was scheduled to land at nine twenty.

"I see you've learned a little more Spanish," Bella commented.

"Couldn't help it. Five months in Mexico will do that to a nigga."

"Hmm." Bella fixed him a plate of eggs, sausages, and blueberry pancakes. She placed it on the table in front of him. "I was not expecting a visit from you. What brings you here?"

"Got some b'ness to handle in Chicago."

"They have that Bud Billiken parade going on out there today." She piled an excessive helping of eggs, eight sausages, and five pancakes onto a plate for herself, then drenched it all with maple syrup. "Pedro and I attended the parade a few years ago, had a blast," she said, filling two tall glasses with frigid Tropicana orange juice.

As she handed him his glass and settled across from him, her smile, a genuine and heart-warming, did not wane; in fact, it seemed to grow wider. Blake smiled back at the portly woman. Aside from her aquiline nose, Bella's corpulent face possessed great pulchritude.

"So," she questioned as they started in on their matutinal meal, "are you planning on driving to Chicago? Because if you are, I'll tell you now, you're not gonna make it out of Texas. Cops are searching everywhere for you."

"I'm thinkin' about payin' somebody to drive me there, in a limo or somethin' wit' tinted windows. That way I can be safe in the back—"

"No, no, no," Bella dissented. "You'd still run the risk of getting caught. What if you are pulled over, and the officer decides to look in the back? And what about when you need to use a restroom?"

"How else am I supposed to get there, then? I can't go to no muhfuckin' airport!"

"You don't have to go to an airport to get on a plane. There are literally thousands of privately owned hangars and landing strips in this country. You can board my Citation-X and be in Chicago in less than three hours."

Blake liked the sound of that. He wolfed down his delicious breakfast while confabulating with Bella. She asked him about King and Savaria; he asked about Antoney and Pedro. She wanted to know why he had brought along four duffle bags; he wanted to know if she could get 500 kilos of cocaine and maybe a few thousand pounds of weed to northwest Indiana or Chicago.

"I'll have a talk to my uncle Papí about that, but more than likely he'll say no. He doesn't agree with doing business with Blacks. Most of them talk too much. We can deal with your people vicariously through the Mexican Mafia, but nothing direct." Bella wiped her greasy, sticky lips with a napkin. "Our family supplies this country with about seventy percent of its cocaine. We get the Acetone and Ethyl Ether from several U.S.-based oil companies. In return, we invest hundreds of millions into their NASA space programs every year. I don't think you understand the depth of detriment our family would suffer if any of this got out."

Shaking his head incredulously, Blake chuckled once. It was a short guffaw of sarcasm. Bella's mother, Mary Jane Patterson, was a 40- something-year old Black woman from Houston, Texas. With both Papí and Flako having children by Black women, the notion of them not doing business with Blacks was indeed ludicrous.

"And another thing," Bella sailed on, impervious to his sarcastic chuckle, "you'd be making the biggest mistake of your life if you give all that money to whoever those people are. $10 million dollars is *way* too much. If they're expecting a hundred grand, give them a hundred grand."

Shrugging off her opinion, Blake finished his breakfast.

About ten minutes later, he was in the back seat of Bella's pearly white Mercedes Maybach 57x, talking on the phone with Lakita as Bella drove him to the airport.

"I got a Lil more than twenty-five racks apiece for y'all," he said. "Oh yeah?" Lakita sounded anxious.

"Yeah. $750,000 apiece."

Lakita Thomas screamed through the phone, and Blake could do nothing but laugh.

Chapter 9

"Ow-ow, cowboy, is that your car?"

The peanut butter-complexioned girl was hanging out the driver's window of a dark blue, newer model Monte Carlo that had just parked a few car-lengths up the street from where Timothy Trice's candy-red 1973 Chevy Caprice was parked.

Tim-Tim was crouched down in front of the rear driver's side tire of his old school convertible, washing its chrome 28-inch rims with a soapy towel. He was tall, dark and not so handsome, shirtless with red Dickies shorts and a white pair of Reeboks.

"I know you ain't just call me no cowboy," Tim-Tim shouted, dropping the towel in a bucket full of soap and water.

He stood and looked back at the red brick two-story home behind him, scanning the first-floor windows to see if his 8-month pregnant girlfriend was peeking out at him. He figured she wouldn't be. E! was airing a Keeping Up with the Kardashians marathon, and Tiffany Jenkins never missed an episode.

Picking up the water hose he'd pulled from around back, Tim-Tim started rinsing the curds of soap off his Asanti rim, watching in his periphery as the nosy girl in the Monte Carlo stepped out and approached him. He was standing in the middle of Wentworth, right off of 109th Street on Chicago's south side.

"Hey, nappy-head, what's yo' name?" The girl asked. She was lithesome and petite, clad in a white halter top and pink Baby Phat short- shorts.

"Meeko," Tim-Tim lied. "Meeko?"

She smiled. "What kinda lame ass name is that? You Chi-town niggas is straight up ratchet, yuh feel me, like? Early, too, yuh feel me, like?" She rested her pert little rump against the side of his Chevy. "I'm Janautica. Most everybody calls me Bird, or Nauti. Just moved here from Durham, North Carolina with my cousin Princess. She got a job as a meteor... somethin', a weather person with MTN News."

"First off, ain't shit lame about me. By the way, I'm not from around here, either. I'm from—"

"Whateva, nappy-head," she interrupted, turning her attention to Chevy's brown leather Louis Vuitton interior. "Can I get a ride to Harold's Chicken Shack? It's over there on 88th and Stony Island, across from Kenwood Liquors."

"I know where it's at. What's wrong with the car you just got out of? It looked alright when you parked it a minute ago."

Nauti sucked her teeth indignantly, and rolled her eyes. "Did I ask you all that?"

"You better have some gas money." He headed around the side of his home with the water hose. Nauti was walking back from her car when he returned. She had a big faux leather purse under her arm, a lit cigarette in her hand.

Tim-Tim stared longingly at her long, sexy brown legs as she went to his Caprice's passenger door. He hastily joined her in the car, started the engine, and disappeared up the street before his girlfriend could peer out and catch him.

"Hold yuh horses, cowboy." Nauti buckled her seatbelt. "Slow this train down, stupid nappy-head! You done lost yo' damn mind."

A smirk fell off his face. "I know how to drive, Lil momma," he said, slowing to a halt at a stop sign. "So how long you been out here, and who you fuckin' with?"

"'About four or five weeks. I don't really fuck with nobody. Cess got a nigga she messes with, but he ain't got no money, yuh feel me? I ain't givin' up the mooncie to no bum-ass nigga."

"Givin' up the what?"

Nauti giggled sweetly. "My mooncie, boy."

"That how y'all say 'pussy' in North Carolina?" He chuckled. "Yes, it is. Got a problem with it, nappy-headed fucka?"

He chuckled again, and she laughed with him, causing him momentarily to escape the reality of what his life had become.

Timothy "Tim-Tim" Trice was practically in exile. The streets had labeled him a snitch. He had informed on his entire crew, the Dub Life Goonz, and gotten most of them murder charges after being busted with seven ounces of heroin on Valentine's Day. Although he regretted snitching on his childhood friends, he knew he would do it all over again if he had the chance. Prison was not on his shit to do list.

"Where you wanna go after we leave Harold's?" He asked the pretty girl next to him, his eyes fluctuating from the road ahead to Nauti's smooth, soft-looking thighs.

She smiled, shrugged nonchalantly, and said, "I don't care. Take me somewhere special."

"Special, like what? You mean special as in hotel-special?" Nauti turned her eyes to his. "What kind of hotel?"

"Ever heard of the Sybaris? They got pools and all kinds of exotic shit in every room." He dug in a front pocket and pulled out a fold of twenties. "This about twenty-two hundred. Room only costs one fifty."

"You stirring my grits," she said, in that euphonious Southern drawl that made Tim-Tim want to pull over and fuck her then and there.

King Rio

The Cocaine Princess 2

Chapter 10

It was 1:45 p.m. when the Citation-X landed on a deserted landing strip in Rockford, Illinois. The runway, flanked on one side by an abandoned airport building and several hangars with a large pond on the other side, seemed to be in pristine condition.

The door on the side of the jet folded down, and Blake descended the stairs first, followed by the Steatopygia, light-skinned Lakita Thomas, who, with all the ass she possessed, had the nerves to wear an obnoxiously tight, pink and white Coogi minidress with a matching pair of Air Force Ones.

Her eyes were hidden behind dark sunglasses. Her hair was a ponytailed mane of micro braids. She had a cheap black gym bag cradled under one arm like an oversized football.

A uniformed chauffeur stood beside a black Cadillac limousine in front of an empty hangar. Blake scrutinized the Hispanic driver's round, battle-scarred face; he had seen the man a couple of weeks prior on the Matamoros estate's 10-acre golf course, teeing off with Santiago Costilla.

"Señor Blake," the chauffeur said, taking Blake's duffle bags. "I'm Jorge Gomez. Bella say to me, um, drive for you, eh?"

Blake nodded and entered the rear of the limo with Lakita, struggling to keep his eyes away from her thick ass. He had had sex with both her and Lakeisha Brown, her older sister, at a Christmas Eve party last year, merely hours before he was gunned down.

The sexual aura between them was palpable.

"You can let go of that bag now," Blake grinned. "It won't disappear on you, I promise."

"Shiiiit," she lengthily replied, "I ain't takin' no chances." She laughed, unzipped the gym bag, and pulled out a $20,000 dollar bundle of bank-new hundreds. "Boy, do you know how hard I've been working to take care of me and my daughter? After all the bills are paid, I'm usually left with only two or three hundred dollas to myself. How am I supposed to survive off that? I've been selling pussy just to pay for clothes and school supplies."

King Rio

"Well, you'll be good now."

"You're damned skippy! $750,000—this kinda money hasn't been seen in my neighborhood, ever. The major dope boys don't even make this much money. Not without gettin' killed."

Blake knew exactly what she meant. In the ghettoes all across America, particularly in cities where gangsterism is a socially accepted ideology, a person's chance of being murdered is already sky-high; having even a few thousand dollars exacerbates that chance substantially.

"Make sure you move out of Gary," Blake wisely advised. "'Cause I guarantee somebody will find out about that money sooner or later. Those niggas who flew to Texas with you might get greedy and come at you for that bread."

"I highly doubt that, since we all got the same amount. However, you're right, though. I was already thinkin' about leaving." She took off her sunglasses and stared out the tinted window across from her.

Jorge was turning onto Des Plaines Road.

"Can he see through that glass?" Lakita asked, motioning toward the black glass partition that separated them from the driver.

"I don't think so," Blake answered. "Look, I brought you here with me for a reason. I want you to start working at this new strip club in the Chi. I'm tryin' to find out the names of all the big-money niggas, all the heavy-hitters."

"Boy, I can't dance. I don't know how to make my booty clap or none of that stuff strippers do."

"You'll learn." Blake felt the iPhone vibrate on his hip. He grabbed it, saw that it was Alexus calling, and said, "You got to be quiet for a minute, Kita. My wife is callin'."

"Nigga, you ain't married."

"Sshhh!" Blake hissed sibilantly. He answered the phone, and a second later, he was gazing at Alexus' somber, tear-streaked face.

"I *hate* rich people!" Alexus exclaimed. "Now I understand why the Bible says it's easier for a camel to pass through the eye of a needle than it is for a rich man to get into Heaven. Rich people are selfish, arrogant punks who care about nothing but them-

54

selves."

'One of the richest people in the country,' Blake thought to himself. 'Calling to tell me she hates rich people.'

He grinned at the irony of her statement. "What's wrong baby?" he asked.

"I just got off the line with Vladimir Khrushchev, the Russian billionaire whose net worth exceeds $200 billion, and do you know he would not agree to donate a single dime to succor all those starving families in Somalia? And it's not only him; I've contacted over thirty of the world' top billionaires, and only one of them, Gates, offered to match my $100 million dollar donation." She sighed despondently, wiped her eyes. "I wouldn't be the least bit surprised if the world did end next year. Maybe the Mayans are right."

"Calm down, baby. Don't let that bullshit get to you." Blake reached into one of his cash-filled front pockets and pulled out an unopened box of Swisher Sweets cigarillos, and a Ziploc bag containing forty-two grams of Purple Kush marijuana. He tossed them to Lakita.

"I can't help it," Alexus complained. "It pisses me off to know that the rich can be so stingy when it comes to aiding Africans. Look at what happened when that earthquake struck Japan earlier this year. They held star-studded telethons on almost every major television network. Celebrities doled out millions."

"You can do the same thing," Blake said. "You *own* the Minority Television Network. Call up some celebrities and get 'em all together for a televised fundraiser. Cryin' about it ain't gon' accomplish nothin'."

Alexus sniffled, dabbed at her leaking eyes with a linen napkin, and softly murmured, "I suppose you're right."

She went silent for a moment, and continued, "I'm on my way to Mogadishu now. It's a 23-hour flight. I have Momma, Tasia, and Britney with me, and a full camera crew. Bella's on a 767 a few miles behind us; Feed The Nation is donating 50,000 pounds of rice and beans to the people of Mogadishu. All of it's on the plane with her."

Alicia Keys' "Superwoman" played suddenly in Blake's head.

He tried, but could not repress the warm smile that burgeoned on his face as he gazed at the comely face of his pure-hearted, selfless woman. "Baby, you must have a thousand hearts packed into that Lil chest of yours."

"Wish I had something else packed into me right now," Alexus whispered salaciously. "Let me see Monster."

Blake laughed and shook his head. "I'm in the back of a limousine.

What if the driver looked back here and caught me with my dick out?"

"He'll probably wish his was as big as yours. Now stop procrastinating and show me that dick."

Conspiratorially, Lakita rubbed her palms together as she watched Blake undo his gray leather Louis Vuitton belt. He knew that she had been listening to his phone discourse. He knew that she had wanted to see Monster ever since he had greeted her at the Brownsville airport. Therefore, he slaked Alexus and Lakita's visual thirsts by whipping out his lengthy love muscle.

"Mmm," Alexus moaned agreeably. "That thing *is* a monster. What did you do, use a penis-pump? How did you make it so big?"

"Same way you made that pussy so wet. Magic." He raised the phone back to his face and attempted to tuck his hardening phallus back inside his gray Louis Vuitton boxers.

However, Lakita did not let him. She moved quickly to her knees in front of him, grabbed the base of his dick with one hand, and sucked it into her mouth, all the way down her throat.

He inhaled deeply, as if he had been splashed with a bucket of gelid water.

"I was just watching one of those Cherokee movies on my iPad,"

Alexus said. "She has a big ass like I do, and she can do anal for hours, even with a dick that's as long and thick as yours. What if you could do that to me? Would you like that?"

"Hell yeah," Blake replied, fighting to keep a straight face.

"Figured you would. I'll have to buy a few toys to practice with first.

Call you back later, okay? I'm about to go to the restroom and get myself together. You've gotten me all wet."

"A'ight, baby. I'll hit you when I get to Chicago."

Blake put the iPhone back in its clip on a case on his hip. For a couple of minutes, he shut his eyes and enjoyed the powerful suction of Lakita's mouth, the incessant flickering of her serpentine tongue, as she glided her lips up and down his engorged shaft. Her gag reflex was obsolete. She deep-throated him easily.

Opening his eyes, he looked down at her. "You tryin' to kill me?"

She popped his saliva-coated dick out of her mouth. "You know, you can fuck me like that if you want to. I'm a pro at that shit."

"You a pro at what?"

"At getting' fucked like Cherokee. My baby daddy thinks I'm better at it than her. Watch." Lakita spit on his dick then mounted him, raising her tight minidress over her knees and pulling aside her floral-print thong. She pressed the hard, wet crown of his dick against the sphincter of her ass, and slowly sank down onto him, impaling herself on his rigid member.

"Put your hands on my hips," Lakita said, "and hold on for the ride."

Blake did as he was told, holding on as the mare-bottomed 22-year old began sliding up and down on him. She moved languidly at first, biting down on her lower lip, squeezing Blake's shoulders, gradually picking up speed until she was bouncing at a jackhammer's pace. The pace with which she rode him was astonishing.

It ended up being an unforgettable ride, in his opinion, one that would forever be etched in his memory.

King Rio

The Cocaine Princess 2

Chapter 11

Trintino "T-Walk" Walkson, decked out in an expensive pinstriped Niemann Elements suit and tie, stalked regally through an obstinate crowd of beautiful young women — Steatopygia Straight Stuntin magazine models — in his penthouse suite at the Four Seasons hotel in New York City. He had an MTN camera crew with him. They were filming video of the women simply due to Rita Mae Bishop's promise that she would look into Walkson's little reality show idea.

All of the models had on bone-white Niemann Elements gowns and dresses. Most of them were sipping Krug Rosé champagne from crystal stem glassware, bobbing their heads to a DJ Kay Slay mixtape that was playing from somewhere near the wet bar, where Kay Slay was sitting in front of a camera being interviewed by an MTN director.

"Excuse me." A dark-skinned woman with 36C-22-48 measurements, tapped on T-Walk's shoulder. "Can I have a moment of your time? I'm interested in knowing more about this show before I sign anything."

"Certainly. I mean, I understand that completely," T-Walk said, turning to the tight-eyed, glossy-lipped woman. "What's your name?"

"Ashley Hunter. My modeling name's Thunder." She beamed.

"Well, Ashley, I plan on executive producing 'Brick House' with Kay—"

"I know that much already," she interrupted. "What I'm concerned about is the image. I don't want to be typecast as some dumb, big-bootied Black girl. I'm an educated Nigerian whose parents moved to Port Arthur, Texas, and worked hard to put me through college. It is an absolute must that I know beforehand the requirements of my role in this TV show"

"First off, let me say that there is nothing wrong with your shape. I don't care how many times you have to watch your favorite artist's video on YouTube because it's been labeled too explicit due to a big booty Black woman shaking her ass too hard.

King Rio

All of you Straight Stuntin models are the epitome of beauty. Why do you think Kim K is so successful? And J-Lo? Think of what the modeling industry would be like if Buffie had been given a reality show."

Thunder assented with a nod of her head and an even wider smile. A dozen models behind her mimicked her actions.

"Here's what I'm thinking," continued T-Walk. "I'm envisioning something similar to….what's the name of that show with all the Italians?"

"Jersey Shore," shouted one of the models.

"Yeah, something like that show. Only you all will be living like Tiger Woods, in a $50 million dollar mansion on Jupiter Island, 10 miles away from North Palm Beach, Florida, which is where the other house will be."

"What other house?" Thunder asked.

"There will be two different shows being filmed simultaneously: Brick House of Jupiter Island, and Brick House of North Palm Beach. One'll air on Sunday nights, the other on Thursday nights after Mariah's Salon. If you remember, the season premiere of The Game on BET had over 7 million viewers; I believe we can double that. In fact, I believe we can easily have 20 or 30 million viewers tuned into every episode. The industry has made it somewhat taboo for men like myself to feel good about seeing women like you. So they avoid showing you to the masses."

"And instead," said Montana, another dark-hued paragon, "they continue to saturate the market with blonde-haired, blue-eyed, skinny little white girls with silicone breasts."

"Or Black girls who are shaped like them," T-Walk said. "Now I'm not saying that White women aren't beautiful; thousands of Black men have jungle fever, and there's nothing wrong with that. But when's the last time you saw a woman shaped like Buffie, or like any of you, on a talk show, or a sitcom, or a reality show? Brick House will not only give all of you that chance, it'll also show us men the kind of women we *love* to see. And we'll all get paid in the process."

For a brief moment, Ashley "Thunder" Hunter scrutinized T-Walk's expression. Then she nodded her head again, and most of the girls began to applaud T-Walk's poignant speech. The fact that Thunder was considered a leader of the group was palpable.

He mingled with the women a short while longer, then headed toward D Kay Slay, ready to work out the final details of their joint contract with MTN.

But his HTC smart phone rang before he made it to the wet bar. "Blake's in Chicago," Tasia Olsen said acidly.

"You sure about that?" T-Walk whispered.

"Yeah, I'm fuckin' sure, yo. I'm on a flight to Somalia with Alexus as we speak. She just got off the phone with him."

"Somalia?"

"It's a long story."

T-Walk took a second to think, a second to ponder and weigh his options. Tasia, his best friend Bookie's girlfriend, had already told him that Blake had said something about giving the $10 million dollars to somebody else. But why would Blake decide to do that? After all, Blake had entrusted T-Walk with the task of eliminating the rats, and T-Walk, a man of his word, had already managed to get one of them eradicated. So what if he had lied to everyone about the price in hopes of pocketing ninety-nine percent of the hit money? He had once read Robert Greene's prolific tome, "The 48 Laws of Power," and in it, he learned the value of taking credit for another's work. It was the same tactic employed by companies all over the world.

Why shouldn't he partake in the universal strategy of success?

"I'm way out on the east coast right now," T-Walk said, smiling and waving at an alabaster-complexioned German model who was stepping past.

"I don't care *where* you're at, yo!" Tasia snapped. "Get your ass on a plane, find that black son of a bitch, and kill him!" She hung up on him.

Frustrated, he grinded his teeth together, put away his phone, and squeezed his eyes tightly shut, gathering his inner self. If Tasia was not so much like a sister to him, he knew that he would have cussed her out a long time ago.

Opening his eyes, he found Thunder standing in front of him. Her eyes were squinted, her arms crossed over twin swells of cleavage.

"How'd you get so dang light-skinned?" She inquired. "You half White or something? Indian?"

"My mom's White. Pops is blacker than you."

"Hmm. Hear you actually used to date Alexus Costilla."

"I did... for a couple of months, anyway. I called it quits when she started sneaking around with Blake."

"Was that before or after she inherited all that money?"

"Before. We broke up in late-December of last year. She inherited the Costilla fortune three months later." T-Walk's brows came together. It was his turn to do the squinting. "Why are you so interested in my life? What's up with all these questions?"

Thunder shrugged dismissively. "Just asking. I think it's somewhat strange that you went from dating Alexus to dating her cousin. That seems a little vindictive to me."

A response was poised on the tip of T-Walk's tongue. But one of the girls summoned Thunder from across the room, and she turned around and headed through the dense crowd of ambulant models, her voluminous derriere undulating from side to side.

As she walked away, T-Walk was reminded of Alexus. He remembered all the special moments they had shared, the laughs, the smiles, the all-night lovemaking sessions. He missed her dearly. If there had been any way for him to speak directly to her, he would have expressed his true feelings months ago. But he no longer had her phone number, and Tasia sure as hell wasn't about to give it to him, not with Kenya and her being so close. Since asking Blake was out of the question, T-Walk's only way of contacting her was via Twitter. But Alexus had nineteen and a half million avid followers on there, and he knew all of his messages were drowning in a sea of others.

T-Walk went to the wet bar and hashed over the "Brick House" contract with Kay Slay. Then he took some pictures with the girls, ingested a modicum of Rosé, and briskly departed from the penthouse suite.

Chapter 12

"We at the Chicago Police Department think it would be wise for you to seek shelter in our witness protection program. The Indianapolis and Michigan City police departments in Indiana feel the same way," said CPD Lieutenant Steve Sawyer.

Timothy Trice was sitting naked in a heated Jacuzzi at the romantic Sybaris hotel, holding his cell phone to his ear while Janautica, seated next to him, fed him chocolate-covered strawberries.

"I'm not doin' no shit like that,' ' Tim-Tim replied vehemently. "I'm cool here in Chicago. Shit, I'll be safe if you muhfuckas quit sendin' me to do all that bullshit."

"Whoa, whoa, you're forgetting the fact that I put my ass on the line to keep you out of prison. There is no other man in all of Cook County who has been busted with seven ounces of heroin and received ten years unsupervised probation. If not for me, your Black ass would be rotting away in Statesville," Sawyer snapped. "And besides, we've had you wire up on, what, twenty-five dealers? That's nothing. We have confidential informants who've brought down entire organizations."

"I don't want to get in no fuckin' program, Sawyer. A'ight? Fuck that. Why can't I stay—"

"I wasn't askin'," Sawyer said. "You're the star witness in what's prob'ly the most high-profile case in Midwest history. The other witness was just murdered in Gary, and we cannot risk losing you."

Timothy dropped his head back, released a deep breath, and sunk deeper into the bubbling water. Janautica pressed a strawberry to his thick lips. He bit into it, and the petite North Carolina girl lapped up the escaping juices from his chin. He thought she looked a bit like Zoe Saldana, and her Lancôme perfume was sensuous and appeasing.

"Well, since I don't really have a choice..." Tim-Tim murmured, "I guess I'll have to say yeah."

"That's good!" Sawyer chuckled dryly. "Meet me at the police station on Harrison and Kedzie in one hour."

"Fuck you, Sawyer."

Ending the call, Timothy reached over the Jacuzzi's side and dropped the phone onto his crumpled pants. When he turned back to his companion, she was sitting on the ledge next to his head, pushing a strawberry into her dripping pussy.

"Who was that?" She asked, circling her clitoris with her middle finger.

"Some punk-ass nobody." Tim-Tim moved between her legs, and began to kiss her inner thighs. He loved the softness of her caramel skin, the smoothness of it. "We gotta get up outta here in a Lil bit. I'm talkin' about within, like, the next thirty or forty minutes."

"Okay, nappy-head," Nauti said softly, as Tim-Tim went to tonguing and sucking her palpitating clitoris.

Seconds before she succumbed to an intense orgasm, she rewarded him with the chocolate-layered fruit she had pushed inside her warm tunnel.

He immediately ate it and got right back to pleasing her with his skillful tongue, sending the sexy young Southern girl into a screaming climax.

Timothy's dick was brick-hard. He was ready to pound her pussy again, just as he had done when they had first entered the room hours earlier.

He picked her up and stepped out of the undulant water. Wrapping her long legs around his waist, her arms around his neck, Janautica kissed his forehead.

"Meeko, you got a ratchet-ass tongue in that mouth of yours, yuh feel me? I mean, like, hard body."

"What the fuck kinda language y'all got down there in North Carolina? 'Cause that shit sound Chinese to me."

"Shut up, nappy head," Nauti fired back.

He nearly tripped over her purse as he set her down on the foot of the round, rose petal-covered bed. Taking a seat next to her, he said, "Do that one thing again."

"I've been waitin' on you to ask," Nauti replied with a wicked smile. Janautica Spalding went to her knees at the foot of the bed as

Timothy eased onto his back and lifted his hairy black legs in the air. Leaning forward, she pressed the flat of her tongue against his asshole and started licking, while at the same time she picked up her toppled pink purse and slipped her hand inside it.

She pulled out a nickel-plated .38 special with a titanium silencer screwed into its barrel, shoved it in his ass, and sent three bullets spiraling through his body. One round punched out the top of his skull, jack-in-the- boxing him. The other bullets tore out of his left shoulder and became lodged in the headboard.

Janautica grabbed a pair of rubber gloves from her purse, along with a rag and a small bottle of Clorox bleach, and for the next forty-five minutes, she slogged around the room, meticulously scrubbing every surface she touched in an effort to erase her fingerprints.

Then she sat on the bed next to Tim-Tim's dead body and called Young-D, Blake King's best friend, from her Blackberry Smartphone.

"I got that sum bitch," she said shakily.

"Just tell me where y'all at, and I'll come blow his shit off," Young- D said.

"I already *got* the sum bitch, yuh he'r me? Only thang I need you to do is get rid of 'im."

King Rio

Chapter 13

Blake was completely disgusted with himself.

For the second time in not even twenty-four hours, he had cheated on his fiancée. The fact that he had failed to use protection on both occasions made matters worse; not only was he cheating, but he was also exposing himself to the risk of catching sexually transmitted diseases.

'How dumb can I get?' He thought staring into Alexus' tired green eyes. He was sitting in back of the limousine, video chatting with her on the iPhone while watching America's Most Wanted on his Infuse.

"This Lil lame ass nigga don't look nothin' like me," he said, watching a reenactment of himself spraying an AK-47 at a crowd of urban- dressed Black men in the parking lot of The Swagger, T-Walk's nightclub in Michigan City, Indiana. Blake had killed four men that night, including two police officers, and he had murdered another young guy earlier that day with the same weapon.

"He looks like you looked back then," Alexus stated with a giggle, "When you were Rick Ross's size."

"I was never that goddamn fat."

"Oh, wait, before I forget," Alexus said, suddenly enthused. "Attorney Vernon Brown sent our lawyer an email this morning. He's the attorney of Slim and Birdman Williams, the CEOs of Cash Money Records. I don't know how they did it, but they've somehow managed to obtain copies of four compact discs full of songs that you rapped in with Young-D and your brother Streets, and they're interested in signing you to their label."

"Hell muhfuckin' yeah. I mean, I know I don't need the money, but I'd rather have them sellin' my music than anybody else. Tell 'em as long as they sign Young-D and Streets with me, I'll sign with them. And we can donate all the proceeds to Somalia."

Their conversation stopped as a reenactment of a shooting in Indianapolis began to unfold on the screen of Blake's Infuse; Alexus tuned in from her iPad.

There were four 70's-model Chevrolet Caprices, each cherry-colored with big chrome rims, lined up along a curbside in the Haughville area of Indianapolis. The character impersonating Blake exited the passenger's door of the first car with a Heckler and Koch MP-5 submachine gun in hand and immediately started arguing with a large group of hustlers across the street from him. A moment later, he waved toward the other Chevys, and machine gun barrels appeared from the drivers windows of all three of them. A hail of fully automatic gunfire ensued.

"That's a hundred percent bullshit," Blake said, breaking the silence. "My jaw was wired shut, and I had twin bullet holes on both sides of my mouth. How could I have been able to scream at them? And I didn't wave at my niggas; they saw them other niggas runnin' to grab pistols, so they started bussin'."

"I can't wait for the day when you finally decide to start using the English language correctly. Now hush, boy."

Blake watched America's Most Wanted all the way up until his impersonator turned around and gunned down a seemingly innocent man who was running out the front door of a duplex.

"He had a shotgun, baby. On everything I love, he had a shotgun. I was gon' kill him, anyway, for fuckin' with my daughter, but I swear that nigga had a shotgun," Blake said. He turned and looked out his window. The passenger's side of the limo was facing a densely populated recreation park at the end of Douglas Boulevard, on Albany Street. Beyond the short steel fence, a bunch of Black people were barbecuing, drinking beer and hard liquor, smoking blunts and cigarettes, and having a good time. Kids were sliding down slides, swinging on swings, and chasing each other around.

"When I get back from Africa," Alexus said, "I'm going to go ahead and get T-Walk to take that paternity test for the baby. I know it's been bothering you."

"Fuck that test. King Neal Costilla is my son, and that's that."

"Now you know that's not fair, Blake."

"What the fuck you mean that ain't fair? T-Walk is fuckin' *Kenya,* your *cousin.* And you want him to be King's daddy? Hell naw! You trippin' hard, baby. On some straight up Jerry Springer shit."

"I didn't say I *want* him to be King Neal's father. But I'm not gonna pretend like what happened between T-Walk and I was a dream, okay? I can't go through life not knowing who the father of my child is."

"Still some Jerry Springer shit," Blake muttered discontentedly.

A black Range Rover Evoque turned onto Albany in front of the limo and parked across from it. Like the three lime-green Dodge Magnums that were lined up behind the limo, and the maroon Chevy Avalanche situated before it, the Evoque boasted a chrome set of 30-inch rims.

"Baby, I gotta go. Reesie Cup and Lil Cholly just pulled up."

"You plan on asking them about those 10 women?"

"We got some b'ness to discuss first. But yeah, I'm gon' get on top of that, too." Blake lit yet another Purple Kush-filled cigarillo—he had already smoked two of them since dropping Lakita off at the Wit hotel—and took a deep toke from it. He coughed thrice. "Love you baby."

"I love you, too, boy. Be safe out there. I'll call you when I wake up."

Blake sat there and stared at his iPhone for a full minute after the call had ended, smoking his blunt, wondering how in the world he'd ended up with the $50 billion dollar woman. He felt unworthy of her love at times, and this was one of those times. Why was she sticking with him? He was far less educated than she was. She had been born and raised in a gated community in Brownsville, Texas; he had been born and raised in a squalid, mostly African American neighborhood full of crack dealers in Michigan City, Indiana. She had traveled the world; he had rarely even ventured out of his hometown, and it was only to Chicago and back whenever he did.

Alexus' mother, Rita Mae Bishop, had a Master's degree from Harvard; Blake's father was a crackhead sanitation worker, his mother an alcoholic grade school teacher. After Alexus' paternal grandmother, Vida Costilla, had passed away and left Alexus the Costilla family fortune, Blake had figured that she would be married to some sort of athlete or actor shortly thereafter. But that had not been the case at all, and the fact that she was still with him, still loved him, spoke volumes.

As he exited the back door of the limousine, eyes low and bloodshot, canary-yellow diamonds aglow, the doors to all the big-rimmed vehicles opened and out- spilled a pack of top-level drug dealers.

The drivers of the Magnums were some of Blake's childhood friends: Maleek "Fly" Harris, a tall, light-skinned nigga in his early twenties who had been a star basketball player in his high school years. Alonzo "Blubbly" Jones, a dark man with a terrible stutter, and a bad coke habit that he won't quit. How could we forget, Dante "Young-D" Roscoe, the brown-skinned, rail-thin 18-year old who was also on the run for the 15 Indianapolis murders. Blake had left the three of them with forty kilos of coke apiece when he had fled the States months earlier, and they had sold every gram.

Altogether, there were six male passengers with Fly and Blub-by, and two young women with Young-D.

Out of the Avalanche stepped four Mafia Insane Vice Lords from Gary, Indiana—Rube and Batman, two dark men with dreadlocks: Pat, commonly referred to as P.A.T. (Pimpin' All the Time), a walnut complexioned man with a baldhead and a muscular physique that rivaled Blake's; and Kenny-Lord, a coal-black, thick-armed man.

Reesie Cup, who could have easily passed as Fly's older brother, hopped out of the Range Rover in a fresh white business suit. He had Lil Cholly and Bey-Bey—two brown-hued Traveling Vice Lords who were also clad in expensive white suits with gold silk ties—with him.

Following Ressie Cup into the park, Blake said, "I like that Range you got. Ain't never seen one like that."

"Yeah, Joe, that's the new one. It's not even on sale yet. Land Rover gave it to me to promote at the club I just opened in Vegas."

"That muhfucka *decent.* And I see you put some thirties on that bitch." Blake hit his blunt a few more times, then passed it to Cup. "Here, get some of this Kush in you."

The 17 men, excluding Blake's chauffeur and Young-D's female passengers, formed a circle in front of a vacant wooden bench. Blake studied their faces for a while before he spoke.

"I need to know y'all names," he said, sweeping his eyes over the six men he didn't know. "Nicknames and cities' do."

However, when the first of them gaped his mouth to talk, Blake changed his mind and said, "Never mind that though. I know that two of y'all are from Indianapolis, and the other four are from South Bend and Fort Wayne, Indiana, and Maywood and Bellwood, Illinois. Another thing I know is that none of you have ever snitched; that fact is what got you all in front of me tonight."

Glancing at his Audemar, Blake saw that it was almost nine o'clock, which meant *America's Most Wanted* was about to go off. He didn't want to be outside for too much longer.

"So," he continued, "I want to bring y'all into the fold on some *real* money. I'm talkin' about bricks of that top-of-the-line dope, ten racks a piece. However, my amigo will start by frontin' fifty bricks to every one of you. If either of you can handle more than that, just hit the connect and let him know."

"Man, are you for real right now?" Bey-Bey scoffed. "Your fiancé is *Alexus Costilla*. She got that Warren Buffett money. Fifty bricks is a lot to us, but you can get us more than that, Joe."

"Did you hear anything I said?" Blake shook his head, incredulous. "If you can move more, you can get more. If you can move two or three hundred key's, he'll give you two or three hundred key's. Pounds of Kush, key's of boy and girl—y'all can get that shit for the low. Every week, too. But if you play, you gon' lay. Everybody understand that?"

"Pardon the body," said Batman. "So, what if you get locked up? Not wishin' bad luck on you or nothin', but half the world know you wanted for all them bodies."

"Don't worry about me. The plug'll fuck with y'all 'til I say otherwise. What's important is that y'all always keep b'ness solid buy a different prepaid cell phone every fifteen days and only use 'em to call the connect, and don't tell a soul."

The conversation sailed on for twenty more minutes. Blake learned the names of the six men he had not known. The Nap-town guys were Baby Mike from 42nd and Post Road, and Lil Dion from Land Life. Hope was a Bellwood native. Snarko was a tall, Snoop Dogg-looking nigga from South Bend. Head Bussa, dark and dreadlocked, represented Fort Wayne. And Jermaine was from Maywood. Blake was surprised to see that, out of the 17 men, 11 of them were wearing Niemann Elements outfits.

Young-D stepped over to Blake and whispered, "Tim-Tim's in Lake Michigan, bruh. I chopped him up, wrapped him in plastic, stuffed him in two suitcases, and dumped him in the lake down by Navy Pier. Tied some bricks to the suitcases so they wouldn't float up to the surface."

"Is everybody into choppin' people up now?" said Blake.

"I had to. It's the only way I could get him out of the hotel. If ol' girl had just set him up like I told her to, shit would've went smooth. But she offed him herself."

"Who is she?"

Young-D motioned toward his Magnum." The skinny lil bitch in the back seat. Janautica. We call her Bird, though." He chuckled. "I still can't believe she offed that hoe ass nigga. Didn't think she had it in her."

"Have you already paid her?"

"I tried. Offered her fifty racks. She turned it down."

"What, she rich or somethin'?"

"Hell naw. Her family's broke as hell. I've been payin' their bills ever since I moved to Durham in March. I just got her cousin Princess a job as a secretary's assistant at MTN, but that Lil fourteen bucks an hour ain't enough for everybody, so I'm still helpin' out."

"I'll be right back." Blake jogged out of the park, his dark brown eyes oscillating left to right as he studied every vehicle on Albany. He was in what the locals called Holy City, the birthplace of Vice Lords, and one of Chicago's most dangerous neighborhoods.

His iPhone sounded off before he made it to Young-D's car. It was T-Walk, calling for the umpteenth time.

"What the fuck you want, ol' lyin' ass nigga?" Blake answered, vexed by T-Walk's incessant calls. "I know you didn't handle that issue in the G, 'cause I know the muhfuckas who did it."

"Calm down, Blake. It's not that serious. I admit I didn't do it,

The Cocaine Princess 2

all right? But I got it done. I spread the word, and it was handled. Is that not what you asked me to do?"

Blake grinded his teeth, clenched his right fist. Last Christmas Eve, T-Walk had sent three masked men, including Reginald "Bookie" Nelson, Alexus' cousin, to murder Blake, and they had come very close to doing just that, shooting him ten times. He had killed one of them during the brief shootout, and that was yet another murder that the D.A. was staunchly determined to pin on him.

"I need some of that money, Blake. I'll pay you back with interest. If you want me to, I'll even sign a contract. But I need that money."

"I'll get at you later, homeboy. I'm on some—"

"Where are you right now? I think it'd be better if we talked face-to- face. Words ain't shit without eye contact."

"I'm in Chicago, at Albany Park." "On my way," T-Walk said, and hung up.

Shaking his head, Blake put away his phone and went to Young-D's Magnum. The two girls — one in the passenger's seat, the other behind her — eyed him as he approached. He opened the rear passenger's side door.

"Scoot over," he grumbled.

Janautica moved quickly to her left, never taking her eyes off him. He got in beside her, closed the door, and looked at her. She donned a white Baby Phat tube-top and a tiny pair of matching cotton shorts. Her hair was in a modest bob. Her mouth was wide open.

"Oh, my God," said the pretty redbone in the passenger's seat. She had her pie-shaped visage hovering between the front seats, gazing at Blake with awestruck eyes. "Blake King! *The* Blake King! In the back seat of my boyfriend's car! This cannot be happening."

Blake laughed. "You must be Princess." He reached out and shook her hand.

"Yes, I'm Princess Spalding. I'm employed at your fiancée's television network." She gave him a cursory glance. "I've always pictured you as being dressed like, I don't know, Will Smith or somebody. Or maybe like George Clooney. Why are you out here walking around as if you're not wanted?"

"Man, fuck those cops."

"Oh, I see you're not into using standard American English, either, huh?"

"What?"

"SAE's the dialect you always hear on the news. It's okay, though,

because although many of those whose dialect is SAE look down on ghetto dialects , there is no such thing as superior and inferior dialects in the linguistic sense. As long as you communicate your intended meaning to listeners, then the words you use or the ways you construct your sentences are as valid linguistically as any other."

Blake did not say anything. He stared at Princess's enthusiastic expression, and she kept right on bumping her gums.

"Here's another fun fact I bet you didn't know. Your fiancée's uncle has three kids, Antoney, Isabella and Pedro, and their mother's an African American woman from Houston named Mary Jane Patterson. Can you tell me where they got their names from?"

I'm way too high to be gettin' quizzed like this, Blake thought about saying. What came out was a simple, "Nah."

"Well, in August of 1619, a year before they celebrated the Mayflower's arrival, a ship containing a stolen cargo of Africans sailed into the harbor at Jamestown, Virginia. The ship's captain traded his human cargo to an Englishman for food, and among those twenty Africans were Antoney, Isabella, and Pedro. They were America's very first Africans"

"Damn, straight up? You just taught me somethin'," Blake said. "Yup. And Mary Jane Patterson is the same name as the first Black

woman to ever graduate from an American college. She graduated from Oberlin College in 1862."

"Shut the hell up, Cess," Janautica snapped. "Sound like a goddamn walkin' 'cyclopedia, runnin' yo' fuckin' mouf."

Blake turned to her with a smile on his face. He tugged a $20,000 dollar rubber-banded bundle of hundreds out of his gray

The Cocaine Princess 2

denim shorts and offered it to her. "Here. Take this money and –"

"I don't want your money, okay? Now, I done told yuh Lil friend fifty-eleven times I don't want nothin' to do with y'all's money. So you can just go on out yonda with all that mess, yuh feel me, like?"

"Maaaan, what the fuck you just say?" Blake burst out laughing, genuine and jubilant. He laughed so hard his ribs ached. Tears grew in his eyes.

"I don't see what's funny," Janautica said. But she and Princess were already beginning to laugh along with him.

"Aw, shit, you just fucked me up with that alien language," he said, wiping his eyes with the back of his hand. "I ain't ever heard nobody talk like that in my *life*."

"You know what, you Lil...black fucka. Can't stand you already, and we ain't met two seconds ago."

Princess said, "Girl, I'd take that money if I were you. You and I both know you need it. Don't be ridiculous." She shifted her eyes to Blake. "And why are you trying to give her all of that cash in the first place?"

"Get you some business, okay, Cess? 'Cause you sho is all up in mine,"

Janautica replied, rolling her eyes and twisting her neck truculently.

Blake knew right then that Janautica had not told her cousin about the murder, which was a good thing. It meant she was capable of keeping her mouth shut about certain things that weren't to be discussed.

"I need to talk to you in private." He grabbed her hand, pushed his door back open, and led her onto the sidewalk. As they walked to his limo, he asked, "Why won't you accept our money?"

"Young-D's been doing everything for my family in North Carolina.

He bought us cars, paid for my mom's medicine, paid for groceries, rent, and utilities. He even got us a big-ol' swimmin' pool for the backyard, yuh feel me, like? I'm rockin' with him, like, hard body. I mean, he straight gets it in *early* on the hustle, yuh feel me? Any fuck-nigga snitchin' on a real nigga like Young-D

75

needs to be dead and gone, anyhow. Fuck'm and feed im beans and colla' greens, yuh ask me."

Chuckling, Blake leaned back against the trunk of the limo, slipping the rubber band off his chunky bundle of cash. He saw that a crowd of girls had migrated over to where his guys were huddled in the park, attracted to the scent of money like sharks to the smell of blood.

"Is them guns, like, real gold?" Janautica asked with her gaze fixed on the twin nines in Blake's shoulder holsters.

"Yup. 24-karat". He flicked his eyes over to a young Black woman who was walking up the sidewalk. She was as black as the night's sky and impishly proportioned, pushing a stroller while three kids-two boys and a girl-ambled nimbly behind her. "Ay, Lil momma, come and grab this," he said, extending his cash-filled hand toward her.

"You talkin' to me?" The girl slapped a palm onto her chest and gasped.

"Yeah, I'm talkin' to you. Don't start that screamin', hoppin', and shit. Just take it and do something good for yourself."

The girl was sobbing even before she had the immense pile of hundred-dollar bills in her hand, and when she fanned through it, she broke all the way down. "Oh, Jesus," she cried as her arms enveloped Blake. "Bless yo' heart, boy. Lord knows I needed this. Mah baby-daddy just got killed a few months ago. It's been hard ever since."

"Yeah, well, make sure you don't go jackin' it off on some nigga. Take care of them kids. Getcha life together," Blake advised. He happily watched the girl turn the stroller around and race off in the direction from which she had come, urging her kids to keep up. "I've always wanted to do somethin' like that. If I could do that every minute of my life, I know I'd be happy."

"Awww," Janautica cooed. "You betta stop yo' shit. That was so nice of you." Then the sweetness in her sugary tone dissipated. "But you still just gave dat bald-headed ho my money."

"Your money? Could've sworn you said you didn't want it."

"So what? That don't mean you give it to the first—"

A sparkling blue Rolls Royce Ghost pulled up beside the limo, halting Blake and Janautica's conversation. The driver's window slid down. Ensconced in the sumptuous white leather driver's seat was T-Walk.

Without giving it much thought, Blake reached for one of his pistols.

Instinctively, T-walk stomped on the gas, and his tires screamed as he started to speed away.

The stentorian reports from Blake's guns were rapid as he ran up the middle of the street firing round after round into the Ghost's rear end, shattering its back window. He watched it swerve from side to side and crash into four parked cars before it finally turned a corner two blocks up and vanished.

He sprinted briskly back to the limo. Janautica crouched down beside it. All around them, people were flooding out of the park, rushing to their cars, running away from the scene of the shooting.

Holstering his pistols, Blake snatched open the back door of the limo and said, "Ay, c'mon, Lil momma."

He got in behind Janautica, and the chauffeur reversed onto Douglas then started toward Kedzie.

"Dang, Nigga," Janautica whispered softly." You straight ratchet like that all the time?"

Blake turned to her just as Jorge made it to the intersection of Douglas and Kedzie…but he did not get an opportunity to answer her. Instead, he shouted, "Get down! Get down!"

Then he wrapped an arm around Janautica's narrow waist and dove to the hardwood floor, praying for God to save him.

T-Walk was wounded.

The first bullet had lanced through the back of his left shoulder and out the front of it, as smoothly and easily as a hot butter knife through a stick of margarine. And the second stinging round had punched an almost see-through hole in the center of his left hand.

"Bitch ass nigga done shot me!" He had snarled as he had stopped the now battered and shot up the Rolls Royce in front of a yellow brick apartment building on 15th and Kedzie. After grabbing his trusty old Mac-11 from under his seat, he'd set it on his lap and again put the gas pedal to the floor, determined to catch back up with Blake and give him a taste of his own medicine.

King Rio

"Yeah, nigga," T-Walk said, glowering at the limousine as he spotted it at the intersection of Douglas and Kedzie. "Gotcha ass now!"

He hit the brake just as he reached the intersection, dropped his right hand from the steering wheel to the submachine gun, raised it, and started shooting out the right side of his windshield, which already had several bullet holes in it. Fire leapt from the Mac-11's barrel. Bullets pounded the limo's left side, first the driver's window and door, then all the way to its trunk. And when his 32-round clip was empty, T-Walk sped away hastily, on his way to Northwestern Memorial Hospital.

Chapter 14
3 weeks later

"If I could get through this glass, I'd fuck you up, Blake. I'd punch you so hard you'd swear I shot you."

"Damn." Blake smiled derisively. "You know what?" "Shut up."

"You look so sexy when you' mad."

"Nothing about this is funny, Blake. Absolutely nothing. So you can wipe that retarded little smirk off your face and get serious," Alexus snapped in a tone that bespoke both anger and vexation.

She was standing in a small, private visiting room at LaPorte County Jail in northern Indiana, staring at Blake through a thick slab of bulletproof glass. She had on a simple white tee shirt, white leggings, and white six- inch heels. No jewelry. No makeup. All pissed off.

It was a few minutes past 10:00 a.m., Saturday, September third, and Alexus felt just as sullen now as she'd felt three weeks earlier when Blake had been captured.

They'd found and arrested him-along with Young-D and some girl named Janautica Spalding-at a comfort Inn hotel in Michigan City, Indiana. Young-D had been foolish enough to order Pizza Hut, and the pizza delivery man had spotted Blake inside the hotel room when Janautica was paying for their order. Needless to say, the pizza man had contacted the MCPD, who had then surrounded the hotel in droves.

Now, as Alexus studied Blake's seemingly nonchalant expression, she became even more disconcerted. He was standing there as if his black and white-striped jail scrubs were comfortable, as if being locked up was the most normal thing in the world.

"It's about time you paid me a visit," he said through the phone. "I was startin' to think you forgot about me."

"I've written letters to you every day since I returned from Africa, haven't I? You asked me to send you a bunch of pictures; I mailed you more than a hundred of them. And we talk on the phone for at least two or three hours every single day."

"So muhfuckin' what? Is that supposed to satisfy me? I'm allowed visits one day per week, right? I've been here for three weeks—"

"Oh, shut up. I'm here now. We could've argued over the phone if that's what you wanted to do," Alexus said. Her eyes were glued to his.

"You're lucky that limo was armored, you know that? You'd appreciate me flying all the way from L.A. to visit your black ass, then."

Blake's smile widened. "You ain't lyin'." He chuckled." I thought I was out the game, baby."

"That limo's a replica of the Beast," Alexus said." Once I saw Obama's armored car, I knew it was worth buying."

"What's up with the Monique show? You been on there, yet?"

"I'll be there tomorrow with the cast of Sweet Licks. Oh, my God, I still can't believe Sweet Licks has five Emmy Award nominations!

Everybody's saying Beharie's gonna nab the Emmy for lead actress in the miniseries."

"Yeah, I like her. She deserves to win that award."

"I hope she does win it. Maybe it'll open the door for a Golden Globe or a People's Choice Award. She's scheduled to appear on Chelsea next week." Alexus paused, leaned her shoulder against the white brick wall.

She moved the phone from one ear to the other." I, um...okay, I know you don't want to hear this, but Trintino has proposed a reality show-well, it's actually two shows-to my television network, and my mother accepted it."

Alexus bit down on her lower lip, squinted her eyes, and tucked her head down to her chest, bracing herself for the invective that was sure to follow.

"I don't care," Blake said with a dismissive shrug." Why didn't you bring the kids?"

A sigh of relief blew from Alexus' mouth." They're with your parents in L.A. Savaria had a dentist's appointment, and she wanted her brother there for support."

"She really said that, too, didn't she?"

"Boy, you know how grown Vari thinks she is. When I woke up this morning, I reached over to hit the snooze button on my alarm clock. But she was already slapping my shoulder before I could even reach it. She said. "Get up and get dressed so you can go see my daddy." That little girl is a piece of work." Alexus laughed. "Sometimes I think she's tougher than you."

"She is tougher than me." Blake lowered the phone and silently mouthed,

"Did…Reesie Cup…get…the…shipment?"

Alexus nodded affirmatively and mouthed back. "One thousand kilos and three thousand pounds of weed."

"What about the ten women?"

"I'll have Britney…tell you…about that…tomorrow."

Blake raised the phone back to his mouth, and the sound returned to his voice. "What's goin' on with Niemann Elements?"

"Everybody who's anybody in the industry's wearing it now, from rappers to country singers to movie stars. We've secured endorsement deals with Venus and Serena, Oprah, Mrs. Obama, Denzel, and Seal. Jeezy and Wayne just recorded a hit song about our new line of duffle bags. And we now have stores in L.A., Chicago, New York City, Toronto, Dubai, and London. Momma wants me to buy the remaining forty percent of the company from Britney and her colleague, but I'm fine with the sixty percent I already own. Britney and Nikki Staples worked hard to start that company; I wouldn't feel right buying them out of it."

"What ever happened with the telethon?" Blake asked.

"It went all right, I guess. We raised a little over $2 million." She shrugged. "I haven't been able to think about anything but Beyoncé ever since I attended the VMAs last week. I'm so happy for her and Jay. I never thought I'd see her pregnant."

"Bitch, shut the fuck up and pull them pants down." "What!" Alexus scoffed. "What did you just say to me?"

"I said I love you, baby. Gi' me kiss," he said with a beaming smile. "That's not what you said, bastard."

"That is what I said." Blake palmed the crotch of his striped pants, and the tone of his voice attenuated to a whisper. "Play with that pussy for me."

"Boy, I'm not about to have my ass all out in this jail."

"Come on, baby." He turned around as a tall, bald-headed white man in a two-tone brown sheriff's uniform appeared at the door behind him.

"Visit's over, King," the man said.

"You's a goddamn lie!" Blake snapped. "I ain't been here for no hour."

"We got an emergency count. Gotta get you back to your cell."

"Man, you got me Fucked up."

Another officer opened Alexus' door and motioned for her to step out into the linoleum-floored hallway.

"Just do what he says, Blake. We'll have you out of here in no time," Alexus murmured. "I love you."

Blake's jaw muscles tightened and loosened, tightened and loosened, as he forced his teeth together and apart. "I love you, too," he said in a defeated tone, then left out. Alexus Costilla was in tears as she breezed out of the LaPorte County Jail. Ten bodyguards surrounded her, and Tasia Olsen was perambulating next to her.

"Yo, they mad played you on the v-time," Tasia said, biting into a chocolate éclair ice cream that she'd purchased from a vending machine in the jail's waiting area.

"They shouldn't be able to lock people up like that." Alexus sniffled and shook her head." If I handcuffed and locked somebody away in an escape proof building, I'd be charged with kidnapping and criminal confinement."

"Mmm-hmm," Tasia assented.

"And they're calling Blake a murderer, right? But if he would've killed for them, he'd be labeled an American hero; you see what I'm saying? What if you went to every house in this state and forced everybody to pay a certain percentage of their hard-earned money to you?"

"I'd probably end up right back in the feds."

"You certainly would. They'd charge you with extortion and send their goons to kidnap you. But you're a "taxpaying American" when they extort *you*. However, if you don't pay up, they'll steal all of your belongings, kidnap you, and hold you for ransom, only they'll call it a "bond" or "bail" instead of ransom. Isn't that something?"

"It's wild, B. Sounds to me like they're the damned gangsters." "The American government is a gangster government, plain and simple," Alexus said as they made it to her white Phantom convertible. "And they are the coldest gangsters on this entire planet."

When they were seated in the Phantom's rear seats and being driven away, Alexus added," The word "law" actually stands for land, air, and water. The government has rules for all of those places, and they'll extort you no matter where you live in this country."

"Gotta give it to 'em, though. They're the best that ever did it."

Tasia tossed her ice cream stick out of the car. "I don't see what you're so upset about, Lex. I mean, it's not like your man's gonna be convicted for all those bodies anyway. They can't even find Tim-Tim." "Attorney Bostic said that Blake will still have to do some time for

shooting Bookie and Craig." Alexus sighed and retrieved her iPad from its black leather carrying case. Logging onto Twitter, she fought back another wave of tears. Three weeks without Blake felt like three centuries.

"Yo, are you even listening to yourself?" Tasia said. "Bookie is your *cousin!* Blake tried to kill your *cousin!* And not just once, either."

Alexus kept quiet. She considered defending Blake, pointing out the fact that he'd been robbed by Bookie and two other masked men, and that was why he had killed the other two robbers and wounded Bookie. Since Tasia was madly in love with Bookie, Alexus decided to silently, pursue her Twitter page.

Aside from her family, her Twitter followers were the most important people in her life. She never in her wildest dreams imagined that nearly 20 million people would be so obsessed with her lifestyle, her beauty, her Steatopygic, her affluence. She knew that a lot of them followed her for the same reason they followed Ice-T's wife—to view her generous curves—but she still loved unprecedented level of attention she was receiving.

The latest topics of conversation among her followers revolved mainly around Irene, a category two hurricane that had ravaged the east coast a week prior; Lady Gaga's transgendered appearance at the VMAs; and the shooting of Trintino Walkson, the latter of which proving to be the most popular subject.

Who had attempted to murder T-Walk? Was it Blake? If so, did it have anything to do with Alexus? The theories were boundless, as were the questions. Everybody and their mommas wanted to know what had transpired on that warm Chicago night, mere hours before Blake's arrest.

They were all certain that Blake had *something* to do with the shooting; the girl he had been arrested with had told officers that the two golden nine millimeters they would found in the hotel room were hers, and ballistics tests confirmed that both weapons had been fired at the Albany Street shooting.

However, Janautica Spalding was not cooperating with the police.

Neither was T-Walk. Shrouded details of the shooting left the public hungry for info.

Following a moment of deep rumination, Alexus composed and posted a poignant tweet:

To the world U may be 1 person, but to one person U may be the world...Luv U Blake!

Chapter 15

"I hate that Blake guy," Juan "Papí" Costilla muttered vacantly.

He was standing on the rear upper-deck of the 470-foot "Omnipotent," the world's largest yacht. He had squandered $600 million dollars on its construction and to him, it was worth every penny.

There were five others on the deck with him: Flako and his two overweight sons, and Savio and Santiago, Jennifer Costilla's sons. All of them were dressed like American politicians in navy business suits and shiny black shoes.

"You shouldn't talk that way about your daughter's boyfriend," Flako admonished. He watched as Papí swung a nine-iron at a golf ball and sent it flying through the air. The ball splashed into the azure water of the Pacific Ocean.

They had boarded "Omnipotent" at a pier in Mazatlán, Mexico, and now they were headed to San Diego, California.

"Blake doesn't love my daughter," Papí said acidly. "He's nothing more than a pugnacious street urchin with an insatiable sex habit. I don't know what Alexus sees in him."

"I agree with you, Uncle Juan," Savio said. "Personally, I liked that other guy she was with. She should've stayed with him."

"Santiago nodded and put fire to the end of a fat cigar." T-Walk was his name. He was a club owner out of Indiana, I believe. Real Business- minded and presentable. I think he's the one they're saying Blake shot a few weeks ago, the one with the WNBA girlfriend."

"The basketball chick is Rita Mae's niece," Flako said. "We'll have plenty of time to talk about all this frivolous shit later. What we need to be discussing is our problem with the Medellin Cartel in Colombia."

"There is no problem with the Medellin Cartel," Papí said, clubbing another golf ball into the sky. "We've been paying thirty-five hundred per kilo for 17 years now, no? If that Escobar wannabe wants to raise the price to $4,000 dollars, then we'll just have to start paying that. It's not like we're losing any real money.

And we've taken the spot as the number one cartel in the world, am I right? We're fucking invincible. An extra $500 dollars per kilo isn't going to kill us."

"Nobody taxes the Costilla Cartel and lives to tell about it, "Flako stated assertively. "Mother would have had him killed, and you know it." Papí turned to Flako, then to the others, wondering if either of them had anything to do with his mother's murder. He was certain that at least Flako was innocent in the matter of Vida Costilla's premature death; they both had been in Federal prison when someone poisoned her. Papí's sister, Jennifer, had set him and Flako up for an arrest by the DEA and FBI, and once that had been accomplished, Jenny had set out to murder Alexus in an attempt to become the sole heir to Vida's multibillion-dollar fortune. She had been shot and captured after being found inside Osama Bin Laden's compound in Abbottabad, Pakistan, on the First of May, and police were holding her at Guantanamo in eastern Cuba.

Nevertheless, there had been some co-conspirators to assist Jenny in framing Flako and Papí, and in trying to murder Alexus. Papí was sure of it. He just didn't know who they were.

"I don't care what Mother would have done," he said, "because she's no longer here to make those kinds of decisions. Somebody killed her. And my daughter isn't old enough to run the family business, so that leaves me. I say we pay the four grand for each kilo."

"Well, what about Gamuza?" Antoney asked. Short and pudgy, with a loud tie and a bent-brim fedora hat, he looked like a modern-day Al Capone.

His brother Pedro did not look much different.

"What's he talking about, Flako?" Papí rarely spoke to his nephews; it was quotidian for him to ask his brother if he had a question for one of his nephews.

Flako took a seat on a lounge chair. "Gamuza has been sending threats to the police in Matamoros. Death threats. Family-death threats. He's interested in knowing exactly how we're getting our dope into the U.S. who's helping us, and how he can get involved."

The Cocaine Princess 2

"The Zeta Cartel has been steadily losing ground in Juarez," Pedro said. "They've lost two tunnels and thirty-seven lieutenants in the past year alone. Evidently, Gamuza's noticed that we have yet to take any losses, and he's willing to murder an entire police force to find out why."

A brief growl rumbled in Papí's throat. "Can anyone explain to me why Gamuza's still fucking breathing?"

"Trust me, Uncle Juan," said Antoney, "we've been breaking our backs trying to locate him. He has all of Juarez petrified. No one will tell us a thing."

Papí was thoughtful for a moment. Finally, he said, "Send a hundred men to Juarez with instructions to murder every Zeta they encounter. And somebody needs to figure out a way to get that T-Walk guy back on my daughter's radar."

King Rio

Chapter 16

Aplomb, Trintino Walkson strolled into the MTN International Tower dressed in an umber linen Niemann Elements suit and brown leather and orange suede Salvatore Ferragamo boat shoes. A sling cradled his left arm, and his left hand bandaged and gauzed, but he had the brightest smile on his yellowish-brown face.

He gave the receptionist his name, showed her his ID, then waited as the lanky Black woman made a phone call. She hung up and said, "Ms. Bishop's ready to see you. Take the elevator to the fifty-fifth floor."

"Thank you, miss," he said, heading for the elevator.

"Nice cologne, by the way," the receptionist added.

T-Walk was too preoccupied with his own thoughts to reply. The impending meeting with Rita Mae Bishop had his full attention.

Three other executives joined him on the elevator. All of them seemed shocked to see him push the button marked 55.

"Sure you hit the right one?" asked one man.

T-Walk nodded and took his phone from his waist. He was watching a video that Kenya had just sent him of her team practicing at the US Airways Center in Phoenix when another man said, "Fifty-fifth is the company president's office."

"I know whose office it is," T-Walk said.

"Don't mind us," said the first man. "We're surprised to see you going up to fifty-five, that's all. Not many men are able to do that."

T-Walk nodded again. He kept quiet and played *Angry Birds* on his smart phone for the rest of the elevator ride.

"Wow. That's quite an eccentric suit," Rita Mae Bishop said as she stood and reached across her large mahogany desk to shake T-Walk's hand. She donned a contemporary light gray Niemann Elements skirt suit over matching four-inch heels. "Have a seat."

She studied the handsome young man as he settled across from her, wishing he and Alexus had stayed together. T-Walk had graduated from Morehouse College in Atlanta, Georgia, with a B.A. in international business. He now owned two nightclubs, a barbershop, and a slew of houses in his hometown of Michigan City, Indiana.

Blake, on the other hand, possessed about as much ambition as a slothful pig. He was a high school dropout, and the only reason he owned a house and a convenience store in Michigan City was that Alexus had given the properties to him.

"So," Rita said, recumbent in her black leather swivel chair, "Long time no see. How's your arm?"

"It's my shoulder, and my hand. I was shot twice."

"By whom?"

He shrugged his right shoulder. "You know how it is out here in Chicago. Innocent people get shot all the time."

"Remember this, T-Walk: The mouth of a righteous man is a well of life, but violence covereth the mouth of the wicked. That's the eleventh verse in the tenth chapter of Proverbs. I'd advise you to incorporate that powerful verse into your life. Nothing good can come from feuding with your brothers."

T-Walk acknowledged the wisdom of her statement with a gentle nod. "I'm trying my best to be successful," he murmured laconically.

"I'm focused on this reality show venture."

"That and my niece, huh?"

"Yeah, I gotta take care of home. Believe it or not, it's kind of hard to support Kenya in her basketball career while at the same time trying to keep my own businesses afloat. We hardly ever see each other. She's always at practice; I'm always here in the Midwest on business. It's crazy."

"Do you ever feel any guilt at having left my daughter for my niece?"

T-Walk sighed, shifted around in the comfortable raven leather chair as if it were laden with thorns, and turned his eyes to a gold-framed picture of Rita, U.S. President Barack Obama, and Alexus. The three of them were clad in dark suite, standing in the Oval Office.

"We took that picture last week before he started his vacation in Martha's Vineyard, a day before Irene struck," Rita said. "Growing up in Baton Rouge, Louisiana, I never thought I'd live to see the day when a black man would be elected President of this country."

"Well, the bottom line is, you and slay need to scrounge up three million dollars apiece to get this show on the road. Everything else has already been set in motion."

"We have that ready now."

"Then we'll be able to begin filming both shows this Friday. I've purchased the Jupiter Island and North Palm Beach estates, and they're being decorated, furnished and laced with cameras as we speak. There will be eight women staying at the Jupiter Island mansion, twelve at the other. If these shows do as well as I think they're going to do, we might be seeing these girls attain supermodel success in as little as twelve months."

T-Walk cracked a smile. "I like the sound of that."

"It's pretty dulcet to me, too", Rita said with a reciprocal smile.

She turned to her computer and replied to some e-mails while T-Walk phoned Kay Slay. Within minutes, the $6 million was wired to an MTN account, officially sealing the reality show deal.

As Rita walked T-Walk to the door, she said, "I'll be debuting my daytime talk show on Monday. Hoping to follow Oprah's example. I'd like you to drop by with the Brick House cast for my first show."

"I'll be here *early*," he said, his tone replete with enthusiasm.

She watched him perambulate past her secretary's desk and board the elevator. Then she went back to her desk, picked up her phone, and called her ex-husband, Juan Costilla.

"Trintino Walkson just left my office," she said. "I booked him for my first show."

"Good, good. Now all you have to do is make sure Alexus shows up."

King Rio

Chapter 17

"Pack up your stuff, King. You're moving to a cellblock," an officer voiced through the intercom.

Blake was sitting on his thin blue mattress on the bottom bunk of the two-man cell, poring over a neatly-written letter he'd received in the mail yesterday from an extraordinarily beautiful Indian and Lebanese woman named Jaclyn Gemayel. She had sent him four provocative pictures of her posing in red-lace lingerie. Jaclyn claimed to be the owner of two luxury car dealerships in Seattle, Washington, and, like the dozens of other women who'd been flooding him with mail since his arrest, she was interested in getting to know him.

"Money-hungry bitches," he grumbled, tossing the letter and pictures into his dark green Rubbermaid box.

Blake packed all of his food—boxes of Little Debbie cakes, bags of chips, tubs of cheese, summer sausages, pickles, and a variety of confections—hygiene items, and mail into the box. He rolled up his mattress and waited for an officer to come and get him. He had been stuck in this cell for three whole weeks, and he was overwhelmingly anxious to get out of it.

The same officer who had brought Blake back from his visit an hour ago was standing outside the big green door when it popped open. He escorted Blake to an elevator, up to the third floor, down a short hallway, and through two more green steel doors into N-8 cellblock.

"You're in Cell 2," the officer said, and shut the door behind Blake.

With only four cells, each holding four men, N-8 was one of the jail's smaller cellblocks. There were three steel tables centered in the dayroom, a television suspended from the ceiling, two shower stalls in the far right corner, and two payphones on the right wall. Behind three large, darkly tinted windows next to the dayroom door was a control room where officers sat and monitored the cellblock.

Remo, a dark-skinned man in his early fifties, was the only

person in the dayroom. He was sitting at a table playing solitaire. "Back already, huh?" he said with a grin.

Blake chuckled and shook his head. He had been in this very same cellblock late last year with Remo. "Yeah, they got me again, old school."

"At least you struck gold before they gotcha. Hell, you're set for life.

Wish I had a woman with fifty billion dollas in the bank. I wouldn't be in here, that's for sho."

Bet you wouldn't want her after you met Papí, Blake thought as he walked to Cell 2 and pulled open the heavy door.

His face twisted into a mask of boiling anger the instant he realized who his cellmates were.

One of them was Dante "Young-D" Roscoe, his closest friend.

The other two were his worst enemies: Reginald "Bookie" Nelson, a dark-hued braided-up young thug; and Craig White, a slim brown-skinned cat with a mouthful of platinum and white diamond teeth. They were the two men he had shot last October for shooting. They were two of the three men T-Walk had sent to kill him last Christmas Eve, the two men who had shot him ten times.

All three of them were shitless and sweating bullets, and Bookie was on the smooth cement floor doing push-ups.

"My motherfuckin' nigga!" Young-D exclaimed jubilantly.

"Dub Life or no life, nigga!" Blake shouted He dropped his box and mattress and shook hands with Young-D. "Man, bruh, they done had me in that punk ass cell downstairs since we got here, talkin' 'bout they feared for my safety."

"They had me trapped, too. I just got in here, like, five days ago, bruh." Young-D canted his head toward Craig and Bookie. "I hollered at them about that bullshit. Muhfuckas ain't on that shit no more. Niggas in here on tryna get some money."

"Hell yeah," Bookie concurred. He stood up, wiping globules of sweat from his forehead with the back of his hand, eyes filled with palpable apprehension. "You engaged to my cousin, T-Walk fuckin' with my sister, I'm about to marry Tasia – we all too connected to be beefin', my nigga.

The Cocaine Princess 2

You shot me in my leg, shot Craig in his wrist, and we shot you up a few months later. Let's leave all that shit alone, my nigga. On Vice Lord, I'm off that shit if you—"

Blake didn't wait for the rest of Bookie's sentence. Pushing past Young-D, he pulled back his right arm and shot his fist straight into Bookie's jaw. Bookie fell back onto a crème-painted steel desk that was welded against the back wall between the four bunks. Blake managed to land three more devastating punches to Bookie's face before Craig's bony fist slammed into the left side of his head. He stumbled aside and was about to start fighting Craig, but Young-D was already exchanging blows with him.

Bookie regained his equilibrium before Blake did. He threw a myriad of sharp, swift jabs at Blake's head, and every one found its mark. The jabs turned into hooks as Blake wrapped his mighty arms around Bookie's waist, lifted him into the air, and flung him across the room. Bookie's head struck the stainless steel sink hard enough to render him unconscious.

"Bitch ass nigga!" Blake snarled at Bookie's stagnant figure. Then he turned around and helped Young-D pummel Craig to the floor.

King Rio

Chapter 18

"Momma, you cannot keep donating millions of dollars of my money to all these churches and organizations. The least you could do is ask me first," Alexus complained the moment she stepped into her mother's office at the MTN tower.

Rita was sitting behind her desk reading a much-abused copy of Barack Obama's *The Audacity of Hope*. She looked up from her book, gazed briefly at Alexus, and went back to reading.

"I'm dead-serious, Momma," Alexus continued, kicking the clouded glass door behind her shut. "$20 dollars to the Salem Baptist Church of Chicago? $35 million to the American Cancer society? We don't even know anybody with cancer."

"And I've never been to the Salem Baptist Church of Chicago," Rita quipped. "Doesn't mean I shouldn't help them."

Alexus went to the huge window behind Rita's desk and looked down onto Wabash Avenue; the Chicagoans traversing the busy street far below appeared to be ant-sized.

"Well, since I have to start asking permission to spend money now," Rita said, "I may as well bring up my $200 million dollar Lawndale reconstruction proposal."

"Bostic told me already. You want to re-open some closed-down schools, buy and renovate a bunch of houses and apartment buildings, create some new businesses and programs for the kids in the Lawndale neighborhood. I am completely on board with that idea. In fact, I've been thinking about doing the same thing for the neighborhoods affected by Katrina in New Orleans." Alexus looked over her shoulder at Rita. "Just start telling me before you decide to write all these eight-figure checks. I don't like finding out about it from my lawyer at the last minute."

Turning back to the window, Alexus roved her eyes over the Chicago skyline and remembered the blissful times she had spent as a child with her maternal grandparents, Hattie Mae Zimmerman-Bishop and George Bishop, and her maternal aunt, Ralla Mae Bishop. All three of them had lost their lives in Hurricane Katrina.

"So, how much are we pledging to these two projects?" Rita

asked. "Half a billion altogether $200 million to the Lawndale neighborhood, and $300 million to New Orleans, mainly the lower Ninth Ward where Grandma Hattie used to live."

Rita walked over to Alexus and stood silently next to her. Together, they stared out into the midday sunshine, lost in their own individual thoughts. Alexus could not stop thinking about Blake. She hoped he was staying out of trouble, but with Blake's volatile temper, she doubted it.

"If you don't mind me asking," Rita murmured affably, "what is it about Blake that has you so glued to him? I'm curious."

Alexus took a moment to reply. "Love," she said, moving her eyes to those of her mother. "I love that boy so much, Momma. He completes me in every way. I know he's not the kind of man everybody wants me to be with, but I'm sticking with him 'til the end, no matter how long it takes for him to come home. I'll just be as loyal to him as Tiny is to T.I."

"But don't you think you should at least find someone who will appreciate your loyalty, someone who'll love you enough to stay out of trouble so that he'll be here for you when you need him?"

"I know where you're going with this, Momma," Alexus said, as her iPhone began singing a harmonic Mary J. Blige song from inside her $40,000 dollar crocodile skin Niemann Elements purse. "I'm not getting back with T-Walk, okay? I'm engaged to Blake, and soon I'll be married to Blake. You or nobody else can convince me to do otherwise."

Shaking her head discontentedly, Rita sat back down in her swivel and spun around to face Alexus. The incessant ringing of her daughter's Smartphone prompted her to ask, "Are you going to answer that?"

"That's the ringtone I assigned to Kenya," Alexus said. "And?"

"I don't wanna answer it." Alexus turned to Rita with a scowl on her visage. "You know, maybe if T-walk hadn't started sleeping with my *cousin*, I might've thought about giving him another chance before Blake and I got engaged. He nailed his own coffin shut with that move. And Kenya buried herself with him."

Rita shook her head again, this time in a gesture of disapproval. "Kenya is my brother's daughter, Alexus. She is family. You don't turn against family."

"Same thing I said." Alexus glimpsed another Barack Obama tome on Rita's desk, *Dreams from My Father*. "How many books has Obamawritten now?" She asked as she bent to pick it up.

But she never received a reply; at that very second a .300 Win-Mag bullet pierced the fifty-fifth floor window behind her and zipped past the left side of her head, missing her by mere inches. It came so close that she felt the intense heat on her cheek, like a searing hot kiss from Satan.

Two blocks down Wabash Avenue, in a presidential suite on the fifty- sixth floor of the Trump International Hotel and Tower, the black-suited sniper was crouched down on one knee with his eye pressed against the scope of an XM2010 sniper rifle. He was an ex-Army soldier and long-time member of the Latin Kings who had been affiliated with Ciudad Juarez, Mexico's Zeta Cartel since he was 20-years old.

Now Emilio Godinez was thirty-nine, and he was on a mission to collect a $5 million dollar bounty for the assassination of Alexus Costilla.

The window in front of him had blown out from the first gunshot. He watched Alexus drop to the floor and, for a second, he thought he had hit his target. Then he saw her rise up on her hands and knees and swiftly crawl around a large desk.

He squeezed the trigger again, knocking a huge hole in one of the desk drawers. The chocolate woman who had been sitting in the chair plunged to the floor. Emilio paid her no attention, though; he fired twice more through the desk, intent on killing Alexus.

It was to no avail.

Dejectedly, he watched as Alexus got to her feet and raced out of the office before he even had a chance to reload.

"*Mierda!*" he hissed, clenching his teeth together.

Emilio immediately started disassembling the rifle. He wasn't worried about the Chicago police finding out anything about him because he'd had the prostitute (she was now tied up in front of one of the Italian leather sofas) order the suite in her name, and he planned to kill her before leaving the room.

But suddenly things went wrong. Terribly wrong.

He heard a noise behind him, felt a bare foot ram into the center of his back, and the next thing he knew, he was plummeting out of the fifty-sixth floor window.

Chapter 19

"Baby, I need to tell you something. But first you have to promise me that you won't get mad."

"I won't get mad. What is it?"

"You promise?"

"Yes, I promise, T-Walk," Kenya said. "What did you do this time?"

"I, uh…I just invested $3 million dollars of our—"

"You just did *what?*" Kenya screamed.

"I knew this was coming," T-Walk thought as he drove his leased, smoke gray Mercedes Benz S550 up to a brownstone apartment building on the corner of 5th and Madison in Gary, Indiana. He parked behind a flashy white Hummer H2 on a matching set of 32-inch rims.

He was smack dab in the middle of the slums, surrounded by a bevy of drug-dealing, gun-toting young Vice Lords. There were nine candy-painted older model Oldsmobile Cutlasses and Chevy Caprices sitting in a vacant lot across the street where three big barbecue grills were set up. A variety of black girls in skimpy little shorts and miniskirts were scattered *all* along the street.

"I said I spent $3 million, baby," T-Walk said into his phone's earpiece. "We'll have the money back in no time, I promise. I'm executive producing a major reality show on—"

"I don't give a damn *what* you're producing! That's all we had left!"

"I know, baby, just listen to—"

"No *you* listen! We already lost $300,000 dollars because you didn't want to tell the police what happened to our Rolls. *You're* the one who wanted to buy that stupid million-dollar condo in Chicago when we already had this $3 million dollar house here in Phoenix. Now you're telling me you've spent our last little bit of money on a damned TV show! Nah. You go and get my fucking money back."

Kenya ended the call abruptly.

"Crazy ass woman," T-Walk murmured, stepping out of his

Benz. He walked to the rear left side door of the Hummer, pulled it open, and got in next to Lil Ant, a dark-skinned twenty-five year-old with a head full of braids and an all blue Coogi outfit. Lil Ant's necklace and watch were replete with blue diamonds. Squirm-G, a similarly dressed brown man who also had braids and blue diamonds in his jewelry, was sitting in the driver's seat. The passenger's seat was vacant.

"S'up, folks," Squirm-G said, twisting his neck to peer at T-Walk through a pair of Gucci shades.

"GDN," T-Walk replied while simultaneously doing the Gangster Disciple handshake with Lil Ant. "Man, what the fuck y'all got me out here in this punk ass Vice Lord neighborhood for?"

"Folks Lil Regg got a baby mama out here," said Lil Ant.

"A bad lil bitch," Squirm-G added.

"Aw yeah?" T-Walk studied their gaudy attire. "I see y'all niggas done came up. Who's Hummer is this?"

"This my shit here, G. and plenty much love on that lick. That nigga ended up givin' us seven hun'ed-fifty racks apiece," Squirm-G said.

"We wanted to off that nigga, anyway." Lil Ant grabbed a blunt from behind his ear and lit it. "That was the same nigga who told on Gusto."

That's when it clicked. T-Walk had told just about every street nigga he knew that there was money on Phillip "Jazzy" Dolton and Timothy Trice's heads. When he had spoken with some GDs in South Bend about the situation, a thick-bodied woman name Lakita had been with them, and she had promised to relay the message to the folks in Gary; she must have given the information— vicariously, at least— to one of the folks he was now in the Hummer with.

"Is that what y'all wanted to talk to me about?" T-Walk asked.

Lil Ant shook his head. "We need you to help us launder this money, fam, so we can get to buyin' houses and shit."

"How much y'all talkin'?"

"1.5."

"1.5? Shit, that's only a million after taxes. $900,000 after I get my cut." T-Walk eyed a maroon-colored Avalanche on chrome

30-inch rims as it turned onto Madison. It was followed by an older-model money-green Delta 88 on chrome and green 26s.

"How long will it be before we get the money?" Squirm-G asked. He pulled a nickel-plated .44 caliber revolver from under his seat and set it on his lap. He glued his eyes to the Avalanche that had just parked across the street from them.

Lil Ant quickly drew a 9mm glock from his lap.

"It'll prob'ly take me about two or three months to run it through my clubs," T-Walk said, grabbing his own formidable pistol – a Sig Sauer 9mm

—from the shoulder holster inside his suit jacket. "What's up with these niggas?"

"That's Rube in the Avalanche," Squirm-G said. "Folks Gusto fell out with that nigga when we was in the joint."

"And that's his guy Batman getting' outta the Delt," Lil Ant added, passing his blunt to T-Walk. "Those niggas been sellin' bricks o'soft for 17 racks apiece. They got Kush, hero'n, pills — damn near every drug you can think of, fam. On Larry. I don't know where the fuck them niggas be getting' that shit from, but they getting' it."

T-Walk watched the two dreadlocked men cross the street. Rube glanced in through the Hummer's windshield, gave a head nod, and then entered the apartment building.

Lil Ant reached over behind his seat and lifted a seemingly heavy Gucci duffle bag back over it. He placed it on T-Walk's lap. "That's all of it, fam. Be careful with this shit."

"I got you, folks." T-walk shook up with Lil Ant "Tell folks Lil Regg I said love, G-ball. I'll be at y'all."

"A'ight, plenty much, folks," Squirm-G said, shaking up with T-walk. "Never too much," T-Walk replied.

His phone rang as he was getting out of the Hummer. Kenya's distraught voice whelmed the line. Her words were bunched together.

"Oh, my God, T-walk, somebody just tried to kill Alexus!"

King Rio

The Cocaine Princess 2

Chapter 20

The tension was thick.

Standing next to Young-D in the back of the cell, arms crossed over his chest, a bellicose expression on his face, Blake stared coldly across the room at Bookie and Craig, who stood in front of the big green door looking just as angry. Ten men separated them, but only one, the eldest of the group, was speaking.

"You boys have lost y'all's goddamn minds," Remo grumbled irritably as he continued his histrionic harangue. "Now, Blake, you're about to marry this man's cousin. If you think for one second that she's gonna be happy with you and Bookie tryna kill each other, you are sadly mistaken.

That marriage will be over with faster than a 20-yard cheetah race. And you can take that to the dope man."

Blake wasn't listening to Remo's prudent advice. He had his mind set on demolishing his foes, making them feel the pain and fear he had felt when their bullets tore through his body. A part of him wanted to end the drama for the sake of Alexus' feelings. But the notion was opposed by his pride and his reputation

All of that changed in one dramatic instant.

Marcus Eastwood, a tall black man who Blake had been cool with since he was 10 or 11 years-old, opened the cell door and poked in his head.

"Ay, Blake and Bookie, y'all need to get out here and check this shit out," Marcus said urgently.

Bookie preceded Craig into the dayroom, and everybody else spilled out of the cell.

Blake's mouth went agape as soon as he looked at the television screen. MTN News was on. The banner at the bottom of the screen read: *BREAKING NEWS – Assassination Attempt on Alexus Costilla.*

"What the...," Blake muttered as he watched and carefully listened to middle-aged black anchor Nat Turner speak about the incident.

"Call Alexus," Bookie said after they had watched the segment. "I'm about to call my Auntie Rita."

As Blake rushed to the pay phone, he dropped his defenses completely. The only thing on his mind was his woman. Nothing else mattered.

He picked up the phone and punched in her cell phone number.

Chapter 21

"Well, well, well," FBI Special Agent Josh Sneed said as he entered the executive lounge on the 13th floor of the MTN tower. "Here we are again."

Alexus was sitting on one of the opulent lounge's white leather sofas, nursing a glass of undiluted Nuvo through a straw. Her momma, Attorney Bostic, and Tasia were seated with her, and all twenty-nine of her bodyguards had stationed all around the large white marble-floored room.

The two CPD detectives who had been questioning Alexus stepped aside after glimpsing Sneed's FBI badge.

"Any idea who's after you this time?" Sneed asked Alexus. He sat down across from her and leaned forward, elbows on his knees, fingertips pressed tightly together. To Alexus' dismay, he looked entirely too much like CNN's Anderson Cooper.

"I have absolutely no idea of who could've sent that man," Alexus said shakily. "Wish I did. I was bending over to pick up a book when the first bullet came flying through the window."

She cringed at the memory, and said uneasily, "It came so close to my face."

"Guess it's safe to say that book saved your life?"

"Yeah, I guess so." Alexus finished her drink – third glass of Nuvo she'd ingested in the past hour—and motioned for the redheaded waiter to bring her another one.

"You've had enough to drink," Rita said, waving away the waiter.

'I could drink a whole bottle,' Alexus thought. She looked around the lounge for her purse before finally remembering that it had slipped from her grasp as she had escaped her mother's office.

"Aren't you about two years too young to drink alcohol?" Sneed asked, squinting his eyes at Alexus. He moved on to Tasia. "And I've been dying to ask you this question for months now, Ms. Olsen. How'd you manage to finagle your way out of federal prison? I've checked with all of my superiors, searched all of our files, and yet I've found nothing. The same thing happened with

Juan and Flako Costilla. It's as if you all were never even arrested."

"What does any of this have to do with today's assassination attempt?" Attorney Bostic inquired silently. "I'd highly appreciate it if you would stick to a more pertinent line of questioning. My clients don't need any more stress than they already have."

With a vapid chuckle, Sneed eased back in his seat, withdrawing a small notepad from the breast pocket of his black blazer. Flipping it open, he said, "The woman our suspect was with has been arrested numerous times in and around the Chicago area for prostitution. She led us to the suspect's vehicle, where we found his I.D. and cell phone. His name's Emilio."

Alexus tuned the FBI agent out. She didn't need Sneed to help her figure out why a sniper had targeted her. When she had first arrived at the MTN tower with Tasia, she had received a call from Papí.

"I'm back to eating those trifling pork burgers again," Papí had said, which meant that the Costilla Cartel was again at war with the Zeta Cartel.

Immediately after ending the call with Papí, Alexus had checked a Mexican news site and saw that twelve men had just been murdered in Ciudad Juarez, Mexico, gunned down in front of a minor league baseball stadium. All were reputed Zeta Cartel members, and one was somewhat of a major figure in the lucrative drug conglomerate.

The assassination attempt didn't really surprise Alexus; however, she *was* surprised by the swiftness of their retaliation, and the fact that they had targeted her first.

She turned to Rita. "Momma, where's your phone?"

"It's in my office," Rita said in her signature whisper. "And I'm not going back up there to get it, either."

Alexus released a drab chuckle. "I don't think I'll ever step foot in that office again," she said.

She sent one of her bodyguards to fetch her purse from the bullet- riddled office, wondering if Blake had called yet.

"Well," Sneed said as he stood to his feet, "I came in here expecting to learn something more about the guy whose body is

splattered all over the middle of Wabash Avenue. I guess I should
have known better than to think I'd get any cooperation out of Juan
Costilla's family."

Rita leapt out of her seat and cast an accusatory glare at the
pallid–faced FBI agent. "Don't you dare insult my family!"

Grabbing her mother's hand, Alexus said, "Ignore him, Momma. You're giving him exactly what he wants."

Sneed departed with a laugh, leaving behind four vexed wom-
en.

"Somebody needs to snipe *him*, yo," Tasia said.

"Forget about him," said Britney Bostic. "We need to get our-
selves to a safe place outside of Chicago. Alexus, I'm canceling
your appearance on The Monique Show. We'll reschedule it for
some time next week."

"No, I don't want to cancel anything," Alexus said, flicking a
tiny piece of glass from the inner thigh of her white jeans. "I'm not
going to let them scare me into seclusion."

The bodyguard returned with Alexus' purse and Rita's phone.

As all of them were leaving the executive lounge, surrounded
by the phalanx of armed, black-suited bodyguards, Alexus checked
her iPhone and saw that she had eighty-six missed calls. Twenty-
five of them were from LaPorte County Jail, and the rest were
from concerned family members and friends.

Alexus dropped the phone back into her purse, grabbed Britney's elbow, and pulled the lithesome young attorney close to her
side.

"Is it possible for me to marry Blake while he's in jail?" she
whispered.

"Of course it's possible. People do it all the time. But I don't
think *you* should do something like that. Not right now, at least.
The media would be all over you."

"The media can kiss my fat ass. I want to marry my fiancé as
soon as possible, and I don't care what anybody has to say about
it."

Britney hesitated. "I'll have to contact the–"

"Whatever you have to do, just do it. I want to be happily married by the end of this month."

"Oh, my Lord," Rita said when they reached the tinted glass façade of the building. The pack of reporters couldn't yet see them, but they could see outside. A uniformed chauffeur stood by after he had parked a white Escalade limousine at the curb. Three white Tahoe's' were lined up in front of the limo. Four more were parked behind it.

Alexus took a pair of sunglasses out of her purse and pushed them delicately over her nose. She took a deep breath, settling her nerves and getting her thoughts together.

"Everybody keep quiet," Britney said. "We don't need to be making any comments. There will be plenty of time to answer questions on Rita's show this Monday."

She went ahead to open the door. Alexus looked over at Momma. "I wish Granny Costilla hadn't left me with all of this money," she muttered.

"Hush, child. As long as we stick to helping those who deserve our monetary succor, we can only expect more blessings to be placed upon us."

Alexus emerged from the building behind a trio of brawny-chested bodyguards. The fear of being the target of another sniper compelled her to duck her head low as she approached the limo. Photographers started snapping pictures. Reporters began firing questions. Alexus ignored every voice, all except for one.

"Alexus!" The familiar voice screamed from behind a police blockade two blocks up Wabash.

She didn't even have to look his way to know that it was Trintino Walkson shouting her name. But she turned and looked anyway.

T-Walk was waving his good arm wildly in the air, trying to get her attention. About a hundred spectators or so had crowded behind the blockade with him.

"Let him through," Rita said to a uniformed officer. "He's a family friend."

The four women piled into the stretch Escalade and T-Walk joined them a minute later.

Chapter 22

Blake grinded his teeth together and pounded the steel table with his palms. He was watching MTN News with everybody else in N-8 cellblock, and he had just witnessed T-Walk get inside a limo with Alexus. Although he felt no dubiety concerning his woman's fidelity, it was still unnerving to know that she was now sitting inside a limousine with an ex-boyfriend of hers.

He stood up and went to his cell. Young-D followed him. "Stuck in this bitch wit' no bail," Blake said, shaking his head incredulously as he paced back and forth in the cell. "Muhfuckas out there tryna kill my bitch, and I can't do shit about it."

"That's crazy as hell, bruh." Young-D sat down on one of the bottom bunks, picked an open bag of cheese popcorn from a box under the bunk, and started munching on them."

"Man, calm down. Ain't you the one who told me how dumb it is to get mad about stuff you ain't got no control over? Get down there on that vent and talk to one of them hoes, nigga. Janautica wanna talk to you, anyway."

Blake moved his eyes to the rectangle of small holes in the white steel wall next to the toilet. He knew that the ventilation system was connected to two other cellblocks—N-5, the women's block on the second floor, and N-2, a men's clock on the first. Hearing women moan through the vent as they supposedly played in their pussies was commonplace.

"Watch the door, bruh." Blake slipped beneath the toilet on his back and turned his face toward the vent. "Ay, Janautica," he shouted. "Bring yo' lil bony ass to the vent."

"Nuh-uh, nigga, who the fuck you think you talkin' to?" She instantly replied. Her sweet, Southern drawl was so clear and distinct that it seemed like her lips were pressed against his ear.

Blake allowed himself a short chuckle. "You know who this is?" She hesitated. "Blake?" She said, sounding uncertain.

"Damn, you remembered my voice, huh?"

Janautica inhaled sharply. Then she lowered her voice to a barely audible whisper and said, "Boy, we gotta come up with a nickname for you. These thirsty bitches in here can't stop talkin' 'bout you."

"Give me a nickname, then. And it bet' not be lame." She was quiet for a moment.

"Bullet face," she finally said, referring to the scars on both sides of his face where two bullets had blown through his left jaw and out his right cheek. "That name would fit you well."

It was Blake's turn to go silent. He was thinking about Alexus, wondering who was after her, and if King was his son or not. *Fuck it*, he thought. *At least I know Savaria's mine.*

"Just got through watchin' MTN News," Janautica said.

"Yeah, that shit fucked me up. I wish I was out there with her. We prob'ly would've been somewhere fuckin' when that shit happened."

"Please don't talk about no sex right now, cowboy. The mooncie is backed up and hungry, yuh feel me? Hard body. I need some dick so fuckin' bad."

Blake's dick twitched and started to swell in his pants. Involuntarily, he envisioned himself slapping the head of his long phallus against her lips, and then watching her suck it into her mouth. He had wanted to fuck the slim little Southern girl ever since he first saw her in the backseat of Young-D's Magnum with those tiny cotton short-shorts on.

"Why haven't you bonded out yet?" He asked, changing the subject. "Judge hit you with no bond, too?"

"Nah, I got a bond. I just don't wanna call my family for the money. Like I told you, my momma's sick, yuh feel me, like? My cousin Princess claims she ain't got it. Plus, that judge gave me that high ass bond, and the white bitch won't lower it for *nothin'*."

Blake sat up and looked at Young-D. "Why the fuck haven't you—"

"I already know what you about to say, bruh," Young-D interrupted.

"I got six hun'ed and forty-thousand put up in one place, though, and I don't trust nobody to fuck with it. That's the only reason I ain't bonded her out yet."

"Man, you could've had Fly or Blubby drop that bread, nigga,"

Blake said, turning back to the vent. "Ay, Lil momma, I'll have you out of here real soon. If not today, it'll be tomorrow for sure. I'ma buy you a house in North Carolina, too. Wherever you wanna move, just let me know."

"Are you serious right now?" Janautica asked.

"Yeah, I'm serious. Fuck, you think this is a joke? Bitch, I'm a hun'ed at all times. If I say I got you, I got you. Let me go out there and get on that phone right quick. You should be outta here tonight."

"Thank you, Bullet face."

'Damn, her voice is sexy,' Blake thought to himself as he got up. He thought about the three Louis Vuitton duffle bags he had stashed at the Michigan City home he owned before heading to the hotel on the night of his arrest. The fact that he had $9 million dollars in cash hidden away in his attic brightened his disposition significantly. It meant that he could buy all the people he needed to buy in order to progress and gain the upper hand in every situation.

"C'mon, Young D," he said, pushing open the cell door.

King Rio

Chapter 23

"You okay, baby?"

"I'm fine, Blake. My nerves are a little raw, but I'm fine."

Alexus gazed down at her engagement ring and sighed. She was sitting next to Tasia in a sumptuous white leather seat inside of her $50 million dollar, 12-passenger private jet. Momma and Britney were seated behind her, both of them were typing on their laptops, and T-walk was sitting directly across from her, grinning his cocky grin, looking as dapper and handsome as a GQ model in his cinnamon brown suit. The pilot was taxing the jet on a runway at Midway Airport, readying for takeoff.

"They got me in here wit' Bookie now," Blake said dryly.

"Please tell me you two aren't in there fighting over that stupid shit from last year."

"We, uh...nah, we cool. We had a long talk about that. It was that other bitch ass nigga who got that drama goin', same nigga I just saw gettin' in that limo with you."

Alexus didn't reply. For a moment, she wondered how he had seen T-Walk getting in the limousine. But then she remembered the cameras, and figured he had watched on the news.

"You with that nigga right now, ain't you?" Blake asked.

"We're on my jet, about to fly to Atlanta. And he's here with my mom. I am not the one who invited him, okay? So don't even start with that mess."

"You bet' not be out there on no bullshit, Lexus. I ain't got time to be dealin' wit' no extra shit."

"Blake, do not start pestering me with this nonsense. You don't have to worry about me doing anything out of the ordinary. I'm not like *you*."

Blake chuckled once. "I love you, baby."

"I just bet you do," Alexus retorted snidely.

The co-pilot, a stout white man, stepped out of the cockpit and asked everybody to turn off their phones and computers.

"Call me back in a few hours if you can," Alexus said.

"A'ight, baby," Blake said. He hung up.

Reclining in her seat, Alexus sat her iPhone on her lap, buckled her seatbelt, and shut her eyes to keep from looking at T-Walk. The Nuvo she'd drank before leaving the MTN tower had her feeling horny, and the lingering scent of T-Walk's Gucci cologne exacerbated that feeling tenfold. Her pussy was hot and wet, her clit throbbing, and her significant other was locked up.

She kept her eyes closed for about ten minutes. When she opened them, she caught T-Walk staring at her thighs.

He licked his lips. "Can we talk now?"

"Talk about what, T-Walk?"

He took off his seatbelt as the plane leveled off in the sky. "Not right here. Let's step in the bathroom. We can leave the door open."

Alexus glanced over at Tasia, who was busy reading Stephen King's *The Dark Half*.

"Go 'head, yo," Tasia said without looking up from her book. "He ain't gonna rape you or nothin'."

'Can't rape the willing,' Alexus thought, then immediately chastised herself for thinking it.

She stood and followed T-Walk to the bathroom, sneaking a peek at the crotch of her jeans to see if her juices had seeped through. Once inside the bathroom, she lifted up onto the granite sink and waited for T-Walk to start talking. But he didn't say a word. He simply chose to stand in front of her, gazing blatantly between her legs, biting his bottom lip.

It was all too much for Alexus.

"Close the door," she said softly, unfastening her jeans. "And lock it."

T-Walk did as he was told, never taking his eyes off Alexus as she kicked off her heels, pants, and white-lace Victoria's secret panties. She rubbed her fingers over her engorged clit, spread her glistening wet pussy lips apart, dipped her middle finger in, and sucked the wetness of it.

"Damn, baby," T-Walk murmured.

"I'm not your fucking baby." Alexus started fingering herself, first with one finger, then with two. "I'm only gonna let you eat this pussy because I'm in dire need of some head. You can save all that *baby* talk for Kenya."

T-Walk's grin returned. He kneeled between her meaty thighs and attacked her clit with his violent, flickering tongue. Pursing his thin lips around it, he sucked and licked and slurped, then dug his tongue deep in her pussy. She palmed the back of his head and forced his tongue deeper into the wet hole. "Mmm...yeah, T....mmm," she moaned, raising her skirt over her head. She freed her D-cup breasts and started pinching her nipples as T-Walk went back to sucking her clit. "Mmmm.....move move, move."

Quickly, T-Walk stood and stepped aside, knowing that his entire face and suit jacket would have gotten drenched had he stayed between her thighs. He'd learned long ago that Alexus was a squirter.

She pressed down on her clit with two fingertips and jerked them around erratically until, a few seconds later, her juices jetted out of her pussy in a short arch. When her climax finally subsided, there was a puddle of her sweet-smelling liquid on the sink top beneath her, dripping down to the floor where a larger puddle lay.

"That is just crazy," T-Walk said, and crouched down to suck the remaining juices from her dripping lips. His talented tongue then danced its way up to her breasts, flapped over nipples.

"Okay, nigga, that's enough," Alexus said, breathlessly, pushing his face away from her. "This isn't a lovemaking session. Pull that fat dick out. I want you to ram it down my throat."

"I see you still got that freak in you." He unbuckled his belt, untucked his shirt, and unbuttoned his slacks.

Alexus dropped down from the sink, her mouthwatering as she eagerly anticipated the taste of his pickle-thick dick in her throat. She squatted before him, yanked his pants and Gucci under wear down to his ankles, and took the head of his 8-inch phallus into her mouth, twirling her tongue over it. Inch by inch she pushed her head forward until his entire length was in her mouth.

"Damn, you can deep-throat now?" T-walk muttered, staring down at her as she pulled back slowly, twisting her head from side to side and sucking him strongly.

She popped her lips off his dick and eased down to her knees. "You ready to fuck my throat?" She whispered salaciously.

"Hell muhfuckin' yeah."

"Grab my hair in the back," she said, reaching to grab the back of her ankles. "And slam that dick down my throat until you're—"she dipped her head forward, licked a dangling string of pre-cum from his dickhead, "—ready to bust."

T-Walk didn't hesitate. He wrapped her long, curly black hair around his hand and started pumping his dick in and out of her throat, gradually increasing his speed until Alexus started gagging. Her eyes watered. Saliva spilled from the side of her mouth.

"Oooh, shit! Damn, girl," he groaned huskily.

A few minutes later, he pulled out and stroked his dick. Alexus opened wide and stuck out her tongue, and he shot ribbons of cum into her gaping mouth. His nut was thick and creamy, and there was lots of it. It filled her throat, covered her tongue. She kept her mouth open as she gulped down his nut, and he filled her greedy mouth again. She swallowed it all down then sucked him dry. She got dressed, dabbed puddles she had left on the sink and floor with a few napkins, and dropped them into the trashcan.

Due to T-Walk's wounded hand and shoulder, it took him a bit longer to get his suit back in order. "I hope this means I have a chance of—"

"This doesn't mean anything, T-Walk. I was horny, you were, too, and we got our rocks off. That's it."

"But, what about the baby? Has Blake taken a DNA test?"

"Yes," Alexus lied. "Blake is my son's father, okay? We did the paternity test two weeks ago. So you might as well have a baby with Kenya and leave Blake and me alone. We're about to get married in a few weeks, anyway."

T-Walk leaned back against the door and laughed.

The next thing Alexus knew, Momma and Tasia were shaking her awake.

"Wake up, Alexus," Rita was shouting. "We're about to land, yo," Tasia said.

Alexus' eyes fluttered open. T-Walk was still sitting across from her with an ingratiating smile etched on his face.

"That dream must've been mad good, yo." Tasia giggled merrily. "The way you was moanin' and groanin'."

118

"Shut up talking to me," Alexus said.

King Rio

The Cocaine Princess 2

Chapter 24

Remo ended up convincing Craig and Bookie into trading cells with two guys in Cell 1. Blake watched them pack up and move their things while he spoke with his parents, Carolyn and Dale, and Savaria on the phone. Then he went back to his cell, squeezed into the snug space between the wall and toilet, and yelled for Janautica.

"Hey, stupid Bullet face!" Janautica answered happily a few seconds later. She sounded excited and out of breath. "We straight in here getting' it in early, yuh feel me, like hard body."

"The fuck is y'all down there doin'?"

"Okay, is yuh listenin'? Okay, so, we got to talkin' 'bout that boy named Blake, 'bout what we would do if the po-leece let 'im in here wit' us. E'rybody think you---my bad, I mean Blake---is gon' just give a bitch a million dollas fuh some mooncie, yuh feel me, like?"

She sucked her teeth. "Anyways, is yuh listenin'?"

"Yeah, I'm listenin'. Quit askin' me that stupid ass question."

"You're the one that's stupid, ol' nappy head fucka," she said. "*Anyways*, we got to p-poppin' and carryin' on, talkin' 'bout how we'd do some real ratchet, nasty shit for Blake."

"You would, too?" Blake asked with genuine interest.

"Hell yeah, I would. That black ass fucka is F-I-N-E!" She paused. "But he wouldn't much fuck wit' me, no how, I ain't got no big basketball booty, like Alexus got, yuh feel me, like? I done played wit' this mooncie a many times thinkin' 'bout him, though. You best believe that."

Blake smiled a little. His dick grew hard. "I think he'd fuck wit' you, if he wasn't wit' Alexus. He loves sexy lil slim bitches like you."

"I gotcho bitch, you nappy head fucka." He laughed.

"So, wussup?" She asked. "Am I goin' home tonight?"

"I couldn't reach one of my niggas. However, I'ma get back on the phone before we lock in. Either way it go, I got you."

"Hold yuh horses, cowboy. This girl gotta use the toilet."

"A'ight. I'll holla at you when we lock in at—"

"No the hell you won't! Yo' black ass is gon' stay right here 'til I get back, yuh her' me?"

"Yeah, right," Blake said dismissively. But he stayed at the vent, anxious to hear the Southern girl's euphonious voice again.

Young-D was sitting on his bunk, finishing off his popcorn. He said, "Man, bruh, you know that bitch Princess crashed my Magnum the other day? Fucked my shit clean up. Now she talkin' 'bout she pregnant."

"You shouldn't have been bustin' loogies in that bitch. That's yo' fault, bruh. But fuck that car. I'ma buy Bugattis for the whole team. Shit, nigga, you remember the picture I sent you of the green one?"

"How could I forget that?"

Blake shook his head. "I'm not even gon' tell you what happened to that muhfucka. It's crazy as hell in Mexico. I still got those Lambos, the Rolls Royce, and the Ferrari. All that shit still down there."

"I bet they got some bad bitches out there."

"Bad ain't even the word. It's some hoes out there look colder than Alexus, bruh. Fucked a badass Brazilian model in our mansion down there. I'm talkin' about *bad!*" Blake said.

He heard the toilet flush through the vent. A few seconds later, Nauti's voice returned. "Hey, nappy head. Is yuh listenin'?"

"If you keep callin' me a nappy head, I'ma start callin' yo' Lil skinny ass Swine Flu," he replied jokingly.

"Swine Flu? Nigga, I ain't got no fuckin' Swine Flu." Janautica sucked her teeth, said something to one of her cellmates, and then mumbled, "I want you to tear this mooncie up, Bullet face."

For a couple of seconds, Blake was stunned into silence. He felt a burgeoning inclination to reciprocate with an equally salacious statement. Still, the assassination attempt on Alexus flashed across his mind like lightening on a tumultuous summer night, powerful and compelling.

"You want to um…" he paused, changing the subject, "to move out here to Michigan City? I already own a house out here, and a convenience store on the corner of ninth and Willard

Avenue. You can get the house, and manage the store. And I'ma get you that news Benz truck—the ML350. I gotta get you right, Swine Flu. Can't have you out there livin' bogus."

"I'll move out here," Janautica said. "Hell, as long's Cess stay wit' Young-D, I'ma pretty much be somewhere near, anyhow, yuh feel me, like? And I'm rockin' wit' you hard body, anyway. Might as well stick by."

Blake smiled generously. 'I'm really startin' to like this country Lil bitch,' he thought to himself. 'wonder if she'll keep shit one hun'ed wit' me when I bond her out of here.'

King Rio

Chapter 25

The following four weeks were excessively busy for Alexus. She had television appearances on The Monique Show, The Wendy Williams Show, Regis and Kelly, Windy City Live, E! News, and The Rita Bishop Show.

She attended the Primetime Emmy Awards in a flowing white Niemann Elements gown with over $10 million dollars' worth of Le Vian chocolate and white diamonds embellishing her ears, neck, and wrists. And, on Thursday, October 6th, she and the rest of her family—her parents, uncles, and cousins—showed up at the Michigan City courthouse in a sparkling white, 10-car fleet of Rolls Royce Phantom Drophead Coupes.

The Honorable Judge Katherine Blagojevich's order sent shockwaves through the media.

"Since the prosecution has failed to locate the key witness for crossvexamination, and since they have also failed to produce any kind of physical evidence against the said defendants in the allotted time, the state has no choice but to drop all charges against Blake King, Terrence King, Dante Roscoe, and Michael Lane."

Alexus was elated when Blagojevich's gavel slammed down. She was the first to run up to Blake, embracing him in an amorous, one-armed hug, holding King in the other. She pressed her succulent lips against his.

Due to Blake's adamant refusal to point out Craig and Blake as the men who had gunned him down late last year, and vice versa with them, the charges stemming from those two shootings were also dropped. Everybody was going home, and Alexus could not have possibly been happier.

Blake picked his daughter up and kissed her, too. Then he hugged her, his parents, and his elite team of lawyers and paralegals from the Bostic and Staples firms. Alexus frowned as a slender-bodied, pretty-faced girl stepped up and embraced Blake. But she didn't say anything. She watched the girl disappear from the courtroom.

"Didn't I tell you daddy was comin' home?" Blake asked Savaria as he smiled widely at the brown little girl's face.

"I knew you was comin' home, Daddy," Vari said in her tiny voice. "I kept tellin' Grandma that my, um, my dream said you and Mommy was comin' home."

Alexus' heart cringed at Savaria's poignant words, knowing that Vari's momma would never come home.

"Ooooh, baby," Alexus said, kissing Blake's lips again. "We have so much planned for you. Your party is already set up at the Wit Hotel in Chicago. Wait 'til you see the list of celebrities I've paid to attend the celebration."

"As long as I have you and my niggas there, I'm good," he replied. Since the judge had known hours before the felony court proceeding that the cases would be dismissed, she had allowed Blake to wear his own clothing, which consisted of an all-white Niemann Elements business suit with a white skirt, a white silk tie, and white gator skin Mauri shoes.

Clad in a white Niemann elements minidress and a 6-inch pair of white diamond-clustered spiked heels, with a matching million-dollar bracelet, $700,000 dollar platinum and white diamond earrings, and a gold- framed pair of Niemann Elements sunglasses, Alexus was the epitome of an American Dream come true. Hand in hand, she sauntered out of the courthouse with Blake and their kids, followed by her family, his family and friends, and a gang of curious Michigan City denizens.

A bunch of news reporters from CNN, MTN, NBC, ABC, and Fox were crowded off to the side of the courthouse's front stairs.

"How does it feel to be a free man again?" shouted one reporter. "Good," Blake said. "Real good." He squeezed Alexus' hand, and together they descended the stairs.

To no one's surprise, the moment they stepped into the foyer of Rita's $9 million dollar Long Beach mansion, Alexus and Blake excused themselves from their mingling families and headed up to the master suite—a spacious, high-ceilinged room with large windows, and white fur carpeting.

Alexus locked the door behind her and leaned back against it. Her mouth began to water as she watched him undress. Gently, she stroked his hardening dick, she sauntered over to him, licking her lips.

"Turn around and shake that ass for me," he murmured, and when she did, he let out a husky groan. "Mmm-mmm-mmm. Ass like Mizz Dr, face like Nicki Minaj, and a bank account like Bill Gates—I still think I'm dreamin'. This shit can't be real."

"Oh, it's real, bae." Alexus spread her feet apart, bent at the waist, grabbed her ankles, and wiggled her ass welcomingly. Her minidress raised up, exposing the nakedness beneath it. "Suck this pussy, daddy."

Blake pushed his face forward, opening her Steatopygic ass with his hands, and dipped his tongue into her wet pussy. He flicked it around inside her for a couple of minutes, lapping up her sweet juices.

Closing her eyes, Alexus started toying with her clit, biting down on her lower lip as the throbbing between her thighs reverberated throughout her entire body. She tried to stop imagining that it was T-Walk licking her down, but the image would not go away.

The freaky little dream she'd had on her private jet about her and T-Walk was only the first in a long list of dreams she'd been having about him, and the fact that they kept bumping into each other—on Rita's show, and sex or seven times at the MTN tower—wasn't making things any better. She had given T-walk her cell phone number after the Rita show, but he hadn't been using it much. He had called thrice times to see how she and the baby were doing, and told her that he still loved her. After each call, Alexus had grabbed her 9-inch battery-operated dildo and made love to it instead, as if it were T-Walk.

She popped open her eyes as she climaxed. Her juices squirted out all over Blake's mouth and chin.

He stood up, massaging his brick hard dick with one hand, wiping her dripping juices from his face with the other. "You know what it is," he said. "Get on the bed. Face down, that ass up."

Submissively, Alexus did as she was told. She crawled onto the furry blanket, spread her knees apart, and lowered the right side of her face to the middle of the bed. Her body tensed and she bit her bottom lip again as his thick phallus penetrated her from behind. He pushed into her slowly, inch- by-inching his long strong pole in until her pussy was at full occupancy.

Then he slapped the palm of his hand across her left ass cheek and watched it undulate.

"You missed this dick, didn't you?" Blake said, easing out, and in again.

"Mmm! Yeah, papí," Alexus replied. Her eyes began to water as he picked up speed. Gripping her waist with both of his strong, vein hands, he established a piston-like rhythm, slamming his dick into her sopping wet pussy. "Ooooooh, fuck…oh, Blake. Tear this pussy up, papí."

"Like this? Huh? You want it like this?" Blake grabbed a handful of her hair—an idiosyncrasy of his that never failed to turn her on—and yanked her head back. 'This the way you wanted it?"

"¡Sí, papí! ¡Sí!" Alexus exclaimed.

The Cocaine Princess 2

Chapter 26

All these muhfuckin' Mexicans, Blake thought to himself as he traversed the expansive dining room floor, halting occasionally to speak with the Costilla's. Each of them said that they were glad to see he was home, that they wished the best for him and Alexus but he knew they were lying. Their expressions told it all.

Centering the white Carrera marble floor were two long dining tables draped in white cloth, one for Blake's family—all of whom had showed up in their Sunday's best—and one for Alexus' family. 8-foot high windows offered an awe-inspiring view of the sandy beach and lucid blue waters of Lake Michigan outback. Five crystal chandeliers hung from the high ceiling. However, Blake's favorite dining room feature of all was a 10,000 gallon fish tank that was built into the south wall. It contained three vicious-looking bull sharks.

When Blake and Alexus walked up, Blake's father, Dale King, a fifty-two year-old, rail-thin dark man in a black Brooks Brothers suit, a matching fedora with a ribbon of Louis Vuitton fabric running around its brim, and a black and brown pair of Mauri loafers, stood in front of the fish tank and stared in at the sharks. He was sipping from a glass of iced Remy Martin.

"I dig that lil look you got goin', Pops," Blake said.

Dale assented with a subtle nod of his head. He had been addicted to crack for the past seven years; hearing him say that he was off it brought a smile to Blake's face.

"We're here for you, Dale," Alexus whispered, squeezing his other shoulder. "You hang in there, all right? You're doing good."

Studying his own reflection in the fish tank's glass, Blake frowned at his clean white suit. It certainly looked nice. But it reminded him of Gucci Mane in that Mariah Carey video; the posh white ensemble didn't match his gritty, dope boy character. He was used to wearing baggy jeans, Air Force Ones, white tees, and fitted caps, with a cluster of small $20 bags of crack stashed in his mouth and a pistol on his hip. This suit-wearing shit was not his style.

"When do y'all plan on getting' married?" Dale asked as he turned to Blake.

Alexus said, "We were going to do it last week. Then our family attorney told us that Blake would be released if the prosecution didn't find Timothy Trice in time for the court date, so I decided to wait. Tasia's working with a celebrity wedding planner and a MTN director to get everything set for the big day, which should be on the 16th of this month. It'll be broadcast exclusively on MTN, like E! did with the Kardashian weddings."

"Where will the wedding ceremony take place?"

"Right here at the mansion..."

While Alexus briefed Dale on the wedding plans, Blake turned his attention to the two men whom he detested most: Trintino "T-walk" Walkson, and Reginald "Bookie" Nelson. The two men were standing across the room in front of the fireplace with Kenya and Tasia. Neither of them were looking at Blake, but he figured they were talking about him.

Isabella Costilla walked over to Blake at that moment, wrapping her chubby arms around him, and kissed him on the cheek. "¿Cómo está usted?"

"Muy bien," Blake replied. "Just ready to get the fuck out of this suit and relax, spend some more time with Alexus."

"I'll bet you are." Bella gave him a knowing smile. Then her eyes moved over to where Blake's mother, Alexus' mother, and another black woman sat at the end of one of the tables. Savaria was asleep on Carolyn's lap. "Your daughter is so smart and beautiful, Blake. My mom's in love with her."

"Yeah, that's my baby. I know I'ma go crazy when she gets old enough to start datin'."

"She'll be fine. When she turns twenty-one, King Neal will be seventeen, and I'll bet my life on it he's going to be harder on her boyfriends then you'll ever be," Bella said.

"Why is everybody using his first and middle name?"

Bella shrugged. "It might have come from Rita Mae. But don't you like the sound of it? It makes *King* sound more like a royal title than a first name."

"I guess so," Blake said drably, still vexed at not knowing if he was King Neal's father.

"Has Alexus told you about the concert?" Bella asked him as she sipped from her glass of red wine.

Alexus stepped around Blake, sucking her teeth, and gently slapped Bella's forearm. "Don't be a snitch, okay, Bella? Some things are meant to be kept secret, you know?"

Bella's expression turned indignant. "Me? A snitch? Aren't you the one who snitched on Bin Laden and Aunt Jenny?"

"They were planning terrorist attacks against the United States, you retard. We'd all be dead if I hadn't—"

"Snitched!" Bella hissed. "So the next time you fix your lips to call *me* a snitch, remember who the real snitch is. Retard!" She threw the drink in Alexus' face. The red wine splashed all over Alexus and Blake.

"Bitch, you picked the right one!" Alexus grabbed a handful of Bella's hair with one hand and punched her cousin square in the eye with the other.

Blake tried separating them slipping an arm around Alexus' waist and pulling her hair back, but she wouldn't relinquish her grip on Bella's hair.

It ended up taking four men—Blake, Dale, Antoney, and Pedro—to finally separate the cantankerous cousins, and by that time, Alexus had landed a good nine or ten uppercuts to Bella's face, leaving it swollen and bloodied.

"You fat ass bitch!" Alexus screamed as she struggled to free herself from Blake's arms. "Throw another drink, you fat funky bitch!"

Blake carried Alexus out to the foyer, which, with her wildly flailing arms and twisting hips, was no easy feat. He pushed her back against the white wall at the rear of the foyer, directly beneath a $175,000 dollar gold- framed painting of Nelson Mandela.

"Calm down, baby. This shit ain't that serious," Blake said, pinning her against the wall.

"Not that *serious*?" Alexus scoffed incredulously. "This is a $12,000 dollar dress!"

"So muhfuckin' what? Like you can't afford another one."

Alexus stopped struggling when Papí entered the foyer, followed closely by Rita Mae, who was holding King Neal in her arms.

"What has gotten into you, Alexus?" Rita asked.

"She called me a snitch, momma. And she threw red wine all over my dress." Alexus glanced down at her heels. "And my shoes! I paid $2 million dollars for these shoes, had 570 platinum-set diamonds put on—"

"I could care less how many diamonds are in your shoes, nor do I care how much they cost. Papí and I raised you better than that. You don't go around fighting your family, Alexus, regardless of what they say to you." Rita's tone of voice was low and stern. "As for Bella calling you a snitch, I've told you over and over again that only God can judge you; all other judgment is irrelevant."

"I know, turn the other cheek and all that," Alexus muttered vacantly. "I'm tired of people thinking they can do just about anything to me and get away with it. Forget turning the other cheek. An eye for an eye is the only concept people respect these days."

"She's your cousin," Rita shot back.

"Savio's my cousin, too, but that didn't stop him from trying to blow my head off earlier this year, did it? Jenny's my aunt, and she tried to kill me how many times?"

Blake was watching Papí, and Papí, through squinted eyelids, was watching Alexus with a quizzical expression on his brown visage.

Shaking her head, Rita Mae Bishop turned and headed back into the dining room, mumbling something about people needing to read the Bible more often. Blake wondered what she would say if she knew her daughter was the Costilla Cartel's official leader.

"I'm on your side, Alexus," Papí said. "Bella was wrong. She got what she deserved." He crossed his arms over his chest, still squinting at her. Then he spun around abruptly and traced Rita's path into the dining room.

"Why did he just look at you like that?" Blake asked gazing into Alexus' frustrated green eyes. He knew the answer before she even said it

132

"Now he knows that it was Savio who shot at us on Valentine's Day," she said. "I hadn't told him before."

'Aww shit,' Blake thought, wondering if Papí would go nuts on Savio with a sharp-edged machete or something crazy like that. There was never any telling with Papí.

Blake looked down at his crimson-stained suit. "Baby, I gotta go change clothes. You comin' with me?"

"No, I have to change, too. Just make sure you come right back. I have a lot planned for us today," Alexus said as she stepped past Blake and started up the spiral staircase. "Come on, your jewelry and car keys are up here."

King Rio

Chapter 27

"Oooh, girl, did you see the YouTube video of that fuck nigga punchin' Waka Flocka?" Janautica asked, pressing a palm over the left side of her full-length black Gucci coat as if she were suffering a heart attack.

She was standing on the corner of ninth and Willard, in front of Bee Kay's, Blake King's greystone convenience store. To her left stood Princess, her cousin, who also donned a Gucci coat.

It was two in the afternoon, and there were close to a hundred people crowded around the store. Most of them were young 'hood niggas, thuggishly comported in baggy jeans, fresh white Nikes, and fitted caps; and inherently ghetto girls in tight jeans, with stylish urban hairdos and impeccably decorated fingernails. They were waiting on Blake, hoping he would swing through the 'hood and kick it with them as he'd done before.

"We talked about that video last week," Princess said. "You're just too high to remember."

"Early, too," Janautica giggled. "Bitch, I been poppin' pills, snortin' up that ow-ow, smokin' Kush, and drankin' e'ry since Bullet face had nappy-headed ass Blubby bond me outta jail."

"Bird, you need to calm down and stop using all these drugs."

"No the hell I don't,' Nauti dissented, taking a drag from her Newport. She was high off two triple-stack X-pills, about a gram of cocaine, and a blunt of Kush. "Ain't nothin' wrong wit' gettin' all the way turned up, yuh feel me? Like, I'm Gucci from head to toe, so I'm Gucci."

And she was Gucci indeed. From her sunglasses to her black patent leather peep-toe pumps, she was Gucci. Even the interior of her brand new black 2012 Mercedes Benz ML350 was Gucci. Like everybody else Janautica knew, Princess had been constantly asking about all the money Nauti was blowing through. Where was it coming from? How had she been able to afford a new Mercedes SUV? The questions were infinite, and Janautica wasn't answering any of them.

With an impatient sigh, Janautica unclipped an iPhone 4S from her black leather Gucci purse and was just about to send Blake another text message (she'd already sent him five others) asking how long it would be before she'd get to see him.

Then somebody shouted, "Man, nigga...I *know* that ain't no lime-green Bugatti!"

The obstinate crowd parted as Blake pulled up and parked his $2 million dollar car next to Janautica's SUV. He had stopped by his Aunt Renée's house and changed into an all-white Coogi sweat suit with a matching skullcap, white Jordan sneakers, and all the platinum and yellow diamond jewelry he'd worn on the day of his arrest.

Stepping out of his Bugatti Veyron Super Sport, smiling emphatically at all of his Dub Life goons and goonettes, Blake felt better than ever.

Cameras started flashing. Girls were shouting his name and recording video of him with their smart phones. He hugged and shook hands and took dozens of pictures with just about everybody, then signaled for Janautica to follow him into the store.

"Took yuh nappy-head ass long enough," she said before the door had even closed behind them. "You 'bout got fucked up, ol' Tyrese-lookin' lil boy. Black ass fucka."

Blake grabbed a 20oz Mountain Dew from the beverage cooler, cracked it open, and turned it up, slaking his thirst.

"And just 'cause you own this Lil dusty ass sto'," Janautica added placing her hands on her hips, "don't mean you can come in here and drank up whatever you feel like drankin' wit'out payin', yuh feel me, like, I'm still the manager. Hmm."

"Damn, you think I look like Tyrese? That's a compliment. Hoes love that nigga," Blake said.

"Well, you must be his ugly twin." Janautica had a sexy smile on her face. "You get some mooncie already?"

Blake hesitated. "Uhh, I don't know. Depends."

"You stupid fucka, you know if you done stuck yo' Lil baby dick up in some mooncie or not."

"I got a bad memory."

Janautica walked over and slapped a warm palm across the

back of his head. "Can you remember now?"

"Bitch, slap me again and see if I don't choke-slam yo' ass on this muhfuckin' flo'."

She gave him a nonplussed look, sucked her teeth, put her shades back on, and walked past him down the first aisle to the back of the store where she stored meat products. "C'mon, nappy head, so I can give you yo' lil money from this stankin' ass sto'."

'This lil bitty bitch won't stop talkin' shit,' Blake thought to himself as he knocked off the rest of the Dew. He had been calling her every day since his nigga had bonded her out of jail. Whenever Alexus was in a business meeting, doing a magazine interview, on a television show, at the guy with Tasia, or at church with Rita Mae, Blake had been on the phone with Janautica, listening to her talk about her family and, mostly, Waka Flocka Flame. He could count on one hand the number of times she had spoken kindly to him, but it did not bother him at all. He actually loved her bellicose attitude.

Blake admired his reflection in the glass door of the cooler for a moment, the sparkling yellow pave diamonds in his necklaces, earrings, pinky rings, bracelet, and watch. Who would have thought that he, Blake King, the same young nigga who'd been riding around the west side of the Michigan City in a rust-laden bubble Caprice last year, would pop back up in the 'hood in a Bugatti, wearing $2 million dollars' worth of jewelry.

He swaggered to the manager's office in the back just as Nauti unlocked the door. Reaching over her head, he pushed open the door for her, and they stepped inside.

The office was small but lavishly decorated with a heavy pink carpet, three pink leather chairs, and an oak desk with a pink HP computer sitting on the left side of it, and a bunch of pink-framed concert photographs of Gucci Mane, Waka Flocka Flame, and OJ da Juiceman on every white and pink-striped wall.

"Don't pay no mind to my Brick Squad pics. Gucci my baby daddy and Flocka my husband, yuh feel me, like?" Janautica went to a small safe that stood against the wall behind her and kneeled in front of it.

"Fuck that money," Blake said, shutting and locking the

fogged glass door. "You can keep that shit, lil momma. I came over here to check on you, that's all. Make sure you was good."

What Janautica did next surprised Blake.

On her hands and knees, she crawled around the desk to him, salaciously licking her beaming lips. She yanked down his sweatpants and boxers, wrapped her fingers around his rapidly hardening phallus, and squeezed it.

"Dang, Bullet face," she softly cooed. "It's so fuckin' *big.*"

"Thought you said I had a baby dick."

"Shut up, stupid," Nauti murmured, flickering her tongue over the head of his dick. She took a few inches of him into her mouth and started bobbing her ink-glossed lips back and forth over it, sucking him so hard that her cheeks became large dimples, indented by the power of her suction.

"How much of my money have you spent?" Blake asked. He looked down at her, mesmerized by her oral talents.

Janautica eased her mouth off him. "'Bout um, two eighty. Yeah, 'bout $280,000, on clothes and furniture mostly. You still got, like, $8 million and some change. I got it all put up in the attic. Had the ceilin' floor reinforced with steel, and the door, too. It got a digital combination that you gotta type in, yuh feel me, like? Now will you hush and let me do what I do best?"

Blake chuckled but kept quiet, reveling in the moment as Janautica went back to sucking his dick. While slurping him, she took off her coat and laid it on the carpet beside her. Then she removed her sunglasses and set them on the coat. She donned a tight black Gucci dress, and a thin gold necklace with a small, heart-shaped diamond pendant.

"That's right there. Suck on this dick like you love it," Blake groaned as she continued servicing him.

A few minutes later, he grabbed the sides of her head, let out an ecstatic growl, and pumped her mouth full of semen.

Chapter 28

By the time Alexus Costilla had showered, changed into a backless white $25,000 dollar Valentino dress, sat in front of a large mirror in her dressing room while two gay male hairdressers worked their magic on her long black hair, and finally made her way back downstairs, nearly everybody had left. Aside from the mansion's full-time staff—two maids, a butler, a chef, and a shark caretaker—and five bodyguards, the only remaining people were Rita Mae Bishop, Papí, and Savio; the three of them were gathered around a gold-trimmed white Italian marble billiards table in the game room when Alexus sauntered into the room.

The game room was a 1,000 square foot, white marble-floored palatial domicile of entertainment. There were four billiards tables, a fully stocked bar, and a long white leather semi-circular sofa that sat poshly before a 100-inch flat screen Sony television.

Alexus walked over to where Rita stood and, for a minute or two, they watched Papí sand Savio shoot pool.

"Both of them are crazy," Rita finally whispered. "They're betting $10 million dollars per game, and Papí's up eight to zero."

Alexus didn't comment. The memory of Savio shooting up her Phantom while she and Blake had been inside it was still vivid in her mind. So, instead of speaking, she smiled, logging on to Twitter from her iPhone.

"I have a question for you," Rita said, moving closer to Alexus. "Britney and I discussed your prenuptial agreement, and, I think you're being way, way, way too generous, Alexus."

"Too generous?" Alexus shook her head. "I don't think so. A million bucks a month to play with, $200 million if we ever split up. Seems pretty fair to me. I really wanted to give him more than that." She decided against telling Momma about the $500 million dollars she had transferred to Blake's bank account a few hours earlier. She would have never heard the end of it.

"What happened to the record deal he was supposed to sign with Cash Money? You should let him do that. Let him make his own money," Rita said.

"We couldn't reach a deal, which is good, because now I'm about to get him a record label. That way he'll be able to generate his own funds. I think he wants to do that anyways."

Papí cracked the eight ball into a corner pocket, threw a 60-year old fist to the sky, and triumphantly shouted, "$90 million! Gonna get me two new Gulfstream Fives with that money." He sat the pool stick down on the table, shifted his ancient green eyes to his daughter's inexperienced ones. "I'll tell you something, Alexus. Take it or leave it, I don't like your fiancé. In my most honest and most humble opinion, I think Blake is a sloth. You can do much better than that, my angel." A second later, he added, "Summer's over, no? I hear it's gonna be a cold, cold winter."

Very suddenly, a fierce, icy chill surged through Alexus' bones. Was Papí making an implicit threat on Blake's life? Sure sounded like it.

"And what exactly is that supposed to mean, Juan?" Rita inquired, planting her hands onto expensive navy skirt suited hips.

Papí's eyes flicked over to Savio, and he regarded his tall, Armani-suited nephew with the same abhorrent glare that Scar gave Simba in *The Lion King*. "Rack 'em up. We got one more."

Savio Costilla's face was unusually pallid. Alexus determined that the vapidity of his skin tone was not due to him losing $90 million to Papí; after all, Savio was #47 on the Forbes list of the 400 richest Mexicans.

What was bothering him had to be something much more profound and disturbing than a monetary loss.

"You listen to me, Juan Costilla, and you listen good," Rita snapped at her ex-husband. "I'm not too fond of Blake myself. But he's who Alexus wants to be with. He is the father of our one and only grandson, and in ten days, he'll be our daughter's husband. So I don't want to hear about *any*- thing happening to him. We clear on that?"

As if on cue, Rita's smart phone beeped, alerting her to an incoming text message. Alexus snuck a glance at the phone and saw that the text had come from Nat Turner, the MTN News anchor Rita secretly and frequently dated.

"I have to get going. Alexus, I'll call you in the morning. And Papí… behave yourself." Rita scampered out of the room.

"*Por favor*," Papí shouted after her, "send the entire staff home before you go. I'm going to need some time alone with Savio and Alexus."

An all-around daddy's girl, Alexus was always eager to spend some quality time with her father. Besides, it was 2:30 p.m. Blake's welcome home concert wasn't due to start until nine. She had plenty of time to spare.

Climbing up onto the billiards table next to the one Papí and Savio were using and composing a Twitter message to her twenty-one million avid followers, Alexus smiled contentedly, wondering if her Goldman Sachs banker had phoned Blake with the $500 million dollar news.

King Rio

Chapter 29

"Didn't I tell you I'd get our money back?" T–Walk said to Kenya as they walked through the door of their million-dollar North Chicago condominium. "I just got an email from Ford Motor Company. They're offering $12 million for the Brick House girls to drive their vehicles, which, after Slay and MTN get their pieces of the cake, will put us up to, like... $7 million. And that's from endorsements alone."

"Okay, I admit, you're smarter than I gave you credit for." Kenya pushed the door shut with the tips of her fingers. In her black cashmere Missoni sweater, blue jeans, and black leather boots, he reminded T–Walk of Chili from TLC. She sashayed across the hardwood floor to the living room, plopped down on their Aztec-patterned sofa. "Do you ever Google your name?"

"What kind of question is that?" T–Walk asked, stepping into the kitchen to grab an MGD from the fridge. A myriad of thoughts ricocheted through his mind as he twisted the cap off his beer and joined Kenya on the sofa. He loosened his gray silk tie, took off his gray Tory Burch blazer, and kicked his feet up on that ottoman. "Why would I need to Google myself? Only people I've ever Googled were Pinky, Buffie the Body, Cubana Lust, and Mizz D.R. You know I don't fuck with the Web like that. I'd rather read a book."

He leaned over and kissed her cheek, then slickly said, "Or lay with your sexy ass."

"Oh really?" Kenya regarded him with an accusatory stare. Then she picked up the remote to their 72-inch flat screen TV, turned it on, and flipped to CNN. An anchor was talking about the cancer-related death of Steve Jobs. Shaking his head, T–Walk took the smart phone from his waist and Googled his name. What popped up surprised him—a report stating:

Trintino "T-Walk" Walkson was recently spotted having brunch with video vixen and urban cover girl Ashley "Thunder" Hunter at Pimp C's, an upscale restaurant in Port Arthur, Texas. The two were what some describe as "extremely flirtatious" during their early-hour date, and emerged hand in hand…

T-Walk didn't finish reading the article. "That was a business meeting, Kenya. I was…"

"You were what? Huh? What's the matter? Complete the sentence."

"I'm sorry, baby."

"A sorry piece of human excrement is what you are. And you can go to hell. Piece of shit boyfriend who will fuck any girl with a fat ass. What do I have to do, get implants?"

"I said I'm sorry, all right? It's not like we did anything. We ate, we talked, and we left. An hour later I was at home with you."

Wishing I was in bed with Thunder, he thought, and gulped down some beer.

"On the BOS, I have *never* cheated on you, Kenya. Not one single time."

For a moment, Kenya became silent and hammered her thumb on the top of the remote, flipping through channels until she landed on Ellen. "Do you remember that girl named Cereniti, the one who stole $5 million from Alexus?"

What T-Walk wanted to say was, *How could I possibly forget a girl who looked almost identical to Alicia Keys, a girl whose derriere was like Buffie's?*

Instead, he said, "Of course I remember her. She died in that earthquake that hit Japan earlier this year, right?"

"Not exactly." Kenya muted the television and turned to T-Walk. "You know, Cereniti was my girlfriend in college. I honestly believed that she and I would be together forever. We were planning to get married and everything." She sighed, and then chuckled once. "Well, to make a long story short, she called me this morning."

"What? She's alive?"

Kenya nodded. "She wants to give our relationship another try, and… I don't know. " A pause. "I kinda want the same thing."

Chapter 30

Janautica's pussy was so wet, so warm, and so unbelievably tight that Blake never even contemplated pulling out before ejaculating. He had her bent over her desk with her dress pushed up to her neck, thrusting his rigid member deep into her creamy center.

"Damn, this pussy is *good*, girl," he said, his toes curling unreservedly in his Jordans. His vice-like grip on Nauti's slender waist tightened, and he spilled a copious nut inside her. A few more pumps ensued. Then he took a step back and watched his cum pour out from inside her.

Nauti breathed heavily. "Oh, my God, Bullet face," she said in the softest tone he had ever heard from her. "You prob'ly had to get a license to carry a dick that big."

"Aww, *now* you wanna talk all nice. Is this what I gotta do every time I want you to shut the fuck up?"

"I'm Gucci with that, yuh feel me, like? I'll shut up quick-fast." Nauti giggled softly.

Blake snatched a tissue out of a Kleenex box on the desk and wiped himself off as Nauti retrieved her purse and swabbed away the viscid strings of cum that were dangling from her lower lips like melted cheese.

"I'ma be outside," Blake said, opening the office door.

He was in the middle of the first aisle when he received a text message from his bank that made his heart drop. It read, "Account Balance- $500,019,237.15."

There had to be some kind of mistake.

His mouth fell open. $500 million dollars was a sight full, and he couldn't take his eyes off the numbers.

"Heeeyy, Blake, wit' yo' fine ass. When you gon' stop by my apartment and get you some mo' of this grown shit?"

Blake knew that voice well. It was the voice of Loretta, a well-known crackhead in her late thirties who had sucked him up about a thousand times over the past five or six years. She was standing right in front of him, clad poorly in a beat up pair of Reeboks, threadbare jeans, and a multi-stained long-sleeved Notre Dame shirt.

He breezed past the voluptuous crack head and several other women who were trying desperately to get his attention. Once outside, Blake looked at his guys' vehicles—two lime-green Magnums on 30-inch rims, a lime-green Chevy Caprice on chrome 28s, three Chargers colored patriotically in blue, red, and white on 28s, a canary yellow Escalade on 30s, a pearl-white 1992 Caprice. He smiled and shook his head.

Young-D, wearing a gray leather Pelle Pelle jacket over baggy Girbaud jeans and gray and white Jordans, walked up to Blake and wrapped an arm around his neck. "Bruh, I thought they was gon' do us like them pigs did Troy Davis in Georgia a few weeks ago," Blake said.

"Fucked up how they killed that man. And they didn't even have no real evidence against him. If I take a life, and you take my life as a consequence, then yours should be taken for killin' me about killin' him."

"And they wonder why we sell dope." Blake shook his head again, this time out of pure disgust. "Fuck I look like payin' taxes for them to keep my niggas locked up?"

Young-D took a pack of Newports out of his jacket pocket, lit one, and offered the pack to Blake, who gladly accepted.

Halfway through his cigarette, Blake said, "What would you do if you had a half a billion dollas in the bank?"

"Half a *billion*? What's that, like, five hun'ed million?"

"Damn, nigga, you can't count?"

"Shit, I ain't never had to count *that* mufuckin' high befo'. I don't know what I'd do with that much money." Young-D puffed on his square. "First thing I'd have to do is look out for Nauti and Princess. They used the Internet to find that nigga Tim-Tim. Then Nauti whacked his hoe ass. If it wasn't for them, we'd be kickin' it wit' Troy Davis."

"Where'd you meet 'em?"

"MySpace. Princess sent me a friend request, and I—"

Blake's smart phone started bellowing out Yo Gotti's "Five Star Bitch," a ringtone that Blake had assigned to Alexus.

"Hold on a minute, bruh," Blake said. He walked to his Bugatti, opened the driver's door, and sat down in his seat with his legs outside the car. Then he answered the call.

Alexus' face filled the screen. "Has the banker called yet?" She

asked.

"You put all that money in my account?"

"Uhh, no, it must have been Oprah," she replied sarcastically.

"Shots fired," Blake teased with a laugh. "I can buy"—he paused and calculated—"like, a thousand Maybachs with that much bread."

"Well, we couldn't celebrate your birthday on September 20th, so I decided to give you a few gifts today. Turn on your car radio, and go to 107.5. I have another surprise for you."

Blake followed her instructions. "Okay, what now?"

"Push the 'map' button, the 'p' button, and the 'sound' button' all at the same time and hold them for 10 seconds."

Again, he followed her instructions, and then watched in amazement as the bottom half of the passenger's seat began to rise pneumatically, hissing like one of those doors on the starship Enterprise. Beneath it was a wide, suede-lined compartment containing a Niemann Elements bulletproof vest, two 9mm glocks, and a necklace full of ridiculously large round-cut white and yellow diamonds with an oversized medallion depicting his face in yellow and black diamonds. What shocked him the most was the yellow diamond-encrusted word under the blinging head: Bullet face.

"What made you put 'Bullet face', where'd you get that?" Blake interrogated as he started to lift everything out of the compartment and moving them to the floor in front of the passenger's seat. He found six long fifty-round magazines underneath the vest.

"Bookie told me that everybody had started calling you Bullet face in jail, so I told my jeweler to incorporate the name into the medallion's design. Do you like it?" Alexus beamed.

"Hell yeah!" Blake was enthused, emphasizing each word. "How do I close this box?" He quickly scanned his surroundings to see if anyone was watching.

King Rio

A phalanx of about twenty girls were standing behind his Bugatti, flashing pictures, talking, and laughing. Since the rear and side windows were so darkly tinted, they could not see him.

"Just push the seat down a little, and it'll finish closing on its own," Alexus said. "There's one under the driver's seat, too. All you have to do is tune to 92.3 and hold the same buttons down. There are some silencers for the guns, a pound of Purple Haze, a fifty-count box of Swisher Sweets cigars, and $40,00 in cash in that one. Ok, and don't worry about the smell of weed being detected if you're ever pulled over; the stash boxes will vacuum-seal automatically when closed."

Setting the phone down on his lap, Black picked up one of the glocks and slid a clip into it, using his right elbow to push down the raised seat next to him. "I didn't even know they made clips this long for handguns. You got me on some James Bond type shit."

"Wait until you use that gun. These are fully automatic Glock 18s. They shoot like Uzis."

"I love you more and more every minute, Alexus. It ain't about the money, either. You're so real, so...solid."

"And I love you for the same reasons. But listen, Papí wants to discuss something with me and Savio, so I'll call you back in a few minutes." Before he could respond, she added, "Oh, and, for the record, I paid $4 million dollars for that necklace and another million for that medallion. I'm expecting full compensation tonight."

Blake smiled. "I got you."

He put the phone back on his hip, put on his new chain, then eased back in his seat and relaxed vibing to the thrumming beat of an Ace Hood song that blared from the back his nigga Fly's Magnum, embracing the Glock 18 in his right hand. He wondered how many black men in America had half a billion in the bank. Probably five or six, he guessed. Certainly not much more than that.

Young-D appeared at Blake's open driver's door. "Who was that?"

"That was Nunya," Blake said, lustfully eyeing a sexy,

longhaired mulatto chick named Tootie who was standing a few feet away from Young-D.

"Who the fuck is Nunya?" Young-D asked.

"Nunya muhfuckin' business, nigga. Fuck is you, a phone patrolman?"

Following a brief, jubilant chuckle, Young-D dipped his head into the driver's door and studied the new bling. His eyes moved from the medallion to the glock and then back to the medallion again. "That chain nasty, bruh. That's prob'ly the coldest piece in the game right now. Only other nigga I done seen with some shit like this was Ross, and I don't even think his was as big as yours." He paused and lit another Newport. "You don't need no guns, though. E'rybody out here got choppas. Muhfucka try somethin' stupid with you, they gotta be retarded."

"I ain't takin' no chances," Blake said as he started the Bugatti's 1200 horsepower W-16 engine. "Niggas shot me up once already. Be damned if I let it happen again."

King Rio

Chapter 31

"I love your mother, Savio. She's my little sister, *la chica bonita* from the great Mexican land of Matamoros, no?" Papí sounded grim. He was standing atop the shark tank's glass ceiling with Savio and Alexus, staring at his nephew with cold eyes. He turned to Alexus, whose head was down, studying the bull sharks. "I'm sure Lexi loved her, too. Until Jenny blew up Rita Mae's house, and shot up Lexi's car on I-94. I think that the proverbial thin line between love and hate was crossed at the point, no?"

"My mother may be *loco*," Savio countered, "but she's still my mother, Papí. And personally, I don't blame her for being upset about Granny Costilla leaving everything to Alexus. We've worked all our lived for those billion. I don't know if you remember or not, but back in '09, my mother invested 2.7 billion in Daimler-Benz for a 9.1 percent share of the German company, and she sold it back to them last year for a little over six, kept three, and gave the rest to Granny Costilla. The least Granny could've done was leave my mother that 3.2."

Nervously, Alexus looked up at Papí who was puffing on a Cuban cigar, squinting his sage old eyes at Savio. He had his thumbs stuck in the front belt loops of his finely tailored slacks.

"So," Papí asked, "you feel that justified Jenny's attempts to murder Alexus Costilla? *My daughter* Alexus Costilla?" A thick plume of tobacco smoke blew from his mouth.

Savio's countenance fell, offering an ill-received apology. Was it defeat? Fear?

Whatever it was didn't matter. Papí drew a golden .45-caliber revolver from his waist, aimed it at the top of Savio's forehead, and pulled the trigger twice in rapid succession.

The reports were deafening. Savio's brains divorced his skull faster than a Hollywood wife does her headlining husband. His lifeless body crumpled to the glass floor, and his brain remarried to the smooth marble wall behind him.

"*Que la chingada!*" Alexus screamed at the top of her lungs. Her eyes bulged. Her palms slapped over the lower half of her face. "Papí!"

"Shhh!" Pressing a forefinger to his thin lips, tucking away the revolver, Papí said, "He tried to kill you, no? Well, no one gets away with trying to kill my daughter. Nobody." "But—"

"No buts, Alexus. I don't want to hear it." He looked down at his dead nephew for an eternal minute. "I need your help getting rid of this body."

"I'm not touching him! Are you crazy?"

Papí shrugged indifferently, waving Alexus off. He was thoughtful for a moment. Then he drew the revolver again and sent three bullets through the big square of glass on which Savio's body rested.

The glass webbed, cracked, and then gave way. Alexus gasped as she watched her cousin's body splash into the water, and when one of the bull sharks bit a huge chunk from Savio's leg, she turned and ran frantically down the narrow steel staircase to the foyer.

Chapter 32

"Have you ever read the *Deadly Reigns* trilogy by Teri Woods?" Nauti asked Blake as she stood next to him on the sidewalk in front of her five-bedroom home on Lincoln Avenue, just three blocks away from his convenience store.

The street was jam-packed from end to end with flashy cars and black folks in 'hood attire. Some of them were engaged in a boisterous dice game a few feet down the sidewalk from where Blake stood with Janautica, his brother Streets, Young-D, and Lil Mike. Some were drinking cups and bottles of Remy Martin (Streets had arrived in his candy-red 1973 Chevy Caprice convertible on chrome 28s with twenty bottles of Remy) and smoking blunts of Kush. Some were on the corner of eighth and Lincoln, dealing crack, heroin, X-pills, and weed to the seemingly endless procession of drug addicts.

Blake didn't hear Janautica's question. What he heard was the trunk-rattling bass of Gucci Mane and Waka Flocka Flame's "Ferrari Boyz," which was screaming from the trunk of some-body's car nearby. He had already smoked eight blunts with Streets, Young-D, Lil Mike, and Nauti.

His eyes were narrowed down to stringent slits, focused on a dark-skinned girl who had just pulled up and stepped out of a silver BMW 750Li. She had on a tight pair of black leather leggings that showed off her massive ass, and Blake couldn't stop staring as she began swaying her hips to the music.

"Hello? Earth to stupid, nappy-head," Janautica said, shaking Blake's shoulder. "Is yuh listenin'? 'Cause it sho don't seem like it."

"Bitch, if you shake me one mo' muhfuckin' time, I'ma throw yo' Lil ass all the way back to North Carolina." Blake shifted his scarlet eyes over to Nauti and was about to say something else when Streets and Young- D started laughing. Janautica and Lil Mike followed suit.

"Dang!" Nauti said. "You was 'bout ready to fuck me up, huh?"

Blake started laughing with them. "Nah, I was just"—he dropped his head and laughed some more—"I was jokin'."

"No the hell you wasn't," Nauti declared.

They all laughed for a minute Blake kept an eye on the big-bootied chick across the street. She had her hands tucked in the pockets of her short, gray fur coat. Her lips were gleaming with gloss. Briefly, her eyes settled on Blake, and she smiled suggestively.

When the laughter simmered down, Janautica repeated her question.

"Nah, I ain't never read no *Deadly Reigns* books," Blake replied. He took a sip from his bottle of Remy. "Think I might've heard somebody talkin' about 'em, though."

"Oooh, let me tell you," Nauti said. "The Reigns family got money like you and Alexus got. I mean, they wasn't in the streets like you, all icy and whatnot, yuh feel me? Nevertheless, they was *ballin'*. Early, too."

Lil Mike was rolling another blunt. Like Young-D, he was slim, brown-complexioned, and tatted from neck to waist. Every tooth in his mouth was covered in gold. He had moved from Memphis, Tennessee, with his grandmother when he was twelve, and had been friends with Blake and Young-D ever since. "Mane," he said to no one in particular. "Nauti's a white girl in a black girl's body, yuh her' me?"

"Fuck all y'all." Janautica looked at her watch. "Well, I got a 4:30 hair appointment. I'll see you nappy-headed bastards later. And Blake, don't be havin' yo' Lil rascals runnin' in and outta my house while I'm gone. I ain't got time to be cleanin' up after no grown ass men."

She walked over to her cousin Princess said, "C'mon, jabber jaws." Then the two of them climbed in her leased Mercedes and vamoosed.

"I like that Lil Swine Flu victim," Blake murmured.

"Bruh, dat bitch got the Swine Flu?" Streets asked with a note of seriousness. He donned a brown leather Louis Vuitton jacket over Red Monkey jeans.

Blake chuckled amiably. "Hell nah, nigga. You think I'd be

fuckin' that bitch if she had the Swine Flu for real? That's just a nickname I gave her."

"That's a fucked up nickname," Young-D noted, turning up his own bottle of Remy. "Man, I can't believe we got all dem murda cases dropped."

"We would've been hit if Alexus hadn't dropped all that money, mane. On my dead brotha," Li' Mike said.

"Fuck all dat," Sweets cut in. "What happened to the record deal with Cash Money? I wrote down near two hun'ed songs in the county."

"We did, too," Blake said. "I'm cool on that deal, though. I'ma start my own record label." He glanced at the extra-large Louis Vuitton duffle bag that was sitting on the hood of his Bugatti, which was parked at the curb in front of them. "Name it Money Bags Music... or somethin' like that. I got the bread to do it now."

Lil Mike lit the blunt. I wish Lil Meach and Straw was out here wit'us."

"Lil Lord, too. You know he'd be out here clownin'," Blake said, fluctuating his eyes from the duffle bag to the BMW girl; she was sauntering across the street toward him.

"Damn!" Lil Mike exclaimed.

"Nigga, she thick as hell," said Young-D.

About fifty or sixty sets of eyeballs were unwaveringly pasted to the girl's ass. She seemed to gain an abundance of confidence and swagger with every tantalizing, hip-swinging step she took.

"I didn't know Buffie had a sister," Blake said to her.

"Hi, Blake, I'm Ashley Hunter, but you probably know me as Thunder," she said as she examined Blake from head to toe.

"Oh shit, y'all," someone yelled from the dice game. "That's whatshername from Brick House."

"Brick House of Jupiter Island," Thunder corrected. "Premieres tonight at eight o'clock on MTN. Make sure y'all watch it, too. It's goin' down!" She turned back to Blake. "Listen, I know you're wondering why I'm here. Especially since I've been dating T-Walk."

"I don't give a fuck about who you datin'. Wussup?" Blake said. Thunder shrugged her shoulders. "I was supposed to meet T-

Walk at IHOP for a late breakfast a few hours ago, but he never showed up. Sent me a text saying his girlfriend had found out about us, and that he couldn't see me anymore. So I went to that mall up the road from IHOP, overheard some girls talking about coming over here to chill with you, and followed them home. You don't mind, do you?"

Lil Mike answered. "Hell naw, you her' me? You can stay here all *year*, you her' me?" He was geeked all the way up, ogling her thick thighs, her wide hips. "Mane, dat ass *can't* be real."

"Oh, it's all real," Thunder said. She flicked her inquisitive umber eyes from Blake to Lil Mike and then back to Blake. "I hear you like your girls with big rumps."

"What's inside matters more to me than what's outside," Blake replied honestly. "Some women are like a hoarder's mansion, you feel me? Pretty on the outside, but filled with trash on the inside. Make you wish you would've just drove past instead of stoppin' to take a look." He accepted the blunt from Lil Mike, sucked in a mouthful of smoke, held it in for a couple of seconds. "But, yeah, I like my women thick... like you."

Planting her hands on her hips, Thunder showed an infectious smile. She owned a dark chocolate face, smooth and unblemished, with full heart- shaped lips and eyes that were both penetrating and picturesque. Young-D stepped behind her to get a closer look at her ass. His mouth dropped open, and he silently mouthed, "Daaamnn!"

"Well, this metaphorical mansion is spick and span," Thunder said. "Aw yeah?" Blake asked.

"Yep. Outside and inside." "I'll try to remember that." "You'd better remember that."

Blake hit the blunt again. "Who gave you that?"—he coughed several times—"that name?"

"Bun B gave me the name a few years ago at one of his video shoots," she explained as Blake's phone began vocalizing "Five Star Bitch." "I was dancing behind him and Pimp C while they were performing—I had on some thong panties and pair of heels—and my ass was clapping. Loud as thunder."

"You knew Pimp C?" Blake asked, unclipping his phone from

the waist of his white Coogi sweatpants. He had been listening to UGK since he was a kid.

"Of course I knew him," Thunder said. "We're from the same city. In fact, I was actually in the studio with them when they were talking about how much they liked your music. That was right before Pimp C passed." She made a cross on her chest, looked up into the cool blue sky, and murmured, "God rest his soul."

Blake held off on answering the phone call. "Wait a minute. So, you sayin' Bun B and Pimp C was bangin' my shit?"

Thunder nodded. "If you want to, you can ask Bun B yourself. He'll be at your concert tonight."

Blake walked to the front of his car, sat on the hood beside his duffle bag, and answered his phone.

"Baby, you *gotta* tell me what's up with this concert I keep hearin' about," he said, staring at Thunder's massive ass and wondering if he could stand his bottle of Remy on it.

"Where are you?" Alexus asked. Sounded like she was crying. "I'm in the 'hood, baby. You a'ight?"

"*No*, I'm not all right!" She screamed. "In fact, I'm a zillion fucking miles from all right, *¿comprende?* My paternal family is full of nut cases. Papí is the biggest nut of them all. And they're beginning to drive *me* nuts."

"Man, you can calm down with all that loud shit. I *can* hear you, you know. I ain't deaf. And why am I not lookin' at you? You on the Internet?"

"I'm on Twitter," Alexus said in a much lower tone. She sniffled. "Big Mark's driving me to our place in Chicago. I'm gonna take a long bath, smoke another joint, and relax. Hopefully, I'll be able to forget about everything that's happened today."

"You talkin' 'bout Bella?"

Alexus hesitated. "No. Something else has happened. I need you here by six-thirty. I'll tell you then."

"You still ain't told me nothin' 'bout the concert," Blake pointed out. "That's why I need you here by six-thirty. We're gonna make an appearance at The Visionary Lounge first for the Brick House premiere celebration. Then we're heading straight to the United Center. It'll be a fun night."

"A'ight, baby. I'll be on the highway in a few minutes."

"Okay. I love you, Blake."

"Love you, too."

Blake clipped the phone back to his hip and looked at his watch. It read 3:55 p.m., which meant he had little over two hours and thirty minutes before he had to be in Chicago. Normally, it took him about forty-five minutes to drive from Michigan City to the chi, but in the Bugatti Veyron SS, the world's fastest production car, he knew he could get there in thirty. Twenty if he floored it.

He sat the bottle of Remy Martin down on the curb, sucking in yet another cloud of Kush smoke. His thoughts quickly drifted to the extensive wardrobe he had in Janautica's basement, clothes that Alexus had bought for him back in February. There were Gucci and Louis Vuitton hats, jackets, sunglasses, belts, outfits, and sneakers; suits by Armani, Brooks Brothers, Tory Burch, and Versace. Blake briefly considered going down to the basemen and changing into a Louis Vuitton outfit, or maybe one of the Girbaud ensembles he'd brought over back then. But since most of the 'hood seemed to be in a Coogi-rocking phase, he decided to keep on the intricately woven sweat suit.

"Pass the muhfuckin' weed, nigga," Young-D said. He was walking toward Blake with his eyes stuck on Thunder's voluminous derriere. He leaned back on the lime-green Bugatti next to Bullet face. "Man, bruh, dat bitch say she done been featured in eight magazines and thirty videos.

Claims she's from Nigeria some muhfuckin' where originally. Bitch damn near got mo' ass than Alexus."

"Damn near," Blake concurred, handing his nigga the blunt. "I'm boutta hit the highway, bruh. Chill wit' wifey in Chicago."

"Fuck Chicago, bruh. How you gon' go out there like shit's gravy after them niggas kidnapped Savaria and killed her momma?"

"Gotta find out who did it one way or another." Blake picked up his Remy and the duffle bag. He flicked his eyes around at all the decrepit old houses lining Lincoln Avenue, and tried to estimate how much it would cost him to fix them up. Then he stepped around to the passenger's door of his car and opened it.

"I'm comin' wit'choo," Young-D said.

Nodding his head, Blake stood the Remy bottle on the passenger's seat, unzipped the long duffle bag, and shouted, "Everybody get in a line on the sidewalk over here. I want the females in front."

When everyone was in line, Blake stood in front of them and passed out $20,000 dollar bundles of hundreds to them. He started with $3 million in the duffle. By the time he was finished handing out the cash, he was down to four rubber-banded bundles of bank-new Franklins.

The 'hood went wild. Every face in the crowd was elated and beaming. Blake caught Thunder smiling at him as she fanned through her twenty grand.

"You might as well follow us to Chicago," he said to her. "That was already my next destination," she replied.

King Rio

Chapter 33

Alexus Costilla reposed on her custom-made white leather Niemann Elements sofa in the spacious living room of her urban Trumbull Street mansion. She had on her favorite robe—a brown fur Louis Vuitton robe that Papí had brought her last year—with nothing on beneath it. With her bare feet curled under her, she held a dog-eared copy of *Deep Throat Diva*—a Cairo novel—open in her hands.

Nevertheless, she could not concentrate on reading it. The yolk of her thoughts was scrambled with impending wedding decisions, Blake's dubious fidelity, tonight's red carpet Brick House premiere, the star-studded concert that immediately followed, and –perhaps the most burdensome of all—the macabre memory of Savio's brains splattering against that wall.

With a frustrated sigh, Alexus closed the novel and set it aside. There was a   100-inch widescreen Sony television on the wall across from her.

Paranormal Activity 3 was playing. She shut it off and then turned on a Cherokee   D'Ass porn.

The movie began with Cherokee standing outside a mansion in a fishnet bodysuit, shaking her ass, making it clap. Alexus slipped out of her robe, stepped into her 6-inch Louis Vuitton heels, and started mimicking Cherokee's movements. She moved in sync with the black porn goddess, clearing her mind, expunging her troubled thoughts a modicum at a time. She sashayed across the heated white marble floor to the east wall bent over with her hands pressed flat against it and wiggled her thighs as Cherokee did the same things against a tall white pillar.

"Damn baby. So, this is what you do when I'm not around," Blake said as he entered the living room.

Alexus turned around. "Wow, you got here fast."

"Don't mind me." Blake took a seat on the sofa. "Act like I'm not even here."

He kicked off his shoes and leaned back, expecting a show.

"Nuh-uh, bay. The only reason I'm naked is because I just got out the tub and I can't decide on what to wear." She walked back to the sofa, picked up her robe, and was about to put it on when Blake snatched it from her and lodged it behind his back. She grabbed her hips belligerently and sucked her teeth. "Don't make me knock you out," she snapped.

"Make it clap for me one time, baby."

"We'll be married in 10 days. I'm saving all my tricks for our honeymoon."

"You got me fucked up," Blake said. He was staring into her eyes, grinning that cocky little grin of his that never failed to make Alexus smile.

"I can't stand your black ass," she uttered and turned her back to him.

She wiggled her thighs and her ass applauded. "Goddamn," Blake murmured.

Alexus looked at the television. Cherokee bent forward in front of a dark-skinned, bald-headed man who sat on a sofa with his face buried between her thick butt cheeks. Alexus swept her arm around, grabbed the back of Blake's head, and pulled his face to her ass.

"Lick my...um....my other hole," Alexus said, too embarrassed to say the actual word.

"Do what?" Blake scoffed and pulled back a little.

She peered over her shoulder at him. "It's clean, boy," she coaxed, swaying her hip salaciously.

That was all the prodding Blake needed. He glanced at the widescreen for a couple of seconds, as if he were seeking confirmation from the porn star, then eased his head forward, spread her big cheeks apart, and said, "Shit, you blessed me wit' a Jay-Z bankroll today. You lucky I feel like I owe you."

He straightened his tongue and poked it into Alexus' asshole. Her pussy was already soaking wet, and as Blake's agile tongue began to flicker around in her sphincter, she grew even wetter. Globules of vaginal juices seeped out of her; her nipples stiffened; her clit palpitated.

When Cherokee straddle the porn actor in a 69, Alexus did the same thing with Blake. She pushed down his sweatpants and

162

boxers, curled the fingers of one hand around the base of his dick, and tapped its head with her tongue.

"What the hell?" Alexus hopped off Blake, snatching up her robe in the process. She put it on and crossed her arms over her chest "What the hell is that on your dick?"

Sitting up, Blake looked down at his hard phallus. "Ain't nothin' on my dick. Fuck you talkin' 'bout?"

"Nigga, you know exactly what I'm talking about. Your dick tastes like funky pussy, and it certainly didn't come from me."

"Baby, you' trippin'," Blake said without much conviction.

Alexus glowered at him for a long moment. She already lamented giving so much to him so soon. Tears burgeoned along her lower eyelids, but she kept a straight face, struggling to keep her emotions in check.

"Who was it?" Her voice was vindictive and frigid, as skin chilling as a Chicago winter. Her hands raced to her hips. "What's her name, and where does she live? And don't lie and say you didn't fuck her, because I was born 19 years ago, not yesterday, not last week."

Blake was hesitant. Tucking away his manhood, he lifted the diamond-encrusted replica of his face from his chest and studied it. Then he looked up at Alexus. "It's the money, baby. I got too much of it. You got me riding around in a Bugatti, breaded up, iced out. Every bitch I ride past tryna holla at a nigga. I ain't never experienced no shit like this." He sank deeper into the white leather and sighed. "I apologize, baby. Swear to God, I'm sorry."

"I don't wanna hear that shit." Alexus pulled a gold-pated .44 Bulldog revolver from a pocket in her robe and aimed it at Blake's nose. "Tell me her name, Blake. Tell me her fucking name."

"You better put that muhfuckin' gun back in yo' pocket where you got it. Make me fuck you up."

"Either you give me her name so I can find her, or you can die for her. The choice is up to you." An infrared beam was attached to the top of the revolver's snub-nosed barrel. Alexus thumbed it on. "I'll murder you, kill myself, and then kill your ghost if I can. Think I'm playing if you want to."

"Put that gun down," Blake sternly demanded. "What's her

name?"

"I'm not playin', Alexus."

"And I'm not playing, either. Tell me her goddamn name."

Blake went silent again. His phone started to sound, but he didn't answer it. He kept fluctuating his eyes from the gold revolver to Alexus, wondering if she really had the heart to shoot him. "Whitney," he finally said. "It was a bitch named Whitney."

He felt bad about the lie immediately after it vacated his mouth, and the fact that Janautica was phoning him at that very instant did not make him feel any better. But, he reminded himself, revealing a name to Alexus might have resulted in Papí learning of the infidelity, and there was no telling how the Costilla Cartel's violent patriarch would deal with the news.

Slowly, Alexus lowered the revolver to her side. The tears started cascading down from her hurt green eyes. "I can't stand you, Blake. I hate you with a passion." Her heels clacked loudly on the polished marble as she stormed out of the living room.

"Baby, I... I said I'm sorry," Blake shouted.

"Get out of my house," Alexus replied from somewhere in the foyer.

Blake stayed seated for three or four minutes, salty at himself for neglecting to clean up after he had fucked Nauti. He decided against sticking around to console his woman. That crazy bitch had a gun. No sense in staying inside to see if she would use it.

He swaggered out the front door, down the gray marble walkway, and pulled open the heavy iron gate without glancing at the five heavily armed bodyguard who were strategically positioned around the yard like *Men In Black* extras.

There were eight more bodyguards on the sidewalk outside of the gate, equally spaced from the corner of Douglas and Trumbull to the other corner on 15th. Blake spotted Young-D and Lil Mike standing next to his Bugatti with Chubb, an overweight hustler and Three Star Universal Elite of the Traveling Vice Lords.

"Look at this Lil nigga!" Chubb said enthusiastically as he yanked a mammoth paw out of his brown leather jacket and shook Blake's hand. "Man, Joe, yo' Lil crazy ass hit the jackpot. How the fuck you manage to pull a bad bitch wit' Bill Gates money?"

"Don't call my bitch no bitch," Blake said, shooting a diagonal glance at the newly built red brick convenience store on the corner of 15th and Trumbull. Bunches of people were hanging out near its entrance.

"You know I ain't mean nothin' by dat, Lil homie. I'm just sayin', Alexus got, like, twenty times more money than Oprah. And she stay right here on my block. Chubb shook his big brown head. "Shit wild, Joe."

"Yeah... shit is wild." Blake's eyes fixed to the corner store. He was wondering who had financed its construction when suddenly Thunder came walking out of it with a bottle of Pepsi in one hand and a bag of Skittles in the other.

Men shouted lustily after her. Thunder sashayed across the street to her car, which was sandwiched between the Bugatti and Alexus' white Phantom.

"Give me Blake my number, Lil Mike," Thunder said, opening her driver's door. "Sorry to leave y'all stranded like this, but I have to get dressed and head over to the Visionary Lounge for the premiere celebration. I'll see your fine ass at the concert... Bullet face."

Blake chucked up deuces and watched her drive off. Chubb started to talk about Lil Lord, a twenty-five-year-old all-around goon who had been groomed by some of Trumbull Street's most infamous gangbangers, gunslingers, and drug dealers. Lil Lord had been bouncing back and forth from Chicago to Michigan City since he was a kid. He had taught Blake everything there was to know about the dope game. He had introduced Blake to the guys in Chicago, showed him how to handle every situation properly and effectively.

"Man, Joe, I remember when Lil Lord first brought you out here," Chubb said as he grabbed a blunt from behind his ear. "I think that was back in '02, right befo' the feds indicted damn near everybody in that 'Operation wild West' bullshit." He slapped his pockets until he found his lighter, then fired up the blunt and continued. "You know we raised that Lil crazy muhfucka. We used to make him beat up all the Lil niggas who thought they were tough. Had him smoke weed when he was five years old. I knew he was gon' end up murkin' muhfuckas when he grew up."

"I watched Lil Lord shoot a nigga 15 times at point-blank range," Young-D said, puffing on his own blunt.

Blake had also witnessed that shooting. In fact, he'd seen Lil Lord gun down several niggas. Now Lil Lord was serving a thirty-five-year prison sentence for murder.

Blake didn't want to discuss Lil Lord's reputation. "Ay, Chubb," he said, pulling his Glock from inside the large front pocket of his hoodie. The bulletproof Kevlar vest he wore beneath it had Velcro straps on both sides that held four of his fifty-round clips. He retrieved one, slid it into the Glock, looked Chubb straight in the eye, and said, "My daughter was kidnapped from that apartment buildin' on the corner of Douglas and Albany earlier this year. You know the buildin' I'm talkin' about, right?"

Chubb nodded, 'yes.' His jovial expression attenuated to a mask of trepidation. "Yeah," he murmured. "I know that buildin'."

Blake cocked the fully automatic pistol and aimed it at the left knee of Chubb's loose-fit Girbaud jeans. "Tell me who kidnapped my daughter."

Chubb's mouth fell open. The blunt secured between his lips dropped to the sidewalk.

"One of you niggas kidnapped my daughter, killed her momma, and got me out of $50 million dollas. And I know it had to be one of y'all niggas off the block right here, 'cause we had the money traced," snarled Blake. He backhand slapped the pistol across Chubb's face and watched the fat man crumple to the ground.

The viscous blow opened a deep laceration beside Chubb's right eye, but he didn't make a sound. He rolled over to his side, lifted himself up on one elbow, and stared up at Blake with blood pouring from his fresh wound.

Lil Mike drew a pair of Mac-11s from inside his blue leather Niemann Elements jacket and gave one to Young-D. Blake took a long black silencer out of his hoodie pocket and started screwing it into the barrel.

"Just tell me who did it, Chubb." Blake pointed the gun at the same knee. "Don't make me—"

166

The Cocaine Princess 2

"Ay, Joe, deez niggas upped strap on Chubb!" Somebody screamed.

Looking up, Blake saw six young niggas in black hoodies jogging toward him. A few others were running into the St. Louis Street alley, presumably to get their weapons.

Blake did not hesitate. Raising the Glock, he squeezed the trigger.

The gun went off like an Uzi, sending a hail of bullets spiraling through all six of the approaching hoodlums. All of them were grounded within two seconds.

Young-D sent a three-round burst of ammo at the sky, and the crowd scattered like roaches when the lights came on.

"On my momma, Joe," Chubb said emphatically. "You know you done fucked up. Wait 'til Cup find out about this shit."

"Nigga, you think I give a fuck?" Blake snapped and moved the gun to Chubb's face. He was just about to pull the trigger when a bullhorn sounded from behind him.

"This is the Chicago Police Department. I need you all to put down your weapons and put your hands up."

The next thing Blake knew, four of Alexus' bodyguards were firing their M-16 assault rifles at a nigga who had just emerged from the St. Louis Street alley holding an Ak-47. Blake looked back over his shoulder and saw that the man with the bullhorn was also a bodyguard. Young-D and Lil Mike seemed to be bewildered; they thought the bodyguards were actual police officers.

Their uneasiness rubbed off on Blake. He scowled at Chubb. "If it wasn't for you knowin' Lil Lord, I'd empty the rest of this clip into yo' face, nigga. Remember that."

Blake rushed over to Alexus' Rolls Royce and peered in through the driver's window. The key was in the ignition, just as he'd thought. He told Young-D and Lil Mike to take the Phantom. Then he hopped in his Bugatti, and they drove away.

King Rio

The Cocaine Princess 2

Chapter 34

Located on the corner of Laramie and Chicago Avenue, the Visionary Lounge, a five-story Yellowstone edifice with wide, darkly tinted windows and a massive outback parking lot, was Chicago's first glitzy Vegas-style day club/nightclub. Half of Hollywood had already made appearances at the opulent establishment. Rappers and singers from all over the world performed there regularly.

But there were no rappers in the building this evening. Nor were there any singers. The Steatopygic cast members of Brick House of Jupiter Island sauntered gracefully across the red-carpeted ballroom on the third floor of the Visionary Lounge. A slew of other MTN reality TV stars had shown up in support of the new reality show, which was receiving rave reviews from some of the industry's most renowned critics.

Not only had Trintino Walkson been listed as an executive producer of The Brick House shows, but he was also credited as the creator, producer, and writer.

Taking occasional sips from his stem glass of Ace of Spades champagne, he moved around the ballroom in a black Armani suit, taking pictures with the girls. No matter how hard he tried, he could not conjure up a smile, and his eyes were vacant behind the dark Gucci shades that cloaked them. Kenya had just left him to be with a woman, and he had screwed his backup plan when he stood Thunder up earlier. To make matters worse, he had been expecting to see Alexus here at the MTN event. He wanted to ask her if she had forgiven him for breaking up with her last year, and, if things didn't work out between her and Blake, would she ever consider getting back with him. However, it seemed like that plan was out the window, too; it was going on eight o'clock and she still had not shown up.

"I've never in my life seen this many big-booty women at once," said a man who had just stopped next to T-Walk. His three-button suit was light gray, with gold cufflinks, a gold silk pocket square, and a gray tie covered with five-point, gold stars and crescent moons.

"It is a beautiful sight," T-Walk said, turning to look at the man. "Do I know you from somewhere?"

"My name's Tyrese, but everyone calls me Reesie Cup." He reached out and shook T-Walk's hand. "I'm CEO of this club and many others. I was there at the park the night you were shot."

"Yeah?" T-Walk squinted at Reesie Cup.

"Yeah. Saw the whole thing. That was some weak shit he pulled." Reesie Cup had a smart phone in his hand. He was watching CNN. "To tell you the truth, I want him dead. He just killed two of my youngsters and wounded four more of them. His girlfriend's bodyguards murdered one of my best soldiers. And he even had the audacity to slap my right-hand man with a pistol. The media's received word from CPD that it was a gang hit. No suspects, no leads."

"You sure it was who you think it was?"

"I'm 100 percent sure it was Blake King. Who else drives a Bugatti in the Midwest, and walks around with, like, 10-mil' worth of jewelry on? And besides, the whole damn block saw him." Reesie Cup flexed his jaw muscles and balled his right hand into a tight fist. "I'm something like a mayor in my neighborhood, you know what I mean? I've been there since day one. My team gets rid of thirty-hundred kilos of girl every goddamn week out there. I pass out fireworks on the 4th of July, turkeys on Thanksgiving, presents on Christmas. They look up to me in a lot of way, you feel me? I can't just let that young nigga get away with killing my people. I believe in justice just as much as I believe in peace."

"Well, murk that nigga. Pay somebody to blow his head off," T-Walk said.

"Easier said than done," Cup replied. "I'd like nothing better than to have him taken care of immediately. The thing is, he's somehow plugged in with the Mexican Mafia, and they're the ones who've been supplying me with the purest white I've ever tasted. If something happens to Blake, I could lose my connect. Gotta keep business first."

T-Walk finished off his champagne in two long gulps. For a moment, he gazed across the room at a widescreen television.

170

Brick House of Jupiter Island was set to premiere in just under three minutes. "So why are you telling me all this shit?" He finally asked. "I want him dead, too. But I'm trying to focus on these reality shows right now. Once I have $40 or $50 million in the bank, I'll take him out the game myself."

"Nah." Reesie Cup was shaking his hand. "That's not the answer. What you need to do is get in good with Alexus first. Get her to plug you with somebody in that cartel. If you can do that, I'll serve you Blake on a silver platter."

King Rio

Chapter 35

Alexus felt her heart slamming against her ribcage. She was so nervous that her hands were shaking. As she strolled up the long hallway beside Blake, dressed in a white-sequined Dolce & Gabbana mini-dress with matching 5-inch Christian Louboutin heels under a full-length ninety thousand-dollar white fur coat, she took a couple of deep breaths and tried to settle her nerves.

They were inside the United Center, surrounded by body-guards. Lil Mike and Young-D walked behind them. Although Alexus was still distraught over Blake's infidelity, she was forcing herself to remain calm and appear emotionless. *Sure,* she kept telling herself, *'he cheated, but criticizing him about it won't make things any better.'* She had a trick for his ass, though. Just thinking about it made her smile.

"Fuck is you smilin' 'bout?" Blake asked. "Nothing," she smiled sweetly.

"You' smilin' 'bout somethin'. Don't nobody smile without a reason."

Alexus' smile widened. "You'll find out soon enough."

After the shooting, she had met up with Blake at a Laundromat on Roosevelt Road and brought him a new set of clothes—he had pistol- slapped somebody and gotten blood on his Coogi outfit. She selected a white leather Gucci jacket with a skullcap, belt, and sneakers by the same designer, white True Religion jeans, and a matching T-shirt. Looking him up and down, Alexus silently cursed herself for choosing such a gaudy ensemble for him to wear. He looked good; especially with those diamonds. She thought about all the gold-digging bitches that were crammed into the sold-out stadium, and her smile vanished.

As they drew closer to a pair of big wooden doors marked CoNFERENCE RooM A, Alexus grabbed Blake's elbow and squeezed it as tightly as she could. He stopped and looked over at her.

"Listen," Alexus said through clenched teeth. "There's gonna be a ton of groupies in there after the show. You can look at them all you want, but if you even attempt to lay a single cell on any ass that ain't *mine*, I'm…" She paused, took in a deep breath, and exhaled. "Just keep your hands to yourself. I hope that's not too much to ask."

"Baby, I'm not on that. I told you it'll never happen again." Blake leaned toward her, pressed his lips against hers. "I love you, girl. Stop trippin'." He kissed her again, this time adding a bit of tongue.

Then Big Mark, Alexus' head of security, opened the wooden doors, and they entered the conference room.

A dense cloud of Kush smoke hung over the room. Baby and Lil' Wayne were seated at one table with Drake, Nicki Minaj, and Rihanna. At another table, Rick Ross was chilling with his MMG team, as well as T.I., Young Jeezy, and Jeremih. In the back of the room, about twenty beautiful girls with small waists and big butts were practicing dance moves.

T.I. was the first to shake Blake's hand. "The King of the Midwest himself," he said. "We finally meet, pahtna. Heard you the man out here."

"Somethin' like that. Shit, we got them brick for the low, too, nigga," Blake said, flicking his eyes around the room. "Come through and fuck wit' me."

Alexus was overwhelmed with excitement as she started getting hugs from all the rappers. She was listening to Blake discuss cocaine prices with Baby, Rick Ross, and T.I. when her iPhone buzzed inside her coat pocket.

The vibration indicated an incoming text message, so she slipped her hand into the pocket, intent to compose a hasty reply. However, Nicki Minaj darted over and embraced Alexus before she could even touch the phone.

"Oh, no, I am not looking at *the* Alexus Costilla," Nicki cooed, pulling back to give Alexus a quick bottom-to-top glance over. "My twin Barbie! You know, people are always saying we look like twins, and now I see what they mean. It feels like I'm looking into a mirror."

"Thanks." All Alexus could do was smile. She had a million questions for both Nicki and Rihanna, but the words were caught in her throat.

They moved to the right corner of the room where another group of rappers—Bun B, 8Ball, and MJG—were seated; the three of them talked about how hip-hop legend Heavy D had killed it at the BET Hip Hop Awards.

The nervousness Alexus had been feeling before she entered the large room gradually faded as she began conversing with Rihanna and Nicki Minaj. She pulled out her phone while they were chatting. "Let's take pictures," she suggested.

So, they did. She took off her coat, handed MJG her phone, and had him take a bunch of pictures of them. It did not take long for Blake to stroll over and add his iced out frame to the photos.

"I gotta be luckiest nigga in the world," he said as he wedged himself between Rihanna and Nicki.

Facing Blake, Alexus squatted down and looked back at her phone. MJG snapped the picture. Then everyone came together for a group photo.

Weezy took Blake over to his table where a laptop computer was set up, and for the next fifteen minutes or so, he played beat after beat until Blake found one he knew would go well with a song he had written titled "Lime-Green Bugatti."

"This beat gon' run you a hundred thousand," Lil Wayne said.

"I got it," Blake said.

"A'ight." Lil Wayne looked at his watch. "It's eight twenty-five.

Show starts in thirty-five minutes. Think you'll be ready by then?"

Blake nodded his head. "I want you to get on the remix: You, Ross, and Yo Gotti."

"I gotchoo," Weezy replied.

King Rio

The Cocaine Princess 2

Chapter 36

There were nearly twenty-two thousand people packed into the stadium. Every single one of the massive monitors suspended above the stage had the same large, lime-green, blinking name stretched across their screens—"Blake." The crowd was chanting his name.

"Got-damn... That's a whole lot of muhfuckin people out there." Blake said as he peeked out from behind the stage curtain. "Ain't no way in hell all of them know who I am."

Alexus was standing next to Blake. She placed her hand on his shoulder and gave it a reassuring squeeze. "Don't be silly. Your songs have already gotten close to forty million views on YouTube. Those people want to hear you. They *paid* to hear you. Now get out there and give them what they paid for."

"We can do dis shit, bruh," Young-D encouraged confidently.

A Kush-filled Swisher Sweets Cigarillo was burning slowly between Blake's thumb and forefinger, sending curlicues of smoke twirling up into the air. Somebody shouted that he had ten seconds until show-time. He raised the blunt to his mouth and took one last pull. Then, gripping a microphone in one hand, he dropped the blunt, extinguished it with the heel of his Gucci sneaker and stepped out onto the stage.

"Born and raised Indian Boy
Got bricks o'dat Indiana girl and Indiana boy Lime-green Bugatti, that's my Indiana toy AK-47's make a lotta Indiana noise
King o'the Midwest, gon' head and ask 'round From my town, to Nap-town, to Chit-own
I got pounds o'dat loud for the low
But if you want that otha smoke I'll give you what cha ask fo'..."

The crowd was going ape shit. A dozen pairs of panties flew through the air and landed at Blake's feet. He swaggered from the left side of the stage to the right side, pouring out his heart and soul through his lyrics. He and Young-D spit the chorus together. When Young-D started in on his verse, Blake took off the Gucci jacket and True Religion tee shirt and showed off his bulging muscles to the screaming ladies. He was immediately rewarded with a second barrage of panties.

Standing there in his bullet-proof vest, with $20,000 stuffed in each pocket of his baggy jeans and $7 million in platinum and diamonds shining brilliantly on his neck, wrists, earlobes, and pinky fingers, Blake did not just feel like he was the shit. He *knew* it.

As the song ended, he took the bundles of cash out of his pockets, removed the rubber bands, and showered the crowd with hundred-dollar bills.

"Money Bags Management comin' soon. My album "Bullet-face" comin' soon. Make sure y'all cop that muhfucka," Blake said.

Then he left the stage, feeling like five-hundred million bucks.

There were tears in Alexus' eyes when Blake made it back-stage to her. "Oh, my God, you are not going to believe it!" She said, waving her iPhone in his face. "I just talked to my mom. Brick House of Jupiter Island pulled in over forty-two million viewers!"

"Is that big for a TV show?" Blake asked as he nodded at T.I., who was on his way to the stage.

"Hell yeah, it's big! That makes it the twelfth most watched television program of all time.

"So what the hell are you cryin' for?"

"Because…Watching you shut it down out there… and then the news about Brick House—it's a little overwhelming."

Blake wrapped his arms around the waist of Alexus' fur coat and kissed her softly. "Calm yo' ass down baby." He glanced around and saw Lil Mike and Young-D leaning back against a wooden fold-out table with a clique of bad bitches standing in front of them. He recognized one of the girls without even seeing her face; the short gray fur coat and tight black leather pants revealed her identity.

Clamping her hand on Blake's chin, Alexus turned his face to hers, "I'm right here," she hissed. "There's no need for you to be looking over there at those gold-diggers."

The Cocaine Princess 2

"That's ol' girl from your reality show," Blake said.

"I don't give a damn who she is. Just keep your eyes on me." Alexus sucked her teeth crankily and crossed her arms over her chest. "Am I not enough woman for you? Seriously, I mean, it's supposed to be me and you against the world. I can understand if you want a threesome with another woman every now and then, but the sneaking around behind my back has got to stop." Blake's iPhone was on vibrate and it was buzzing away nonstop on his hip. His reply to Alexus was nearly drowned out by the music as T.I. began performing "Flexin".

"I promise," Blake said as he eased forward and kissed her again. "I'll keep my dick in my pants from now on, okay?" Another kiss ensued. "Now let's slide off into one of these restrooms and get it in real quick."

Alexus smiled. "Alright. We can't be long, though. I'm hitting the stage with Nicki for "Superbass," and then you have to go out there with Ross and Meek for "I'mma Boss.""

Blake followed Alexus to a dressing room that had originally been designated for him. It was right next to Rihanna's dressing room. Alexus shut the door on her bodyguards and draped her coat over the back of the chair. As she was taking a container of baby wipes out of her croc skin purse, Blake thought about asking her why women carried around wet wipes. He canceled out the question before the obvious answer came to him. What if she asked who the other women were? What then?

Out of the blue, Alexus threw the flattish container at his head and cracked him an inch above his right brow. "Clean off your nasty little dick," she said.

Grinding his teeth together, he crouched and picked up the container. "That's what we on?" He locked the door, keeping an eye on his scornful bride-to-be. "You on your period or something?"

"I'd sit on your face if I was."

"You got me fucked up." Blake stripped down to his boxers and socks and started rubbing a wet wipe back and forth along the length of his long black shaft.

Awestruck, Alexus could not stop her mouth from watering as

she swept her green eyes up and down Blake's powerful, dark body. All the weeks he spent exercising in the gym at her Matamoros mega-mansion had paid off. His physique was Herculean: hard, chiseled, and packed with muscles. His hair was cut low, with an impeccable line-up that accentuated his handsome black face. The four diamond necklaces he wore gave him the look of an ancient Egyptian king.

"You're kind of like King Aahmes the First," Alexus murmured, hiking up her mini-dress and pushing down her panties. "And I guess I'm Nefertari, the most respected figure of Egyptian history."

"Don't start with that black history shit. Come over here and get this dick." Blake was stroking his erection with a hungry look in his eyes.

Alexus' smile returned as she stepped out of her panties, tossed them atop her coat, and strolled slowly over to him, moistening her lips with her tongue. She turned her back to him and bent over. He grabbed her waist, guided his dick into her wet pussy, and fucked her senseless until someone knocked on the dressing room door about ten minutes later.

"Nicki Minaj is about ready to perform," said an unknown man. "They need you out here, Ms. Costilla."

"Fuck," Alexus said, pulling away from Blake and snatching up her panties. "I'll be right out," she half-yelled.

"Aww, hell naw," Blake said with a brief chuckle. "Baby, you just gon' leave me like this? What if I get blue balls?"

"You'd deserve it." After swiping a wet wipe across her pussy, Alexus put her panties back on. "We're all heading to The Wit after the show, anyway. I got us a penthouse suite. All he rappers will be across the hall from us. We can party with them for a while, then go right to our suite and get busy."

"I hope you know you owe me for this."

"I'll pay whatever it is I owe," Alexus wisecracked.

"Ain't this about a bitch," Blake muttered to himself the moment Alexus departed from the dressing room.

He pulled his pants on, stepped into his sneakers, then sat down on a cushioned bench in front of a row of lockers and scanned through the missed calls on his iPhone.

Janautica had called him twelve times already. He also missed three calls from Lakita, one from his mother Carolyn, and one from his daughter. He called Savaria first. She answered on the first ring.

"Hey, Daddy." Her small, pretty brown face filled his phone screen.

She was beaming. "Did you get my phone call? 'Cause I called you, Daddy, and you didn't answer the phone when I called you."

"I was busy, baby girl. You okay?"

"Is you comin' home before I go to sleep?"

"Nuh-uh. I'll be there to pick up you and your brother first thing in the morning, though. We're going to Disney World for the whole weekend." He knew she'd like that.

"For real, Daddy? Is, um, Minnie Mouse gonna be there?" "I believe so. You want me to call and ask her?"

Savaria bunched her eyebrows together. "You don't got her phone number, Daddy. You can't call her."

"I might not have her number, but Goofy's my nigga. He lives with her. I can call and tell him to make sure she's there."

Savaria hesitated. "No...you don't have to do that, Daddy. Her might has a cold or something. If her not there, I'll just ask somebody is her okay."

"A'ight, baby, go to bed so you can be rested up and ready for tomorrow."

"I'm already in bed."

"You know what I mean. Go to sleep."

"I love you, Daddy," Savaria said, giggling groggily. "I love you, too. Goodnight.

He ended the call and was just about to call Carolyn when a light knock came from the dressing room door.

"Blake? Are you in there?"

It was an exotic-sounding female's voice.

'Is that Rihanna?' Blake asked himself.

"Yeah, I'm in here," he said. "The door's unlocked. Come on in."

King Rio

Chapter 37

Nat Turner was five feet, six inches tall, dark-skinned, with a neatly trimmed mustache and a sparse crop of hair on his chin. His demeanor was fearless and commanding, respectable and spiritual. At thirty-one, he was thirteen years younger than Rita Mae Bishop, who was sitting across the table from him.

He watched her eat a chicken salad while he devoured an appetizing Angus beef burger. She donned a fuchsia colored one-shoulder Gucci dress with a matching wide brim hat and snakeskin Prada heels. The dress squeezed her thick figure in a snug embrace. The burn scars on the side of her head were mostly hidden by the long black hair of an expensive wig.

By contrast, Nat was short and robust. The black three-piece Niemann Elements suit he wore did not disguise his pronounced beer belly. But it had not been his physical attributes that attracted Rita Mae to him four months ago. Her interest had been piqued by Nat's extensive knowledge of Black history, and his seemingly inherent way of teaching it to everyone he knew.

They were dining at Great-Aunt Micki's, an upscale restaurant in downtown Chicago. The atmosphere was affluent. The private room they were in was red all over. "This place is beautiful, isn't it?" Rita said.

"Not as beautiful as you are."

Rita Mae lifted her eyes to her companion. "How did I know you were going to say something like that?"

"I don't know. Maybe you're a psychic. Or maybe we've grown as close as George Jackson and Angela Davis were before those San Quentin pigs murdered him back in August of seventy-one." Nat shrugged his shoulders. "Whatever the case may be, we're close enough for you to read my mind. I think that says a lot about our relationship."

"Yeah?" She eased back in her seat, eying him.

"Absolutely. It shows how compatible we are. Just think, if we were married, you'd be able to read your husband's thoughts. Would that not be interesting? And the great thing about it is I would sign a prenup stating that I get nothing if we ever split."

This was Nat's seventh or eighth time broaching the subject of marriage, and Rita truly wanted to take him up on his offer. She knew deep down in her heart that his intentions were pure and genuine, that he wanted her for the strong, black woman she was and not for the fifty-billion dollar corporation she presided over. The only reason she had yet to take their relationship to the next level was because she feared for his safety. She wasn't sure how Papi would take the news. She didn't want Nat getting hurt.

"Speaking of George Jackson and Angela Davis," she said, switching gears, I finally got a chance to finish reading Soledad Brothers last night.

That man was a literary genius."

"A revolutionary genius. He'd be the leader of the Occupy Wall Street movement if he were alive today. Wait until you read his second book, *Blood In My Eye*. It is going to blow you away."

Rita pushed aside the plate and reached for her glass of red wine. She swished the first mouthful around before gulping it down. "I wish my daughter would pick up an Assata Shakur or George Jackson book. All she reads are those urban novels. I think that's why she's so into Blake; he pretty much embodies that whole street element."

"There is nothing wrong with reading urban novels. A lot of those stories capture the essence of Black America. I mean, take Mario Bardlett's *Sweet Licks* novel for example. Every week, over four million people tune in to watch that show. In fact, it's not only one of the highest rated shows on MTN; it's one of the highest rated shows on television *period*. And it all began with one well-written urban novel that he utilized to express his vision to the world. So what if he's a bit long-winded when it comes to drugs and sex. That's what he grew up around, you know? A Tyler Perry-like environment is about as real to him as Santa Claus is to us."

"Still... I just don't think it's right to jot down wicked tales and publish them, but I see what you mean. It's essentially a different facet of America, one that I've never really experienced."

"Exactly. Only God can judge him. All he and other urban

authors are doing is shedding light on the darkness of our ghetto streets in their own little ways. Personally, I admire their creative imaginations. Donald Goines, Eric Jerome Dickey, Mario Bardlett, K'Wan, Teri woods, Iceberg Slim— they're some of my favorite writers of all time."

Rita sipped her drink. "I suppose you're right." She paused for a couple of seconds. "Can you believe that Alexus actually had five-hundred million dollars transferred to Blake's account earlier today?"

"Are you serious?" "As a heart attack." Nat was speechless.

"I'm just as astonished as you are," Rita said. "That is entirely too much money to give to anybody, let alone a wild young thug like Blake. In my opinion, he's far too immature to handle that kind of money. He's going to blow right through it. Mark my words."

"Don't be so hard on him Rita. These kids nowadays are a heck of a lot smarter than we give them credit for. Mark Zuckerberg is only, what, twenty-seven? Facebook made him fifty billion dollars, but you don't see him squandering away his wealth, do you?"

"Zuckerberg is a Harvard graduate. You cannot compare him to my son-in-law. Blake doesn't even have a high school diploma."

"You're also a Harvard graduate, Rita, and Blake *is* your son-in-law. It is your responsibility to teach him whatever it is he needs to know. Show him how to manage that money. Teach him to be an entrepreneur. If you don't show him the way, then who will?"

Rita Mae Bishop listened to Nat Turner's prudent advice for another thirty minutes or so. She liked listening to him. He seemed to have an answer for every challenge. His soothing baritone drifted effortlessly from one subject to the next. With his precise diction and Colgate smile, it was no wonder why he was MTN News' most famous and highest paid anchorman.

After a quick dessert, four bodyguards escorted them outside to Rita's car, a black Mercedes Maybach 62 with pitch black windows. A uniformed chauffeur was standing beside its already open rear door. Rita stopped to take pictures with a group of Michigan Avenue pedestrians, and then she and Nat got in the backseat. She shrugged out of her pale-gray chinchilla coat while the bodyguards climbed into the black suburban that was parked behind her car.

"We have to come here again," Rita said.

"There's no place like Great-Aunt Micki's. I've been eating here for years. My mom says the food reminds her of Virginia," Nat replied.

"Oh, that's right, you are from Virginia. I don't know why I keep forgetting that."

He nodded his head. "Southampton County kid, born and raised," he said, and then got quiet as the chauffeur started the car and drove off. Rita grabbed his hand and interlaced her fingers with his. A contented smile spread across his face. "Mind if I tell you about this recurring dream of mine?" he asked.

"Go right ahead. I'm all ears." She looked over at him.

"Well… There are always these black and brown spirits wrestling in the sky. Then the sun goes dark, and blood pours down from the heavens."

"What do you think it means?"

"I'm not sure. I've been praying about it, asking, God to—"

An Aretha Franklin ringtone suddenly bellowed from Rita's iPhone. "I have to get this," she said apologetically. "It's my daughter."

She answered the call.

"I'll never in my life listen to another Rihanna song," Alexus said.

She was sobbing uncontrollably. "What's wrong, Lexi?"

"I just *caught* Blake cheating on me! Oh, my God, I am *so* done with him. The wedding's off, mom. This relationship is over."

Chapter 38

The days crawled by. Alexus spent most of her time taking care of King Neal at the Matamoros mega-mansion. She ended up sending her best friend, Tasia, to pick him up after the concert while she herself had boarded her Gulfstream VI and waited at O'Hare Airport for Tasia to arrive with the baby. Then they had flown straight to Matamoros, Mexico and they'd been there ever since.

At first, Alexus had been deeply wounded by Blake's betrayal. She'd left the stage with Nicki and headed back to Blake's dressing room, only to find him pounding his dick in and out of another woman. He had tried to apologize, but an apology was the last thing Alexus wanted to hear. She turned around and rushed out of the stadium in a fit of tears, feeling as if her heart had just been ripped from her chest and stomped on. Images of her tear-streaked face landed on TMZ the following day, which only served to intensify her pain. She changed her phone number due to Blake's nonstop calls. When he showed up at the estate four days later, she had her security personnel turn him away.

Then her pain turned into boiling hatred. Barely two weeks after the dressing room incident, a video of Blake throwing $250,000 in singles at a trio of strippers at an Atlanta strip club popped up on YouTube and went viral. The next day Entertainment Weekly reported that Blake had just purchased a twenty-million dollar mansion in Miami, a two-million dollar condo in Indianapolis, and a twenty-million dollar private jet—all in the same day. He was then spotted at the Grand Wailea Resort in Maui, Hawaii, with two women who were seen "kissing all over him" be several eyewitnesses. The latter transgression inevitably resulted in countless news stories concerning Alexus and Blake's obvious break-up; stories that blazed through the media like a California wildfire.

Another news story that was receiving a lot of attention from the media was "The Whitney Murders."

While Alexus and Blake had been enjoying themselves at the concert, eight women, all of whom were named Whitney, were shot to death in Blake's hometown of Michigan City, Indiana. Alexus had ordered the hits after Blake confessed to cheating on her with a chick named Whitney.

Now she regretted doing it. She believed that the killings might have somehow fueled Blake's recent escapades, and although she hated him for all the pain he put her through, deep down she longed for his presence, his voice, his touch.

"You haven't gotten over him yet, have you?"

Alexus raised her head. Her cousin, Pedro had come into the living room without her hearing him. "I'm fine," she said with a gloomy smile.

"No you're not." He lowered his chubby body into one of the easy chairs. "I know you're upset, Lexi. I've been around you all your life."

"I'll be okay, Pedro. It's just bothering me that I…" "You miss being with Blake."

"Of course I miss him. Every second of every day I miss him. He was supposed to be my husband. I gave that bastard a half a billion dollars, and this is how he repays me?" She sighed and then glanced over at the baby. He was wide awake in his custom-made Versace car seat, smiling around his pacifier, opening and closing his hands on his chest. "I'm too young to be a single parent, Pedro," she muttered faintly. "I'm a nineteen year-old multibillionaire. I should be in college somewhere, studying global economics and hanging out with a well-educated sorority, not changing diapers and fixing bottles and waking up in the middle of the night to rock a baby to sleep."

"I agree with part of that; you are too young to be a mother, especially a single mother. But you have to get it out of your mind that college is a necessity. By reading studiously, taking notes, expanding your vocabulary, and testing yourself, you will be able to absorb more knowledge than a lot of college graduates. Colleges are merely slave schools. They teach you how to slave for some billion-dollar company who slaves for the government, and if you're intelligent enough, you just might be able to start your own company and slave for the government yourself. You don't need to do any of that. You already own one of the most popular television networks in the world; Niemann Elements accounted for thirty-nine percent of third quarter clothing sales in the UK alone; the Costilla's restaurants are doing great; Urban Housing Development is doing alright."

"Okay, okay, I get what you're saying." An iPad computer tablet was resting on her lap. She was doing some on-line shopping.

"I don't think you do," Pedro said, loosening his tie. "You are the richest woman on this planet. Sure you've just had your heart broken, but you can't let it kill you. Learn from it and move on. There are literally millions of men who are dying to get to know you. Get out there, meet some new people. You can even make your own little "I Love New York" kind of reality show if you want to."

"I'll keep that in mind."

Alexus looked up at the hundred-inch television and watched about two minutes of "*12 Corazones*" on Telemundo while Pedro did something on his smartphone. She had on her comfortable pink Hello Kitty sweatpants, with white anklet pom-pom socks and a sleeveless white tank. Her long raven hair was pulled back in a modest ponytail.

"I think Papi might have done something to Savio," Pedro said. Alexus' heart dropped. A grim astonishment locked her face. "Don't be silly, Pedro. You know how Savio is. He's probably somewhere in El Salvador with that girl he's been dating."

"It's not like him to just disappear without contacting the family. He would have at least told Santiago where he was going. Last time any of us saw Savio was at your place, right after you kicked my sister's ass."

"She started that fight."

"I'm not talking about the fight, Alexus. Our cousin has gone missing. No one's seen him in weeks. I think that takes precedence over everything else." A note of seriousness intensified his voice. He moved forward to the edge of his seat and stared at Alexus. "Savio didn't leave with us that day. He stayed at your mansion in Indiana with Papi."

Alexus shrugged her shoulders. "I left for Chicago tight after you guys left. If I knew where Savio was, I'd tell you."

A few seconds later, Tasia waltzed into the living room with Bookie, his friend Craig—and T-Walk.

Chapter 39

Blake's 16,800 square-foot Mediterranean-style Miami estate was the home of his dreams. It had set him back $19.8 million, and for the price he got nine bedrooms, twelve bathrooms, four fireplaces, two kitchens, a gym, a steam room, and a private theater. The backyard boasted rolling lawns, a hotel-like pool with a spa, a waterfall, and outside cabanas. The circular tan-brick driveway in front of the lavish mansion had room for fifteen cars.

"You can't tell me that this ain't the life," Blake said, raising a Swisher Sweets cigar full of Purple Kush to his mouth. He was standing next to the pool with Young-D, peering through the dark lenses of the gold- framed Louis Vuitton sunglasses at Janautica, Princess, Lakita and two strippers he picked up at an Indianapolis strip club as they tossed around a beach ball in the pool.

"All real niggas should live like this," Young-D said. He was rocking a white diamond necklace with an eighty-thousand dollar diamond- encrusted MBM (Money Bags Management) pendant over a Pacers jersey, Evizu jeans, and Air Force Ones. He paid for his own gear with part of the five-million dollar check Blake had given him two weeks ago.

Blake donned his bullet-proof vest, a black wife beater, black-and-red Red Monkey jeans, and black and red Jordan's. He held an AK-47 with a 100-round drum in his left hand, its perilous barrel pointing at the ground.

He had all of his jewelry on; the clunky diamonds sparkled in the midday sunlight. The left canted Bulls cap he wore matched his outfit.

"Man, bruh," Young-D laughed, "I can't believe Alexus had dem hoes murked just 'cause you said the name Whitney when she asked who you was fuckin'. That's crazy as hell. I couldn't fuck wit' no bitch like that, bruh. She nuts f'real."

"Nigga, you don't know the half of it. Them Mexican mu-hfuckas ain't got no sympathy for human life."

"And we do?"

Blake grinned behind a cloud of smoke. "That's different," he

said, flicking his eyes over to Lakita, who had just climbed out of
the pool. As she began drying off, he gawked at her leopard-print
bikini bottom and all the ass it embraced. "Oh, my God," he
whispered, taking a corner of his full lower lip between his teeth.

Lakita had been staying with Blake ever since the morning
after the concert; so had Janautica. Blake felt it was his personal
responsibility to take care of the two women who saved him from
spending the rest of his life in prison. He brought them along with
him and Savaria to Disney World, which worked out well, because
Lakita's daughter was the same age as Savaria. Now the two little
girls were inseparable.

Another plus to having Lakita around was that she had established friendships with a long list of Chicago's most prominent
hustlers while dancing at Redbone's, the new strip club on the
corner of 16th and Trumbull that Blake convinced her to work at.
One hustler in particular, a lame-ass nigga nicknamed Tongue, told
Lakita everything there was to know about the kidnappings of
Ashley Joy and Savaria King, and of course Lakita repeated every
juicy detail to Blake. He rewarded her with a brand new, yellow
Lamborghini Gallardo, a yellow pave diamond Tiffany bracelet,
and an appearance in his very first music video, "Beat it up",
which featured Keri Hilson, Young-D and T.I., and had cameos of
Bun B, Rick Ross, Baby, and Young Jeezy, all throughout it. The
video was shot at Pure Passion, the same Indianapolis strip club
where Blake picked up two sexy strippers— Mocha and Play-
Thang—who were now stepping out of the pool with Janautica and
Princess.

"Boy, you know you need to put that gun down," Lakita said
as she sashayed toward Blake. "Ain't nothin' but rich white folks
live out here. The hell is you worried about?"

"I'm worried about that pussy you gave me this mornin'."
Blake flashed an pleasant grin. "You can't keep wakin' me up like
that. I'll fuck 'round and have a heart attack."

Lakita smiled wickedly, "I know I got that wet-wet, nigga, you
ain't gotta tell e'rybody." Fingering an errant lock of hair from her
face, she stood facing him, her hands mounted on her hips.
"Between me, Nauti, Mocha, and PlayThang, who do you think

has the best pussy?" she asked, abruptly.

"You and Nauti," Blake lied. Janautica had the tightest juice box he'd ever delved into, and he liked her way more than he did Lakita.

"You can only pick one of us, Blake." "I can't choose just one."

"Well, you have to."

Always the voice of outspokenness, Young-D chuckled and said, "Bitch, get off that weak-ass shit. You fucked our whole squad last night, just like bofe o'dem stripper-bitches over dere."

"Did I ask you?" Slowly, she turned to face Young-D. "I bet you'll never get that treatment again, ol' disrespectful-ass nigga. Come through Gary talkin' like that. I triple dare you, Wit'cho Wiz Kalifa-lookin' ass."

"Don't get mad at me 'cause I'm slim and you a Twinkie away from two hun'ed pounds," Young-D shot back.

Blake choked on the potent smoke he was inhaling as he started laughing. He motioned for Janautica to follow him into the mansion, then turned and strolled to the patio, vigilantly fluctuating his eyes across the thick floor to ceiling windows and keeping his forefingers a half an inch away from the AK-47's trigger.

Ever since Alexus caught him cheating, Blake experienced an overwhelming sense of dreadful paranoia; especially, after the Whitney murders. He knew how the Costilla cartel operated. They were cold, calculating and malicious. They had slain those eight innocent women simply because Alexus had been angry at an imaginary girl named Whitney. Blake knew that all it would take was a few words from Papi or Alexus for him to end up on a hit-list.

So he kept choppers with him everywhere he went. There were caches of fully-automatic assault rifles stashed away in each of his seven homes.

He opened one of the tall glass doors and preceded Janautica into his luxurious man-cave. Spacious and elaborate, with shiny hardwood floors and whitewashed walls, the room had expensive butternut leather furniture, several large flat screen televisions with PS3s hooked up to them, a wet bar with fifteen leather-cushioned stools lined up in front of it, a state of the art surround sound Sony music system, and five intricately carved Honduran mahogany and gold-trimmed billiards tables. This is where Blake sought refuge when he wasn't in the upstairs studio recording songs, or traveling the county in his private jet.

Janautica went straight to the bar and fixed herself a glass of Ciroc vodka on ice. Her tantalizing walk stirred up a carnal craving deep in Blake's loins as he admired her slender, model-like figure. She wore a black one piece Gucci swimsuit that accentuated her long caramel legs. Her shoulder-length hair was black with lime-green highlights.

"What the hell you want, Bulletface? And if it's 'bout that rich bitch, I ain't even much tryna listen, yuh feel me?" Janautica said, dropping her hand at her hip.

"It's not about Alexus." Blake pulled out a stool and took a seat. Just hearing himself say his ex-fiancée's name struck an emotional chord in his heart. Trying to ignore the heartache, he put the chopper on the granite countertop before him and drew in another mouthful of Kush smoke. "I'm still trippin' off that Lawndale restructuring shit they got on," he said.

You ol' nappy-head fucka, this is about that bitch." "No, it's not."

"You's a got-damn lie and the truth ain't in you. I do watch the new, you know. I'm not full-the-way retarded."

Blake burst out laughing. "The hell you just say?"

"Stupid fucka, you heard me," Janautica replied with a subtle smile. "Baby, it ain't no such thing as 'full-the-way'."

"So fuckin' what? It wasn't no such thing as 'bling' til Lil Wayne said it, yuh feel me, like? I can make up some shit, too?"

'This bitch is crazy.' Blake thought. *'Full-the-way crazy.'* But, he had to admit, Janautica was the realest chick he'd ever had. If not, then she and Alexus were running neck and neck. In Blake's opinion, Janautica had all the ride-or-die characteristics that real 'hood nigga looked for in a woman. The fact that she had kept nine-million dollars of his cash without disappearing with it while he was in jail, spoke volumes about her loyalty.

Plus, she had voluntarily taken the rap for the two handguns a few months ago. Another thing that he dug about her was how she carried herself.

Unlike Lakita, who had already managed to fuck seven of Blake's friends, Janautica strongly refused to have sex with anybody else. Every night when Blake went to bed, whether in a jet, a hotel suite, or one of his homes, Janautica was there beside him.

She walked around the bar and stood in front of Blake. A seraphic expression burgeoned on her sweet caramel face. "Okay, the rich bitch just invested two-hundred million dollars into fixin' up some ratchet-ass ghetto in Chicago. Whoopty-got-damn-doo. What's so important 'bout that?"

Stifling a laugh, Blake said, "I ain't trippin' about her helpin' a ghetto. But she shouldn't be helpin' the Lawndale neighborhood. That's where the nigga who kidnapped my daughter lives."

Janautica's eyelids came together in a conspiratorial squint. "Mmm- hmm. I know that rich bitch was up to somethin'. Her mammy, too. Like my grandpa Funky Feet always said: 'Never trust a rich bitch wit' a big butt and a smile'; yuh feel me, like?"

Blake cracked up laughing again. "Funky Feet?! That's his name?" "Don't start wit' me, you Lil black sumbitch."

His laugh was jovial and constant. "Shots fired. Your granddaddy's name is Funky Feet." He shook his head. "And you' lyin', too. Yo granddaddy ain't never said no shit like that."

"How you gon' tell me?" Janautica pressed a palm to her waist and sucked her teeth. "Don't be tryna make light o' me 'cause that rich bitch done pissed in yo' Cheerios. I ain't that bitch; I'll buss you upside yo' head wit' this glass." She sipped some vodka through a pink straw, scowling at him.

"You ain't gon' do shit," Blake said, grabbing her waist and pulling her to him. "Hit me wit' that glass if you want to."

"Think I won't?"

"I *know* you won't." He dipped forward and kissed her lips. "Getcho mooncie munchas off me, stupid nappy head fucka,"

Janautica said, twisting her face into an expression of disgust.

But she offered no resistance when Blake kissed the left side of her neck. His big hands crept up her back, then cascaded down to her lovely lady lumps. He squeezed and caressed until his hands were content, licking her neck on the spot she called her 'all-duh-way-turnt-up button'."

Janautica pulled back and studied Blake's face. She touched the two bullet scars on the left side of his jaw. "Stop tryna turn me up, you lil pervert," she murmured. "You like the green skreeks?"

"What?"

"The lime-green skreeks in my hair, jackass. You like 'em?"

Blake chuckled again. "You need to start readin' some books."

"Hush, cowboy, I'm ser'ous. Is yuh listenin'?" she beamed. "Aaany-ways, like I was sayin' fore you opened yo' Lil stankin'-ass mouf, I got the skreeks to match our cars, yuh feel me, like, lime-green e'rything."

She was referring to the expensive fleet of luxury cars that were parked in the driveway out front. There were four 2011 Bentley Mulsannes, a Mercedes-Benz SLR McLaren, two Ferrari's—a 430 Scuderia and a 458 Italia— and two Mercedes Maybach 63s, and all of them were lime-green in color. Blake had purchased the Bentleys for Young-D, Streets, Lil Mike and Blubby. The Scuderia and one of the Maybachs belonged to Janautica. The other three cars were Blake's.

"Just make sure I don't find nothin' green down there," Blake said, grabbing the pussy that had instantly become his favorite.

"Ain't nothin' down there but tight wet mooncie, yuh feel me, like? And you know it, too. That's why yo' Lil ugly-ass face always screwed up when I put it on you."

Blake shrugged. "I don't know. I hear that Swine Flu shit can give you green bumps if you don't get it treated. You might wanna go and get that shit checked out."

"I ain't got no fuckin' Swine Flu, you nappy head—"

"Mr. King," said the thick-bearded Freddy Douglass as he barged into the room with his briefcase in hand. Tall, dark and stern-faced, Freddy was the music manager of Money Bagz Management, Blake's new record label. "I have some good news and some bad news. Which would you like first?"

"Hit me with the bad," Blake said.

"Your video for "Beat it up" is apparently too explicit for 106th and Park. They're not going to air it. They say it's too much like Nelly's "Tip Drill" video." Douglass pulled a smart phone from his hip and maneuvered his thumb over the screen. "It's really nothing to stress over. "Lime-Green Bugatti" is heating up the airwaves all over the country. The *Goon Musik* mixtape has already sold three-hundred and forty thousand copies, and it's only been out two days. What we'll do is shoot the "Lime-Green Bugatti" video sometime within the next couple of days and get it to them, have you make an appearance on 106th for the world premiere."

"What about the other video?" Blake asked.

"We'll put it up on YouTube, let the fans eat it up. They'll love it."

Blake nodded his head in agreement. At first, he'd been reluctant to start his own record label. There were too many risks. But Douglass was a juggernaut in the music industry. He assisted Blake in hiring all the right people, ensuring that MBM would be able to hold its own in corporate America.

"So, what's the good news?"

"Good news is, Jay and Kanye sent us a track that they want you to get on. The song's pretty much done already. All you have to do is lay the first verse, maybe throw in an ad-lib or two, you know. And they've offered you an opportunity to open up for them when their Watch The Throne tour hits the United Center on November thirtieth and December first."

"I'm with that." Blake began rubbing his palms together.

"That's not even the half of it," Douglas boasted. He tugged his tie straight in a prideful gesture. "XXL Magazine wants you on their cover next month, and so does Don Diva, F.E.D.S., Street Elements, ASIS and... I forgot the name of the other magazine. Of course they want interviews, too. Nine times out of ten they're gonna ask about your relationship with Alexus."

"And I'ma plead the fif."

"If that's what you want to do, then do it. The interviews aren't that important. What we're looking for is exposure. Let's get your face on those magazine covers. We need to take full advantage of these promotional opportunities. People are fascinated by your music, your lyrics, and your grimy street mentality. You're the talk of the industry right now."

Rolling her eyes, Janautica sucked her teeth and said, "Oh, my lord, is you, like, ser'ous right now, Docta Cornell West? You know damn well dey only want some words 'bout that rich bitch."

A bubble of laughter grew in Blake's chest, and it was difficult to repress. He turned to Janautica and gave her a rigid stare. "Go back outside till we're gone talkin'."

"She's all right," Douglass said, seemingly impervious to Janautica's pessimistic jape. "I'm about to go up to the studio and make a few calls. Lil Webbie and some other rapper named Two Chains left messages on my voicemail asking if you'd be interested in making a few songs with them.

I'm considering turning their offer down—"

"What?! Man, you' trippin'. Tell 'em I got 'em. No charge," Blake said, regarding his music manager with an are-you-crazy look. "Shit, we just got started. We can't afford to be turnin' down nothin'. Besides, all my Nap-town niggas fuck wit' Boosie and Webbie."

"We've just lined up an unprecedented distribution deal with Universal Records—" Douglass stopped talking mid-sentence and turned to look at the elderly Mexican man who was walking up behind him, carrying a backpack.

As soon as Blake saw who it was, he snatched up his chrome-plated AK-47 and aimed it at the old man's face.

"Do you always keep your door unlocked?" Papi asked.

Chapter 40

T-Walk dropped the GQ magazine onto the glass-topped white marble table in front of Alexus, smiling beneath a fashionable pair of Marc Jacobs shades. Then he handed her the bouquet of red roses.

"You look amazing," he said, lifting his eyes to graze over the thirty- foot high ceiling. "And this mansion... it's like a castle. How much did you pay for this place?"

"I didn't pay anything," Alexus murmured gently as she inhaled the scent of the roses. She got up from the sofa and wrapped her arms around the lower back of T-Walk's gray pinstriped Gucci tuxedo, her eyes cast down at the magazine cover. "My grandmother left it to me. It's worth ninety-five million, though, if that's that you're asking."

She went back to the sofa, and T-Walk plopped down next to her. "Who'd you have to screw to get on the cover of GQ Magazine?"

Alexus asked. A wide smile was pasted on her face.

"I didn't have to screw anyone. I bumped into one of GQ's senior editors in Hollywood at Lexington Social House a few weeks back. She took a picture of me and sent it to her boss, and that was that. They contacted me a week later and paid me two million for the cover shoot."

"Why didn't you tell me? I would have stopped by the shoot if I'd known you were going to be on the cover."

"I've been so busy with the Brick House girls, you know. Bouncing back and forth from North Palm Beach to Jupiter Island can be a headache." T-Walk let it out a chuckle. "There's so much money coming in, though. It's crazy. We were just on Wendy's show yesterday."

"I know, I saw it." Alexus glanced around the huge living room at everyone else. They were all smiling happily. Even Pedro was beaming.

"Can I hold the baby?" T-Walk asked. He wanted to scrutinize King Neal's infantile visage, to see if any of the baby's features were similar to his.

"Let's leave these two love birds alone," Tasia said as Alexus lifted her son out of the car seat. "We're about to go horseback-riding anyway." "Guess I'll get going, too." Pedro stood up. "Bella and I are hosting the Race to Erase MS Gala at the Hyatt Regency Century Plaza in L.A., I'll call you later."

In his periphery, T-Walk saw that Alexus was checking out his expensive Gucci suit as he held King Neal out in front of him. When everybody was gone, Alexus softly said, "Is your shoulder feeling any better?"

"It's alright. My hand's been bothering me a little, but it's not that bad. Nothing a few Tylenols can't take care of." T-Walk laughed at the grinning baby. "Is he always this happy?"

"I wish," Alexus replied with a sigh. "That little fucker keeps me up all night. He's like a real-life Stewie."

"Don't say that. He's just a baby." He handed King back to Alexus, then took off his sunglasses and looked at her. "So, um… did you ever get that paternity test done?"

"I haven't gotten around to doing it yet."

A deafening silence fell upon them. Alexus took longer than necessary putting the baby back in his car seat.

"Blake didn't want me to do it," she finally said. "I think he was afraid that you might be the father."

"So there's still a chance that King is my son? And you're just now telling me this?"

"I know, T-Walk. If you want to, we can go and get it done today. I shouldn't have waited this long in the first place." Her voice cracked. Tears sprang forth from her emerald eyes. "I'm sorry. I don't know what I was thinking. Blake had me wrapped around his finger."

"Sshhh." T-Walk pulled her head to his shoulder and let her cry, administering a light-handed rub to her back. "Everything's gonna be okay. We both have some things to apologize for. Nobody's perfect."

Alexus sniffled. "I treated him so *good*," she bawled. "I gave that cheating bastard over five hundred million dollars. When his daughter and her mom were kidnapped, *I'm* the one who paid the fifty-million-dollar ransom. *I'm* the one who paid off those judges to keep him from getting the death penalty."

Grabbing Alexus by her shoulders, T-Walk raised her up to face him. "Stop cryin' about that nigga. I'm here now, Lexi you can trust me."

Chapter 7

"Put that gun down, Blake. I'm allowed to stop by and see my son- in-law every now and then, no?"

"I ain't goin' for that shit," Blake said, keeping the chrome Kalashnikov AK-47 trained on Papi's face. "What's in that bag?"

Juan Costilla exposed a wicked grin on his leathering old face. He looked down at the black backpack that was hanging from his right hand and chuckled. It was a gelid, maniacal chuckle, and Blake didn't like it one bit.

"Get out of here, Douglass. I'll call you later," Blake said.

As the music manager was leaving, Flako Costilla and his son Antoney entered the room with eight more Mexican men, all of whom were holding MP5 submachine guns, which they immediately aimed at Blake.

Suddenly, an ear-piercing scream sounded from outside near the pool.

Blake and Janautica flicked their eyes that way and saw that Young-D, Princess and the three strippers were being held at gunpoint by yet another team of Mexican gunmen.

"We don't want any trouble," Flako said. "We're here to talk money, my friend; Pesos, dollars, francs, pounds, big piles of American cash. If we wanted trouble, you'd be in an unmarked grave somewhere in Mexico by now."

"What's in the bag?" Blake repeated, impervious to Flako's excuses.

Papi unzipped the backpack and turned it upside down. A severed black human head tumbled out of it. It was a young man's head, wrapped in the same greenish-blue colored cellophane as the massive cubes of cash in the mysterious vault at the Matamoros mega-mansion. Blake did not recognize the blood-covered face.

"Oh, shit," Janautica gasped.

Slowly, Blake lowered the assault rifle. "Y'all are some sick-ass Mexicans. Why do you always gotta chop muhfuckas up?"

Some guy proposed to my ex-wife on her talk show yesterday," Papi said. He kicked the head across the hardwood floor and cackled again when it landed in front of Blake. "That's his little brother. I paid his family a visit in Virginia right before I came here. Figured I'd keep myself a souvenir, you know? A keepsake."

"You's a fucked up individual, Papi." Blake turned to Flako. "Whatever you got to tell me, make it fast, 'cause I ain't wit' this crazy shit."

Flako had a fat cigar clenched between his teeth. He puffed on it, took it out of his mouth, and blew out a ring of smoke. "Who's the girl?" he asked, eyeing Janautica.

"Nunna yo' gotdamn business," Janautica snapped.

Papi scowled at her. "You left my daughter for this scrawny little whore?"

"Listen here, you Lil wetback motha—"

"Go outside, Nauti," Blake said, cutting her off before she got herself killed. "They'll be gone in a few minutes."

The Costillas watched Janautica as she headed back outside, but Blake's eyes were glued to the bloody head.

"One of these days," he said, "y'all gon' fuck wit' the wrong nigga, cut off the wrong head."

Flako laughed. "I see you still think you're a walking jewelry store," he joked.

Blake looked up at him. "What the fuck y'all want?"

"The drug shipments, Blake. The Midwest drug shipments. Why'd you cancel them?"

"'Cause I wanted to."

"We were moving two-thousand kilos of coke every month out there. A hundred key's of heroin, ten-thousand pounds of Mary. You can't just stop that kind of business. You're taking money out of our pockets."

"And *nobody* takes money out of our pockets," Papi added.

"Look, man," Blake said, taking a seat on the stool behind him, "the nigga who was movin' most of that shit is the same muhfucka who kidnapped my daughter and slit her momma's throat. He already got us out of fifty million for the ransom. I'm not about to be feedin' that nigga."

"You have to learn how to keep your personal life separate from business," Flako said, walking closer to Blake. "Later on down the road, when that guy no longer matters, he'll disappear without a trace. But right now we need him. Your little Midwest crew had us raking in fifty million a month. We have to keep that going."

Blake picked up Janautica's glass of vodka and drank down the remainder of it in one big gulp. The fiery liquid played like a flamethrower in his throat. His face tightened then relaxed. "A'ight... check this out," he said, flicking his eyes from Papi to Flako. "I want half of that fifty every month. As long as we can agree to that, I'm all in."

"You're out of your fucking mind, kid," Papi said.

Flako and Antoney laughed skeptically.

"I'm dead muhfuckin-serious," Blake said. "I didn't get a dime out of all that dope money. Only reason I set up that Lil connection in the first place was 'cause I was with Alexus at the time, and I knew she'd get most of the money. But shit's different now. We ain't together no more."

Flako shook his head. "We're only charging you ten grand per kilo of coke, a hundred per kilo of heroine, and two-hundred for every pound of Purple Kush Mary. You can easily make whatever you want to make by charging your guys a few extra grand."

"I said half of what y'all get," Blake sternly replied. "If I move fifty million dollars' worth of product, I want twenty-five million in my pocket."

Papi moved across the room to one of the tall glass windows and peered out at Janautica, who was standing on the patio with her arms crossed and her back to him. "I have a better idea," he said as he reached inside his black suit jacket, pulled out a gold-plated .45 revolver, and pointed it at the back of Janautica's head. "We'll give you fifteen million out of every fifty million. Now, either you accept that or your scrawny little girlfriend gets it."

King Rio

Chapter 41

There were seven MTN executives and ten of the network's most distinguished anchorpersons—Not Turner included—seated around the long mahogany conference table when Rita Mae Bishop walked into the room.

"Good afternoon, ladies and gentlemen," she said, taking her place at the head of the table. She beamed at all of the inquisitive black faces. "I know you all are wondering why I called this meeting. As I said in the email, there are about to be some major changes to our newscasts, and we're getting ready to launch two more television networks."

Rita's assistant placed a steaming-hot cup of Starbucks coffee on the table in front of her. She took a few tongue-searing sips of caffeine to awaken the rest of her mind. Yesterday morning, during a live taping of The Rita Bishop Show, just as she was wrapping up an interview with New York Times best-selling author Wahida Clark, Nat had come out onto the stage and proposed to her with the flawless twelve carat white diamond and platinum engagement ring that was now sparkling on her ring finger.

Afterwards, they had headed to Rita's multi-million dollar Victorian style Chicago home, where they'd celebrated their engagement with Krug champagne, catered soul food, and splendidly appeasing episodes of raucous love-making that lasted most of the day and half of the night.

Releasing a tired yawn Rita adjusted her black leather swivel chair to a more comfortable level and mumbled, "God, I am so fatigued."

A bevy of knowing smiles blossomed around the table.

"As I was saying," Rita continued, "from now on, our newscasts are going to be structured around the true core of urban America. No more stories about the wars transpiring overseas. I mean, I love our American soldiers, and we are forever indebted to them for protecting our country from terrorists, but there are thousands of wars being waged all across the

U.S. that are essentially being swept under the rug. Every time

King Rio

an American solider is killed, it's an international news story; however, when a Black or Latino is murdered, they're lucky if their story gets fifteen seconds on a *local* news station. That kind of injustice is unacceptable."

"I absolutely agree," Nat Turner said, nodding his head. He was seated to the right of Rita. "Twenty-four hour coverage of the tragedies and triumphs of urban America—that sounds like a dream come true, like a CNN for the ghettos. Maybe now we can get someone to tell us why it's illegal for the families living in those urban war zones to wear body armor, or why police officers harass Blacks and Hispanics in low income communities, yet cruise through wealthier neighborhoods as if everyone residing there is drug-free."

Rita turned to him. "Or why insurance costs for minorities are substantially higher than they are for whites."

Halfway down the table, an MTN anchorwoman named Nikole Giovanni eased forward in her chair and asked, "Mr. Turner, what do you mean by 'twenty-four hour' coverage?"

"He's referring to MTN News which, beginning January second, will have its own network," Rita said. "The other new network will be sort of like HBO or Showtime. It'll be entitled iBlack, and it's set to debut in the second quarter of twenty-twelve. I'm also launching a newspaper, magazine and book publishing company, a motion picture company, and a social networking website within the next five or six months. Of course each one of the companies will be a part of the already flourishing Costilla Corporation."

Giovanni began taking notes on her iPad2. "Keep it up Ms. Bishop and you'll make this corporation grow to the size and success of Time Warner Inc. It will be like cotton candy on a rainy—"

Nikki Giovanni went silent as Nat's phone started buzzing. "Excuse me for a moment," he said as he stood and stepped over to one of the thirty- eighth floor windows to answer his smartphone.

Picking up her cup of coffee, Rita studied Nat's appearance for a brief moment. She like the way he looked in his dark Tom Ford suit. If not for the room full of colleagues, she would have told him so.

Suddenly, Nat dropped down to his knees. His smart phone clattered to the floor. He pressed his palms against his eyes and shook his head from side to side. *"God, no!"* he groaned in a pained, guttural voice. *"Not my family!"*

Rita moved hastily to his side. Consolingly rubbing her hand cross his back, she murmured, "What's wrong, Nat? What happened?" When he didn't reply she grabbed his phone from the floor and put it to her ear. "Hello?"

"Who am I speaking with?" a man asked. "I'm Rita Mae Bishop, Nat's fiancée."

"This is Homicide Detective Jeff Diehl out of Southampton County Virginia." He cleared his throat and continued. "A little over an hour ago, we received an anonymous tip that there had been a break-in at the Turner residence. The responding officers discovered, um...four dismembered bodies. They were Nat's parents, his aunt, and his younger brother. Their limbs appear to have been hacked off with some type of machete. We're still searching for the little brother's head, but I'm certain it's him. My family's always been pretty close with the Turners. I knew them well."

Rita gasped. "Lord Jesus," she whispered.

"I know. It's pretty gruesome. I have a team of voice analysts going over the recording of the anonymous caller. Sounds like an older man, with a Spanish accent..."

Twenty minutes later, Rita and Nat boarded the company's Bell helicopter on the MTN tower rooftop. Aside from the chopper's roaring blades, it was a silent ride. Rita gazed at the pristine Chicago skyline through her window and asked herself why she'd accepted Nat's proposal. She'd known that Papi—a Mexican drug lord, a habitual murderer—would not take too kindly to her being engaged to another man. But she had not even considered the thought that he'd go so far as to murder her lover's family.

Nat cried with a stone face all the way to O'Hare Airport and Rita held his hand the entire time. As soon as the pilot landed and they stepped off the chopper, Rita said, "I know exactly who killed your family."

"I know, too," Nat said. "And he's going to pay for it."

The Cocaine Princess 2

Chapter 42

"Oh, my God...you got the sexiest body I've ever seen, Lexi. On the BOSS," T-Walk said. He was sitting on the side of the vintage claw-foot tub in the spacious bathroom of Alexus' master bedroom suite, watching her as she rinsed bubbly curds of Dove soap off her naked skin in the shower across from him. "Why are you torturing me like this? Is this my punishment for leaving you?"

She looked at him and smiled. "I do look good, don't I? I've gotten my waist down to twenty-four inches. Double that and you have my ass measurement."

"Damn." T-Walk shook his head in disbelief. "Forty-eight? Ain't that thicker than Deelishis?"

"Don't get yourself all worked up for nothing, porn star. We're business partners now. You should be focused on creating another hit reality show."

"Just because we're business partners doesn't mean we can't fuck.

We can be friends with benefits. I promise not to kiss and tell." He paused. "I know you remember how good this dick is."

Alexus stepped out of the shower and grabbed a gold-stitched white bath towel from the gold rack that stretched across the sliding glass shower door. Drying off, she danced her eyes over his face and bit down on the corner of her lower lip. "Got condoms on you?" she asked.

"You know it," T-Walk said, and grinned.

Alexus curled his tie around her hand and pulled him close. His triumphant grin expanded. He moved in to kiss her, but she evaded his lips by turning her back to him and sauntering out of the bathroom, yanking him along behind her.

"No kissing," she said. "Why not?"

"Because I don't want to kiss, I want to get eaten and fucked. Is that okay with you?" She pushed him down onto the snow-white faux fur blanket on her oversized circular bed.

"I'm cool with that...for now." T-Walk undressed in a hurry, gazing attentively at his ex's Brazilian-waxed pussy as she cupped her big breast into her hands. "If you don't mind me asking, why can't I get a kiss? We used to kiss all the time."

"Because...Just because. Put the condom on," Alexus demanded, sounding vexed.

Rolling a Trojan down his erection, T-Walk said, "So, I guess some head is out of the question, too, huh?"

"And I guess you're a psychic," Alexus replied.

In street vocabulary, yellowish-brown-hued women are often referred to as yellow-bones, and Cereniti "Tee-Tee" Stingley was among the finest specimens of yellow-bone New York City had ever birthed. A few years ago, she and Tasia had been dancers at one of Harlem's most popular strip clubs, taking home upwards of two grand a piece each night they worked, rubbing shoulders with big-name celebrities and professional athletes on a daily basis, all in hopes of one day engaging a baller whose money was long enough to set them for life.

But things hardly ever go as planned, Cereniti and Tasia had teamed up with a local dopeman to cop a million Ecstasy pills from some Canadians in Manhattan, and the drug deal had gone sour. Cereniti had been shot twice in the stomach. Two others were killed, and the Canadians ended up getting away with all of their money. After that Cereniti had fled to Michigan and matriculated into Michigan State University, where she'd met and fell in love with Kenya, her roommate. Shortly thereafter Kenya had introduced her to Alexus, and that he'd been the end of college for Cereniti. She dropped out and started moving bricks of heroin and cocaine for Alexus.

She called Tasia, who'd been dancing at Kamal's 21 in Atlanta at the time, and brought her into the dope-dealing clique, too. The money had been way sweeter than strip club dollars, but after the Costilla family had tried to kill Alexus on several occasions, Cereniti decided to call it quits. She stole five million dollars in cash from Alexus, stashed most of it in the densely crowded basement of her maternal grandmother's Brooklyn home, and then boarded a plane to Fukushima, Japan, with a Japanese model chick she'd met on Facebook.

However, tragedy struck again in early March when a catastrophic combination of earthquake and tsunami wiped out Fukushima. Cereniti was one of the few people who survived the disaster. Her Japanese girlfriend wasn't as fortunate.

"Alexus is going to kill me for stealing that money," Cereniti concluded as she stood between Craig and Tasia behind the horse stables, watching Kenya and Bookie gallop around the equestrian course on horseback. "I *know* she is, yo."

Tasia shook her head. "She's probably already forgotten about that little piece of change by now. What's five million to fifty-six billion? A drop of piss in the Hudson River's what it is. Word is bond."

"Did she say that?" Cereniti asked.

"She hasn't even mentioned it, Tee Tee. That bitch drops a quarter million on one bottle of perfume. She has four pairs of diamond-covered shoes that cost about two mill' a piece. Trust me; Alexus isn't thinking about that money you took. She'll probably cuss you out, but that's about it."

A quiet moment passed. Craig took a step back and let his eyes roam over the girls' voluminous derrieres. Tasia's stylishly faded blue jeans were as tight-fitting as a leotard, and her bow-legged stance accentuated her shapely lower half. Her hair, parted down the middle, was shoulder length and curly. Her pink tee shirt read Viva La Mexico across the back. On the other hand, Cereniti's hair was long and straight, and her dull gray tube dress made Craig salivate. "Did Alexus really pay a fifty-million dollar ransom to get Blake's daughter back?" he inquired, breaking the silence.

"What?" Cereniti said.

"She sure in the hell did," said Tasia. "They had her wire the money to some bank in Panama. I guess they thought that wiring it there would make it untraceable, but she still managed to get it traced."

"And she didn't report it to the law?" Craig asked.

"Alexus would commit suicide before she calls the cops about anything." Tasia pushed her fingers down into the back pockets of her jeans. "Don't tell her I told y'all this, but she has, like, a billion dollars in cash hidden somewhere here in Matamoros. I don't think it's in the mansion. I've been in every room already, and I have yet

211

to find a single dollar."

"So," Cereniti asked, "how do you know about it in the first place?" "Because… A few weeks ago, Alexus and I were having dinner out

in the courtyard. Halfway through the meal, she started crying, telling me how much she loved and missed that punk-ass nigga Blake, and how—"

"Don't call him that, Tasia. Blake's mad real, yo," Cereniti reprimanded.

Craig scoffed. "Man, that hoe-ass nigga shot me in my wrist, shot Bookie in his leg, shot T-Walk *twice*, killed K.G., Johnny, and two more of my Lil niggas. Fuck that nigga."

"Sounds to me like he fucked y'all up, son," Cereniti laughed. "That shit is not funny Tee-Tee, so peel that stupid smirk off your

face." Tasia glowered at her childhood friend. "Anyway Alexus said she showed Blake where her safe was hidden, and that it contained almost a billion dollars."

'Damn…that's alotta muhfuckin money,' Craig thought to himself. He looked through the tall white fence to his right. A white Maybach had just pulled up in front of the mansion and parked beside Alexus' Phantom, blocking his view of the Rolls. Tapping Cereniti on the shoulder, Craig said, "Ay, whose car is that?"

By the time Cereniti and Tasia turned their heads to look at the Maybach, it was already vamoosing down the long driveway.

The Cocaine Princess 2

Chapter 43

T-Walk had Alexus lying on her back, her knees pushed up to her ears, and he was long-stroking her dripping-wet juice box as if it had disrespected him in some way. The feel of her fingernails digging into his back excited him.

"I love you so much," he said in a breathless whisper.

Alexus continued moaning beneath him, not saying a word. Though he didn't show it, her failure to reciprocate his statement of love hurt him. He wanted to try and kiss her again, but he decided to hold back. Right now she seemed to only want sex, and he was content with that.

They went hard for almost an hour, switching positions several times.

Whenever T-Walk felt himself on the verge of coming, he pulled out and sucked on her swollen clit until her inner juices squirted out onto his face. Alexus was bouncing up and down on his dick in the reverse cowgirl position when he ejaculated, filling the condom with cum.

"That's the shit I miss right there," T-Walk said as Alexus fell over next to him. Both of them were covered in sweat.

"My legs are shaking," Alexus noted. Snickering softly, she moved from her back to her side and rested her chin on his chest. She gazed into his eyes, her breathing growing slower and slower. "Bet you wish you'd have never left me now, don't you?"

"I did, at first," he admitted. "Not as much now, though."

"Whatever, negro. Stop trying to be so insensitive. You missed me just as much as I missed you."

"Of course I did. But my dreams and aspirations are everything to me, and I can't let you or anyone else get in the way of me achieving them. I'm hoping to leave as big a footprint in the television industry as Tyler Perry's doing with TBS," he said, removing the condom from his softening penis.

"What is that, a month's worth of cum?" Alexus grabbed the rubber from him and held it up, examining it closely. The latex sheath was extra-large, and nearly half of it was full of semen. "I cannot believe you

came this much. I don't even think my horses can nut like this." She tied the condom in a knot, sat up, and tossed it into a trash can on the side of her bed.

"I've been meaning to ask you," T-Walk said. "Why didn't you show up for the Brick House premiere at The Visionary Lounge in Chicago?"

"Well, I was actually going to come. But then Blake shot those boys in front of my house. Reesie Cup, the owner of The Visionary Lounge, has five houses on Trumbull Street. He runs that whole neighborhood. I couldn't show up at his club after my boyfriend had just killed two of his men. I'm a little bit smarter than that."

"You still could have called and told me that you weren't coming." "Last time I checked, my father's name was Juan Costilla," Alexus

said as she stood and strolled back into the bathroom. "Come on; let's get all this sweat off of us before we leave."

"Give me a few minutes. I have to make a phone call." He said, picking up his BlackBerry from where it lay at the head of the bed.

He phoned Reesie Cup "Hello?"

"Is this Reesie Cup?"

"Yes, it' me. What's the thought, Joe?" You holla at that bitch yet?"

"Holla at her? Nigga I just tore that pussy up! I'm in Mexico with her right now," T-Walk whispered. "I'm pretty sure I can get the connect. I'll ask her about it later tonight."

"Man, Joe, we need that plug. *Bad*. The Mexican Mafia done stopped fuckin' with me, and now I'm coppin' from some Dominicans for twenty- six racks a piece. And that's only fifty bricks at a time. Fuck am I supposed to do with that?"

"You're saying too much over the phone, Cup." "My line's secure."

"I don't give a fuck if it's secure or not. We still don't talk like that on the phone. Anybody could be listening."

"A'ight, Mr. Hollywood," Reesie Cup muttered "Hit me up later, Joe.

One hun'ed."
"One hun'ed."

King Rio

Chapter 44

After showering again and applying her makeup, Alexus stepped into her massive walk-in closet, selected a white one-shouldered Niemann Elements mini-dress, a white Himalayan crocodile-skin Hermes Birkin bag with diamond hardware, and a pair of Dolce & Gabbana shades. She dressed hurriedly and then performed a runway walk through her bedroom for T-Walk, who had been standing in front of the big flat screen television watching ESPN.

"How do I look?" she asked with an amicable smile. "Like the baddest bitch on Earth."

"Badder than Kim K.?" "A thousand times."

"What about that model you used to have on your phone's screensaver back when we first met?"

"Who, Mizz D.R. or—"

"Yeah, that's her," she said, opening the glass-fronted yew wood jewelry cabinet that stood next to her dresser.

"I can't lie, both of you are dime pieces. But I love you, so I can't say you and her are equal."

"Good, 'cause I'd fire your high-yellow ass in a heartbeat."

They shared a jubilant laugh. Then Alexus put on a sparkling platinum Le Vian necklace, encrusted with triple bands of white marquise diamonds, a matching pair of heart-shaped earrings, and four white diamond ball bracelets. As they left the bedroom, she sent a text message to her head of security and Tasia telling them to meet her out front.

"So, where are we going?" T-Walk asked

"I have a restaurant a few miles down the road from here. We're gonna stop there for a bite to eat before we head to Chicago for a tour of the neighborhood we're renovating."

"That's a great thing you're doing for those people, Alexus. You're probably the only billionaire in the world who actually gives a damn about the ghettos of America."

"I try my best," she said, stopping at King Neal's race car themed bedroom, which was two rooms down the hall from hers.

She stuck her head in the door. Anita Ortega, the fifty year-old nanny, was moving back and forth in a rocking chair, perusing a Michele Dominguez Greene novel. King Neal was asleep in his crib. In Spanish, Alexus told the nanny that she'd be back to pick up the baby in about an hour. Then she continued up the marble floored hallway, tantalizingly swaying her hips.

"To be honest," she said, "sometimes I feel bad about my people moving so many kilos into the states. Twenty-two tons every week is an awful lot of coke. That's more than all the other cartels combined, and all of it's damaging the very same neighborhoods that my mom and I are working earnestly to improve."

"Wait a minute," T-Walk said, halting just as they reached the top of the spiral staircase. She turned to face him, and he inspected her expression to see if she was kidding. "Did you say twenty *tons?*"

"No, I said twenty-*two* tones. Comprende?" She started down the stairs, glancing at the Costilla family portraits on the wall to her left. "The only reason I'm still participating in the drug trade is because I'm afraid of what the CIA might do to my family if I walk away from it."

"The CIA?"

Alexus, looking over her shoulder at the clueless man behind her, shook her head and emitted a sigh. She could not tell him that the U.S. government was indirectly responsible for every single gram of cocaine and heroin produced in South America, that without the Acetate and Ethyl-Ether provided by the U.S. based oil companies, cocaine and heroin would not be able to be manufactured at all. She could not tell him that the so-called "War on Drugs" was a complete sham, that guns and drugs were intentionally sent into poor African- and Latin-American communities not only to continue the worsening of their environments but also to keep the prisons populated so that the government could continue to make slaves of prisoners, who were paid fifty cents to a dollar a day to build products for billion-dollar companies. More than likely T-Walk was hip to the U.S. government's lucrative prison hustle, but the CIA had warned the Costillas not to break down the scheme to anyone.

"Have you ever read *Behold a Pale Horse*?" she asked him.

218

The Cocaine Princess 2

"Hell nah, but I'll read it tonight if it'll teach me how to get twenty- two tons of dope."

Like a sincere gentleman, T-Walk opened the front door and let Alexus walk out ahead of him. She appreciated the masculine gesture. *'So, chivalry isn't dead,'* she thought.

And then she froze.

Cereniti, who was standing in front of Tasia's pearly white Porsche Panamera, froze, too. She stared emptily at Alexus, and Alexus stared back. Emotions began to churn in Alexus' chest.

"You're alive," she muttered matter-of-factly.

"I'm sorry, Alexus. All I can say is I'm sorry I wish I could take back what I—"

Alexus reached in her Birkin bag and pulled out her gold-plated .44 Bulldog, a collective gasp was heard from Tasia, Kenya, Bookie and several bodyguards. She turned on the red laser sighting, centered it on Cereniti's forehead, and released a drab, nasal chuckle. "You have the nerve to show your face—on *my* property, at that—after you've stolen five million dollars of my hard earned money?"

"Put the gun down, Lexi," Kenya nervously coaxed. Cereniti started crying as Alexus walked towards her.

"Give me one good reason why I shouldn't blow your brains all over the Porsche," Alexus said, touching the barrel of the revolver to the tip of Cereniti's nose.

"Calm down, Alexus," Tasia pleaded.

"No, I won't calm down. I want this bitch to tell me why she stole my fucking money, and she'd better hurry up."

"Your family was trying to kill you, by any means, and... I got scared, yo," Tee-Tee explained. "Especially after your aunt Jenny shot up your Bentley on the highway. Any one of those bullets could have taken my life."

Out of the corner of her eye, Alexus saw her driver get in the Phantom. She put the gun back in her bag, cocked back her left arm, and punched Cereniti as hard as she could in the mouth. Cereniti fell back onto the hood of the Porsche.

"Get the hell off my property, you thieving—"

Twenty feet away from Alexus, a sudden explosion sent her

King Rio

Rolls- Royce soaring high up into the air atop a mushroom of flames.

Chapter 45

"Wake yo Lil ugly ass up, Bulletface," Janautica said, poking a long, lime-green painted fingernail against the side of his neck.

"Ten seats on the muhfuckin jet, and you just had to sit by me." He kept his eyes shut. "And I'm not sleep anyway; I'm resting my eyes."

"Res' my ass, nappy-head bastud. I'm *tryna* show you what done happened at the rich bitch house in Mexico. But it's cool, yuh feel me, like? I don't even much care, no how. Is yuh listenin'? Is yuh listenin'? I know you heard me, stupid fucka."

She sucked her teeth, got quiet for about *half* a minute, and then said, "Okay, just listen to this: 'Mere hours after MTN News anchorman Nat Turner's family was found brutally murdered, his billionaire daughter-in- law, Alexus Costilla, is now dealing with her own devastating loss following a bombing outside of her home in northern Mexico that has reportedly resulted in the deaths of her driver and two bodyguards.'"

Blake popped open his eyes and glanced over at Janautica's iPhone.

She was reading from the MTN News website. "Ratchet ass Mexicans," she mumbled, shaking her head. "Them muhfuckas got steroids in they' water or somethin', yuh feel me, like? 'Cause they be goin' ham. Early, too."

"Does it say what time it happened?" he asked, snatching his own iPhone from his waist.

"Five o'clock Central Time."

"Shit, that was only three hours ago." "No shit Sherlock."

"You' better watch yo' muhfuckin mouf."

"Or what?"

Grinding his teeth together, Blake ignored her and stared at his phone screen. On it was a picture of Savaria holding King Neal in her arms. Blake scrolled down his list of contacts and called his mom, his heart pounding with dreadful worry at the thought of someone harming his family. The first four rings went unan-swered, and a profound sense of panic overcame him. A sigh of relief blew from his mouth when Carolynn finally picked up.

"Well, hello there, stranger," Carolynn said. "You okay, Momma?" he quickly asked.

"I'm fine, baby. Sitting here having dinner with your father and my grandbabies. Your brother brought the twins over with their costumes so I will take them tick-or-treating after the Halloween party tomorrow. We're gonna walk through Beverly Hills and West Hollywood."

"Did you get Vari's costume yet?"

"Yeah, I got her a nice little Minnie Mouse costume. Looks real cute on her. She wants you to come trick-or-treating with us."

"I'm on my way out there now. My plane should be landing at LAX in about forty-five minutes."

"Oh, well, you'll run right into Alexus."

"Why you say that?" he asked.

"You haven't heard about the bombing? It's all over the news." "I just found out about it."

"She called me maybe twenty minutes ago and said she was on her way over to drop King off, said she's gonna leave him here until she finds out what's going on in Mexico."

Blake put the tip of his thumb between his teeth and lightly bit down on it, wondering what he could possibly say to Alexus to get her back. "You got her phone number?" he asked.

Carolynn hesitated. "I think I might have erased it already."

"Don't lie to me, Momma."

"Who said I was lying?"

"I know when you're lyin', and right now you're lyin'."

"She asked me not to give it to you. And I can't say that I blame her.

She told me what happened at that concert. You ought to be ashamed of yourself, Blake. We raised you better than that."

"A'ight, Momma. See you in a Lil bit."

Ending the call, Blake reclined in his comfortable leather seat. Due to his steadfast love for Louis Vuitton, he had the interior of the Gulfstream customized by the designer. There were LV logos everywhere. Forty-inch flat screen televisions hung in front of the soft brown seats.

The Cocaine Princess 2

Young-D was reclining in the seat across from Blake, getting a blowjob from Princess, whose head was hidden beneath a thick blanket.

"I'm sorry, Blake," Janautica whispered, placing her hand on his knee. "I know I be talkin' shit all the time but.. it's not... you know I rocks witchoo, like, hard body. And it ain't even much about the money. I straight, like, digs ya, yuh feel me? I ain't never fucked with no nigga like I fucks witchoo. F'real."

"I know, Nauti. For the most part, I like that tough attitude, but you can't do that shit all day, every day. You be blowin' me wit' that shit."

He shut his eyes again, and Janautica undid his white 8732 jeans, pulled out his flaccid dick and sucked it into her mouth. A great apology.

King Rio

Chapter 46

Following the bombing, half of the bodyguards had rushed Alexus and her son to the two-mile-long landing strip that lay behind the mega- mansion and onto her Gulfstream VI jet, while the other half escorted everyone else to the Matamoros airport, where they set them up on a flight to Miami. Both T-Walk and Tasia had tried calling Alexus several times since then, but it was to no avail; they got her voicemail every time.

"Ain't this about a bitch?" T-Walk said as he paced the floor of his
$10,000-a-month penthouse suite at the
Fontainebleau hotel in Miami. "I was so close to getting that connect, bruh. On Larry Bernard Hoover, Alexus said they've been moving twenty- two tons of dope every fucking week! You know how much cocaine that is? Nigga, that's twenty thousand key's!"

Craig was sitting on the arm of the sofa with a short glass of Hennessy in his hand. Cereniti and Kenya had gotten their own hotel room, and so had Tasia and Bookie.

"I can believe that," Craig said. "Shit, if I was Reesie Cup, I would have made Alexus pay *way* more than fifty million. I heard she got, like, a billion in cash stashed somewhere down there in Mexico."

T-Walk stopped pacing and stared at Craig through squinted eyelids. "What are you talking about?"

"Tasia said Alexus told her about the stash when—"

"No, I mean about Reesie Cup."

"Oh." Craig sipped his cognac. "I thought you knew 'bout that."

"About what?"

"'Bout the fifty million he got from kidnapping Blake's Lil girl." "He told you that?"

"Nah, I don't even know that nigga. Tiff-Tiff told me he was the only nigga who didn't have a mask on when they ran in that apartment she had in Chicago and tied up her, Ashley and the Lil girl. They originally came to rob Tim—remember, Tiff was

225

fuckin' with that clown while I was locked up—but when Cup figured out that Ash was Blake's baby-momma, and that the Lil girl was Blake's daughter, he kidnapped 'em, and Alexus dropped fifty million to get 'em back. I think the only reason he killed Ash was 'cause she knew who he was."

"Aww, okay," T-Walk said, slowly nodding as the pieces came together in his head. "So, that's why Blake shot up them niggas in Chicago. It all makes sense."

"Know what else would make sense?" "What's that?"

"If we kidnap Alexus' son."

***

A TMZ cameraman was standing outside of the airport when Alexus and her security team emerged from the front doors at LAX. She had the baby nestled against her bosom, and her eyes were vigilantly sweeping the passing vehicles as Enrique Aleman, her head of security, urged her toward the waiting Escalade limousine.

"Alexus, can you tell us anything about the bombing?" The cameraman asked, aiming his shoulder-mounted camera at her face.

She ignored him and the many other people whose video phones were fixed on her and climbed into the limo. Enrique got in next to her, and the remaining six bodyguards hopped in the black Suburban that was parked behind the stretch Escalade.

There was an app on Alexus' iPhone that allowed her direct access to the state of the art camera system at her Matamoros estate. She selected it and then watched for the second time as her cousin Isabella pulled up in her white Maybach, got out, and planted a small black box on the underside of the Phantom. Alexus turned to Enrique and regarded him with an angry scowl.

"Explain to me why I'm paying you a hundred thousand dollars per month," she said. "Is that not enough to finance an effective security team? Let me know if it's not."

"Come on now, Lexi. There is no way we could have known *what* Bella was up to. I was your grandmother's personal security for many years, and not once have I encountered a cowardly Costilla Cartel member until now. When my men at the front gate asked her why she was leaving so suddenly after having just got there, she told them she'd forgotten her purse."

Shaking her head and rubbing King Neal's back, Alexus said, "I want my security doubled—no, quadrupled. I'll write you a check to cover the expenses. And from now on, I want to be advised every time someone steps foot on my property. No exceptions."

"Yes, ma'am. I'll implement the changes immediately."

Alexus dialed Papi's mobile number, but he didn't' answer, so she called Rita.

"Why haven't you been answering your phone, Alexus?" There was an underlying gloominess to Rita's commanding tone.

"Enrique asked me to forward all calls to my voicemail until we could determine who planted the explosive."

"Have you learned anything yet?"

"No, not yet. The police are investigating. Our camera system was down when it happened," Alexus said, hating herself more and more as the lies spilled out of her mouth. But she had to abide by the Cartel's rules, and the rules stated that issues were to be handled internally, with no assistance from non-members. She changed the subject before Momma could question her further. "How's Nat doing?"

"Believe it or not, I'm more distraught than he is," Rita said. "Nat is as angry as a raging bull. I think he's going to retaliate, to tell you the truth. We're at his Uncle Will's house with the rest of his family. He and will are in the kitchen talking." She paused for a couple of seconds then whispered, "Will's a gunsmith. He owns a gun store here in Virginia."

"In my opinion, he should kill whoever did that to his family."

"I'm not going to let him throw his life away, Alexus. And don't ever mention something as insane as that again."

"Why not? What do you think the authorities are gonna do to the killer if they ever catch him? They're gonna give him the death penalty, Momma. They're gonna kill him by injecting poison into his veins. A killing is a killing, no matter how kindly you word it."

Rita whispered, "Your father murdered these people. I'm certain of
it."

For a long moment, Alexus was quiet. She looked at King Neal's
innocent little form and hoped that he would never have to endure the iniquities of life. "Papi didn't do that, Momma," she finally said.

"Don't be so naïve. You know these murders have *Papi* written all over them. It is not a coincidence that dismembered bodies keep popping up all around us. I remember what happened to Raul. That boy didn't kill those girls. And you know it."

"I don't know what happened."

"Well, you aren't as aware as I thought you were." Alexus sighed. "I'm gonna call Papi."

"Tell him I said that if he ever contacts me again, I'm going straight to the FBI and telling them everything I know."

"Don't say that, Momma."

"I say what I mean," Rita countered. "Kiss my grandson for me, will you? And get him somewhere safe. I'm about to go out to our rental car and pray for a little while."

"I'll call you in the morning." "Where are you staying?"

"I'm dropping King Neal off with Blake's mom." "In L.A.?"

"Yeah. I might stay there for the night."

"Just make sure my little nugget is safe. Love you."

Alexus set the phone down next to her, moved to the longer section of seats, and eased down onto her back, kicking off her heels in the process. She sat King Neal up on her stomach.

"Hey, little man," she said, smiling at him. "Somebody tried to kill us today, you know that? My fat-ass cousin tried to take our precious lives."

"Want me to call Papi?" Enrique asked.

"Go ahead. Put him on speakerphone," Alexus replied. "You don't really want me to call him, do you?"

"Not really, but I have to at least let him know that I'm alright."

Reluctantly, Enrique took a smart phone from the waistline of his black Armani suit and called Juan Costilla, putting it on speakerphone as Alexus asked.

"Where's my princess?" Papi hastily inquired.

"I'm right here, Papi. The baby and I are safe. I'm on my way to drop him off at…an old friend's place."

"Who did it?"

"The same fat whore I beat up a few weeks ago."

Papi chuckled sarcastically. "So, that's why she called me." He laughed again. "My niece is truly a complex woman, isn't she?"

"What?!" Alexus was disbelieving. "You are going to kill her, right?" "Of course not. I don't get involved in cat fights. That's between you

and Bella. I love my niece just as much as I love you."

"You didn't say that when you blew Savio's brains out!" "I have no idea what you're talking about, Alexus."

"I'm sure you don't," she snapped, a note of defiance lacing her tone. "Listen, Alexus, I'm not getting involved, and that's that. If you want her dead, you're going to have to kill her yourself."She turned and glared at Enrique as if he were the source of her anxiety. "Why'd you do that to Nat Turner's family?" She asked Papi.

Enrique glanced down at his phone. "He just hung up."

King Rio

Chapter 47

Dressed in a white 8732 t-shirt, matching baggy jeans, and a white Louboutin red-bottom sneakers, Blake mobbed through the Los Angeles airport, rolling a heavy Louis Vuitton suitcase behind him. He was expecting to go unnoticed by the hundreds of late night travelers, but the majority of them recognized both him and Young-D, which resulted in a bunch of autographs and pictures with the bustling crowd of fans.

One fan in particular—a tall, slim black guy in a tight yellow shirt and skinny jeans—said, "Damn, Bulletface, what happened with you and Alexus? There's no way I would've broken up with her. She's as thick and pretty as that girl in French Montana's "Shot Caller" video, and she's rich as shit!"

"You need to break up with them tight-ass pants," Janautica said, stepping forward with her hands on the hips of her twenty-five-hundred dollar beige Valentino dress.

Blake and Young-D laughed as the disgruntled fan turned around and stormed off. Janautica flipped him the middle finger as he was leaving.

"Fruity fucka," she muttered.

A black-suited chauffeur was standing near the airport entrance holding up a black-lettered sign that read, Blake King. After taking one last picture with a middle-aged black couple, Blake and his entourage walked over to the chauffeur, and he preceded them outside.

Sporadic flashes from paparazzi cameras illuminated the darkening night. The entire Kardashian clan had just arrived at LAX, and Blake felt grateful; he wasn't in a mood to be dealing with paparazzi.

They departed from the airport in a long white Escalade. Young-D jotted down rap lyrics on a white college-ruled notepad while listening to music on his iPod via a pair of Beats headphones. He was putting the finishing touches on his verse to Blake's "So Much Ice," which featured Lil Webbie and Gucci Mane.

Janautica rested her head against Blake's shoulder. "So, whatchoo gon' tell the rich bitch?" She softly asked, rubbing her fingertips across the diamond-encrusted buckle of his Louis Vuitton belt.

"I'ma tell her the truth. Either she can accept it, or she can move one." "What's the truth?"

"Shit, I don't know. It'll come out when I talk to her," he said.

Blake was surprised to find a black suburban blocking the entrance to his parents' driveway when he arrived at their Brentwood mansion. Two burly bodyguards were standing side by side in front of the tall iron gates.

An escalade limousine was parked at the curb.

As Blake and Young-D were helping the chauffeur unload their luggage from the rear of the SUV, the gates opened, and Blake's father, Dale, walked out wearing a tailored gray business suit. Savaria streaked past him in a plum-colored sundress and leaped into Blake's arms.

"Daddy!" She yelled, and kissed him on the cheek. "Hey, baby girl! You miss me?"

"Mmm hmm. And guess what, daddy. My step-momma just got here, and I ask her to stay and her said yeah."

Dale walked up and gave Blake a fatherly hug. "Alexus just found out you're here. She ain't lookin' too pleased."

"Oh well. I'm sure people in hell ain't too pleased about the heat, but they gotta deal wit' it," Blake said.

Young-D tipped the driver two hundreds and they all headed inside. During the brief walk, Savaria told Blake how much fun she'd been having at her new school, how many new friends she had, and *who* she was going to be dressed up as for Halloween.

Carolynn and Alexus were admiring the framed portrait of Nelson Mandela that was hung over the fireplace when Blake stepped into the living room. Alexus turned to Blake and regarded him with an ice cold, scornful stare. Then she flicked her eyes over to Janautica.

"Isn't this the same chick who hugged you that day at the courthouse?" She asked Blake.

Carolynn crossed the room and grabbed her granddaughter's

hand. "Come on, Vari. Let's get you in the tub. Dale, show our guests to their rooms."

"I'm Janautica Spalding, by the way," Janautica said, smiling and waving at Alexus. "I'm Blake's assistant." She fell in line behind Princess and Young-D, and the three of them followed Dale out of the living room.

Blake strolled over to the L-shaped black leather sectional sofa and sat down, trying to decide if he should go along with Janautica's lie or simply tell his ex the truth.

Planting her hands on her hips, Alexus said, "She's not really your assistant, is she?"

"She is my assistant." Technically, he wasn't lying. Janautica did handle a lot of his business.

"I would say I believe you," Alexus said, "but I'll never, *ever* believe you again."

"You still love me?" "Fuck you, Blake."

"What? I'm only askin' a question. All you gotta do is say yes or

no."

"That's it? Fine. No." She crossed her arms over her chest. "Any

more questions, sir? Because I have some important phone calls to make, and I don't have time to—"

"Man shut the fuck up with that bullshit. You done fucked some niggas just like I done fucked some bitches, and don't lie and say you haven't"

"See—" she pointed a forefinger at him, dropping her other hand back to her waist—"that's your problem right there. You don't know how to treat a woman. You talk to me like I'm some kind of prostitute, you lie to me, you fuck every bitch who's dumb enough to spread her legs for you, and somehow you expect me to just overlook all of that, to keep on loving you while you treat me like shit? Ha! That'll *never* happen again. I mean, I love you, but I am not going to be your personal little rug. Find yourself another woman to walk on."

Blake smirked. "So, you do love me."

"Agh!" Alexus exclaimed, rolling her eyes. "I fucking *hate* you!" "Make up your mind. Which one is it?"

"Do you see a smile on my face? Stop taking everything I say as a joke." A single tear drop slid down her left cheek. "You don't love me.

You've never loved me. Our entire relationship was a joke to you."

"No it wasn't," Blake said, his tone shifting to a more serious note. "Baby, I love you more than anything in the world. You don't know how many times I done woke up in the middle of the night wishin' you was there layin' next to me. I know I fucked up that night at the concert. Ain't nothing I can do about that 'cept apologize and hope you forgive me. If I could take it back, I would. Swear to God."

He got up and walked to her.

"Don't touch me, Blake," she said, taking a step back.

"Let me get just one kiss, baby."

"Kiss my ass. Better yet, why don't you go out and kiss on of those strippers you've been throwing all your money at. I'm sure they won't mind." Tears began skating down both sides of her face and her lower lip was trembling.

Blake paced his hands on her hips, "Listen, baby. I'll do whatever I can to fix this relationship, a'ight? Whatever it takes." He gave her hips an affectionate rub, his intent gaze fixed on her sexy green eyes. "Can I get a kiss now?"

"Hell no," she murmured.

"What about a hug? Can I get a hug?" He didn't wait for an answer. Wrapping his arms around her, he pulled her close, squeezing her tightly.

Alexus surrendered to his affectionate embrace and hugged him back.

Blake smiled widely. Although it pained him to see the girl he loved so much looking hurt, it still felt good having her in his arms again. He swept his lips across her neck, inhaling through his nose the intoxicating scent of her costly perfume. Pulling his head back, he studied her sullen expression again, wondering how he'd been dumb enough to cheat on Alexus Costilla.

"I love you," he said.

"You have a funny way of showing it," she retorted, thumbing away her tears. "We're gonna have to get you checked into some kind of sex addiction center; Dr. Drew, or something like that."

"I don't need no sex addiction classes. All I need is the squirt-squirt you got down there." Slapping his muscular black hands onto her phat ass, he kneaded the meaty cheeks with his fingers. Then he pressed his lips against hers, and they kissed for a long while until Alexus jerked her head back and smiled at him.

"If Tasia knew I was standing here kissing you right now, I would never hear the end of it," she said.

"So what...? Baby, don't start lettin' muhfuckas dictate what goes on in our relationship."

"I'll never do that." She wiped the glossy remnants of her kiss from Blake's lips. "Can you believe that Bella's fat ass actually bombed my car? If I hadn't taken the time to punch Cereniti in her mouth, I'd be dead. We were just about to drive down the road to my restaurant when the explosion happened."

"Cereniti? You talkin' 'bout Tee-Tee? I thought she was dead."

"So did I. Not many people survived that earthquake and tsu-nami in Fukushima. I guess she was one of the chosen few."

"What's up wit' Bella? I figured y'all had made up by now."

"I don't know what the hell's wrong with her. I'm gonna have a long conversation with Bella first thing in the morning, though."

Beyoncé's "Single Ladies" ringtone sounded from Alexus' Birkin bag, which was sitting on the sofa. She peeled away from Blake and went to answer it.

"Change that ringtone," Blake demanded with a chuckle. "And let me hear that phone call, too.

Alexus looked over her shoulder at him, "You can trust me, Blake. I'm not the one who's been sucking on strippers every damn night," she reminded him.

But she put the call on speakerphone anyway. It was from a seven- seven-three area code. Chicago.

"Hello? Is this Alexus Costilla?" Said a young female voice. Alexus frowned. "May I ask who's calling?"

"I need to know that I'm speaking with Alexus before I give

my name. This is a very, very personal call."

"I'm Alexus Costilla."

A sigh drifted through the phone. "I'm…Mercedes. Mercedes Costilla. I'm your sister."

"Sorry, I think you've mistaken me for someone else. I'm an only child," Alexus said, getting ready to end the call.

"This isn't a mistake. Unless there are two sixty-year-old men named Juan Miguel Donaldo Costilla from Matamoros, Mexico, which I'm absolutely sure there isn't, you and I are sisters."

The Cocaine Princess 2

Chapter 48

T-Walk had been staying at the Fontainebleau, in his grand two bedroom penthouse suite, ever since his split from Kenya. He'd chosen to reside in Miami not only because of the plethora of beautiful women and celebrities he often mingled and networked with at the LIV nightclub downstairs, but also because the hotel was within driving distance of the North Palm Beach and Jupiter Island estates where his hit reality shows were filmed.

Occasionally, when Thunder wasn't busy partying and arguing on the set of Brick House, she'd show up at T-Walk's door unannounced, usually clad in something that looked to have come straight out of a porn stars closet. And tonight was no different.

When T-Walk answered the door at a few minutes past midnight, he found Thunder standing there in a white lab coat, a nurse's hat, and a tall pair of transparent heels. A stethoscope hung from her neck. Through the eyeglasses that were perched low on the tip of her nose, she seemed to be reading from the clipboard in her hand, licking her red-painted lips.

"Mr. Walkson?" Thunder said, lifting her eyes to his. "I'm Dr. Wet Cat, Chief sexologist at the Southern Institute of Sexual Deprivation. Mind if I step inside?"

Chuckling to himself, T-Walk turned around and walked back to his sofa. He heard the door click shut behind him. About ten minutes earlier, he had changed into a sky-blue three piece Gucci suit, intending to head down to LIV and hopefully get a word with Trina, who was hosting a party at the gaudy nightclub.

"I was just about to leave," he said, taking a seat.

"Are you nuts? Sexual deprivation is a very contagious disease, sir.

You could infect half of Dade County."

Thunder stepped in front of him and took off the lab coat, revealing her naked body. The nipples of her big chocolate breasts were pierced, as was her tongue and clitoris, and she smelled good enough to eat. She kneeled between his legs, set the clipboard down on the floor next to her, and started unbuckling his belt.

"So," T-Walk asked, "what do you suggest I do to overcome this terrible disease? You got some kind of medicine for me?"

"A minor blowjob treatment should suffice." She twisted her tongue ring, and it began vibrating. "If that doesn't work, we may have to rush you to the Emergency Room for immediate sexual healing."

A smile of pleasure spread across T-Walk's mulatto face. He dropped his head back and reveled in the moment as Thunder's tremulous tongue touched the crown of his dick. She took it into her mouth, fluctuating her lips up and down its length.

'One billion dollars in cash,' T-Walk thought to himself. 'And all I have to do is kidnap a baby to get it.'

He'd been pondering the kidnapping scheme ever since Craig had mentioned it a few hours ago, and he had to admit, it didn't sound like a bad idea. Sure, it would be extremely difficult to launder that much money, but that was nothing compared to the benefits he'd reap from having a billion dollars at his disposal. The only thing holding him back from drawing out an actual kidnapping plot was the fact that King Neal might be his own son.

'I gotta hurry up and get that DNA test done,' he told himself.

The Cocaine Princess 2

Chapter 49

"Everything she's saying is true, Alexus. I've been going over the paperwork with Mercedes all day. She was born exactly one year and three days after you were born," Britney Bostic said through the speakerphone. "Your father even signed her birth certificate."

Alexus' opened-mouthed, wide-eyed expression told it all: she was shocked beyond belief. She turned to Blake and saw that he looked just as shocked.

"I was sorting through some of my mom's stuff after the funeral when I came across an old picture of her standing with Juan beside a big swimming pool," Mercedes said. "Momma showed me the picture a long time ago—I think I was around eight or nine then—but I never bothered to ask about him, because I didn't know him. I *still* don't know him. He left my mom 'cause she was addicted to crack."

Blake plopped down on the sofa behind Alexus and pulled her down onto his lap. "Well, nice to meet you, sister-in-law," he said to Mercedes.

"Is that Blake?" Attorney Bostic asked.

Ignoring the inquiry, Alexus combed her fingers through her hair and mumbled, "I have a sister." She couldn't believe it.

"You are not going to believe how much she looks like you," Britney said. "Only difference is she's a tad bit shorter and about two shades darker."

"Where do you live...Mercedes?" Alexus asked.

"I've lived with my mom for most of my life, but I moved in with my boyfriend when I turned eighteen earlier this year, and my mom moved to Indiana." She sniffled audibly. "I wish I'd have just stayed with her, you know? If I hadn't left, she and I would still be together in that raggedy old house on Ridgeway."

A grim silence filled the room. Mercedes was obviously crying. Five seconds later, she shakily murmured," My mom was killed a couple of weeks ago in Michigan City, Indiana. Some guy knocked on her door, asked her name, and when she said it, he shot her in the face."

239

"Oh, my God!" Alexus exclaimed. "What's her name?"

"Whitney Clark," cried Mercedes. "Whoever did it must've had something against women named Whitney, 'cause seven others were killed that night, and all of them had the same name."

The Cocaine Princess 2

Chapter 50

Blake watched as the color drained from the beautiful face of his favorite woman. Her body went limp. She pressed her back against his brand-new trio of platinum and white diamond necklaces.

"I'll um… be in Chicago tomorrow afternoon," Alexus murmured, finger-combing her hair again. "Do you need some cash?"

"Girl, I'm flat-broke," Mercedes said. "I have an eleven-month-old daughter and a two year-old son, I got laid off from my job at Church's Chicken for being late five days in a row, and I spent the fifteen hundred I had saved up on my mom's funeral. My man was helping out, but he got busted the other day with five ounces of cocaine in the trunk of his car," she paused for a moment then added, "I don't want you to think I'm contacting you to get some money—"

"No, it's fine. Britney, wire her ten grand. I'm, um, I have to go.

Whose phone number is this?" "It's mine," Mercedes said.

"Okay, I'll call you as soon as I get up in the morning, and I'm going to make damned sure Papi's on the phone, too."

Alexus was quiet for a minute or so after the call. Rubbing his hand across her stomach, Blake wondered what she was thinking.

"You did it," she finally said.

"Nah, nigga, don't blame that shit on me," Blake countered. "I didn't tell you to have somebody go out and whack them hoes."

"Shut up talking to me, Blake." She stood up. "Come on, let's go to bed. I need some rest."

"You need some help."

Following her out of the living room, Blake couldn't keep his eyes off her backside. "You do look kinda like that video chick," he said.

Alexus sighed. "Who do I look like this time?"

"That thick-ass girl in the French Montana video." He reached out and squeezed her big, soft ass. "I want you in my video with some tight jeans on too. We'll be shootin' the video for "Lime-Green Bugatti" in a few days."

"I'll think about it." "Fuck you mean?"

"I said I'll think about it. For all I know, you might be fucking somebody else by then."

Just as they were approaching Dale and Carolynn's master bedroom, Savaria stepped out into the hallway in her Minnie Mouse pajamas, holding a stuffed Minnie Mouse doll under her arm. Her brown eyes lit up at the sight of Blake and Alexus together. She raised an index finger to her lips. "Sshhh."

Squatting down to the little girl's level, Alexus whispered, "Hey Vari.

What are you shushing me about?"

"My grandma just tucked me in, and her don't know I'm out here. Her think I'm sleep, okay? So we just have to be quiet."

Blake laughed as he picked up his daughter and set her on his hip. "It's bedtime, baby girl," he said, heading toward Savaria's bedroom.

"Is you and my step-momma gon' stay together again? I hope you to stay with her, Daddy. I love my step-momma."

"Aww," Alexus cooed. "I love you, too." She looked at Blake. "And I love daddy....sometimes."

Savaria's bedroom had pink walls, pink faux fur carpeting, and a stage that sat against the wall beneath an ever spinning crystal ball. There was a big Minnie Mouse face stitched into the middle of the two-toned pink blanket that rambled across Savaria's king-sized bed, with a dozen matching pillows lined up at the head of the bed. A pink four-step staircase was set next to the bed.

"I see you've been busy in here," Alexus said, looking around. Blake laid Savaria down in bed and pulled the covers up to her neck. "You like it, step-momma?" Savaria asked.

"Of course I like it, I wish my room had been like this when I was a kid. Did you pick out the colors yourself?"

"No. Grandma paid a lady to fix all the rooms good like this, and the lady fixed all the rooms."

"Good night, Savaria," Blake interjected. He kissed her fore-head. "I love you, daddy."

"I love you more."

Savaria's eyes moved to Alexus. "Step-momma, can I just call you Momma now? I don't want you to be my step-momma no more."

Alexus smiled. "I'm okay with that." She bent over and gave Savaria

a hug.

Blake felt a distinct warmness in his chest as he and Alexus were leaving the bedroom. It was a wonderful feeling that he never experienced before. Alexus grabbed his hand, interlaced her fingers with his.

When they made it to his bedroom, Blake opened the door and found Enrique Aleman sitting on the Italian leather sofa that sat a few feet away from the foot of Blake's king-size bed. Enrique was typing something on a laptop computer. King Neal was asleep in his glass crib.

"We now have sixty-five men here in Brentwood, and I've ordered eight armored Excursions and an armored Hummer limousine to be delivered here at zero five hundred hours. It'll cost us about a hundred and twenty grand extra if you're trying to get them flown to Chicago tomorrow," Enrique said, getting to his feet. He walked over to Alexus and hugged her, glanced at Blake, and then disappeared from the room without another word. Blake locked the door behind him.

"What's up wit' him? Blake asked. He sat down on the side of his bed and started taking off his jewelry and laying the expensive pieces on his bedside table.

"He's alright, just a little overprotective." Staring at the platinum and white diamond watch Blake was taking off, she said, "Is that a Hublot?"

"Yeah, I heard Jay-Z say somethin' 'bout a Hublot, so I said fuck it and bought three of 'em. Fo' hun'ed racks a piece."

There was a fully-automatic Uzi submachine gun taped under the bedside table. Blake ripped it loose and set it up on top of the table. He took the twenty-thousand dollar bundles of rubber-banded hundreds out of his pockets and tossed them on the table, too. Then he got naked and stretched himself out in the middle of the bed.

"You do know it's past midnight, right?" Alexus said, pulling off her

dress.

"And...?" Blake looked down at his dick, which was growing long

and harder by the second. "What's that s'posed to mean?"

"It's officially Halloween." She peeled off her white lace bra and panties, kicked off her heels, and hopped on top of him. "And tonight, I'm gonna make you think my name is Superhead."

She lowered her mouth to his, and they shared a passionate kiss, her tongue wrestling with his, his strong, black hands rubbing all over her ass. He slipped a hand between her thighs and massaged her clit.

"Mmm..Shhh....," she moaned, raising up to look at him. "Keep... doing that... right there." She pinched her nipples and mashed her breast together. "I'm gonna cum. I'm gonna..."

Her creamy juices spilled out onto his dick. She moved his hand and slid her dripping pussy back and forth along the under-side of his thick pole. "Damn," Blake said with a chuckle. "That was quick. You missed me that much?"

"I *love* you that much," she corrected.

Then she went down on him. Like Lakita, Alexus could take his dick to the very back of her throat without choking, and she did exactly that. She held it hostage in her throat for a couple of seconds, twisting her head clockwise and counterclockwise to get a few more inches of him into her mouth. Slowly, she skated her lips up to the head, sucked on it as hard as she could, then popped it out of her mouth.

"Put your jewelry back on," she said, stroking, and squeezing his dick, a string of pre-cum dangling from her bottom lip.

There were two hundred carats of chunky round-cut diamonds in each of Blake's three necklaces. His bracelet also boasted two hundred carats of white diamonds, as did his custom-designed Hublot. He sat up and put it all back on as Alexus went back to sucking him, including his two platinum and white diamond pinky rings and his ten-carat, round-cut white diamond earrings.

Leaning back on his elbows, Blake watched as Alexus bounced her sultry lips up and down his dick so rapidly that she seemed to be moving in fast-forward. Sucking sounds filled the bedroom. The seventy-five inch widescreen was on and tuned to MTN, and the volume was muted. Light from the television reflected off Blake's plethora of diamonds, creating a shimmering effect.

Alexus' killer head-game took a toll on Blake a mere ten minutes after it had begun. She must have sensed his imminent eruption, because suddenly she deep-throated his dick and kept it there as he ejaculated, letting the cum drop down onto his shaft before sealing her lips around it and ascending up to its gushing head. She sucked and tongued the rest of his semen into her mouth, then dropped her head back and showed him the glue-like pool of cum that covered her tongue.

"Ugh, you's a nasty muhfucka," Blake said, wincing in disgust. "How am I nasty? You're the one who shot his gunk in my mouth."

With her fingernails, Alexus grabbed a thick ribbon of cum off her tongue, stretched it away as if were a piece of chewing gum, and then laid it back on her tongue and started gargling it in her throat. Finally, she swallowed it all down in two long gulps. "Still think I'm nasty?"

"You ain't kissin' King Neal no more, I'm tellin' you dat now." Blake moved her onto her back.

She snickered as he kissed her navel. "Go on down there and get your mouth nasty, too. See how you like it when I bust one in your mouth," she said, pushing his head further down.

Blake didn't argue with that. Nor did he remove her hands from his head. The delicious aroma of her pussy beckoned him, and he had already been waiting weeks to get another taste of her.

Puckering his lips around her throbbing clitoris, he sucked and licked and swished a bunch of saliva over it while slipping two fingers in and out of her pussy, a well-honed technique of his that Alexus had named the "washing machine." It usually brought her to orgasm within five or so minutes, but this time she barely lasted two before she began squirting onto Blake's chin. He lapped up her sweet juices, and then rose up on his knees, stroking his hard dick.

Blake fucked her for a good hour after that—missionary and doggy-style, cowgirl and reverse cowgirl—and when he was ready to explode, Alexus deep-throated his dick and drank his cum again.

Chapter 51

Juan Miguel Donaldo Costilla was awakened the following morning by the sound of his brother's voice. "They're here Papi," Flako whispered.

Papi opened his eyes inhaling the lingering scents of multiple perfumes, hairsprays, cigarettes, and alcohol. There were four sexy young girls—all of them African-American and in their twenties—in the bed with him.

Last night, with the assistance of two Viagra pills and a bottle of his favorite Brandy, Papi had been able to last quite a while with the four girls.

He sat up wiping his eyes, "What time is it?" He groggily asked. "It's seven o'clock here in South Beach. Enrique just called and said

he's somewhere in L.A. with Alexus and that she's back with Bulletface." Flako was looking worried. He helped Papi out of bed and into a heavy black-and-gold Versace robe.

Working the kinks out of his tired old body, Papi went to his walk-in closet and opened his safe. He grabbed a ten-thousand dollar stack of bank wrapped hundreds, a gold, razor-sharp machete, and a gold-plated .50 caliber Desert Eagle with an already attached titanium sound-suppressor.

He set everything down on top of the safe, took a deep breath then roved his eyes across the many expensive suits that lined the wall to his left.

Flako appeared in the doorway. "I can't lose my daughter, Juan. Not over something as stupid as this."

"That's between Bella and Lexi. You have my word; I won't get involved in any way." Papi pulled two suits—a dark-gray Niemann Elements and a navy-blue Brooks Brothers—from the rack and showed them to his brother. "Which one do you think I should wear to the Halloween massacre?"

"What are you talking about?" Flako asked, lighting a cigar.

"I'm gonna pay another visit to Virginia, see if I can find the rest of that black guy's family. Rita has no idea who she's fucking with, vato. I was good to her." He locked eyes with Flako. "Was I not good to her? Did I not take care of that woman? *I'm* the reason she's rich. If not for our mother, there would be no MTN. There would be no Niemann Elements. Blake wouldn't have that stupid record company. Rita wouldn't have that talk show." He threw the gray suit to the plush black carpet and spit on it. "I'll blow up that fucking MTN tower!"

"We're not going back to Virginia, Papi. Leave Nat Turner and his family alone. Killing them won't make Rita re-marry you."

"Yeah? Well I disagree," Papi said. He picked out a tie, shirt, underwear, fedora, and a silk pocket square to go along with his Brooks Brothers suit. "What's with the new guys in Columbia? Two grand per kilo?"

Flako nodded his head. "The North Valley Cartel is offering us a much better deal than the one we have with that wanna-be in Medellin. The new deal would only cost us two hundred million a month."

"For a hundred thousand kilos?"

"Yep. And they're guaranteeing the bricks will be one hundred percent pure, not that ninety-seven percent garbage from Medellin. North Valley even has the United Self-Defense Forces of Columbia protecting its drug routes and laboratories. I hear they have good heroin, too. We could maybe grab ten thousand of them at ten grand apiece, put a hundred thousand dollar price tag on each one, no? We'd make a nice profit."

"What about the Medellin Cartel?" Papi asked.

"Who gives a shit? I'm worried about the Costilla Cartel, making sure we're eating." The fervent tip of Flako's cigar brightened as he puffed from it. "I see a lot of potential in Blake's little Midwest crew. He reminds me of that guy from Detroit we used to do business with; the flashy guy."

"You're talking about Meech."

Papi handed the suit and all its accessories to Flako; he then picked up the cash and the machete with one hand and the .50-caliber with the other. He breezed past Flako and shouted for the girls to wake up. Once he had their attention, he tossed the stack of hundred dollar bills onto the bed with them.

248

"Each one of you gets twenty-five hundred. I need you all to stay in here until I get back. Should be no longer than five minutes," Papi said, glancing at the panties, bras, and empty Rosé champagne bottles that littered the floor around his huge bed. "Clean this room up and I'll double it."

While Flako was draping his brother's outfit over the arm of a honey- colored easy chair, Papi told the two men who were standing outside his bedroom door to watch the girls. Then he and Flako left the bedroom.

"When do you plan on selling this place," Flako asked. "I paid a million and a half for this mansion, back in nineteen seventy. Now, almost forty-two years later, it's worth twenty-eight million. Why should I sell it? It might be worth fifty million forty years from now."

"That's a big leap."

Papi lifted his shoulders, "You never know."

A small group of Costilla Cartel henchmen were huddled around two chairs in the four-car garage when Papi and Flako walked through the door. The two men tied to the chairs had black pillowcases pulled down over their heads. They were the same men who'd been stationed at the front gate at the Matamoros estate when Isabella planted the bomb on the phantom.

"Incompetent workers will never rank high on my list of favorites," Papi said, raising the Desert Eagle. "And unfortunately, you two didn't make the list at all."

King Rio

Chapter 52

Alexus was jolted awake at 5:50 a.m. by the sound of her iPhone vibrating on the bedside table. Not wanting to disturb Blake's sleep—and certainly not wanting to startle her son into a screaming fit—she picked up the phone and tiptoed to the adjoining marble-floored bathroom, narrowing her eyes as she found the light switch and flicked it on. The call was from Tasia.

"How you doin' girl? Are you okay?" Tasia asked. "Bitch, do you know what time it is?"

"Depends on where you're at. It's almost nine here in Miami."

"Well it's going on six here in L.A." Alexus squatted over the toilet

to relieve her bladder. "Oh God, I have so much to tell you. You're not going to believe this. I got a call from some girl named Mercedes last night. She claims to be my little sister and she has the birth certificate to back it up. Britney was on the line with her and everything."

"You've got to be kidding me. Yo, that's *mad* crazy."

"I still can't believe it. I'm flying out to Chicago to meet her in a few hours," Alexus said with a yawn. "Sorry for not calling you after we left Mexico. My chief of security had me forward all my calls to voicemail, and by the time I turned the call-forwarding off, I was ready for bed." She chuckled lightly. "Shit, after Blake pounded this pussy, I thought I'd sleep for two days straight."

Tasia sucked her teeth. "You gave that punk-ass nigga some coochie?

Are you serious? Have you lost your damn mind?"

"Bitch, you know how much I love that boy. I had to give him another chance," Alexus said, flushing the toilet.

"What about T-Walk?"

"What about him? He's a successful producer with a great vision, and I'm hoping he'll be able to crank out a few more hit shows for MTN. Other than that, we're pretty much done. He's my plan B for now, you know what I'm saying? Boyfriend number two."

"Have you ever ridden the short bus?"

Alexus laughed. "Fuck you, Tasia. I am not slow; I'm in love, and I refuse to let anything or anyone get in the way of me having that love. So, please, if you're not going to support me—"

"Whatever, whatever, whatever. Ain't nobody tryin' to hear that.

Blake cheated on you once, and you know he'll do it again. But since you don't want to talk about that, tell me who put that bomb in your car."

"We'll discuss that later. Just get yourself a ticket to Chicago. I'll be there in about four or five hours."

"You bringin' King, too? I mean, I would if I were going to meet my sister for the first time. I'm sure she'll want to meet her nephew."

Alexus went to the bathtub and turned on the water. "I guess I'll bring him. Girl, let me get myself together."

"A'ight, bitch. I'll call you when I get to the Chi."

Chapter 53

"She's bringing the baby." Tasia said, setting the phone down on her lap. She was sitting in the passenger's seat of T-Walk's powder blue Bentley Continental GT, puffing on a robust blunt of Purple Kush.

T-Walk clenched his teeth together and kept his eyes on the road as he drove up Brickell Avenue. Craig and Cereniti were tailing him in a rented Cadillac CTS Coupe. They had just had breakfast at a fancy restaurant inside the Four Seasons, and now they were headed out to do some shopping until Kenya and Bookie got back from visiting their family in Fort Lauderdale.

"I can't stand that dumb bitch," T-Walk said. He had heard the entire conversation between Tasia and Alexus, and he wasn't happy.

Tasia offered him the blunt. "Don't let that shit get to you, big bruh. So what if she calls you boyfriend number two? If we can snatch that baby and get Alexus to pay us a *billion* dollars—in *cash*—we'll be set for life!

Let's stay focused on gettin' that money."

"What was she saying about her sister? I didn't know she had a sister." T-Walk toked on the blunt, pondering the kidnapping scheme.

"She didn't know about it either."

They were quiet for a moment. In the back of his mind, Trintino kind of regretted telling Tasia about the planned kidnapping. Not only was she best friends with Alexus, she was also engaged to Bookie, Alexus' cousin. But T-Walk trusted her. She was like a sister to him, and he knew she was just as eager to get her hands on that cash as he was.

"So," Tasia asked, "do you really think it'll be that easy? And even if we do manage to get the money, where can we hide it? How will we launder it? And how will they even get the money into the States?"

"If they can move twenty two tons of dope every week without getting caught, I'm pretty sure they'll be able to move a billion in cash," T- Walk reasoned. "What you need to be worried about is how you're gonna get the baby away from Alexus and past those bodyguards. Everything else will fall in place after that."

"I sure hope so," she said, rubbing her hands together.

Chapter 54

"Blake. Blake, get up." Dale was shaking Blake's shoulder. "Nigga, you ain't *that* damn sleepy. Wake up."

Vexed, Blake rolled over onto his back, struggling to open his eyes.

He studied the vacant left side of his bed, then the white marble-topped Honduran mahogany bedside table where Alexus' smartphone and Birkin bag had been last night, and finally his dapper father, who was dressed in a clean black suit with a dark blue tie.

"Where Alexus go?" Blake asked. He reached down to the floor next to his bed, picked up his Louis Vuitton boxers, and put them on under the black and white Scarface-themed blanket.

"Nigga, you should've seen how she left a few minutes ago," Pops said, lighting a Newport. "It was like the Secret Service out there, a bunch of cocky-ass Mexicans in Men In Black suits." He grabbed Blake's watch. "Man, is this a real Hublot?"

Blake climbed out of bed and took his iPhone off the charger. There were twelve new text messages: one from his music manager, one from Alexus, one from his mother, and nine from Janautica. He read the one from Alexus first:

'Good mornin, hubby! Gotta go take care of something. Be back @ 7:30-8:00 a.m. Mwah!'

Then he read the message from his music manager:

'Money Bagz Management tour is set to begin Dec. 2nd! 56 cities, 80 shows, North American tour. First three shows at Madison Square Garden. Lime Green Bugatti video shoot this Thursday in your old Michigan City neighborhood, remix vid shoot w/ Weezy, Kanye, and Ross scheduled for Friday night at Miami mansion, and 30 Inches vid to be shot on popular 38th strip in Indianapolis on Monday. Afterwards we'll have radio and television appearances and magazine interviews to promote the tour and album (we need to get the album done ASAP). Have yourself a Happy Halloween, because the schedule will get hectic starting Nov. 3rd!'

"How much did you pay for this watch?" Dale asked.

"Too much," Blake answered abruptly. "Man, Pops, I got this tour coming up in December. Fifty-six cities, eighty shows. That'll have me all over the *country*." He grinned at Dale. "I'm in the rap game, Pops."

"I always knew you had it in you, son. I am not the least bit surprised at your success. As long as you remain true to what you believe in and give back to the ghetto, I'm with you all the way."

Blake went into the bathroom to brush his teeth and take a piss. "Where is King Neal? Lexi took him with her?"

"Nah. Your mother took the baby, Vari, and the twins out shopping. Left me here with you and your brother," Dale said. "He's out there in the pool with Young-D and those two girls you brought with you. Oh, and your Uncle Noble just got here. That's why I woke you up. He wanna see you."

A subtle grin appeared on Blake's face as he brushed his teeth, gazing at his reflection in the oval mirror above his Carrera marble sink. He'd always favored Uncle Noble over his other two uncles. Uncle Noble was an old-school player out of Detroit, a drug dealer and pimp turned adult film company CEO. He had invested half of the two million dollar check Blake gave him a few weeks ago into the failing porn company, moving its headquarters from Detroit to Pasadena, California.

After putting on his jewelry and stepping back into his baggy white jeans and red-bottom sneakers, Blake returned the four bundles of hundreds to his pockets, tucked the Uzi behind the Louis Vuitton belt, and followed Pops out to the sitting room, checking his other text messages as he went.

Carolyn had texted him at 6:48 to let him know where she was going and that breakfast was on the stove. Janautica's messages were densely laced with threats. *'Umma buss yo stupid azz fohead!'* Said one of them. Another read, *'I hope you catch AIDS and die... BITCH!!'* And her last text read, *'I FUKN H8 U!! U LIL FUCK-NIGGA!!!'*

Blake laughed to himself. "Crazy Bitch," he mumbled.

Uncle Noble was leaning back on the rear side of the leather sofa, flipping through one of the many XXL magazines that were always laying on the glass coffee table. He wore a black Brioni suit and Mauri shoes like his older brother Dale, only Noble's silk tie was yellow with white pinstripes, accentuating his light brown complexion and gold-covered teeth.

Dale poured them each a glass of cognac on ice and they sat down to
chat.

"I can't thank you enough for that money, nephew," Noble said as he
eyed the thick diamonds in Blake's necklaces. "Everything's goin' good now. Got some real stars on the Lucid Entertainment roster. I'm tryin' to get Montana to do a movie for me, ya smell me, young pimp?"

"I smell you, unc," Blake said, chuckling at his uncle's antics.

Serious-faced, Noble moved forward to the edge of his seat. He locked eyes with Blake and said nothing for a couple of seconds; then, "Young pimp, you got the baddest bitch I've *ever* laid eyes on, and she got damn-near *sixty billion* in the bank." He paused. "What are you doin' fuckin' anotha bitch? You mean to tell me you're cheatin' on the sexiest bitch on the *planet*, nigga? The same bitch that bought you a Bugatti and *gave* you a *half billion*?! Tell me what that equals, 'cause it ain't addin' up to me."

Dale nodded his head in agreement. "Alexus is in love with you, Blake... and you're in love with her. And she's King Neal's mom—"

"That baby might not even be mine," Blake interrupted.

"So what?" Said Noble. "I wouldn't give a damn whose baby it is. You better step yo' ass up to the plate, swing til you can't swing no mo', ya smell me, young pimp? That bad bitch chose *you*, nigga. Not a nigga that look like you, not a nigga that smell like you, young pimp. You'd better take advantage 'fore y'hoe meet a savage. Ass around and get her passed around."

"I got this, unc. Trust me. I'm about to make a billion myself wit' my record label. Wait and see."

"Oh, I got faith in you," Noble said with a Kool-Aid smile. "This family ain't raised no fools. I'm just tryna make sure you make y'next move y'best move. You ain't gotta fake it to make it, but y'gotta gotta bake it to cake it, church?" He raised his glass for a toast.

Repressing a chuckle, Blake touched glasses with the old guys. He told Uncle Noble about the upcoming tour, and about his nearly completed freshman album.

"Just make sure you get Face and Mary J on that album," Noble advised. "And if I ever catch you wearin' some skinny jeans, or a colorful- ass Mohawk, I'm fuckin' you up."

They laughed jubilantly, three kings in a castle.

"You got me fucked up, unc. I'm trapped up and strapped up til I'm dead, nigga. Ain't shit changed," Blake said, sipping his Hennessey. "I'm done cheatin' on Lexi, though. I can't be fake wit' my bitch and real wit' my niggas."

"It's not about being fake, son," Dale said. "It's about morals. Be a man. Real men take care of their women. They love their women until the end of time, you know what I mean? You're supposed to be making Alexus feel like she's First Lady Michelle."

"Tabernacle," Noble agreed. "It's cheaper to keep her. If you cain't keep that sweet cat on track, bring 'er back and let a mac teach 'er howda act, y'smell my pimpin'?"

"All day," Blake said, getting to his feet and walking to one of the long floor-to-ceiling second-floor windows. From there he could see

Young-D and Streets mingling with about twenty sexy-bodied black women in the pool out back. "Damn unc, you brought all these bitches?"

Noble joined Blake at the window. "Yep. Those are the Lucid Entertainment girls, all twenty-six of 'em. Porn superstars."

"You got the best job ever, unc." Blake scanned the pool until he found Janautica. She was reclined in a lounge chair beside the pool, a dark pair of shades shielding her eyes from the sun as she chatted with Princess, who was sitting up in the lounge chair next to her. They were getting manicures and pedicures by a team of Asian women.

With a sigh, Blake phoned Janautica, expecting to get snapped on as soon as she answered. He watched her pick up her iPhone from between her thighs and put it to her ear. She had on a black two-piece bikini, and her flawless caramel skin seemed to glow in the sunlight.

"What the hell you want, stupid nappy-head fucka?" Janautica said acidly.

King Rio

Chapter 55

The stomach-turning stench of burnt flesh hung over the basement.

Isabella Costilla was naked and lying flat on her back on the rusted springs of the old bed frame. A strip of duct tape sealed her mouth shut, and her wrists and ankles were tied to the corners of the steel frame. Enrique Aleman sat on two stacked crates a foot away from Bella. The jumper cable in his hand was attached to the new car battery at his feet, and every time he rubbed the cable against the steel bed, thousands of volts of electricity coursed through Bella's body.

"You still want to blow up cars?" Alexus taunted, arms crossed over the chest of her bone-white Pucci dress. She was standing next to Enrique, towering over him in her six-inch Christian Louboutins. "Juice this fat bitch again, Enrique. Make her wish she was dead."

Enrique touched the cable to the steal for the fifth time in less than a minute. Sparks jumped from the springs. Bella groaned miserably.

"Don't cry now, Miss Piggy. You didn't cry when you tried to blow me up, so don't cry while I try to blow you up. Juice her again."

The three of them were alone in the basement of Alexus' sixty-two million dollar, eighty room Beverly Hills mansion. She bought the place on her birthday—April twenty-first—after seeing it on dupontregistry.com, originally planning to wed Blake at the lavish Tuscan-style estate.

Ripping the tape off Bella's mouth, Alexus sneered at her cousin. "How dare you plant a fucking bomb on my car! Have you lost your mind?! I'm the queen of this cartel, queen of the fucking world, you got that?

Nobody fucks over me." She moved her face close to Bella's. "If the family tunnel was not connected to your home, I'd murder you right now."

All Bella could muster up was a painful gurgle that barely escaped her throat, but her eyes were full of dread, an absolute fear to the highest degree.

Beyoncé began singing from Alexus' iPhone, which was resting atop her Birkin bag on the table behind her. She slapped the tape back onto Bella's lips. "I'm not through with you," she hissed, turning around.

The 4,000 square-foot white marble-floored basement was more like a night club than anything. Semicircular white leather sofas encompassed nineteen tables, including four on the elevated VIP platform. There were seventy stools wrapped around the U-shaped, fully stocked bar; eight stripper poles with stages, and enough open floor space to accommodate a large crowd.

Alexus looked at her phone screen and saw that the caller was her mother. Turning back to glare at Bella, she answered the call. "Good morning, Momma. Did you sleep well?"

"Considering the circumstances, yeah, I slept alright," Rita Mae said. "How's my grandson?"

"He's fine. Carolyn took him shopping." Alexus put her thumbnail between her teeth and lightly bit down on it. "Momma... have you ever known of a woman named Whitney Clark?"

"Sure, I know Whitney Clark. Haven't seen her in about twenty years, though. She used to do my hair and nails before you were born. I heard she moved to Chicago and started using drugs. Hey, speaking of Chicago, we have to show up for a walk-through of the Lawndale restructuring areas. We were supposed to do it yester—"

"Hold on a second," Alexus said. "I think Papi pulled an Arnold Schwarzenegger move on us."

"What do you mean?"

Reluctantly, Alexus explained the conversation she'd had with Whitney's daughter, and the revelation silenced Rita for a long moment.

"That ungodly man," Rita finally said.

"I know, Momma." Alexus paused. "Listen, I'm meeting up with the girl when I get to Chicago. I'm gonna take her shopping and then bring her with me for the Lawndale walk-through. She said she has two kids, too. I'll order them some things online."

"Call me when you get here. CNN, BET, and MTN camera

crews will be set up on the corner of sixteenth and Millard in the parking lot of that high school by six o'clock Chicago time."

"The one we're reopening?"

"Yeah. I renamed it Shirley Earl High School. There's an old wise woman by that name who dedicated her life to the enrichment of that community. Nat told me about her."

"How's Nat doing?"

Rita sighed despondently. "He's staying in Southampton for a few weeks. I suggested he take some time off."

"That's good. Tell him I said hi next time you talk to him."

"Just keep him and his family in your prayers. God will eventually clean this mess up. Love you, baby."

"Love you, too, Momma." Alexus ended the call and checked to see what time it was.

7:27 a.m.

Looking over his shoulder at her, Enrique said, "Again?" Bella weakly turned her head from left to right.

"No," Alexus replied. "I believe she's learned her lesson." Dialing Blake's number on her smartphone, she shouldered her big white Himalayan croc-skinned bag and headed for the elevator.

Enrique zapped the bed frame twice more, and Bella's fat body bounced and twitched atop a shower of sparks. Alexus watched the final attacks unfold in the golden reflection of the elevator doors. Then Enrique picked up his gold-plated AK-47 from the table and followed her to the elevator.

"I said *no*," Alexus whispered to Enrique as Blake answered his phone. They were connected via FaceTime and were immediately able to see one another.

"You on your way?" Blake asked, breathing hard, with water dripping from his face. "I just hopped out of the shower."

"I'll be there in about forty-five minutes," Alexus said as the elevator doors slid open before her. She and Enrique stepped inside. "My family's here and I have to discuss some business with them. We'll be heading back in five or ten minutes."

Blake quickly told her about his upcoming video shoots and concert

tour.

"Which video do you want me in?" She asked.

"The original "Lime Green Bugatti" and the remix. I done already

bought two more Bugattis—the Grand Sport convertible and another Super Sport. I'm thinkin' about just drivin' all three of 'em for the first video, then I'll have all my cars on set for the remix in Miami." Blake suddenly frowned at her. "What happened to the cars you bought for me in Mexico?"

"They're still in the garage. How much of that money have you blown through already? It sounds like a lot."

"I ain't spent that much." "How much?" She repeated.

"Bout ninety million. I looked out for a buncha people, mostly my niggas, my family, and some people I went to school wit'. Bought like forty Chevys for my Dub Life niggas, got 'em all candied and rimmed up."

"Stop wasting money on all those people," Alexus scolded, turning to Enrique, who was motioning for her to hang up. "See you in a little while boy. With your crazy ass." She blew Blake a kiss.

"And you love my crazy draws." Blake smiled, and then hung up. Just then, the doors separated.

Pedro and Santiago Castillo were standing right outside of the elevator, both looking angrier than Alexus had ever seen them. There were ten black-suited men lining the walls on the sides of the long hallway and every one of them carried military-issue FN P90 machine guns.

Through clenched teeth, Santiago said, "Tell me what happened to my brother."

"And what did you do to my sister down there?" Pedro added. "She tried to kill me yesterday," Alexus said, shifting her eyes from

Pedro to Santiago. "And I've told you all a million times already, I don't know anything about Savio's disappearance. I'd tell you if I did."

Pedro got on the elevator as Alexus walked up the hallway and turned into the lounge, an extravagant space of luxurious white leather furniture, white fur carpeting, and massive white marble pillars. A square- shaped marble Jacuzzi was built into the middle of the floor.

The ten armed men from the hallway spilled into the room behind Enrique and Santiago, and Alexus sank down into an easy chair. "I don't have much time," she said to Santiago.

He scoffed in disbelief. "Who do you think you're talking to?" His face turned red. "Grandmother is flipping in her grave right this second, you know that? Cartwheels and fucking somersaults!"

Santiago started pacing left and right in front of Alexus' chair, motioning wildly. His aggressive demeanor frightened Alexus. Over the years, she had witnessed him murder numerous men in Mexico, and once, at a gas station in Nogales, Mexico, she'd seen him empty a hundred and twenty rounds from an AR-15 into a carload of rival cartel members and drag the five bullet-riddled corpses out of the shot-up Bentley. Then he'd beheaded all of them with Papi's gold machete.

Alexus crossed her legs. "Calm down, Santiago. Tell me what you're so worked up about."

"What am I so worked up about? You want to know what I'm so worked up about?!" Santiago shouted, yanking loose his tie. "My brother's been missing for weeks! My mother's been in a fucking fed joint since May! And there's a nineteen year old cousin of mine who's in charge of a cartel that she knows absolutely *nothing* about! Not to mention the fact that she's squandering our family's fortune on some nigger rapper, and on fixing up neighborhoods in the fucking United States!"

"Will you please lower your voice?"

"I don't take orders from kids," he replied, but his voice did weaken. "Listen," Alexus said, "I didn't ask for any of this. Grandmother left
me in charge and I'm doing the best I can, okay?"

"For Christ's sake, Alexus, you're a got-damn celebrity! You can't be a celebrity and a fucking cartel boss at the same time!"

Alexus sighed, "Is that all?"

The redness on Santiago's face deepened. He stopped pacing and offered his nineteen year old boss a hostile glare. Then he turned and stormed out of the lounge without another word.

King Rio

Chapter 56

When Blake had answered his phone and told Alexus that he had just gotten out of the shower, he hadn't exactly lied. He'd actually had Janautica bent over in the shower, fucking her in thug fashion, when his phone rang.

Afterwards he sprayed on a mist of Cool Water cologne, rummaged through his Louis suitcase, took out a black pair of baggy True Religion jeans, a black t-shirt with MBM stretched across the chest in big lime-green letters, and a Louis Vuitton belt and skullcap to match the brand-new LV sneakers he would wear with the outfit. He was fully dressed and on the phone with Lil Mike when Janautica returned to his bedroom in a pink and white Prada jogging suit. She stood next to him, hands on hips, as he studied his reflection in the dresser mirror and told Lil Mike to meet him at the airport in Chicago.

Blake clipped the phone to his waist, looked over at Janautica, and grinned. "My lovely assistant," he joked.

"Shut the hell up, stupid," she retorted softly, her sparkling brown eyes descending to the gravid bulge in the front right pocket of his jeans. "How much money you got in there?"

"Twenty racks." "Give it to me."

"For what?" You finally gon' get that Swine Flu vaccine?" Blake said, chuckling aloud. He tugged the rubber-banded bundle of hundreds out.

"I'm serious, you stupid fucka. You always think somebody playin' wit'choo. Ain't nobody playin', yuh feel me, like? Gimme the money." Janautica raised a demanding palm.

Blake laid the cash in her hand. "You need it for real?"

"Of course I need it. I gotta get me a place to stay, pay my bills, get some furniture, pay for the abortion, yuh feel me, like? Since you back wit' that rich bitch."

"Abortion? What abortion?"

"*My* abortion, you fuckin' jackass. I'm three weeks pregnant," she said, fanning through the cash. "I ain't raisin' no baby by myself."

"Is it mine?"

"Duh! I ain't did it alone, genius."

Blake stared at her, eyebrows knitted, and said, "First of all, you already got a house, and I'll buy you another one if I need to. And you ain't gotta get no muhfuckin' abortion. Fuck is you thinkin'?"

"I'm thinkin' I caught two gun cases and killed a fuck-nigga fuh yo' punk ass. *That's* what I'm thinkin', if you really wanna know, *Einstein*. I ain't even much trippin', though, yuh feel me, like? 'Cause I knew it was comin'. I knew you was gon' go back to dat bitch. But guess what, cowboy. Is yuh listenin'?" Her hands returned to her hips. "Next time she leave yo' ugly ass, don't come callin' me 'cause I ain't goin' fuh dat bullshit again.

I'm goin' back to Norf Carolina where I came from, yuh feel me, like? Mind my got-damn marbles and let choo mind yours. Punk!"

"Stop callin' me out my name."

"Or what? Whatcha gon' do hit me?"

"Hell nah I ain't gon' hit you. Baby, listen, I'm not tryin' to hurt you, a'ight? Alexus was already my girl when I met you. I wasn't supposed to be with you in the first place. I'm not sayin' I regret it, but—"

"Fake you, Blake," Janautica said, flipping him the middle finger.

She stomped out of the massive bedroom and vanished, only to reappear at the doorway seconds later. "I got just one question fuh yo' stupid nappy- head ass. Did you really shoot all them niggas in Indianapolis?"

Momentarily, Blake was silent. He'd actually only shot and killed one of the fifteen men who had been murdered that night, and that was because the guy had been abusing Savaria. But what the hell did any of that have to do with Janautica? He knew she'd taken care of the snitch for him, and he assumed she might be feeling self-conscious about taking the snitch's life.

"Don't ask me no police-ass questions," he said, lifting an unopened pack of Newport's from the bureau.

Janautica disappeared again.

Slapping the top of the cigarette pack against his palm, Blake left the bedroom, intending to stop her and perhaps talk her into going to Chicago with him.

But he suddenly found himself face-to-face with Alexus.

"What's wrong with her?" She asked, looking back at Janautica, who was speed-walking up the hallway.

"I fired her," Blake replied as he leaned forward and kissed Alexus. "She'll be a'ight, baby. That bitch just crazy."

"I think your uncle's the crazy one. Carolyn's out there screaming her head off. She said he'd better get those whores out of her swimming pool and back onto that tour bus before she calls the LAPD on his ass." Alexus giggled. "I've rented a Boeing 747 to ship your cars from Matamoros to Miami for your video shoot, and Enrique's renting one for my security team and their SUVs."

"Have you talked to Bella yet?"

"Yeah, we caught up with her. She won't be blowing up anything else. Not for a while, at least." She hopped up and wrapped her legs around his waist. "Wanna get a quickie before we leave?"

King Rio

The Cocaine Princess 2

Chapter 57

The Rita Bishop Show began on a gloomy note.

Standing in front of her big black easy chair in an extravagant, embroidered Tulle Marchesa dress and Guiseppe Zanotti heels, Rita wandered her desolate eyes across the many painted and costumed faces of her studio audience, all of whom were dead silent. They knew all about the tragedy that had befallen her fiancé's family. Half the country knew. It was the top story on every major news station.

"As you all know," Rita began, "Nat is going through the very, very devastating loss of his parents, Martin and Sojourner Turner, his younger brother, Travis Hark Turner, and his maternal aunt, Bessie Smith. I ask that you all keep Nat in your prayers. And cherish your family while you still have them; tell them how much you love them. Those profound feelings of friendship that are so hard to express—feelings of love, of appreciation, of understanding—are really the feelings we should tell our family and friends about most directly. So I say we love everyone and judge no one. Do not partake in the hate. Love thy neighbor. It's what God wants us to do."

The audience applauded loudly. Rita wished everyone a happy Halloween, turned to the teleprompter, and introduced her first guest, a compassionate Haitian-American woman named Fabiola Montgomery.

Fabiola was the co-founder of the Restavek Liberation Foundation, a non-profit organization that offered assistance to hundreds of children in Port-au-Prince, Haiti, children who were forced to walk miles several times a day just to get water, children whose families could not afford school tuition and supplies. Rita admired humanitarians like Fabiola. They sat and talked until there was only forty-five seconds left to commercials. Then Rita's staff brought out a seven million dollar check for the Restavek Liberation Foundation, and Fabiola cried tears of joy.

Rita rushed backstage to use the restroom during the commercial break. She was stopped by her personal assistant as she exited the private restroom in her magnificent office.

"Rita your ex—I mean Juan Costilla's on line one," said the slender female assistant. "Would you like me to tell him to call back after the show?"

Looking at her watch, Rita saw that she had about a minute left before she had to return to the set. She picked up the phone from her large mahogany desk and put it to her ear.

"Don't you *ever* call me again, Juan," Rita said tightly.

"I need you, my queen. We were twenty years strong," he replied. Rita slammed the phone down and got back to work.

The Cocaine Princess 2

Chapter 58

There were eight armed Costilla Cartel members packed into each of the seven black Suburban's that pulled to a stop behind Papi's black Porsche Cayman-R. Inside the Porsche, Papi was fighting back tears and grinding his teeth as he stared at his phone screen.

"She hung up on me," he said, glancing over at Flako, who was seated next to him. "Told me not to call her again."

"What did you expect? Rita's not your wife anymore. You messed that up when you lied about your occupation."

"She wouldn't have stayed with me if she'd known. No Christian wants to be with a fucking cartel boss."

"Well, killing her boyfriend's family won't bring her back."

"I'll see about that, my dear brother," Papi said, opening his door. He stepped out of the car and gazed straight ahead at the big Victorian-style home that sat on a cul-de-sac at the end of Natchez Place, just off Warren Road in Southampton, Virginia. The place belonged to Mary Turner, a thirty year old stockbroker originally from Buffalo, New York.

Mary was Nat Turner's sister.

Papi grabbed his Machete from between the front seats, and minutes later he was standing in Mary's back yard beside an old, tall tree, watching as two of his men dragged the pretty black woman out the rear patio door of her home. She looked to be about eight or nine months pregnant. The men tied her hands and ankles together with a length of rope and hung her upside down from the tree while another man doused her clothes with gasoline.

"Please, don't do this to me," she cried.

But Mary's words ended abruptly as Papi stuffed a handkerchief in her mouth. He took a scalpel from his breast pocket and cut off both her ears, cut out one of her eyes, then got a lighter from one of his men and set her clothes on fire.

"Come on, Juan. That's enough," Flako said.

Ignoring his brother, Papi cut open the woman's abdomen with the golden machete. The infant dropped to the grass, and Papi crushed the baby's head beneath his shoe. He then had his men fire over three hundred bullets into Mary's body.

"Now..." Papi said, flicking the eyeball into the air, "*that's enough.*"

Chapter 59

Nat Turner, dressed in a custom-made dark blue bulletproof sweatshirt, with an AR-15 assault rifle stretch across his lap, had been sitting quietly in the back of his Uncle William Still's brown Chevy van, reading his bible, when he heard the gunshots. Four of his cousins—Henry, Nelson, Sammy, and Frank—were with him in the rear of the van. They too were armed with AR-15s and Kevlar sweat suits. Nat had gathered them for the sole purpose of patrolling the Cabin Pond neighborhood where the majority of his family resided. He wanted to protect them from Juan Costilla, the man who'd already been arrested and accused of being the leader of Mexico's deadliest drug cartel by the FBI, DEA, and ATF.

Now after hearing the gunfire as his Uncle Will drove the van up to Warren Road, Nat prayed for his sister Mary's protection. He cocked the fully automatic assault rifle, then looked around at his cousins as they cocked theirs.

"Don't you think we should let the cops deal with this?" Henry asked.

No one offered a reply.

Will turned left onto Natchez Place and pulled over to the curb. Heart

pounding, adrenaline surging, Nat stared coldly at the group of Mexicans who were loitering near a line of SUVs in front of Mary's home. He tried not to dwell on the loss of his parents, the loss of his little brother, the loss of his Aunt Bessie. Instead he focused on the pot of fiery anger that was boiling in his chest. The two large gasoline-filled titanium containers strapped to his back were attached to the MCGI-219 flame-thrower that lay behind him, and he was more than ready to use it to protect his sister.

He draped the AR-15's shoulder strap around his neck, cradled the chrome-plated flame-thrower in his hands, and addressed his cousins in a resolute tone.

"I fear my sister may be dead already. These guys are heartless animals, and the only way to handle them is to kill them. I need all four of you to come out of this van with your guns blazing. Any questions?"

There were none.

Henry "Box" Brown pushed open the rear doors, and they cascaded out of the van in Navy SEAL-fashion.

"Try to get them into the street," Nat said. He estimated the distance between himself and the SUV that was farthest from him to be about thirty-

five or forty feet. Since the flame-thrower could only reach twenty-five feet, he had to get closer.

A cacophony of thunderous gunfire ensued. Nat made a bee-line toward the Suburban's, studying the black-suited Mexicans with genuine intrigue as the bullets tore through their bodies.

It was then that Nat remembered his dream: black and brown spirits wrestling in the sky, a dark sun, gushing streams of blood. This was it. This was the vision.

He unleashed the flame-thrower on a dozen wounded cartel henchmen. The twenty-five foot rope of fire instantly set the men ablaze. Their blood chilling screams were drowned out by more rapid gunshots, and Nat did not feel even a drop of remorse.

Chapter 60

"Oh my God, Blake. You seriously bought all of these books? I didn't know you liked to read urban novels," Alexus said as she sat next to Blake, scanning through a Barnes and Noble bag that was full of 'hood books.

They were on her seventy million dollar Gulfstream VI, soaring through the clouds on their way to Chicago. Savaria was sitting across from them with the baby pulled tight against her chest and Enrique was reclining in one of the other seats.

"All of 'em ain't urban novels," Blake said. "I got some of James Patterson's and John Grisham's in there, too. And I just bought that Angela Davis autobiography the other day. I try to keep 'em wit' me everywhere I go so I can have something constructive to do while e'rybody else on bullshit. If I ain't readin' or recordin', I'm listenin' to some Weezy or Gotti and thinkin' about yo' muhfuckin ass."

"Stop cursing so much." Alexus lifted a Leo Sullivan novel out of the bag and read the back cover. She had changed into a white belly shirt, snug white jeggings, a white Bulls cap turned to the left, and white diamond-covered five-inch Prada heels. "I've been reading these urban novels for years. A lot of them are antinovels, but I still like the stories."

"Antinovels? What the hell dat mean?" Blake asked.

"Poorly written novels. You know, some black publishers accept every book that's sent to them, and they don't even bother to edit them. That's why the urban book market is so saturated with antinovels." She shrugged. "Leo's a pretty good writer, though."

"Yeah, I dig his books," Blake said and turned to look out his window.

Alexus dropped the book into the bag, interlaced the fingers of her right hand with his left hand, and tilted her head onto his shoulder. Timidly, she said, "I'm worried about you going back to Chicago. Those Vice Lords can't be happy about what happened earlier this month."

"I'll be a'ight, baby. Them niggas ain't gon' do shit. And the Bugatti bulletproof anyway, right?"

"Yeah... But still... they could get you when you're not in it. I, um... I want you to stay with me the whole time we're in Chicago. My men will be able to keep you safe."

"I'm cool with that. I don't need no security, but I'ma be with you. I'll never leave your side again." He kissed the top of her head. "We gotta make this work, baby. We got to. I *have* to be a good example for Vari and King Neal."

"Speaking of King Neal," Alexus said, sitting up to look at him. "I'm getting that paternity test done sometime this week. Hopefully, we'll be able to do it today or tomorrow."

Blake shrugged but did not reply. He was still gazing out the window.

The notion of T-Walk being King Neal's father disturbed him greatly. Just pondering it made him tense all over.

He thought about Janautica's pregnancy. She was on his private jet with Young-D and Princess. She'd decided to accompany them to Chicago after all, but only to pack up the clothes she had at her Michigan City home. It hurt Blake's heart to know that she was really leaving him, but he loved Alexus much more than he did Janautica, so he was content with the split from Nauti; or at least that was what he was making himself believe.

Savaria shattered his introspection. "Daddy is we going to, um, be back to my grandma house for Halloween and trick-or-treating?"

"We should be," he said.

"I hope so, Daddy, 'cause I don't wanna trick-or-treat without my grandma, 'cause her bought me a Minnie Mouse costume for Halloween and I want her to see me wear it." Savaria kept rubbing King Neal's back, holding his head against her shoulder.

"She is so cute," Alexus murmured. She told Siri, her iPhone 4S's computerized assistant, to call Britney.

The attorney answered, "Hey, Lex. I've been waiting on you to call.

Have you spoken with your father about Mercedes?"

"No. I haven't even called Mercedes yet. We're headed to

Chicago now, though, so I'll just call her when my plane lands."

"Is Blake still with you?"

"Yup, and I'm listenin', too," Blake interjected.

Britney laughed. "I knew you two would end up getting back together. You love each other too much."

"Listen," Alexus said, "I need you to stop by the Trumbull Street mansion and grab our furs out of my closet. There's no way I'm getting off this jet in Chicago without a coat. I am not trying to catch pneumonia."

"I'll go over there now." Britney ordered her driver to take her to the Trumbull residence. Then she said into the phone, "Your Rolls Royce Phantom Limousine is finished. It arrived yesterday evening, and I've been rolling around in it ever since." She let out another lively chuckle. "You have to let me use this for my wedding."

Reciprocating a laugh, Alexus turned to face Blake. He applied his lips to hers and held them there for a brief, loving moment.

"We'll let you use it after *our* weddin'," Blake said.

King Rio

The Cocaine Princess 2

Chapter 61

The kids were napping when Mercedes got up at 3:00 p.m. and opened the blinds on her bedroom window. Sunlight poured into the small room. She went to the bedside table, unplugged her BlackBerry, and checked to see if Alexus had called. There were several missed calls from her boyfriend Duke's sister, two from Mutulu, her fifty year old sugar- daddy, and a few from some local girls who wanted their hair done by the best hairstylist in the 'hood.

Mercedes Costilla—short, bronze, gorgeous, and Buffie-bodied— was the baddest young chick on the west side of Chicago, so exceptionally fine that she stopped traffic everywhere she went; especially whenever she chose to rock a tight pair of jeans to show off her rotund derriere. Hustlers all over the Windy City were after her, but she'd only been sexually involved with a handful of them; four to be exact.

One of them, a handsome brown-skin twenty-eight year old named Lil Cholly who was also her boyfriend's drug supplier, knocked at her front door as she was walking to the bathroom.

She opened the door and gave him a tired smile. Standing there in a brown leather jacket with a matching skullcap and loose-fitting Polo jeans, he smiled back at her. She looked at the big round-cut brown diamonds that sparkled in his earlobes, then dropped her eyes to the McDonald's bag he was holding with both hands.

"Breakfast?" Mercedes asked.

"I got you a lil something'," Lil Cholly said, handing her the bag and stepping into the apartment.

On her way to the bathroom, Mercedes put the bag on her kitchen table. She knew without even looking that Lil Cholly was gawking at the meaty cheeks of her ass as they bounced around in her pink boy shorts.

After receiving the ten thousand dollar check from Alexus' lawyer last night, Mercedes had called Lil Cholly and ordered nine ounces of cocaine for sixty-five hundred. She had planned to cook the coke up into eleven ounces of hard and grind it off to pay the ten percent on Duke's bond, which amounted to fifteen grand.

But now she had other plans.

After brushing her teeth and freshening up, she clicked into the Google app on her phone and typed in: *Alexus Costilla net worth.* What popped up made her mouth drop open. According to Forbes Magazine, Alexus was currently worth $57.9 billion!

Mercedes was smiling beautifully when she walked into the living room. Porsche, her sixteen year old sister, was sitting on the tan-colored love seat feeding Mercedes' and Duke's daughter, Meyoncé Sky, a bottle of Enfamil. Counting through a large stack of twenties, fifties, and hundreds on the sofa across from Porsche, Lil Cholly glanced up at Mercedes and scrunched his brows together.

"What the hell you cheesin' about?" Porsche asked.

"I was gon' ask the same thang," said Lil Cholly. "You ain't even looked in the bag yet, have you? That nine piece in there."

"Forget about that nine piece," Mercedes said. "Lil Cholly, do you remember who you said I looked like when you first saw me?"

"Hell yeah, I remember. You still look like her. Shit, y'all got the same last name. Y'all might be related." He continued counting the bills. " I done been face to face wit' Alexus twice before, and I swear, y'all could almost pass for twins."

"What if I told you I really am her sister?" "I wouldn't believe you."

"Why not?" Mercedes was enjoying the suspense.

"Cause you drive a Ford minivan," Lil Cholly reasoned, pocketing his cash. "Man don't tell me I done weighed and bagged up that work for nothin'."

Oscillating her eyes from her dark-skin, thin-framed sister, to Lil Cholly, Mercedes struggled to suppress her sheer excitement. She picked up an old manila folder from the coffee table and gave it to Lil Cholly. "Read that," she said and sauntered to the living room window to peek through the blinds and get a glimpse of his triple-black Range Rover Evoque, which was parked behind her minivan on the corner of Lake and Lockwood.

Members of the Four Corner Hustler street gang were already

out in full force in front of the dilapidated red-brick apartment building. Although there weren't many Halloween decorations up on the street, every day was like October thirty-first. Many L-town residents were confronted by scary masked men in the dead of night, only instead of butcher knives and axes, these menacing creatures wielded Glocks, Rugers, and machine guns.

"Hell mothafuckin' naw," Lil Cholly emphatically stated.

"What?" Porsche nosily asked. She hopped up and rushed to Lil Cholly's side. "What's so important about a stupid birth certificate?"

Mercedes was just about to turn and answer her sister when two white Ford Excursions rounded the corner on the street below, followed by a long white limousine, two more Excursions, and three lime-green Bugattis.

"You're about to find out," Mercedes said.

King Rio

Chapter 62

The 122-inch, 13-passenger 2012 Rolls Royce Phantom limousine was, in Blake's opinion, a work of art. It's hardwood maple floor was painted gloss white. It's ceiling was mirrored, as was the bar. The seats were white Italian leather. There were three fold down flat screen televisions, a twelve-disc Pioneer CD/DVD changer, an additional single Sony CD/DVD player, and an incomparable sound system. Bone-white 24- inch Lexani rims and Dunlop tires completed the look of the most stunning limousine Blake had ever seen.

Hidden behind the darkly tinted windows, Blake was rocking to the beat of Lil Wayne's "Racks" remix and sweeping his eyes up and down Lockwood when they pulled up in front of the run-down tenement. The leering eyes of the gangbangers did not worry him, for he had already gotten his Kelvar vest, shoulder holster, and Glock 18 out of the Bugatti that Lil Mike was driving. Blubby and Fly were pushing the other two Veyrons, and their passenger seats were occupied by a trio of sexy black women, all in their early- to mid-twenties.

"Why isn't Papi answering his phone?" Alexus muttered in frustration. She was staring at her iPhone, wrapped in a plush white fur coat. "I've called him five times."

"You need to get that old muhfucka checked into a mental hospital," Blake said, bouncing King Neal on his knee. Blake's fur coat was a thick, gray-black chinchilla.

Savaria was fast asleep in her seat. She had dozed off shortly after they'd dropped Young-D and Princess off at the Sybaris in Northbrook.

Janautica had opted for a taxicab from O'Hare airport.

"Don't talk about my father." Alexus scrolled down her phone's list of contacts until she reached Mercedes and tapped the screen to send. A Wiz Khalifa call-tone sounded in her ear.

"Yeah," said Attorney Bostic, who was sitting a few seats away from King Neal's car seat, looking as chocolate and comely as Kelly Rowland in her gray floral print Dolce & Gabbana dress.

"He is your father-in-law, Blake. Whenever you and Alexus decide to jump the broom, he'll be the one walking her down the aisle."

Blake shrugged off the lawyer's comment and put the baby back in his car seat. He listened to Alexus and Mercedes as their dialog began, while in the back of his mind he pondered the possibility of having both Alexus and Janautica to himself. Shit, if Hugh Hefner's old ass could do it, Blake knew that he could definitely do it.

"Hey, girl," Alexus said, taking off her gold-framed Channel shades. "I'm down here now. Want us to come up?"

"Trust me, you don't wanna come up here. This tiny little apartment is probably smaller than your closet," Mercedes said.

"You haven't seen a "little apartment" until you've seen Somalia.

Our people over there are starving to death, sleeping in roofless little aluminum huts. But that's another story. Are you dressed yet?"

"No, but it won't take me long. I'll just throw on some sweats." "I'm coming up; at least for a few minutes."

"I'll meet you downstairs."

Alexus clipped the iPhone to her Birkin bag then pressed the button on her door that lowered the black privacy glass. Up front, Enrique was next to the driver.

"I'm going up there," Alexus stated.

Enrique nodded and said something into his earpiece's slender microphone. Seconds later, sixteen men in black trench coats emerged from the two SUVs that were parked behind the limo. One of them pulled open Alexus' suicide-door and helped her out onto the sidewalk while the others drew subcompact machine guns from inside their coats and formed a human shield around her.

"Come on," Alexus said, looking back at Blake.

"I'm good right here, baby. Go on up there and meet your sista."

Sucking her teeth and rolling her eyes, she put her sunglasses back on and headed into the apartment building with her security team. Enrique took her spot next to Blake, shut the door, and raised the privacy glass to exclude the driver from what he was about to say.

"We've secured a stash house for your crew out in River Forest, a nice, secluded mansion. There are two thousand kilos of pure Colombian coke, a hundred kilos of heroin, and ten thousand pounds of Kush piled up in the living room. Now we can't have you going anywhere near the product, not with you and Alexus being together, and definitely not with you being involved in the music industry. We went through that once with Big Meech, and it didn't turn out too good."

Blake nodded his head. "I'll have one of my niggas move that shit."

"Make sure he's in no way involved with your legitimate businesses. His only job should be to deliver the product to two or three to distributors and have a few others drive the money to someone who will deliver it to—"

"I got it, man. You don't have to worry about that. Just let me know how to wash all dat dirty money."

"Why try to launder it at all? You're worth five hundred million dollars. I say you should keep the cash and spend it in the ghettos, you know? Let your crew get about a one or two year run, you walk away with a couple hundred million, everybody's happy." Enrique retrieved a folded piece of paper from the inside pocket of his black Brioni suit jacket, unfolded it, and gave it to Blake. "There's the address. Your man will find two Hummer H2 limousines parked in the driveway. Both have secret compartments that can hold up to three hundred and twenty-five kilos. The instructions on how to open them are attached to the key rings on the foyer wall."

Is that how y'all got those guns through LAX and O'Hare?"

"Works every time." Enrique said as his phone began ringing.

Blake cast a suggestive glance at the lawyer's scrumptious ebony thighs while she had her eyes on her iPad. Then he swiftly turned his attention back to the head of security as Papi's angry voice boomed from Enrique's phone.

King Rio

Chapter 63

Alexus had made it only four or five steps up the ramshackle wooden staircase when she came face to face with Mercedes Costilla, and there was not a doubt in her mind that the girl she was staring at was indeed her sister. They had the same long, curly black hair; the same feline-green eyes;the same high cheekbones and unblemished skin. Even their smiles were similar. Mercedes was wearing a pink Niemann Elements t-shirt, black sweatpants, and Air Max sneakers.

Both of them were speechless. They wrapped their arms around each other and hugged for half a minute before Alexus pulled back and murmured, "God... this is so crazy. I've had a sister for eighteen years and I'm just now finding out about it."

"I can't believe it myself." Mercedes rubbed her forearms. "Let's get inside. It's freezing down here." She glanced warily at all of the armed men, then turned and started up the stairs.

Just then, Beyoncé's "Who Run The World" sang from Alexus' smartphone. The call was from Tasia.

"We just left Midway airport," Tasia said. "Where you at, yo?" "Are you in a taxi?"

"Yeah."

"Have him bring you to the corner of Lake and Lockwood. I'll be here for about thirty or forty-five minutes."

"Is that where your sister lives?"

"Mmm hmm. I'm on my way up to talk to her now."

"Check out CNN when you get a chance. Some wild shit just popped off in Virginia. Buncha motherfuckas got killed," Tasia said before hanging up.

Alexus felt her heart drop to her stomach as a stream of daunting questions skated through her mind: More murders in Virginia? Was Papi responsible for those, too? Was that why he hadn't answered his phone? Had the rest of Nat Turner's family been wiped out?

She went to her smartphone's CNN app and quickly perused the story.

'At approximately 11:30 a.m., the usually tranquil Cabin Pond neighborhood of Southampton, Virginia, was rattled by the sounds of several machine guns firing simultaneously. A minute or two later, more gunfire erupted as a shoot-out began in the middle of Natchez Place between two groups of heavily-armed men. When the smoke cleared, fifty- five men were dead in the street...'

Alexus stopped reading as they walked into the living room of Mercedes' dreary little apartment. She ordered all but two of her men to remain in the hallway. Flicking her eyes around the room, her gaze landed on Lil Cholly. *"What's he doing here?"* She asked herself.

Last year, back when she'd been only a millionaire drug-trafficker, she had sold hundreds of kilos to Lil Cholly and his gang's chief, Reesie Cup. In fact, Blake had proposed to her at Reesie Cup's nightclub. What worried her about seeing Lil Cholly was the Trumbull Street shooting. She knew that he was a legend in that particular neighborhood, and she logically assumed that the homicide victims had been friends of his.

"This here is my sister," Mercedes said, gesturing toward the thin dark-skin girl on the love seat. "My momma let Juan name me at birth, and I guess she wanted to keep the car names rollin' after that 'cause she named my lil sis' Porsche. Should've named her ass Pinto."

Smiling, Porsche flipped the middle finger at her sister.

"Her daddy's in Stateville doing ten for a bank robbery," Mercedes continued, picking up a crawling baby girl from the carpet. "And this is your niece, Meyoncé Sky. Baby Duke's still taking a nap. His lil bad ass'll be up in a few minutes, runnin' 'round and breaking everythang in sight."

Alexus took off her sunglasses. "Can I hold her?" She asked, reaching for the infant. She put Meyoncé on her hip and studied the little girl's face until Lil Cholly stood up.

"Oh and that's Lil Cholly," Mercedes said. "He's a friend of my boyfriend."

"We've met a couple times." Alexus squinted at him.

He flashed a diabolical grin. "Where my nigga Blake at? That nigga done got rich and forgot about us."

"He's down there in the car. And believe me, he hasn't forgotten about *anything*." The contempt in Alexus' voice was noticeable. She glared at Lil Cholly as he walked to the kitchen, grabbed a McDonald's bag off the wooden table, and left out the open front door.

"What was that all about?" Mercedes asked.

"It's a long story." Alexus crossed the room and sat down on the sofa. The little girl slid off her lap to the floor and began crawling again. Eyeing the infant, she said, "You might as well start packing up all the things that are most important to you, because I'm not letting either of you stay here."

Excitedly, Porsche blurted out, "You and Bulletface got back together?"

"Yeah. We're trying to work things out. I think we'll stay together for good this time. At least that's what I'm hoping for."

"I hope this means I can get some free concert tickets."

Mercedes gave Porsche an irritated look. "Getcho lil dirty ass up and go get Baby Duke dressed, witcho lil thirsty ass." She turned to Alexus. "Excuse my French, but she be blowin' me wit' that thirsty-ass shit. Always want XXXsomething' for free. Bitch need to get a job."

Impervious to her sister's harsh criticism, Porsche sailed on. "I read an article on InFlexWeTrust.com that said Bulletface's first album might sell more than Eminem's because he's dating you. They said it might be the highest selling rap album of all time if it's anything like the Goon Musik mixtape. Oh, my God, I'm the biggest Bulletface fan on Earth! Is he really outside right now?"

"The faster you get dressed and ready to leave," Alexus said, "the faster you'll get to meet him."

Porsche got up and sprinted out of the living room, dialing a number on her cell phone as she went. Her skimpy halter and cut-up denim shorts left little to the imagination.

"Watch her around your man," Mercedes warned as she plopped down next to Alexus. "I had to beat her ass the day after Momma's funeral. Walked in on her, my boyfriend, and his brother having a threesome."

"You should've kicked his ass."

"I did. Mased all three of 'em, busted his head wit' a Seagram's Gin bottle, stabbed him twice, blacked his eye, and then stabbed his brother in the face. *Then* I beat the brakes off Porsche."

This elicited a nervous laugh from Alexus as she contemplated the grim notion of what Mercedes would do if ever she discovered the culprit behind her mother's murder.

There was an old polaroid picture jutting out of the side of a manila folder on the coffee table. Another photo—one of Papi sitting on the hood of his old 1988 Rolls Royce Silver Spur with a curvaceous dark-skin woman in a blue sequin dress leaning back against him.

"That's my momma right there," Mercedes said. "She said it was taken in ninety-two, right around the time they started datin'."

"Right around the time he *married my* mom." Shaking her head in disbelief, Alexus turned and eyed Mercedes' wounded expression. "I wonder if all men are dogs. I think it's—I don't know—some intrinsic trait they learn from rap music; or maybe it's hereditary."

"Who you tellin'? And I took Duke's tired ass back. Can you believe that? I'm about ready to give up on love."

"I tried calling Papi. He hasn't been answering his phone." "Is that his nickname?"

Alexus nodded yes and lifted the other picture from the folder. It was the same dark woman, lying flat in a hospital gown on a large bed, and Papi was standing off to the side, cradling a blanket-wrapped baby in his arms with Flako and Granny Costilla standing on each side of him.

Opening the folder, Alexus found further evidence that Mercedes Costilla was actually her sister: Papi's distinctive signature on Mercedes' birth certificate, and a paternity test dated March 13, 1995.

She quickly put the photos and documents into the folder and shut it before the guilt of Whitney Clark's murder could overwhelm her. "Well," she said, emitting a big breath, "this should make for a high-rated episode of my mom's talk show. The media will be in a frenzy. They'll be offering you millions for interviews."

"I'm not interested in all that Hollywood BS. I'm from right here on the west side, and this is where I wanna stay."

"Here? In this apartment?"

"No, I'm just sayin' here in Chicago; or at least in the suburbs, like Bellwood or Des Plaines somewhere. I have to stay within driving distance of the 'hood."

Alexus did not agree. "We have homes all over this country. There's no way you're gonna stay in just one spot. I'll get you a place out here, though, if that's what you want. I don't mind." She looked over at Mercedes and added, "It's the least I can do."

King Rio

The Cocaine Princess 2

Chapter 64

Blake had just stepped out of the limo and waved for his three guys to exit the Bugattis and join him on the sidewalk when Lil Cholly exited the building and stopped on the concrete doorstep. He stared at Blake, and Blake, standing a mere five feet away from him, stared back.

A treacherous grin spread across Blake's face. "What's up, nigga?" He intoned. "I ain't seen you in a minute, pimp. Fuck you niggas been up to? I know y'all still got Chi-City on lock."

"Don't hit me wit' that sarcastic shit, nigga. You bogus as hell for that shit you pulled on Trumbull." The corner of Lil Cholly's mouth rose into a contemptuous sneer. "Then you turned around and shut down the plug we had with the Mexican Mafia, too? What the fuck kinda shit you on?"

Still grinning, Blake shook his head. "Let's leave all dat alone and talk about some millions. Whatchoo tryna do?"

Lil Mike and Fly were walking toward Blake, while Blubby was speaking to one of the hoodie-wearing gang members. On Lake, a crowd of 'hood chicks had already begun to form.

"I'm supposed to trust you?" Lil Cholly said.

"Have I ever broke bad on a business deal? Just let me know how many y'all want 'fore dem hoes get over here."

"Thirty-six a thousand times'll do a somersault."

"You can get that. I know a muhfucka who'll give 'em to you for fifteen apiece. Kush for twenty-five honey buns. Dog food for a hun'ed fifty a block, and you can dance on that thirty times."

"How many Kush pounds can we grab?" Lil Cholly asked, glancing at Fly and Lil Mike as they halted beside Blake.

"As many as you can pay for."

Lil Cholly took a set of keys from his jacket pocket and hit the alarm on his Range Rover Evoque. "A thousand soft, a hundred blocks of dog food, and two thousand Kush thangs. We got the thirty-five million ready right now."

"The alley on fifteenth and Trumbull? Tonight at ten?"

"That's the thought," Lil Cholly said. He walked backwards to his SUV, keeping his eyes on the Dub Life crew. Behind him, fourteen 'hood chicks swarmed in from the corner, their vivacious stares unwaveringly fixed on the man they knew only as Bulletface.

"Mane, it's groupie time," Lil Mike said, flashing his mouth full of gold teeth at the approaching flock of girls. Both he and Fly were clad in black Gucci jackets with matching skull caps, sweaters, baggy jeans and sneakers, and their platinum chains were lined with two-carat round-cut black diamonds, as were their bracelets and Audemars watches.

The girls became ecstatic. They screamed, "Bulletface!" They asked for group pictures and autographs. And Blake, being the wealthy rap star that he was, honored every request.

Chapter 65

Squirm-G's pearl-white Hummer H2 crept to a stop one block over from Lake and Lockwood, but it's brand new set of 32-inch DUB rims kept spinning.

T-Walk sat quietly in the passenger's seat next to Squirm-G, gazing down at the .40-caliber Glock on his lap and puffing on a Swisher full of dro.

"I'll walk from here," said Tasia, who was sandwiched between Lil Ant and Reggie in the back seat.

All four of the men wore light blue Armani business suits, and all of them had Glocks with thirty-round magazines resting on their laps.

"We can't afford to mess this up, Tasia," T-Walk said. "Hundreds of millions of dollars are on the line. As soon as you get that baby, call me, and we'll come and pick him up."

You don't have to keep tellin' me that. I want that money just as bad as y'all want it."

Squirm, the most dangerous of the four Gangster Disciples, turned to Tasia and said, "On GDN, if you fuck up this lick, I'm murkin yo' whole family. I ain't come all the way out here for XXXnothin'."

"I got this a'ight?" Tasia replied, rolling her eyes and reaching past Reggie to open his door. She climbed out behind him and started off toward Lockwood.

Reggie hopped back into the Hummer and pulled the door shut. "That bitch bet' not play no games, G-ball," Squirm-G said.

"She won't," T-Walk said as he activated a GPS tracking device on his BlackBerry that was connected to Tasia's iPhone.

"Ay, Folks, let me ask you somethin'," Lil Ant said, nudging the back of T-Walk's seat. "What made you get us for this lick? Why you ain't get some niggas outta yo' city?"

T-Walk shifted in his seat and looked back at Lil Ant. "I'm from the same city as Blake. Trust me, he'd find out who did it if I had some niggas from out there help me pull this off. And for two, y'all are much more used to bodyin' muhfuckas than the niggas in my city are. I'm willing to shoot everything in sight for that money and I know y'all are, too."

"On the BOSS," Squirm-G concurred, taking a hit from his own blunt. "Just make sure we get that twenty million apiece you said we was gon' get."

"That won't be a problem," T-Walk said.

Fifteen minutes later, the pulsing dot on his phone screen started moving. Two white excursions turned onto Lake, then a Rolls Royce limo, then two more Excursions and three Bugatti Veyrons. He reclined his seat and waited for the motorcade to pass.

Then Squirm-G made a hasty U-turn and followed them.

The Cocaine Princess 2

Chapter 66

"I have bad news. Fifty-five of our men were just found dead in Southampton, Virginia. Nat Turner and four of his cousins ambushed them with a flame-thrower and a couple M-16s. Flako and Papi got away without being hit, and the feds are scouring the East Coast for Nat Turner and his four cousins as we speak."

"What were they doing there in the first place?" Alexus asked.

"You know how Papi is. He's still upset about Rita and Nat's engagement. They went out there to speak with Nat's sister about it, and when they were getting ready to leave, they were ambushed," replied Enrique.

They were speaking in Spanish and everyone else was silent. Perhaps it was the grave undertone in Alexus' voice that hushed them. Or it might have been the disturbing MTN newscast that was playing on the three flat- screen televisions, the gruesome description of Mary Turner's murder.

Alexus closed the privacy glass on Enrique and immediately phoned Papi. She briefly admired a gaudy white Hummer H2 on big chrome rims as her chauffer cruised up Lake Street. Then Papi answered and her attention fell on him.

"My little princess," Papi said.

"I'm not your little princess today," Alexus snapped. "What is wrong with you, Papi? Are you mentally ill? Do you have any idea how much heat that Virginia incident is going to bring to the family business?"

"It's your mother's fault. She's being hard-headed. She won't listen to anything I have to say."

"Why should she? Especially after I told her about Mercedes." Papi did not reply.

"You could've at least told *me* about her. I've wanted a sibling ever since I was a little girl, and you know that."

Still, he was silent.

Shaking her head, Alexus handed the phone to her newfound sister and turned to Tasia. "I hate that old fucker," she whispered.

"That's mad wild, yo," Tasia said. "I hope my daddy ain't

hidin' no secret kids. I'm already having a hard enough time dealing with you and Cereniti's crazy ass. I thought you were really gonna blow her head off in Matamoros."

"I wish I had the guts to actually shoot somebody," Alexus said looking over at Blake, who was talking on his phone. "I'd have shot him by now if I did."

"Just give me the word, Lex. I'll shoot his got-damned nuts off. You know I can't stand his ass no way. Now, tell me where the hell we're going."

"I'm gonna take them"—Alexus nodded her head toward Mercedes and Porsche—"Shopping on Michigan Avenue. I'm supposed to attend the re-opening of a high school with my mom at six, but there's way too much going on for me to be showing my face to the media. I'm just gonna fly us all out to Jamaica for a few days, or maybe the Bahamas, get us away from this madness."

"Why don't you and Blake go somewhere by yourselves and spend some time together? Britney and I can handle the shopping."

Alexus had already pondered this idea when they dropped Young-D and Princess off at that romantic hotel a short while ago, so it didn't take her long to make a decision.

The Cocaine Princess 2

Chapter 67

Tears were streaming down Janautica's face as she raced her black Mercedes SUV down I-94. She had given the cab driver a thousand dollars for the ride to her home in Michigan City, Indiana, and now she was on her way back to Chicago.

Next to her sat twenty year old Christopher Trooper, a light-skin young hustler who had just so happened to be in need of a ride to the Windy City when Janautica stopped on Patrick Street, where he and his guys hang out, to buy a quarter-ounce of dro and four triple-stack Ecstasy pills.

"Slow down a lil bit 'fore we fuck 'round and get pulled over. I'm strapped *and* I got some dope on me," Chris said, rolling a blunt. He was slim and kind of short, about 5'7", wearing a red Coogi sweater over a brand new pair of baggy jeans and black-white-and-red Jordan's.

Janautica slowed the SUV from ninety MPH to fifty. She slipped a hand into her black Gucci dress and retrieved a pill from behind her bra. "Open that glove compartment," she said, popping the pill into her mouth.

"Can't you see I'm rollin' up?" Chris asked.

"Well when you get done, stupid ass, open the damn glove box." She wiped away the tears, turned up the volume on Meek Mill's "Tupac Back" and let it rumble through her sound system. Then she said, "What kinda gun you got?"

"Why?"

"Cause I wanna buy it. I'll give you whatever you want for it."

Drying the wet blunt with his lighter, he glanced over at her. "You still fuckin' wit' my nigga Blake?"

"How the hell is he yo' nigga and you ain't even got no whip?" "My car in the shop, while you talkin'. I got a brand new twenty

eleven Camaro sittin' on chrome thirties," Chris said as he lit the blunt. He pulled a long chrome revolver from under the left side of his sweater and laid it on his lap. Then came a black semi-automatic pistol from his other side. "Why you need a strap anyway?" He asked.

King Rio

But Janautica never answered.

The Cocaine Princess 2

Chapter 68

When Blake and Alexus stepped out of the million-dollar limo in front of the lavish Sybaris Hotel in Northbrook, Savaria crossed her arms over her chest, twisted her face into a confrontational pout and threw a tantrum.

"I'm not staying here wit' these people," Savaria stiffly declared, her bottom lip poked out. "I wanna go with you and Momma, and my brother, him wanna go wit' you and Momma too."

Blake lifted his grumpy little angel out of the limo and squatted before her. "It'll only be for an hour or two, okay?" He coaxed, rubbing her shoulders. "As soon as you get back, we're goin' straight back to California to go trick-or-treating wit' Grandma."

"No. I wanna stay wit' you, Daddy." "What if I buy you your own horsie?"

Instantly, Savaria's livid expression turned into a delighted one. "My own horsie? A little-bitty pony horsie, with pink hair and a pink tail?"

"Yup, I promise." He opened his arms for a hug, but Savaria spun around and climbed back into the limo.

"You'll get a hug when I get my horsie," she said and used all her strength to pull the door shut.

Enrique got out of the limo before it drove away, followed by one of the Excursions. The twenty-four men from the other SUVs were already spread out in front of the hotel.

Ending a phone call with her mother, Alexus looked at Blake and shook her head, smiling vacantly. "You shouldn't bribe your daughter," she chastised as they headed into the Sybaris. "You're going to end up spoiling her."

"Don't worry about how I treat my daughter. What's up with my momma-in-law? Is she a'ight?"

"Hell no, she's not alright. She hasn't heard from Nat since this morning. The FBI is checking her office and home computers for clues as to where he might be hiding." She grabbed Blake's hand and squeezed it, taking a deep breath. "Where did your boys go?"

"I sent them to do somethin' for me," Blake said. He had ordered Lil Mike, Fly, and Blubby to ditch their companions and get to the River Forest stash house to load up the Hummer limos for tonight's drug deal with the Traveling Vice Lords. Then he'd called Young-D and told him to rent out another couple's suite at the Sybaris.

Young-D was waiting in the lobby with the keycard to Alexus and Blake's room. He had on a heavy white robe that was as bright as his smile.

"This shit right here, nigga!" Young-D said in his Katt Williams Voice. "Man, these white muhfuckas got Jacuzzis and swimming pools *inside* the rooms. Waterfalls, rose petals on the beds, glass walls, good- cookin' ass chefs—this shit wild, bruh." He gave the keycard to Blake. "Now, if y'all will excuse me, I got some wet pussy to slide up into."

They followed Young-D to the elevator and up to the top floor where their suites were located. Blake entered the room behind Alexus. Looking down at the red rose petals that led the way to a round, red-blanketed bed; he took off his fur and sighed in relief.

He sat down on the bed. Alexus tossed her coat on a chair and went to the bathroom.

"I'm getting out of the cartel business," she said. "It's about time that I stopped praising Jesus Malverde and started praising Jesus Christ. My mom's been a Christian her whole life, and she's the kindest, most loving person I know. I want to be like that, you know what I mean? I don't want King Neal to grow up around a bunch of murderers and drug dealers."

"Who is Jesus Malverde?" Blake asked, lighting a Newport.

"He's the legendary cocaine god of Mexico. A lot of drug smugglers wear necklaces with pictures of him framed in the pendants, or they hang them from their rearview mirrors. I'm surprised you never heard of him."

Blake lay back on the bed and gazed up at the mirrored ceiling. He blew a neat ring of smoke into the air and said, "What's wrong wit' Papi? Is he really dat fucked up in the head?"

"He watched his father get beheaded when he was a kid."

"By the leader of the Zeta Cartel. He told me about that."

"Gamuza wasn't actually the leader then, but yeah, I think that's what did it." She paused, and then changed the subject. "Have you heard the news about my clothing line? We sold more than Louis Vuitton and Gucci combined. I know that French guy's pissed."

"Who you talkin' 'bout?"

"I'm talking about the guy that owns Gucci, Louis Vuitton, and Converse. I forget his name. He and Salma Hayek used to date." Alexus sauntered out of the bathroom in a white bra and thong, her diamond- covered five-inch heels sparkling on her feet. "How do I look?" She asked, turning a slow three-sixty.

Blake stood up smiling speechlessly. His iPhone began ringing on his hip, but he paid it no mind; nothing in the world could possibly be more important than the woman standing before him. He put out the cigarette. "Close your eyes," he said as he moved forward and kissed her lips.

"I got a lil surprise for you." She closed her eyes and he kissed her again, rubbing his palms up and down her generous derriere.

Then he got down on one knee, fished a small gray Le Vian jewelry box out of the front right pocket of his jeans, and flipped it open revealing a platinum ring with a twenty carat flawless white diamond bulging up from its diamond-encrusted band. He had paid seven million dollars for the dazzling engagement ring five days after Alexus had caught him cheating at the concert, hoping that she'd take him back. Luckily, he'd left it in his top drawer at his parent's Brentwood mansion, and it had stayed there until he pocketed it this morning.

"You can open 'em now," Blake said, his voice an octave low with emotion. He saw the shock register in her eyes when they opened.

She inhaled sharply, slapping her hands over her gaping mouth as if her tongue was about to fall out.

"Blake!" She exclaimed, eyes watering.

"Listen, baby," he said. "I love you. I mean, I really, really love you, Alexus. I know my past infidelities may have made you build security walls around your heart, but like Angela Davis wrote in her autobiography, *'walls turned sideways are bridges.'* All I ask is for you to let down that wall, turn it sideways, and I'ma run across that bridge faster than Derrick Rose to get back that heart of mine." He took her left hand. "So," he added, taking a deep breath, "I ask you again. Alexus Costilla... will you marry me?"

Chapter 69

Tasia Olsen wandered aimlessly through Earl's Jewelry on Michigan Avenue, occasionally glancing at the four bodyguards who were following her around the high-end jewelry store. She was holding King Neal on her hip. Mercedes, Porsche, and the other children were somewhere up the street at another store with Britney.

'Where the hell are you, T-Walk?' Tasia thought. She had sent him a text message fifteen minutes ago letting him know that she had the baby, and that she was in the company of four mean-looking bodyguards inside the jewelry store.

So where the hell was he?

"Excuse me, miss," said the middle-aged, well-dressed Black man who was standing behind the counter. "Can I help you? If you give me an idea of what you're looking for, I'm certain we'll be able to find you something."

Resisting the urge to roll her eyes, Tasia smiled at the man. "I'm looking to buy a watch, actually."

"For you?"

"No, it's for my boyfriend. He wants another Audemars and a new Rolex. I figured I'd get him one today."

Officially employed as Alexus Costilla's publicist, Tasia was currently being paid a hundred fifty thousand dollars a month, so paying a hundred grand on a watch wouldn't hurt her too much.

But, as it turned out, she wouldn't spend a dime in Earl's Jewelry.

The bell over the store's front door jangled lightly as the employee led Tasia toward a section of the glass counter that was full of expensive watches. She looked back and saw that T-Walk and his three comrades had just entered the establishment.

With the speediness of trained assassins, they drew their Glocks and blasted holes through the skulls of the four bodyguards.

King Rio

Chapter 70

"Damn baby, this ass so fat," Blake murmured as he kneeled on the bed behind Alexus, gripping her hips and rapidly slamming his stone-hard erection in and out of her juicy pussy.

He could not keep his eyes off her ass as it bounced wildly with every stroke. The two big reddish-brown cheeks jiggled like twin mounds of Jell-O. Alexus had her head down with her hand between her ample thighs, massaging her clit.

"I'm about to...mmmmm...," she moaned gutturally. "I'm cummin', I'm cummin', I'm... ah, ah..."

Blake poked his thumb into her asshole and held still as her body convulsed. He felt her inner muscles contracting around his dick. Her orgasmic juices poured down onto the bed, wetting the rose petals beneath her.

"I *love* when you do dat," Blake moaned, slapping a hand across her ass. He pulled out and rolled over onto his back beside her. "You ready to ride it?"

"I can't feel my legs," Alexus mumbled in between breaths.

But only seconds later, she rose up on all fours, turned so that her head was hovering over his crotch, took his dick in her hand, and forced it into the very rear of her throat.

It wasn't long before her mouth was overflowing with cum.

Swallowing his gooey cream, she mounted Blake and gazed down at him, rubbing her hands up his tight six-pack. She squeezed his strong pectoral muscles, and he wondered what she was thinking.

"Will I have to pay taxes on all that money you gave me?" He asked.

"No. Britney took care of that for you. She went through all kinds of legal disputes to get it done, so I'd thank her if I were you."

"Aw, I'ma do that ASAP. I'll go out and get 'er somethin' tomorrow."

Alexus sighed, cradling Blake's three diamond necklaces in the palm of her hand. "Let's go to Vegas and get married. I don't want a big wedding anymore. I just want to get it done and over with so we can move on and enjoy our lives as a happy family. Kelly Rippa did it with her husband. Coco and Ice-T did it too."

"I ain't trippin', baby. Whatever you wanna do, I'm witchoo a hun'ed percent." Blake slapped his hands onto her ass. "As long as you' happy, I'm happy. I just wanna see you smile."

"You're really pouring it on today, aren't you?" She beamed. Blake's iPhone rang again, eliciting A$AP Rocky's "Peso" ringtone. "Oh my God, Blake. Why won't you cut off that phone? I turned mine off."

"Grab that for me."

Sucking her teeth, she got up and handed him the phone. The call was from Young-D and his voice was frantic.

"Man, bruh, hurry up and get the fuck over here," Young-D said. "This crazy ass bitch Nauti in here wit' a gun to her head. She talkin' 'bout killin' herself."

Chapter 71

Blake dressed hurriedly; boxers, jeans, and sneakers.

"What's going on?" Alexus asked as she covered her naked-ness with the snow-white fur coat.

"Don't worry about it, baby. Just stay in here," Blake said, rushing to the door.

His mind was racing faster than his feet were moving. He snatched open the door and quickly crossed the hall to Princess and Young-D's suite, noticing the absence of Alexus' security team but not paying it any attention.

He walked into the room and stopped abruptly.

Janautica Spaulding was standing next to the Jacuzzi, holding a black Ruger nine-millimeter pistol to her temple. Princess, clad in red lace lingerie, had her arms wrapped tightly around Young-D, her face pressed against the shoulder of his white robe.

"Put the gun down, Nauti," Blake said in a cautious tone. He moved a step closer. "What's wrong? I know you ain't that got-damned crazy." Another step. "We can talk this shit out."

Suddenly, a frigid smile crossed Janautica's face. She turned the gun on Blake, wiping tear from her face with the back of her hand.

"I been waitin' a long time fuh dis," Janautica said.

Blake lifted his hands in surrender. He didn't know what to say, so he said nothing. Out of the corner of his eye, he saw Young-D push Princess to the side.

"Ay, get that gun out my nigga face," Young-D demanded. Janautica's diabolic smile widened as she swung the gun around to Young-D and shot him in the chest. Princess shrieked.

Deciding to make a move while he had the chance, Blake lunged toward Janautica, but she had the pistol back on him in an instant. The barrel flashed twice, and he collapsed to the floor, bleeding from his shoulder and abdomen.

"I bet you' wonderin' where yuh little flashlight cops done went off to, huh?" Janautica dropped her head back and let out a mean, mad, maniacal laugh. "Well, guess what. I called the *real* cops, told 'em they had some wannabes in the hallway out here wit' machine guns, yuh feel me, like? They took 'em down stairs to question 'em."

"I thought we agreed not to do this," Princess whined. She was crouched down beside Young-D, holding a blood soaked towel to the expanding crimson spot on the chest of his robe.

"Shut the hell up, Cess," Janautica snapped. "These fuck-niggas killed my daddy ten got-damned months ago! We was s'pose to get in good wit' 'em and kill 'em, but yo' stupid ass done fell in love."

Blake rolled over onto his back, clutching the bullet wound in his stomach and trying to figure out what exactly Janautica was talking about.

"I ain't... killed... nobody," he sputtered, looking up at her.

"Yes you did!" Janautica shouted. She aimed the Ruger at his face. "The judge might've thrown the cases out, but I know you did it. My daddy was one of them niggas y'all killed in Indianapolis. Cess was there. She saw it!" Janautica smiled again. "Tell my daddy I did this for him."

Three more gunshots rang out, thunderous and deafening.

Two of the bullets punctured Janautica's forehead, and the third one entered just below her left eye. She fell to the floor, unmoving. Dead.

Blake looked back over his shoulder and breathed a sigh of relief. Standing there in the doorway was Alexus Costilla, her fur coat half-

open, exposing her nakedness. Smoke curling up from the barrel of her .44 Bulldog revolver.

Chapter 72

"Everything's gon' be okay, baby," Blake said as the hotel's medical staff loaded him onto a stretcher.

Alexus took his hand in hers and squeezed it. Although she had been involved with several murders, she had never actually taken a life until now, and it was bothering her more than she thought it would; she couldn't stop crying and her entire body was trembling.

"Ma'am, we have to get him out of here," said one of the medical
staff.

Alexus bent over and molded her lips around Blake's. Then she
watched the medics roll him and Young-D out of the room. She badly wanted to go with them, but the police detectives had already told her that she would have to stay put for questioning.

She turned and stared at Janautica's stiff corpse. A slender-built old white detective approached her.

"I'm not saying a word until my attorney is present," Alexus said. "You have his number?" the detective asked.

Nodding her head yes, Alexus pulled her phone from her coat pocket, suddenly remembering that she had turned it off. It began ringing as soon as she cut it on.

It was her lawyer.

"King Neal has been kidnapped," Britney Bostic stated.

To Be Continued...
The Cocaine Princess 3
Coming Soon

King Rio

Lock Down Publications and Ca$h Presents assisted publishing packages.

BASIC PACKAGE $499
Editing
Cover Design
Formatting

UPGRADED PACKAGE $800
Typing
Editing
Cover Design
Formatting

ADVANCE PACKAGE $1,200
Typing
Editing
Cover Design
Formatting
Copyright registration
Proofreading
Upload book to Amazon

LDP SUPREME PACKAGE $1,500
Typing
Editing
Cover Design
Formatting
Copyright registration
Proofreading
Set up Amazon account
Upload book to Amazon
Advertise on LDP Amazon and Facebook page

***Other services available upon request. Additional charges may apply

The Cocaine Princess 2

Lock Down Publications
P.O. Box 944
Stockbridge, GA 30281-9998
Phone # 470 303-9761

Submission Guideline

Submit the first three chapters of your completed manuscript to ldpsubmissions@gmail.com, subject line: Your book's title. The manuscript must be in a .doc file and sent as an attachment. Document should be in Times New Roman, double spaced and in size 12 font. Also, provide your synopsis and full contact information. If sending multiple submissions, they must each be in a separate email.

Have a story but no way to send it electronically? You can still submit to LDP/Ca$h Presents. Send in the first three chapters, written or typed, of your completed manuscript to:

LDP: Submissions Dept
Po Box 944
Stockbridge, Ga 30281

DO NOT send original manuscript. Must be a duplicate.

Provide your synopsis and a cover letter containing your full contact information.

Thanks for considering LDP and Ca$h Presents.

NEW RELEASES

JACK BOYS VS DOPE BOYS by ROMELL TUKES
KILLA KOUNTY 2 by KHUFU
IN A HUSTLER I TRUST by MONET DRAGUN
THE COCAINE PRINCESS by KING RIO
TOE TAGZ 4 by AH'MILLION
A GANGSTA'S QUR'AN 4 by ROMELL TUKES
THE COCAINE PRINCESS 2 by KING RIO

King Rio

318

The Cocaine Princess 2

KINGPIN KILLAZ IV

STREET KINGS III

PAID IN BLOOD III

CARTEL KILLAZ IV

DOPE GODS III

Hood Rich

SINS OF A HUSTLA II

ASAD

RICH $AVAGE II

MONEY IN THE GRAVE II

By Martell Troublesome Bolden

YAYO V

Bred In The Game 2

S. Allen

CREAM III

By Yolanda Moore

SON OF A DOPE FIEND III

HEAVEN GOT A GHETTO II

By Renta

LOYALTY AIN'T PROMISED III

By Keith Williams

I'M NOTHING WITHOUT HIS LOVE II

SINS OF A THUG II

TO THE THUG I LOVED BEFORE II

IN A HUSTLER I TRUST II

By Monet Dragun

QUIET MONEY IV

EXTENDED CLIP III

THUG LIFE IV

By **Trai'Quan**

319

King Rio

THE STREETS MADE ME IV

By **Larry D. Wright**

IF YOU CROSS ME ONCE II

By **Anthony Fields**

THE STREETS WILL NEVER CLOSE II

By K'ajji

HARD AND RUTHLESS III

THE BILLIONAIRE BENTLEYS III

Von Diesel

KILLA KOUNTY III

By Khufu

MONEY GAME III

By Smoove Dolla

JACK BOYS VS DOPE BOYS II

A GANGSTA'S QUR'AN V

By Romell Tukes

MURDA WAS THE CASE II

Elijah R. Freeman

THE STREETS NEVER LET GO II

By Robert Baptiste

AN UNFORESEEN LOVE III

By **Meesha**

KING OF THE TRENCHES III

by **GHOST & TRANAY ADAMS**

MONEY MAFIA II

LOYAL TO THE SOIL II

By **Jibril Williams**

QUEEN OF THE ZOO II

By **Black Migo**

THE BRICK MAN IV

The Cocaine Princess 2

THE COCAINE PRINCESS III

By King Rio

VICIOUS LOYALTY II

By Kingpen

A GANGSTA'S PAIN II

By J-Blunt

CONFESSIONS OF A JACKBOY III

By Nicholas Lock

GRIMEY WAYS II

By Ray Vinci

KING KILLA II

By Vincent "Vitto" Holloway

Available Now

RESTRAINING ORDER **I & II**

By **CA$H & Coffee**

LOVE KNOWS NO BOUNDARIES **I II & III**

By **Coffee**

RAISED AS A GOON I, II, III & IV

BRED BY THE SLUMS I, II, III

BLAST FOR ME I & II

ROTTEN TO THE CORE I II III

A BRONX TALE I, II, III

DUFFLE BAG CARTEL I II III IV V VI

HEARTLESS GOON I II III IV V

A SAVAGE DOPEBOY I II

DRUG LORDS I II III

King Rio

CUTTHROAT MAFIA I II

KING OF THE TRENCHES

By **Ghost**

LAY IT DOWN **I & II**

LAST OF A DYING BREED I II

BLOOD STAINS OF A SHOTTA I & II III

By **Jamaica**

LOYAL TO THE GAME I II III

LIFE OF SIN I, II III

By **TJ & Jelissa**

BLOODY COMMAS I & II

SKI MASK CARTEL I II & III

KING OF NEW YORK I II,III IV V

RISE TO POWER I II III

COKE KINGS I II III IV V

BORN HEARTLESS I II III IV

KING OF THE TRAP I II

By **T.J. Edwards**

IF LOVING HIM IS WRONG...I & II

LOVE ME EVEN WHEN IT HURTS I II III

By **Jelissa**

WHEN THE STREETS CLAP BACK I & II III

THE HEART OF A SAVAGE I II III

MONEY MAFIA

LOYAL TO THE SOIL

By **Jibril Williams**

A DISTINGUISHED THUG STOLE MY HEART I II & III

LOVE SHOULDN'T HURT I II III IV

RENEGADE BOYS I II III IV

PAID IN KARMA I II III

322

The Cocaine Princess 2

SAVAGE STORMS I II

AN UNFORESEEN LOVE I II

By **Meesha**

A GANGSTER'S CODE I &, II III

A GANGSTER'S SYN I II III

THE SAVAGE LIFE I II III

CHAINED TO THE STREETS I II III

BLOOD ON THE MONEY I II III

A GANGSTA'S PAIN

By J-Blunt

PUSH IT TO THE LIMIT

By **Bre' Hayes**

BLOOD OF A BOSS **I, II, III, IV, V**

SHADOWS OF THE GAME

TRAP BASTARD

By **Askari**

THE STREETS BLEED MURDER **I, II & III**

THE HEART OF A GANGSTA I II& III

By **Jerry Jackson**

CUM FOR ME I II III IV V VI VII VIII

An **LDP Erotica Collaboration**

BRIDE OF A HUSTLA **I II & II**

THE FETTI GIRLS **I, II& III**

CORRUPTED BY A GANGSTA I, II III, IV

BLINDED BY HIS LOVE

THE PRICE YOU PAY FOR LOVE I, II ,III

DOPE GIRL MAGIC I II III

By **Destiny Skai**

WHEN A GOOD GIRL GOES BAD

By **Adrienne**

323

King Rio

The Cocaine Princess 2

GANGSTA SHYT **I II &III**

By **CATO**

THE ULTIMATE BETRAYAL

By **Phoenix**

BOSS'N UP **I , II & III**

By **Royal Nicole**

I LOVE YOU TO DEATH

By **Destiny J**

I RIDE FOR MY HITTA

I STILL RIDE FOR MY HITTA

By **Misty Holt**

LOVE & CHASIN' PAPER

By **Qay Crockett**

TO DIE IN VAIN

SINS OF A HUSTLA

By **ASAD**

BROOKLYN HUSTLAZ

By **Boogsy Morina**

BROOKLYN ON LOCK I & II

By **Sonovia**

GANGSTA CITY

By **Teddy Duke**

A DRUG KING AND HIS DIAMOND I & II III

A DOPEMAN'S RICHES

HER MAN, MINE'S TOO I, II

CASH MONEY HO'S

THE WIFEY I USED TO BE I II

By Nicole Goosby

TRAPHOUSE KING **I II & III**

KINGPIN KILLAZ I II III

King Rio

STREET KINGS I II

PAID IN BLOOD **I II**

CARTEL KILLAZ I II III

DOPE GODS I II

By **Hood Rich**

LIPSTICK KILLAH **I, II, III**

CRIME OF PASSION I II & III

FRIEND OR FOE I II III

By **Mimi**

STEADY MOBBN' **I, II, III**

THE STREETS STAINED MY SOUL I II III

By **Marcellus Allen**

WHO SHOT YA **I, II, III**

SON OF A DOPE FIEND I II

HEAVEN GOT A GHETTO

Renta

GORILLAZ IN THE BAY **I II III IV**

TEARS OF A GANGSTA I II

3X KRAZY I II

STRAIGHT BEAST MODE

DE'KARI

TRIGGADALE I II III

MURDAROBER WAS THE CASE

Elijah R. Freeman

GOD BLESS THE TRAPPERS I, II, III

THESE SCANDALOUS STREETS I, II, III

FEAR MY GANGSTA I, II, III IV, V

THESE STREETS DON'T LOVE NOBODY I, II

BURY ME A G I, II, III, IV, V

A GANGSTA'S EMPIRE I, II, III, IV

The Cocaine Princess 2

THE DOPEMAN'S BODYGAURD I II

THE REALEST KILLAZ I II III

THE LAST OF THE OGS I II III

Tranay Adams

THE STREETS ARE CALLING

Duquie Wilson

MARRIED TO A BOSS I II III

By Destiny Skai & Chris Green

KINGZ OF THE GAME I II III IV V VI

Playa Ray

SLAUGHTER GANG I II III

RUTHLESS HEART I II III

By Willie Slaughter

FUK SHYT

By Blakk Diamond

DON'T F#CK WITH MY HEART I II

By Linnea

ADDICTED TO THE DRAMA I II III

IN THE ARM OF HIS BOSS II

By Jamila

YAYO I II III IV

A SHOOTER'S AMBITION I II

BRED IN THE GAME

By S. Allen

TRAP GOD I II III

RICH $AVAGE

MONEY IN THE GRAVE I II

By Martell Troublesome Bolden

FOREVER GANGSTA

GLOCKS ON SATIN SHEETS I II

King Rio

By Adrian Dulan
TOE TAGZ I II III IV
LEVELS TO THIS SHYT I II
By Ah'Million
KINGPIN DREAMS I II III
By Paper Boi Rari
CONFESSIONS OF A GANGSTA I II III IV
CONFESSIONS OF A JACKBOY I II
By Nicholas Lock
I'M NOTHING WITHOUT HIS LOVE
SINS OF A THUG
TO THE THUG I LOVED BEFORE
A GANGSTA SAVED XMAS
IN A HUSTLER I TRUST
By Monet Dragun
CAUGHT UP IN THE LIFE I II III
THE STREETS NEVER LET GO
By Robert Baptiste
NEW TO THE GAME I II III
MONEY, MURDER & MEMORIES I II III
By **Malik D. Rice**
LIFE OF A SAVAGE I II III
A GANGSTA'S QUR'AN I II III IV
MURDA SEASON I II III
GANGLAND CARTEL I II III
CHI'RAQ GANGSTAS I II III
KILLERS ON ELM STREET I II III
JACK BOYZ N DA BRONX I II III
A DOPEBOY'S DREAM I II III
JACK BOYS VS DOPE BOYS

The Cocaine Princess 2

By **Romell Tukes**
LOYALTY AIN'T PROMISED I II
By Keith Williams
QUIET MONEY I II III
THUG LIFE I II III
EXTENDED CLIP I II
By **Trai'Quan**
THE STREETS MADE ME I II III
By **Larry D. Wright**
THE ULTIMATE SACRIFICE I, II, III, IV, V, VI
KHADIFI
IF YOU CROSS ME ONCE
ANGEL I II
IN THE BLINK OF AN EYE
By **Anthony Fields**
THE LIFE OF A HOOD STAR
By Ca$h & Rashia Wilson
THE STREETS WILL NEVER CLOSE
By K'ajji
CREAM I II
By Yolanda Moore
NIGHTMARES OF A HUSTLA I II III
By King Dream
CONCRETE KILLA I II
VICIOUS LOYALTY
By Kingpen
HARD AND RUTHLESS I II
MOB TOWN 251
THE BILLIONAIRE BENTLEYS I II
By Von Diesel

King Rio

The Cocaine Princess 2

BOOKS BY LDP'S CEO, CA$H

TRUST IN NO MAN

TRUST IN NO MAN 2

TRUST IN NO MAN 3

BONDED BY BLOOD

SHORTY GOT A THUG

THUGS CRY

THUGS CRY 2

THUGS CRY 3

TRUST NO BITCH

TRUST NO BITCH 2

TRUST NO BITCH 3

TIL MY CASKET DROPS

RESTRAINING ORDER

RESTRAINING ORDER 2

IN LOVE WITH A CONVICT

LIFE OF A HOOD STAR

XMAS WITH AN ATL SHOOTER

King Rio